Praise for

The Women of Primrose Square

'Full of **warmth**, **humour** and **compassion** . . . perfectly lovely'
FROST MAGAZINE

'**Challenging perceptions and celebrating friendship**.
Claudia Carroll's latest read is touching,
funny and insightful'
WOMAN'S OWN

Praise for

The Secrets of Primrose Square

'It is **layered**, **tender**, **warm**, **funny** and **heartbreaking**. A truly
wonderful book by an **immensely talented writer**'
SINÉAD MORIARTY

'A warm, **insightful** novel'
WOMAN AND HOME

'A **wonderful read** dealing with all of our human frailties
through a prism of warmth and compassion . . . **Funny,
smart and thoroughly engaging**'
LIZ NUGENT

'A **wise**, **warm** and **witty** gem . . . **I loved it**'
CARMEL HARRINGTON

Praise for

Claudia Carroll

'It **bubbles and sparkles like pink champagne**'
PATRICIA SCANLAN

'Modern, **warm**, **insightful** and **filled with characters that felt like friends** at the end'
EMMA HANNIGAN

'Original, **poignant** and **funny** . . . [full of] **wit** and **humour**'
SHEILA O'FLANAGAN

'Full of **warmth, humour and emotion** . . . I guarantee **you'll love it**'
MELISSA HILL

'Claudia Carroll is a master of creating **a great story** . . . A **brilliantly readable, funny** novel. **Highly recommended**'
FABULOUS

'An **emotional roller-coaster** . . . Hilarious, effervescent, heart-warming'
IRISH INDEPENDENT

'**Brilliantly funny** stuff'
SUN

Readers love

The Women of Primrose Square

*****

'A beautiful book that I didn't want to put down'

*****

'Utterly believable and totally magical'

*****

'A deliciously heart-warming enlightening tale . . . This book is
like unwrapping a beautiful present each layer at
a time to get to a treat in the middle'

*****

'Uplifting and emotional'

*****

'A fantastic book. I absolutely love it'

*****

'A heart-warming read'

*****

'What a wonderful cast of female characters!'

*****

'I could not put this down'

*****

05297791

*****

'I thoroughly enjoyed this book'

*****

'Well crafted with the layers and layers that Claudia
writes so well. This book is an absolute joy!'

*****

'What a lovely, warm, heartfelt read . . . It really
made me think'

*****

'Beautiful'

*****

'I really enjoyed this . . . it dealt with very emotional
subject matters in a warm and witty way'

*****

'Skilfully written with believable characters'

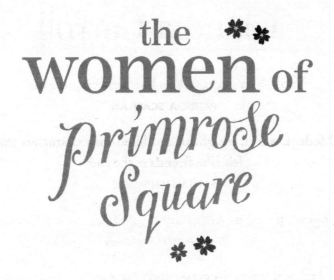

the women of
Primrose Square

Claudia was born in Dublin, where she still lives and works as an author and actress. She's a *Sunday Times* top ten bestselling author in the UK and a number one bestselling author in Ireland, selling more than half a million copies in paperback alone.

To date, Claudia has published fourteen novels, five of which have been optioned, two for movies, two for TV and one for a stage play. She's currently hassling producers for a walk-on role, and is hoping they might even let her keep the costumes for free.

 @carrollclaudia

 @claudiacarrollbooks

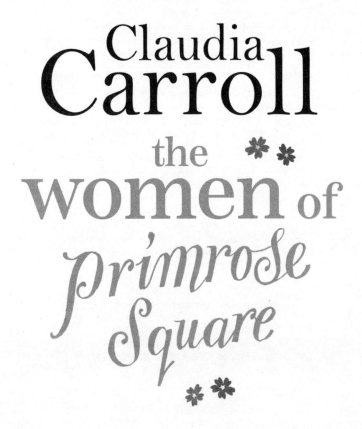

Claudia Carroll

the women of

primrose Square

ZAFFRE

First published in Great Britain in 2019
This edition published in 2020 by
ZAFFRE
80–81 Wimpole St, London W1G 9RE

Copyright © Claudia Carroll, 2019

All rights reserved.
No part of this publication may be reproduced,
stored or transmitted in any form by any means, electronic,
mechanical, photocopying or otherwise, without the
prior written permission of the publisher.

The right of Claudia Carroll to be identified as the Author of this
work has been asserted by her in accordance with the
Copyright, Designs and Patents Act, 1988

This is a work of fiction. Names, places, events and
incidents are either the products of the author's
imagination or used fictitiously. Any resemblance to
actual persons, living or dead, or actual
events is purely coincidental.

A CIP catalogue record for this book is
available from the British Library.

Paperback ISBN: 978–1–78576–776–0
Hardback ISBN: 978–1–78576–778–4
Trade Paperback ISBN: 978–1–78576–777–7

Also available as an ebook

1 3 5 7 9 10 8 6 4 2

Typeset by IDSUK (Data Connection) Ltd
Printed and bound by Clays Ltd, Elcograf S.p.A

Zaffre is an imprint of Bonnier Books UK
www.bonnierbooks.co.uk

Frank

Imagine if it was your fiftieth birthday party and absolutely no one wanted to come. That on its own would be bad enough, but even worse were the excuses Frank Woods was given, most of which bordered on pathetic.

Time and time again, he was told, 'Aww, thanks for asking me to your fiftieth, Frank, but . . . hang on a minute, did you mean the twenty-ninth? Nah, can't make it, I'm afraid. I've got to . . . emm . . . babysit that night. No childcare. Sorry!'

More watery excuses flooded in thick and fast.

'Yeah, fifty is a big deal and all that,' said Phil from next door, snapping on his bike helmet as he and Frank left their respective houses on Primrose Square for the dawn commute to work. 'You know I'd really love to be there, but the match is on that weekend and I've got tickets. Cost me a fortune too and it's the final, you know how it is.'

Frank smiled quietly and said he understood. But the thing was, he didn't really understand at all. The big match was on in the afternoon; surely it was possible to go to both? He sighed and said goodbye to Phil, who just grunted and cycled off, wobbling his way into the early morning traffic.

Before he got into his car, Frank took a moment to breathe in the mild, fragrant spring air. It was May and he'd always thought that Primrose Square looked its absolute best at that time of year, when all the buddleia and camellia lining its well-tended pathways were in bloom and when you could smell the fresh, scented air the minute you stepped out your front door. The party was to be held at number seventy-nine, the fine Victorian townhouse where he lived with his family – a house big enough to hold about a hundred guests at a squish, except now it looked like there'd barely be enough people to fill his downstairs loo.

At the company where Frank had worked calmly and efficiently for over twenty-five years, it was exactly the same story, with slightly different variations.

'Oh, for fuck's sake!' said Florence from finance, clamping her hand over her mouth when Frank handed her a neatly written invitation. 'Is it really your fiftieth birthday? I'm *so* sorry, but I'm going to be away playing golf that weekend. Can you believe it, the very same shagging weekend?'

'Can't make it, Frankie boy,' shrugged Joe, the sales director who went to so many company functions, the running gag was that he'd turn up to the opening of an envelope. 'But I'm sure you'll have loads of other mates to have a few beers with; sure you'll hardly even notice I'm not there!'

Frank sighed quietly and took off his glasses to give them a little rub. Then he took a good, long look around at his work colleagues.

He thought of all the vouchers he'd shelled out for, for their thirtieths and fortieths – even when no one had bothered to invite him. He remembered all the office weddings that he hadn't been asked to, but had still chipped in for a present anyway, never once complaining. He just did it because it was the right thing to do, the kind thing to do.

He thought of countless work dos where he'd invariably end up being the designated driver for his colleagues, ferrying everyone home at all hours without as much as a thank you. How he'd nurse fizzy water for the whole night, while everyone around him partied like there was no tomorrow. Not to mention all the nights out after work, which somehow everyone would forget to include him in.

Frank had often overheard the younger staff members chatting about him behind his back like he wasn't even there. He knew perfectly well that his nickname was Mr Cellophane – from the musical *Chicago* – because no one ever seemed to notice whether he was in the room or not. Not that he minded, really. He'd always assumed it was an affectionate nickname, given fondly.

Now, though, he wasn't quite so sure.

Was it really possible, he wondered sadly, that not a single one of his workmates would come along to his fiftieth birthday party?

Even his nearest and dearest were at it.

'Oh Frank, does it have to be on the twenty-ninth?' his wife Gracie had sighed. 'You know I'm in court that day and it'll be insane. Sorry, love, but this case is make or break for us and I can't just drop everything to organise a birthday party in the middle of it all. Tell you what; why don't we do something when it's all over? A family dinner, anywhere you like? I'll even pay, and I'll let you pick the poshest restaurant you like. How about that?'

Frank had two kids – a teenage son and an eleven-year-old daughter – who told him in no uncertain terms that they'd both be off doing their own thing the night of the birthday.

'I'm going to an end-of-term party that night, Dad,' Ben, his eldest, told him, pulling out an earbud and momentarily glancing up from his phone, as Frank uncomplainingly drove him to school. 'All my friends are going, and I can't cancel now, just to go to some lame-o fiftieth.'

'But this is a very special occasion,' Frank said, as his heart sank. 'It would mean so much to me if you were there, son. Surely just this once—'

'Come on, gimme a break, Dad,' Ben interrupted. 'You and Mum never let me out, like *ever*. I don't even bother asking anymore, because you keep saying: "Not until after the Leaving Cert". But you both swore blind to me that if I got good grades in the mocks and mowed the lawn for a full month that I could go to this party. And now you seriously expect me to give up the chance of a night out with my own gang, just to go to some old people thing where I won't even know anyone?'

'Don't be so mean; he's sitting right beside you!' Amber, Frank's daughter, piped up from the back seat of the car.

Frank smiled fondly at her through the rear-view mirror. Amber was his little princess. Eleven years old and the light of his life. His ally at home. The one person who didn't treat him like he was a complete pushover.

'So, what about you, Amber, love?' Frank asked her, as she munched into a granola bar she'd grabbed on her way out of the house, somehow managing to get more fruit and nuts all over the car seat than anywhere else. Frank's car was barely a year old and it was his pride and joy, but he still didn't utter a word of complaint. Instead he caught her eye when the car was stopped at lights and gave her a little wink. 'At least I can count on you to celebrate with your old dad, can't I?'

'Oh Dad,' Amber said, biting her bottom lip. 'I'd really love to, but I can't. Your birthday is on a Friday night and you know I always have piano lessons on a Friday.'

'But just this once, can't you make an exception?' Frank said. 'It wouldn't be the same if you weren't there, love . . .'

'You know I'd far rather be at your party,' Amber said, looking a bit guilty, 'but my piano exams are only two weeks away and I'm on Grade Two now, and that's a really big deal and I might fail my exam if I miss class.'

'Okey dokey,' Frank said quietly from the driver's seat.

'Jesus, Dad,' said Ben, rolling his eyes, 'do you really have to say "okey dokey"? That is like . . . seriously embarrassing.'

'Sorry,' said Frank, in a small little voice.

He probably should have been an awful lot sterner with Ben for being so rude, especially in front of Amber, but he knew he'd be wasting his time. Ben wouldn't have listened to him anyway. No one ever did.

I'm about to be fifty, he thought, inching his way through bumper-to-bumper traffic. He was about to hit the half-century. The Big One. Never once in the entire course of his life had Frank ever thrown a birthday party for himself, and now the one time he actually wanted to mark the day, there were absolutely no takers.

So he swallowed his disappointment and let everyone at home and at work buzz about him, ignoring him, as usual. Mr Cellophane.

But, he thought calmly, *if that's the way it's going to be, then it's not the end of the world.*

I'll be fifty this Friday and I'll have the whole house to myself. Time to execute Plan B.

The day of the Big Birthday turned out to be a Nothing Special Day in the life of Frank Woods of number seventy-nine Primrose Square. Gracie seemed particularly preoccupied and tense that morning, barely pausing to give him a quick kiss at breakfast as she gathered up a mound of court briefs and documents, stuffing them into her briefcase.

'Happy birthday, love,' she'd said, gulping back a scalding cup of tea he'd made for her, then pulling her coat on. 'We'll celebrate properly soon, OK? When this case is over.'

'Whatever you want, love,' Frank said, quietly loading up the dishwasher, completely understanding why she hadn't made much of a fuss. Gracie was a lawyer and was working on a high-profile financial corruption case just then, so she was bound to be a bit preoccupied.

'Don't worry,' she said from their little hallway, 'when I'm a bit less stressed, we'll do something.'

Except, Frank thought, *that was never*. These days, Gracie was stressed all the time. She didn't even take holidays anymore, her job was so pressurised. The best thing he could do, he knew of old, was to keep the housework ticking over, keep well out of her way and try his best not to get on her nerves.

'Just don't take the M50,' he called after her. 'There's a road closure at junction ten and a seven-minute delay, according to Google Maps. Take the N11, you'll be far quicker.'

For some reason, though, Gracie didn't thank him for this useful nugget of information. Instead she stopped in her tracks, gave him an apologetic smile, then banged the hall door behind her.

Ben seemed to have almost forgotten what day it was too. He barely even thanked his dad as Frank passed over the sourdough and avocado sandwich he'd painstakingly made for his lunch.

'Happy birthday, Dad. See you over the weekend,' was all Ben grunted as he grabbed the sandwich and bolted out the door, late for school as usual.

But what stung Frank most of all was Amber, his little princess, who normally went to such particular bother over everyone else's birthday. This was the girl who once threw a party to celebrate the cat being ten years old. She'd invited in a few neighbours on Primrose Square – Susan Hayes and her daughter Melissa, who were both noted cat lovers – she'd even moulded a birthday cake for the cat out of tins of Whiskers. Yet Amber just gave him a quick hug as she grabbed an apple to eat on the bus.

'We'll make a big fuss of you very soon, Dad,' she promised, rushing out the door. 'When my piano exams are over, OK?'

Never mind about a big *fuss*, Frank thought, scrupulously clearing up the mess his family had made in the kitchen, even though they'd only been in it for approximately five minutes between them. Just a *little* fuss today of all days would have been nice.

He walked to his car – a neat, practical little Prius – and waved across Primrose Square at Jayne Dawson, a lovely neighbour who'd lived on the square since Old God's time and who seemed to be out for an early morning jog.

'Happy birthday, Frank!' Jayne called over cheerily, as Frank smiled and waved back at her, marvelling that someone of Jayne's age – she had to be seventy if she was a day – could still seem so youthful and energetic.

Then he stopped in his tracks. *How did she know it was my birthday?* Jayne was the sweetest soul you could ever meet, but they weren't exactly close friends. There was no way he'd have expected her to know that the day was special for him.

Odd, he thought, strapping himself into the car and waving at Jayne as he drove off to work, taking the correct lane and staying well within the speed limit, as always, punctual to the dot.

No one at the office remarked on the day, not even at lunchtime when Frank slipped out and bought a fresh Victoria sponge for the staff to share.

He wondered if it seemed a bit sad that he was left to go out and buy his own birthday cake by himself. Then he wondered if it was even sadder that not a single soul in the office took a single slice when he offered it around. Instead, there was a whole chorus of excuses.

'Oh, cake! A lovely thought, but you know I'm gluten free right now . . . Sorry.'

'What class of a fucking idiot brought in cake,' griped Florence from finance, 'when I'm trying to stick to a sugar-free diet? Are you shower of bastards trying to torture me or what?'

Even kind-hearted Tracey, the office receptionist, joined in. 'No, take that vile thing away from me!' she yelled theatrically, like it was made of nitro glycerine and not just a humble cream sponge. 'I'm doing the Slimming World plan and I've already had all five of the sins I'm allowed for today!'

'Rightio, sorry about that,' Frank said apologetically, lifting the offending cake safely out of harm's way. He nibbled at a tiny slice of it himself on his own at his desk, then threw the rest of the cake into the brown bin – the correct bin, as he was constantly having to remind the others, for food waste disposal.

Oh well, he thought. *Never mind. Chin up.* After all, what did it matter really? It was only a bit of cake. Besides, he'd already silently made his own plans for that evening and a full, bloated stomach certainly wouldn't be of any help to him. Not with what he had in mind.

Ordinarily, you could set your watch by the time Frank's spotless Prius would trundle up Primrose Square at the end of a working day. The neighbours often said that the only two things you could depend on around there were bin day on a Monday and that Frank Woods from number seventy-nine would arrive home at 7 p.m. every night, punctual to the dot, parking in his usual spot, with the correct resident's permit prominently displayed against the dashboard.

But that particular night was different. If you were watching Frank's movements closely, you'd know that something was up. For a start, it was later, far later than normal, well after 9 p.m., when Frank finally did get home. He'd purposely waited until dark, when he hoped Primrose Square wouldn't be too busy with neighbours coming and going. Less chance of being seen, he figured, a mix of excitement and anxiety bubbling away in his belly.

The weather had changed dramatically, and the mild spring day had given way to a miserable, rainy night. Still, though, you could never fully count on privacy around the square, whatever the weather. You'd often see hardy late-evening joggers puffing their weary way around the perimeter, or Becky from number forty-two out walking her yappy little terriers that barked a lot and always went for your ankles.

The last thing Frank wanted that night, of all nights, was to bump into a single soul. It was absolutely critical that he get home unnoticed and unobserved – any witnesses would be a potential disaster. So switching off the engine, he took a cautious peek all around before daring to get out of the car. It seemed that his luck was in – the coast was clear. There wasn't a single soul around, just lights peeping out through the curtains from lots of neighbouring houses and a Deliveroo guy pedalling furiously down the square with the smell of Thai food wafting after his bike. It seemed everyone was having a cosy Friday night in with takeaways in front of the telly.

Frank's home was the only gloomy-looking one, with not a single light on. No one was home. Gracie was still at work, Amber had gone to her piano lesson, and Ben was hopefully not going too wild at his end-of-term party. The place looked utterly deserted.

Perfect, thought Frank. *So far, so good.*

Gingerly, he stepped out of the car, a bit wobbly on his feet, but still. Frank felt fantastic. He'd made up his mind to do what he was doing and it felt utterly sensational, he thought, enjoying a freedom he so rarely got to savour. He clipped up the three neatly scrubbed stone steps that led to his own front door, thanking his lucky stars his hands weren't trembling as he put his key into the lock. Speed was of the essence here.

One heart-stopping moment later and Frank was safely inside the privacy and comfort of his own hallway, which was in pitch darkness. With a sigh of relief, he fumbled about for the light switch, finally grasping it and switching it on.

'SURPRISE!!!!'

'HAPPY BIRTHDAY, FRANK!!!!'

Frank heard the cheers in deafening loudness, but somehow his brain couldn't quite process what he was seeing. Now the house was bright – full-on fluorescent bright. There were people stuffed into his sitting room and hallway, and no matter where he looked, every single face was focused on one person and one person only – him.

There was a giant banner over the fireplace that read: HAPPY 50TH FRANK! Helium balloons were floating all throughout the hall and up the staircase, and everywhere Frank looked, he recognised someone. Old school friends he hadn't seen for years, almost every one of his Primrose Square neighbours, including Susan Hayes and her husband, the square's other Frank, his parents-in-law, and his only brother who lived in London and who must have flown over specially. It was like Frank was standing before a parade of his entire life to date, past and present.

But the cheering and clapping had died out now, and every eye seemed to be staring at him in mute, sickening horror.

On the stairs was Gracie, looking breathtaking in a skinny cocktail dress that he'd never seen on her before. *She must have gone and bought it new,* Frank thought, from the tiny part of his mind that could still function. *Just for me. Just for this.*

Behind Gracie, Ben stood with his two best friends from school, all three of them gaping at him dumbly, mouths hanging open like pictures in old comics, registering crude shock at what they were seeing. Images were beginning to waft past Frank now, as he began to feel almost suspended in time. He saw Jayne from number nineteen with her husband Eric, and the confused, mortified look on their faces. Old college pals who he hadn't seen in decades, were now trying to suppress snorts of snide, vulgar laughter.

Beside them in the living room, Frank could make out a few of his work colleagues, the very same team who'd lied through their teeth about their plans for the night. Joe from sales with a beer clamped to his hand, Florence holding what appeared to be a gift-wrapped set of golf clubs, Tracey from reception, even Margaret the office gossip – all of them in perfect freeze-frame, staring at him in open-mouthed disbelief.

And one last, final image that would probably haunt Frank till the end of his days. Amber, his little princess, bursting out of the kitchen, in her good party dress, clutching bright blue helium balloons that read: *50 today!*

'Oh Dad!' she exclaimed, weaving her way through the throng before she could get to him. 'I'm so sorry about all the lies we've told you – as if I'd ever go to a boring piano lesson on your big day! Mum and Ben and me have been planning this for weeks and weeks and we wanted it to be a proper surprise for you . . .'

But then Amber's voice weakened and slowly trailed away as she looked at her father in utter confusion.

'Dad . . . ? Dad, why are you dressed like that?'

The penny slowly dropped as she took in what Frank was wearing. The tight satin dress, the high heels, the wig, the faceful of makeup that he'd applied as painstakingly as he always did, but which probably looked harsh and unforgiving in the glaring overhead lights.

'Dad?' his daughter's voice rang out, clear as a bell, through the pin-drop silence. 'Why are you dressed as a woman?'

Emily

'Welcome to the first day of the rest of your life!'

'And remember what Abraham Lincoln said: "Determine that the thing can and shall be done, then find the way"!'

Emily was standing on the steps outside St Michael's Wellness Centre, on the happy, glorious day when she'd finally been discharged and let loose into the world again. The other patients only meant well, she knew, as they clustered around her taxi, to wish her a fond farewell. Emily had really got to know them all over the past few months and they certainty weren't the worst bunch. Still, she thought, forcing a tight grin through clenched teeth, she could gladly have dispensed with ninety-nine per cent of the happy-clappy, vomitty shite they were all coming out with now.

Emily had clambered into the back seat and was dying to put as much distance between her and the nuthouse as possible when Chloe, one of the newer inmates, almost threw herself over the bonnet of the cab. An annoyingly thin woman in her early twenties, Chloe had pretty much driven everyone mad since she first checked in with all the patronising drivel she was constantly coming out with.

'I'm only really here because of my stress levels, you know,' she was forever reminding her fellow patients in a whiny voice that almost made Emily want to smack her. 'It's not like I'm . . . some kind of sad-case *addict* . . . I'm just here to rest, really.'

'Where do you think you are, anyway?' Emily would snap back. 'A fucking health spa?'

'Emily, wait!' Chloe was squealing now, thumping on the car bonnet as the taxi driver tried his best to drive away. 'I just have one last thing to say to you and it's, like, *SOOOO* important.'

'Do you have to?' Emily sighed, sticking her head out the back window.

'Well, you know I'm reading a lot of Paulo Coelho right now?' Chloe said, ignoring the jibe. 'He's, like, this really famous author.'

'Is that a fact?' Emily said dryly, itching to be gone.

'And he says: "When we strive to become better than we are, everything around us becomes better too." Isn't that so beautiful?' Chloe sighed happily. 'I just thought I'd share it with you before you go. To wish the new you well in your life of sobriety.'

'Oh, would you ever fuck off with yourself,' Emily said, rolling up the back window and getting the hell out of there as fast as was humanly possible.

Later that night, Emily lay fully clothed on the top bunk of her eight-year-old nephew's bed. Lego Minecraft featured prominently in Jamie's room; just about everything seemed to be covered in it, from the sheets she was lying on, to the posters on the wall.

Meanwhile, Jamie lay on the bunk bed directly below her. The fecking monkey should have been long asleep by then, as it was well after his bedtime, but something about sharing the room with his wicked Auntie Emily had made him as high as if he'd eaten an entire bag of Haribos.

'Auntie Emily?' his little voice piped up for the nine hundredth time.

'Go to sleep,' she barked, not meaning to sound grouchy, but not exactly bothering to check herself either.

'Why are you here, Auntie Emily? I mean, like, in our house, sleeping in my room tonight?'

'Because I'd nowhere else to go. It was a toss-up between this or sleeping on a park bench.'

'Do you not have a house of your own?'

'I had, but I drank it.'

'That's silly, Auntie Emily!' He giggled. 'How can you drink a house?'

'It's easy enough if you know how.' Emily shrugged as she stared up at the ceiling, bored witless and wondering if Sadie, her younger sister, would have a complete meltdown if she lit up a fag.

Jesus Christ, she thought. *It's nine o'clock on a Friday night and here I am, being quizzed by an eight-year-old I'm sharing a bedroom with. Could it possibly be any worse?*

'But . . . you could have stayed in a hotel,' said Jamie, sounding puzzled.

'Believe you me,' said Emily flatly, 'I'd kill to be in a hotel right now. I'd kill to be anywhere, except stuck in here.'

Jamie thought about this for a second. 'Then why don't you just go?' he asked, poking his head out from the bottom bunk. 'You're a grown-up. You can do whatever you want.'

Emily stared across the room at a Minecraft poster and sighed. 'In the first place,' she said, 'I've no money for hotels, and secondly, your delight of a mother is the only relation I have who'd take me in. So here I am.'

'How long are you going to stay in our house for?'

'Not long at all, I hope,' Emily said, 'but when you're in recovery like I am, you're supposed to stay with someone responsible. I don't like it any more than you do, kiddo, but you might as well just get used to it.'

Bit of a harsh way to talk to an eight-year-old, she thought, *but what the hell*. In St Michael's, patients were constantly being bombarded with shite like: 'tell the truth and it will set you free'.

'What does "in recovery" mean?' came Jamie's annoyingly persistent voice through the darkness.

Emily sighed. 'It means when you're not allowed to have fun anymore,' she said.

'Is that because you're an alcoholic?'

'Recovering alcoholic,' she said. 'Get your facts straight, kiddo.'

'What's an alcoholic, Auntie Emily?'

'It's when someone drinks a pint for breakfast and they think it's normal.'

'A pint?' said Jamie innocently. 'A pint of what?'

'Vodka.'

'What's vodka?'

'It's something you shouldn't touch till you're at least eighteen. Jesus, are you ever going to go to sleep?'

'Were you eighteen when you first had vodka?'

'No, I was fourteen.' She could have also told him that she regularly passed out in a pool of her own vomit at that age, but decided against it.

'Mum says you're trouble,' said Jamie after a thoughtful pause. 'Big, big trouble.'

'Did she, now?'

'She says you can only stay with us for a little while, till you're all better, but then you have to go.'

'Fine by me.'

'I don't think Dad likes you all that much either,' Jamie said.

'I'd say he doesn't.'

'He says once when you were drunk, you hit on him.'

'I probably did.' Emily shrugged.

It certainly sounded like the kind of thing she would have done. God knows, she'd certainly done a lot worse than hit on Sadie's pillock of a husband, Boring Brien, current holder of the grand title: Unsexiest Man on the Planet.

'But Auntie Emily,' came Jamie's disembodied voice, 'why would you hit my dad? Hitting people is wrong. Everybody knows that.'

'I didn't actually *hit* him the way you might think,' Emily tried to explain, growing more and more desperate for a fag the more this inane conversation went on. 'I didn't punch him in the face or anything. I just . . . misread signals, that's all. Booze makes you do crazy stuff like that.'

'Dad says you made a show of yourself on the night of his fortieth birthday. He said you ruined all the fun for everyone.'

'Believe me, I was the only bit of life in the place,' Emily said, hauling herself up onto one elbow, so she could get at the emergency cigarette she kept rolled up at the back of the knapsack lying on the bed beside her. The one that was only to be used in the event of a crisis. 'If memory serves, that party was complete shite.'

'Auntie Emily! That's a bold word! You're not allowed to say bold words.'

'Your dad just has a bit of a sense of humour bypass, that's all,' she said, feeling around the canvas lining for the cigarette and filching it out.

Then she lay back on the bed, wondering if she dared light up in Sadie's perfect two-bed dormer bungalow with its bang-on trend Farrow & Ball wall paint, underfloor heating and tastefully displayed artwork on the walls, in the heart of nameless, soulless commuter-land. This was a house where you were told to take off your stilettos before you were allowed to walk on Sadie's beautifully waxed wooden floors. The rebel in Emily almost wanted to smoke purely to see Sadie's shit fit of a reaction.

'Don't be mean about my dad,' Jamie said stoutly, peeking out at her from the bottom bunk. 'My dad is my bestest friend. He plays soccer with me every evening and he's taking me to Tayto Park this weekend.'

'I'm not being mean,' said Emily through the darkness. 'I'm just telling it like it is. Mark my words, kiddo, by the time you're sixteen, your dad won't be your best friend anymore. If you're even halfway normal, you'll want to get as far away from Stuck Up Sadie and Boring Brien as humanly possible. Then you'll be delighted to have an auntie like me, because I've been there, seen it all, done it all and got the T-shirt. When your parents are driving you up the wall, you'll be able to tell me anything. I'm unshockable.'

'Mum says you were born bad,' said Jamie, 'and that you were always trouble. She says you used to have loads of good things in your life, and you ruined every single one of them.'

'Your mother only thinks that because she's a sanctimonious prude.'

'Auntie Emily! Talk in words that I understand; I don't know any long words.'

'Time you went to sleep, kid, OK?' said Emily, breathing in the lovely, fresh tobacco smell of the cigarette in her hands. *Sod this anyway*, she thought. *I'm exactly nine hours out of hospital and I deserve this. I've earned it.*

'Mum says you can share my room,' Jamie said seriously, 'but that I'm not allowed to hang out with you.'

'Well, that's something, I suppose.'

'It's because of what happened the time you took me to the panto when I was six. Do you remember, Aunt Emily? You promised to take me to *Jack and the Beanstalk*, but instead we went to that horrible, smelly dark place with the bar and the high stools, and you gave me Club Orange and you drank four drinks in the same time that it took me to drink only one. I was really bored, so I counted. We never got to the panto at all in the end, did we?'

There was a long pause before Emily could answer.

'No,' she said, in a much, much smaller voice, mortified that he could still remember. 'No, Jamie, we didn't.'

Weird, how the innocent questions of an eight-year-old had the power to sting her just as much as any full-on therapy session.

'After that, Mum and Dad said you weren't allowed to take me out ever again,' he said sadly. 'Mum said you broke Granny's heart too, back when Grandad died and went to heaven.'

Oh, fuck this, Emily thought. *Enough is enough.*

She couldn't take another word, so she leaped out of bed and scooped her jacket up off the floor, knowing there was a lighter buried deep in there somewhere. Then she threw open the bedroom window, stuck her head outside and lit up. Two puffs later and she felt a bit more relaxed.

'Auntie Emily!' Jamie said, totally shocked. 'You're smoking! Mum is going to kill you!'

'Shut up and go to sleep.'

'I'm telling on you!' he said, hopping out of bed and padding out the door in his bare feet.

And that's when Emily saw it. Half hidden on a bookcase behind a stack of Harry Potters, right beside the bedroom door.

Her nephew's piggybank. It had been his birthday just the previous week and there were lots of lovely, crisp, fresh notes sticking out of it, just waiting to be pocketed. Emily didn't know what came over her and she didn't particularly care. All she knew was that two minutes later she was pulling her coat on and tiptoeing down the hall in pitch darkness, banging the front door behind her.

Emily had had some pretty meteoric rows with Sadie in the past. But nothing, absolutely nothing, compared to the one they had the following morning.

Sadie purposely waited till Jamie was safely at school and Boring Brien had gone to work before launching into the mother of all rows. Up till then, she'd been frosty and cool, but the minute it was just her and Emily, boy, did she really let rip.

'I want you to listen to me very carefully,' Sadie began, abandoning the washing machine she'd been loading. 'Because I'm only going to say this to you once.'

'OK, OK, I get it, I fucked up last night,' Emily said, putting her hands up in an 'I surrender' gesture, as she perched on a stool at the kitchen counter, drinking strong black coffee. 'Calm down, dear. Won't happen again.'

'Too bloody right it won't happen again!' Sadie snapped. 'Because as of today, you can pack up your bags and get the hell out of my house. Jesus Christ, Emily, have you any shame? You stole from an eight-year-old! I just drove Jamie to school and he was desperately upset—'

'I didn't steal,' Emily interrupted. 'I *borrowed*. Big difference. Besides, it was only a few quid. It's not the end of the world. Jamie will get it back, won't he? It's not like he's going to miss it or anything; it was just sitting there in a piggy bank.'

'Not even a full day out of rehab,' Sadie said, her voice choked with anger and frustration, 'and you steal cash, then go straight to the nearest pub? Why, Emily? Why?'

Emily just shrugged back at her.

'All that time you spent in therapy,' Sadie went on, 'and then you just go and piss all over it? You've destroyed those months when you worked so hard to dry out, just like you destroy everything!'

'You really need to get your facts straight here—' Emily tried to say, but Sadie was in no mood to be interrupted.

'I mean, what kind of a person *does* that?' she asked furiously. 'It's like wherever you go, disaster follows.'

'But you're missing one crucial point,' Emily said, when she was finally able to get a word in edgeways. 'OK, so I may have gone to the boozer last night, but I didn't drink. Not a single drop of alcohol passed my lips. I sat there till closing time with one fizzy water after another in front of me, and nothing stronger than that. Just to see if I could. And I did. And you know something else, Sadie?' she added. 'I'm kind of proud of myself. So you can drone on and on all you like, dearest, but actually, last night was a bit of a breakthrough.'

'Last night was a breakthrough for me too,' said Sadie, sounding sad now, rather than angry. 'You know why? Because all my life, I actually looked up to you, Em. You were my cool big sister. Even when you were drinking, even when you were at your very worst, even when you'd broken Mum's heart,

I was the only person in this family who stood up for you. I was there for you when your marriage broke up and you basically turned into a full-time alcoholic. No matter how bad things got, I was the one who always stuck up for you and tried to reach out to you. And what happens? I take you in after you're released from rehab and not twenty-four hours later, you've upset my son, you've betrayed my trust, and you've gone and ruined it all. Just like you ruin everything.'

'Oh, for fuck's sake,' Emily sighed, 'there's no need to act the martyr. I'll be a good girl from now on. Will that get you off my back? I faithfully promise not to sneak out in the middle of the night again, and I'll obey all your stupid gobshite house rules, and I'll even take my shoes off on your precious wooden floors. Will that keep you happy?'

But this time Sadie just looked at her, with deep exhaustion in her eyes. 'Everyone warned me against this, you know,' she said. 'Brien, Mum, everyone. They all told me the exact same thing. "Emily might be sober for now," they said, "but she certainly won't have changed."'

'Oh come on, I'm crawling over hot coals here to apologise to you,' Emily said, rolling her eyes. 'What more do you want me to do?'

'I'll tell you exactly what I want you to do,' said Sadie, banging the washing machine door shut and clicking it on. 'I want you out of here and gone by the end of the day. And after that? Don't ever *think* about contacting me again. Mum always says she only has one daughter – me. And as of today, I have no sister.'

Gracie

Of three things, Gracie was absolutely certain. That every single soul who'd crammed into her packed hallway for Frank's surprise party was now staring at the Birthday Boy in horror. That *Shotgun* by George Ezra was blaring out of the iPod speakers, a song that months later still had the power to make her physically nauseous. And that Frank Woods, her husband of over twenty years, was standing in the doorway dressed from head to toe as a woman.

Not in any kind of a drag queen way, mind you; that was almost the most surprising thing of all. The exotic creature, who every single eye was riveted on, was elegant, graceful, beautifully made-up and wearing a long, black satin coatdress that looked far more expensive and well cut than anything Gracie herself owned. It almost looked like it could be Givenchy.

Bastard must have done this before, was the first thought that went through her quick, lawyerly mind. *There's no way Frank would fork out on a dress that pricey if this was a one-off.*

Long, agonising seconds passed, then she became aware of heads, lots of heads, swivelling her way, dying to see what her reaction would be. So what did Gracie Woods do? What any well-brought-up, middle-class woman would, of course. She smiled. She reminded herself to breathe. She'd been holding the birthday cake on a serving platter this whole time, so with unnatural calm, she found a free space on the hall table and gently placed it there.

With typical efficiency, Gracie had lit the candles just moments before, as soon as she got the cue that Frank's car had pulled up outside. The idea was that she'd present the cake to him when he came in the door, so he could blow out the candles himself. So he could enjoy the surprise. *Dear God,* she thought, *surprise didn't even begin to cover it.*

Now, though, all she could think of was that someone had better blow out all fifty of the candles before her expensive wallpaper caught fire. Clearly not Frank, who just stood uselessly by the door, surrounded by family and friends, utterly poleaxed, unable to move. So Gracie did it herself, taking care to blow out every last one.

What a waste, she thought, with the tiny part of her brain that was still functioning on autopilot. *All that money to have the bloody cake custom made, and no one's going to eat it now.*

A bubble of chatter began to grow, which quickly swelled to nervous laughter. Then smart-alec comments began to come in thick and fast.

'Jesus, Gracie, you never told us it was fancy dress!' said Joe from Frank's office. Gracie had never really liked Joe; she'd always considered him a loud-mouthed boor and now she remembered exactly why.

'Always the quiet ones, isn't it?' muttered Phil from next door. Gracie heard him quite clearly though, and vowed to give his precious bike that he kept chained to the railings outside a right good kicking next time she got the chance.

Then, slowly and serenely, she glided through the crowd till she was standing right beside Frank. Everyone was watching her, and at all costs, she had to keep up appearances. So, leaning over, she gave her husband of twenty years a little kiss on the cheek, even though the caked-on foundation he was wearing stuck to her lips and she got a distinct whiff of her own good perfume from him – Jo Malone Peony & Blush.

Unimaginable fucker, she thought. *He must have filched it when my back was turned.*

'Happy birthday, darling,' Gracie said, good and loud so they could all hear her back in the cheap seats. She even managed a tight little smile as she said it.

'G-Gracie . . .' Frank began to stammer, but then Frank always stammered whenever he was agitated. It was one of the things about him that particularly grated on her nerves.

'Not now,' she said coolly. 'We have guests, or hadn't you noticed? Go upstairs and change, and we'll talk later.'

'But . . .' Frank mumbled, looking like he could pass out, 'this is . . . I hadn't expected . . . that is, I never thought . . .'

'I said later, Frank. We'll discuss it later.'

Being in court was always an act, but for this, Gracie thought, she deserved a fucking Oscar. Gliding as though on castors, she effortlessly turned into a 1950s housewife, topping up glasses, passing around platters of mushroom vol-au-vents, gently chiding her guests: 'not to eat too much. The caterers are making the most divine chicken korma; you have to save your appetite!'

If her laugh was too forced and tinny, that was the only flaw in an otherwise perfect performance.

Maybe everyone will forget, she thought. *Maybe people will think they were seeing things. Maybe they'll all treat it as a big joke. If I act cool about it, maybe everyone will take their cue from me.*

So Gracie forced herself to have polite, inane conversations with everyone she could. Jesus Christ, did she really manage to have a full, in-depth discussion with that snowflake Tracey from Frank's office about which brand of Charlotte Tilbury foundation was the best? She dashed around her living room, topping up drinks that were already full to the brim, then busying herself in the kitchen, even though the caterers had everything under control.

And all the while only one thought ate away at her. Ben and Amber. Where were the kids and what in God's name did they make of this? She could barely take it in herself. How must it have looked to an eighteen-year-old and a child of just eleven?

Only Jayne Dawson, a kind, compassionate neighbour, who Gracie was deeply fond of, called it like it was. Gently, she gripped Gracie's arm and steered her away from the throng into a quiet little alcove just off the main hallway.

'Are you OK?' Jayne asked softly. 'I can help clear the room if you like? We can tell people you're not feeling too well and drop hints that the party is over?'

'Ben and Amber,' Gracie said weakly, her command performance falling apart when she came face to face with genuine concern. 'I'm so worried. I don't know where they are or how they're taking it. I don't even know what to say to them . . .'

'Find them,' Jayne said firmly. 'And don't worry a bit about the party. I'll tell everyone here it's time to go home.'

❦

Gracie found her daughter lying behind a pile of coats in the spare room.

'Oh, my little sweetheart,' Gracie said, tenderly lifting Amber up and carrying her into her own room, just like she used to when she was a tiny child. 'Come to bed, pet. You can share with me tonight.'

'The party's ruined now, isn't it, Mum?' Amber said in a wobbly voice that cracked Gracie's heart. 'Why was Dad dressed up as a woman? Why would he do that?'

In her whole life, Gracie had never felt so useless and pathetic, because for once she had absolutely no answers to give. How was she supposed to answer a question like that, when she could barely process it herself? So she shushed her daughter and smoothed down her hair, then tucked her up in her own bed, doing her best to reassure her that everything was OK and that they'd talk about it in the morning.

Finding Ben was a much tougher job. Gracie had to search the house high and low, weaving her way in and out of drunken party stragglers before she eventually discovered him.

He was in the downstairs loo, being violently sick into the toilet bowl.

And a very large part of Gracie Woods knew exactly how he felt.

Violet

It was the talk of Primrose Square: Frank Woods from number seventy-nine and the night of his birthday party. Of course, Violet herself hadn't been invited, but then she never was invited anywhere, was she? Although Jayne Dawson was there all right, Violet thought crossly, not to mention that new age hippy husband of hers who went around the place ponging of incense and curry. The pair of them had front row seats for all the juicy drama, didn't they?

Not that it was much good pumping someone like Jayne to get the full story of what had or hadn't happened at the party. Everyone was always saying what a lovely woman Jayne was. 'She never has a bad word to say about anyone,' they said. 'She's such a trooper for her age.'

Personally, comments like that made Violet want to vomit. Violet was about the same age as Jayne, both of them pensioners, but in the whole course of Violet's life, she was pretty certain that no one had ever used the word 'lovely' to describe her.

'So, is it true then?' Violet asked, when Jayne called around to her house to drop off a particularly pungent dinner.

'Is what true?' Jayne asked, taking off a ridiculous pair of pink sunglasses, as she stacked the Tupperware containers she'd brought into Violet's decades-old fridge. The two women were in Violet's kitchen on Primrose Square, with its peeling wallpaper, overriding smell of damp and lino that curled up at the corners.

Violet beadily looked her old neighbour up and down.

You'd want to take a good, long, hard look at yourself in the mirror, she thought bitterly. Jayne was dressed in what young ones these days called 'athleisure', or some ridiculous, made-up word like that. Leggings with jungle print all over them, with a bright neon pink fleece top. Someone Jayne's age should have been ashamed of herself. *You're a pensioner*, Violet thought. *You should be at home saying your prayers, not bouncing around the place in neon pink Lycra. It's obscene, that's what it is.*

'Anyway, I'm just back from my Reformer Pilates class,' Jayne chattered away, deftly changing the subject, 'and as I was passing your front door, I thought I'd drop off some leftovers of the lentil stew Eric made last night. Maybe you'd like some later on?'

'Never you mind about your stinky aul' stew.' Violet sniffed distastefully. 'What I really want to know is: what happened at number seventy-nine?'

'Oh, never mind about that,' said Jayne tactfully. 'That was nothing.'

'Doesn't sound like nothing to me,' said Violet, pulling out a chair at the top of the kitchen table and staring expectantly at Jayne. 'I heard that Frank Woods walked in on his own surprise fiftieth birthday party dressed head to toe as a woman. Well, I nearly passed out with the shock, I can tell you. Mind you,' she added, 'I always knew there was something weird about that fella. Not quite right in the head, if you ask me.'

'Really?' said Jayne. 'Because I've always thought Frank was a great neighbour. Quiet and reserved. The type of fella who'd do anything for you.'

'Well, he certainly never lifted a finger for me. And if him and that uppity wife of his think it went unnoticed that I was the only neighbour on the square not invited to the party, then they're quite wrong. I was greatly offended, I don't mind telling you.'

'Frank and Gracie are lovely people,' said Jayne kindly. 'I'm sure the last thing they'd ever want to do was cause offence. It must have been an oversight on their part, nothing more. No harm meant.'

'Hmph,' said Violet.

'As a matter of fact,' said Jayne, sitting down opposite her, 'it's actually Frank Woods that I came to talk to you about.'

'A man dressed up as a woman,' Violet said, barely even listening. 'Did you ever? Mind you, it's always the quiet ones, isn't it? So, I presume that wife of his has turfed him out? Good enough for him, if you ask me. And his kids are trouble too, mark my words. Only the other day, his son Ben flicked me the two-finger sign. The one shaped like a V,' she added bitterly, 'which I know for a fact means something horribly rude. Impudent little pup. I put him on my list.'

Violet's list was famous throughout Primrose Square, though possibly not for the reasons she supposed. A keen observer of what went on up and down the square, whenever anything annoyed her – which was most of the time – it was added to 'the list'. Snotty letters would usually follow, all handwritten in Violet's scrawling, spidery writing, outlining her complaints point by point.

Becky Mulcahy from number forty-two, for instance, had been on the receiving end of one of these missives because those yappy dogs of hers had the cheek to wee repeatedly all over Violet's front steps. Not that Violet's letter had the desired effect at all; in fact, the very next morning, she peeked out her front window to see the steps strewn with little plastic bags stuffed with dog poo. The wet, runny kind.

Similarly, when sixteen-year-old Phoebe Miller from number seventeen received one of Violet's letters griping about the shortness of her school uniform, Phoebe posted it on Twitter, where it quickly gained considerable traction.

'People are tweeting about you,' Susan Hayes, from number eighteen across the square, warned her.

'Oh, don't be so ridiculous,' was Violet's crisp retort. 'Tweeting? I never heard such nonsense. Where do you think we're living – a bird sanctuary?'

'As a matter of fact,' Jayne said, steering the conversation back on track, 'I'm glad you brought up the subject of Frank Woods. Because he's in a bad place, as you can imagine, and you might just be able to help him.'

'Let me guess,' said Violet sourly. 'He wants to borrow one of my support girdles?'

'No, nothing like that at all,' Jayne said patiently. 'It's just that . . . well, things are a little ropey between poor old Frank and Gracie just now. Gracie is taking the whole thing very badly.'

'Serves her right,' muttered Violet. 'I never had any time for Gracie Woods. She once took my parking space right outside the door. I'll never forget it. The barefaced cheek of the little madam. Just because she's a lawyer doesn't mean she's a cut above the rest of us.'

'But Violet, love,' Jayne said gently, 'you don't even drive.'

'That's beside the point. She got a right stinker of a letter from me after that, I can tell you.'

Jayne sighed. 'It's actually Frank that I wanted to speak to you about.'

'What about him?' Violet asked, a little intrigued in spite of herself.

'I bumped into him earlier and you can imagine how upset he is after all this.'

'So he should be.'

'The thing is,' Jayne said, ignoring her, 'given the tensions at home, I suggested to Frank that he might think about moving out for a bit. Just till the dust settles, that's all.'

'Oh really?' said Violet suspiciously. 'And what can this possibly have to do with me?'

'Well, do you remember how you used to take in lodgers?' Jayne said. 'Anyway, I thought maybe you might like to offer Frank one of your spare rooms. Wouldn't that be perfect? Frank would be nice and close to Gracie and the kids, yet he'd have all the time and space he needs. And you'd have a bit of extra cash coming in . . .'

Violet sat bolt upright, a study in wounded pride.

'And what, Jayne Dawson,' she spluttered, 'makes you think that I'd have the slightest interest in taking in lodgers?'

There was silence at the table. Jayne was far too tactful a person to answer, but still. Violet could see her taking in the cracked ceiling that leaked and the blue/green mould that was starting to creep up the walls. The thought was unspoken between them.

Because you need money badly, that's why.

A moment later, Violet had risen to her feet.

'How dare you,' she said crisply, a monument of threadbare dignity. 'How dare you come into my private home and presume to tell me that I'm indigent? What do you think I am anyway, some kind of a charity case?'

'Oh now Violet, love,' said Jayne, flushing furiously, 'come on. We've known each other most of our lives. Surely you don't need to be like this with me?'

'I'm a piano teacher, you know,' Violet snapped. 'I teach privately and I earn my own living, thank you *very* much. Not that it's any of your concern, Jayne Dawson.'

'Forgive me if I was being insensitive,' Jayne said, backpedalling as fast as she could. 'I just thought . . . well, we could all do with a spare bit of cash these days. It was only a suggestion, that's all. No harm intended. There's no need to be cross with me.'

'I'll behave any way I like,' Violet retorted briskly. 'Coming in here like Vincent de Paul and treating me like some kind of charity case, with your meals on wheels. I'll thank you to leave now,' she added, picking up the thick orthopaedic walking stick that went everywhere with her. 'I've been patronised by you quite enough for one day.'

'I really am so sorry, Violet,' Jayne said, mortified. 'You know I only meant to be helpful.'

But Violet was already at the hall door, holding it open for her.

'And one more thing,' she said, as Jayne got up to go.

'Yes?'

'You can take that stinky lentil curry or whatever it is with you. I'm not having that garlicky smell destroying my house, the way it's destroyed yours.'

A hurt look from Jayne, which Violet chose to ignore.

'And you can tell that new age hippy husband of yours,' she added witheringly, 'that he can keep his vegetarian lentils to himself, thanks all the same.'

Later that evening, there was an urgent rapping at Violet's heavy, peeling front door. She grumbled as she pulled back lock after lock and latch after latch with arthritic fingers, snapping, 'Will you kindly hold your horses; I'm going as fast as I can!'

Who, she wondered, had the barefaced cheek to hammer on her door like this? During *Coronation Street*? Well, whoever it was, she thought, hauling back the heavy metal bolt at the top of her door, they were in for a right lash of her tongue.

'Conor Nugent,' she said, seeing who it was on the other side. She knew Conor only slightly; his son Ted was one of her piano students. One of the very few.

'Miss Hardcastle,' said Conor, looking thunderous, with his arms folded as he stood in her doorway, framed by hanging cobwebs.

'What on earth do you want at this hour?' she demanded, peering at him through the tiny chink of space that her lock and chain allowed. 'Lessons are over for today and I won't see your Ted till next Wednesday at five p.m. sharp. Kindly be punctual this time, please. I'm a very busy woman and I won't be kept waiting.'

'I'm here about Ted, actually,' Conor said sternly. 'Because I'm not bringing him back to this house ever again, and you, Violet Hardcastle, can consider yourself bloody lucky that I don't take legal action against you.'

At that, Violet stood up to her full height – which, given that she was long and thin and well over five feet ten, was fairly intimidating.

'And what do you mean by that, may I ask?' she demanded.

'You know exactly what I mean!' Conor barked back. 'My Ted came home earlier bawling his eyes out, because you were abusive to him! You should be ashamed of yourself!'

'How dare you come in here and start throwing accusations like that around!'

'Did you or did you not,' Conor went on, 'call my son retarded?'

At that, Violet went silent.

'Have you any idea how offensive that is? You do realise I could report you for this, don't you?'

'Your son,' said Violet, clawing back her dignity, 'was supposed to be learning Bach's *March in D Major* for his piano exam at the end of the term. Instead, that young man had the barefaced cheek to come in here and demand that I teach him some kind of ridiculous pop song. Utter nonsense about a personage who claims that liking something is conditional on putting a ring on it.'

'It's a Beyoncé song,' said Conor crossly. 'It's a perfectly reasonable request.'

'It's vulgar, vulgar, vulgar,' Violet snapped. 'And how dare your impudent pup of a son tell me what I can or can't teach!'

'You called my son retarded!' Conor yelled. 'Are you completely insane? You can't speak to a child like that! Ted certainly won't be back for any more of your poxy piano lessons.'

'Is that meant to be some kind of a threat?' said Violet, trying to close the door, only Conor had wedged his foot inside, so she couldn't. 'Because that's absolutely fine by me,' she went on. 'I have plenty of other piano students, you know. The loss of one cheeky and talentless pupil will have no effect on me whatsoever.'

'Oh, listen to yourself,' said Conor, shaking his head in disbelief. 'You're just a bitter, deluded aul' one and you're as mad as everyone says you are. When I tell the other parents what you did, you're going to lose the rest of your students too. All three of them. Don't you get it? It's over for you. If you think any parent will allow their child to be verbally abused by you, you've another thing coming.'

Violet stared at him in shock. Because she needed those students, badly. She was depending on them. They were a horrible little bunch of misbehaved primates, but they did at least pay her in cash.

Then she remembered herself.

'Get your filthy, dirty boot out of my doorframe,' she snapped. 'And if I find out you've damaged my paintwork, you'll have to pay for it.'

⚜

The following morning, yet another scary-looking bill arrived through Violet's letterbox. A mere glance at the very first line was quite enough to put her off her hard-boiled egg.

**FINAL NOTICE: ELECTRICTY SUPPLY WILL BE DISCONTINUED
IF PAYMENT DUE IS NOT RECEIVED BY RETURN.**

All typed in bold, black print. So very cheap and classless. Violet tore up the demand, tossed it on the floor, and tried to go back to her breakfast and an out-of-date copy of *The Lady* she'd been trying to read.

But by then, the thought had lodged in her head and wouldn't budge.

Moments later, she was on the telephone to Jayne from across the square. Violet didn't own one of those mobile phones that everyone seemed to be so utterly dependent on these days; she used the landline in her dust-covered hallway, which was perfectly satisfactory, thank you very much.

'Now, Jayne, I don't want you to go seeing this as some kind of moral victory for you,' she began, as soon as the telephone was answered. 'But I've decided, just this once, that ridiculous friend of yours, the transvestite, or whatever he calls himself, may indeed rent out my spare room. Not the good one, mind you – he can have the little box room on the top floor, where I don't have to look at him. Seven hundred euros a month, payable in advance.'

'That's wonderful, Violet,' Jayne said warmly from the other end of the phone. 'I'll let Frank know right away.'

'But if I catch him dressed as a woman, or if he even thinks about touching anything belonging to me, he's out on his ear. Got it?'

Frank

Frost. Not outside, though. Outside it was beautiful, late spring. The cherry blossoms that lined Primrose Square were in full bloom, and everywhere you looked, locals had begun to enjoy lunchtime or weekend picnics, the braver ones already out in their flip-flops and sun cream.

At number seventy-nine on the north side of the square, however, it might as well have been deepest, darkest winter. The atmosphere inside the house was so glacially cool, you could almost have got frostbite from it.

'Can we at least talk about what happened?' Frank said quietly to his wife Gracie, as she stood at the kitchen table stuffing her briefcase full of case notes. It was a few days after the infamous party and she had yet to utter a single, solitary word to Frank on that, or any subject.

'Gracie?' he repeated gently.

Silence.

'Please, love,' said Frank, donning a pair of rubber gloves and beginning to clear up the remains of her breakfast, same as he did every morning. 'I think the least we should do is talk.'

More silence, but this time Gracie stopped dead in her tracks and really paused to look at her husband of almost twenty-one years, as if he were a complete stranger. Frank stood opposite her, his neatly pressed work suit utterly incongruous against the bright yellow Marigolds he was wearing, as the pair of them locked eyes.

This, he thought, *is a breakthrough.* This was the closest they'd come to communicating since The Night Of.

'I know what happened was a huge shock to you,' Frank said, grabbing his chance, his speech sounding a bit pre-prepared and rehearsed, because that's precisely what it was. 'But we can't continue to ignore the elephant in the room, can we?'

Then he bit his lip as he waited for her response. Tension always made him edgy and twitchy, and he'd been a complete ball of tension for the last few days.

There was a throbbing moment as Gracie eyeballed him, and Frank prayed she'd speak. Anything, absolutely anything was better than the cold, silent treatment he'd been enduring.

She looks pale, he thought, *and she's got bags under her eyes from lack of sleep.*

It crushed him to think that he was the root cause of it all. Part of Frank wanted to hug her and hold her and tell her that everything would be all right. But that, he knew, was out of the question. The mood Gracie was in now, it would be like hugging a Doberman.

'I want you to listen to me very, very carefully,' she eventually said, in a dangerously low, threatening voice. 'You have to understand that I'm working hard to hold it together here. Ben is about to start his Leaving Cert, Amber will be on her school holidays very soon and I'm in the middle of a huge trial with a lot of clients depending on me.'

'Yes, I know all this, love—' he tried to say.

'Don't you *dare* interrupt me.' Gracie spoke with authority, just like she always did in court.

'Sorry. I'm sorry,' he said meekly.

'So somehow, Frank,' she went on, 'in spite of what you did and the sheer mortification you've put this family through, somehow I have to find the strength in me to park this. I have to put my kids first and my job second, and I'll deal with you when I deal with you.'

There was a tight pause.

'Oh,' Frank said, visually deflating. 'All-righty then.'

Had he really thought that Gracie would talk about this? He should have known better. Gracie was a wonderful mother, like a mother tiger with her cubs, and if you were ever up in court on a drunk-driving or violent disorder charge, then Gracie Woods was the woman you wanted in your corner.

But she had a unique ability to compartmentalise her life. She'd always done it, and now, Frank knew only too well, she was doing it with him too.

'Oh, and another thing,' she added, on her way out the kitchen door to the hall.

'Yes?' Frank asked, looking up at her hopefully.

'If you want to move out,' Gracie fired back, 'no one in this house will stand in your way.'

'Oh. I see.'

'It would certainly go a long way towards lightening the tension around here.'

'Rightio.'

'We're agreed, then?'

'Whatever you say.'

'Good,' said Gracie briskly. 'The sooner you start looking for somewhere to rent, the better. And before I forget . . .'

'Yes?'

'The U-bend in the upstairs loo is blocked again. Can you fix it before you go?'

Frank sighed, went back to loading the dishwasher and said what he always said: 'Okey dokey.'

If Frank thought the silent treatment from his wife was bad, it was nothing compared with how Ben was dealing with him. For days now, Frank had tried his very best to reach out to his son, tapping gently on his bedroom door time and again, only to be told: 'If that's you again, Dad, you can fuck off and leave me alone.'

'Please, Ben,' Frank persisted softly from the other side of the door. 'I only want to talk to you.'

Then one night, to his astonishment, Ben actually unlocked and opened his bedroom door, glowering down at his dad, as Frank looked nervously back up at him. Ben was already over six feet tall and Frank hadn't quite realised how truly terrifying his son could be when he was angry. But then, he reminded himself, he'd never really seen Ben angry before. Not like this, not on this scale.

'I have nothing to say to you,' Ben said coldly. '*Nothing*. So stop tapping on my door night after night and just PISS OFF!'

'B-But Ben,' Frank stammered, 'we can't go on like this. All I want to do is try and explain . . .'

'Explain what? That you're some kind of a fucking freak show? That you're not who any of us thought you were?'

'Please, son,' Frank begged. 'I know you're angry and upset . . .'

Ben was having none of it. 'Angry?' he spat, as a vein started to throb dangerously at the side of his temple. 'You haven't a clue! As far as everyone we know is concerned, you're a fucking joke. Word has gone all around my school and now I'm getting roasted, because no one wants to be friends with the guy whose dad goes around dressed as a woman!'

'Please, just let me explain . . .' Frank tried to say.

'And what about Mum? Have you any idea what she's going through? Do you even care?'

Frank opened his mouth, but it was as if the power of speech deserted him. How could he put it into words? How could he explain that he'd give everything he had to put the clock back to that awful night? That he'd been stuck in a living hell ever since? That the very last thing he'd ever wanted to do was cause pain to his family, who were his whole world?

He didn't get a chance to say a single word, though.

'Oh, just fuck off and leave me alone!' were Ben's last words, before he slammed the door right in his father's face.

'Okey dokey,' Frank sighed quietly from the other side of the door.

Then he felt a gentle arm slip silently around his waist. It was Amber, his baby, his little princess. His ally in the house and the one person in his life who still gave him the time of day.

'Don't worry, Dad,' she told him. 'Ben might be cross, but I still love you.'

'Thank you, love,' Frank said hoarsely.

'Even if everyone says you are a freak show.'

The following morning, Frank took Amber out to brunch, ostensibly for French toast and waffles, but really to get out of the line of fire and the unbearable tension back at Primrose Square.

'Did you think the party was fancy dress, Dad?' she asked him straight out. 'Is that what happened?' She looked across the table at him, all wide-eyed and confused. 'Dad? Did you just make a mistake?'

Oh Amber, Frank wanted to say to her, as the smell of maple syrup on freshly made waffles turned his stomach to ash. *If only you were older, maybe I could make you understand.*

There was so much he wanted to say, not just to her, but to Gracie and Ben too. He wanted to explain how trapped he'd felt. Not just recently, but always, ever since he was a small child. He wanted to tell her how he'd never really known confidence or self-esteem or what it felt like to actually be valued as a human being.

Mr Cellophane. That was what he was called behind his back at work, and even though it was meant as a harmless joke, it still bloody hurt.

Of course, Gracie and his children had always been a source of huge joy to Frank, but they all had their own lives to lead and the older they got, the more marginalised he became in theirs. Gracie had her own highly successful legal work, while Ben was a bit of a sports star at school, with a better social life than anyone else Frank knew. So that just left Amber, who was now looking at him over her waffles in the cheesy 1950s diner where they'd gone for brunch, wanting adult answers to her child-like questions.

'But why, Dad?' she kept saying. 'If it wasn't for a joke, then why did you do it?'

Because it makes me feel free, Frank wanted to tell her. *Because you think you know your old dad, but I'm not this person at all, really. I'm not the boring, predictable, staid Mr Cellophane that everyone thinks I am. When I'm dressed up, when I release the female in me, I can take on the world. I'm unstoppable. I'm a better person as a woman than I ever was as a man.*

Maybe one day, when you're older, I can make you understand, my darling. But till then, all I can do is feed you waffles, and drive you to play dates, and take you to the movies, and be here for you, and love you unconditionally.

'Daddy?' Amber's worried face was frowning up at him. 'You've gone all quiet. Are you OK?'

'I'm fine,' Frank said, with a sad little smile. 'Would you like anything else to eat, pet?'

'No thanks,' she said, pushing away a plate of waffles that she'd barely even touched.

'If it's cool with you, Dad, I'd really like to go home now.'

'Okey dokey.'

I've failed her, Frank thought as he pushed back his chair. *Just like I've failed everyone else. The whole point of this brunch was to reach out to her and put her mind at rest, and I can't even get that much right.*

He got up to pay the bill, standing quietly in line as a gang of rowdy teenagers cut in ahead of him, feeling useless, pathetic, so full of self-loathing that it was almost frightening.

Emily

The evening had barely begun and already Emily had a grand total of:

- Five missed calls on her phone.
- Two further rows with her sister and temporary hostess, Sadie.
- One major guilt trip from her brother-in-law, Boring Brien.

Oddly enough, though, the worst thing of all wasn't any of the above. It was the massive big hug her nephew and temporary room-mate Jamie gave her when he got home from school.

'I don't mind that you stole money from my piggy bank, Auntie Emily,' he told her gravely, his pale, serious little face looking up at her. 'Mummy said you're very sick and that's why you did it.'

'Is that what Mummy said?' Emily asked, as she shoved a few crumpled T-shirts and a spare pair of jeans into her rucksack.

'She said you had demons inside you,' Jamie said. 'And that's what makes you do bold things. So don't be sorry, Auntie Emily, because I really don't mind about the money.'

'I'll pay you back, kiddo,' she said, abandoning her packing and stooping low so she could look him right in the eye. 'That's a promise.'

'I know you will.' Jamie nodded wisely. 'And just so you know, Auntie Emily – I think it's kind of cool to have demons inside you. It's like you're possessed or something. I can't wait to get into school tomorrow to tell all my friends that my auntie is possessed.'

With that, he gave her a big, warm hug and headed outside to play on his bike.

The one family member I have, Emily thought, *who'll actually miss me.*

'So, I'll be off then,' Emily said to Sadie not long after, as her sister stripped the bedsheets off the top bunk with unnecessary aggression.

As if I've contaminated her precious sheets, Emily thought, *just by sleeping on them.*

'I said I'm leaving,' she said to Sadie.

'I heard you.'

'I've left your keys on the hall table for you.'

'Fine,' said Sadie crisply, not even looking at her.

'And I've promised Jamie that I'll repay every penny I owe him.'

At that, Sadie stopped yanking pillowcases off the bed and stood still.

'The greatest favour you can do my son,' she spat, 'is to get the hell out of our home, out of our lives and never come back again.'

'Which is exactly what I'm doing,' Emily replied. 'Look at me: here I am, backpack in hand, on my way out your front door. Happy now?'

But Sadie had always been a great one for getting the last word in.

'For God's sake, Emily,' she said, 'are you ever going to wise up and take a good, long, hard look at yourself in the mirror? You used to have a husband, a home, a job, a family and friends who cared about you. And look at you now. You're forty years old and you're nothing more than a washed-up, lonely, pathetic alcoholic who steals from kids.'

Even though her words stung like merry hell, Emily had too much pride to let it show.

'*Recovering* alcoholic,' she tried to interject, but Sadie was in no mood to listen.

'I had hopes for you,' she said sadly. 'I really thought you'd come out of rehab cured and that I'd have my big sister back again. But you're not recovered at all, are you? If anything, you're even worse.'

Emily opened her mouth but there was nothing left to say. Sadie went back to stripping the bed as Emily left the room, the house, the road and the neat, suburban area where Sadie lived, vowing never to come back.

Never, never, never, not as long as she lived.

You might be right about a lot of things, sister, dearest, Emily thought. *But there's one thing you're quite wrong about.*

As it happened, Emily did have one friend that she could turn to. Forty years of age with just one single friend to your name mightn't have been much to brag about, but by Jesus, it really meant something to Emily.

'Oh honey, what have you done to yourself? You look like total shit.'

Susan Hayes, of number eighteen Primrose Square, had never been one to pull her punches, and she certainly wasn't reining anything in now. Emily had met Susan months before, when the two women had shared a room together at St Michael's rehab centre. Susan had lost her eldest daughter to a drugs overdose and was in the throes of a full mental breakdown back then, but the pair had bonded and formed an unlikely friendship. In fact, Emily often thought the one good thing that came out of that miserable hellhole was that she'd actually met someone as sound as Susan.

Because Susan just got it. She'd had her own demons to wrestle with, but even during her darkest days back at St Michael's – and there had certainly been plenty of them – she'd never been anything less than warm, compassionate, supportive, and a great friend to Emily, just as Emily had tried to be for her. Susan knew what it was like to be at rock bottom. She was one of the first people to call and offer support when Emily was released, and Emily vowed never to forget her for it.

She had joined her old pal for dinner at the beautiful Victorian house where Susan lived with her family, and afterwards, because it was a warm, sunny evening, they decided to take a stroll across the road to Primrose Square.

'I know from bitter experience exactly what it's like to get out of a place like St Michael's,' Susan said, as the two women drifted over towards a quiet park bench, under a wisteria tree. Primrose Square was beautiful at any time of year, Susan always said, but particularly on a mild spring night like this one, when it was still bright at eight o'clock. 'The worst part is that you're just expected to start a brand-new life, like nothing had happened. Not easy, is it?'

'You said it.' Emily sighed, stretching her long legs out in front of her as they sat down.

'So, come on then, out with it. How bad has it been?'

'Well, as my delightful younger sister took great pains to point out,' Emily replied, 'I'm a forty-year-old divorcee; I'm childless, unemployed and homeless. I've basically lost the last decade of my life to booze, and you know what?'

'Tell me,' Susan said gently.

'I thought being in St Michael's was rock bottom,' Emily said, looking straight ahead of her, where two boys were kicking a soccer ball around the grass. 'I really thought that was it, that there was no lower I could possibly sink. But it seems I was wrong; turns out there was a whole other strata of deepest crap I still had to look forward to.'

'That bad, huh?'

At that, Emily's phone started to ring, but she resolutely ignored it.

'Would that be important, do you think?' Susan asked tentatively.

'They can piss off, whoever they are,' Emily said, feeling the warm evening sun on her face. 'The only person I want to talk to right now is you.'

Susan had always been a great listener, and more than anything, Emily needed someone who'd listen. Without judgment, without saying 'I told you so' – all she wanted was a sympathetic ear.

Susan sat back, deep in thought. Then she sat bolt upright, as if something had just struck her.

'Well, here's a suggestion for you,' she said. 'You might be single and you might not have a job just yet, but there's at least one thing that I might be able to help you with . . . If you trust me, that is.'

'What's that?' asked Emily. 'Jesus, you're not about to suggest I go back to St Michael's, I hope?'

'No, nothing like that,' Susan said thoughtfully, looking straight ahead where the kids who'd been playing soccer had kicked their football into the rose bushes and were now getting a right ticking off from their mum.

'What, then?' Emily said, as her phone started to ring yet again. 'Oh piss off, whoever you are,' she muttered, fishing around in her pocket for it and this time switching it off properly.

'It's actually about your living arrangements,' Susan said. 'Because there at least, I might just be able to help.'

'Susan,' Emily said, turning to face her, 'if you're offering me a bed on your couch for a few nights, it's really sweet of you, but I'd drive you insane within about twenty minutes. I know I would. And your friendship means too much to me to ever put you through that.'

Anything good in my life, I sabotage, Emily thought. But by God, she was determined not to let anything sabotage her friendship with Susan Hayes.

'So, where will you stay for the next few nights?' Susan asked her.

'I've got just enough dosh to cover me for a B & B for the next week or so, till I find somewhere affordable.'

'Supposing I had an alternative idea for you?'

'You do?'

'There's actually a neighbour here on the square who I hear is about to take in one lodger,' Susan said, with a sly little smile, 'and who might just be amenable to taking in another.'

'Really? And it wouldn't be too expensive, do you think? Scraping a deposit together is going to be challenging enough as it is.'

'Trust me,' Susan said dryly, 'you'll be well able to afford this place.'

Emily was intrigued now. The vast majority of houses on Primrose Square were stunning Victorian terraced homes with at least three bedrooms apiece, gorgeous living rooms with high ceilings, and beautiful basement kitchens with good-sized gardens to the rear. You only had to look around the square to see how well maintained and gentrified the whole area was. Was it actually possible that this could be within her reach?

'Now wouldn't that be something?' Emily said, her mind racing ahead. 'You know how much I've always loved it around here. I'd kill to live on Primrose Square. I'd be close to you and to the centre of town. It would help me so much in getting a job. In fact,' she added, turning to Susan, 'this could be the answer to my prayers. And if this worked out for me, I'd faithfully promise not to fuck it up.'

This could just be the golden ticket for her, she thought, really allowing herself to get excited. With a great place to live, she might even be able to get a job. Not at the events management agency where she used to work, of course; that was out of the question after how she'd behaved before they'd fired her.

That was almost three years ago now, when the binge-drinking Emily had been doing ever since she was a teenager had escalated into full-blown, full-time alcoholism. But surely it wasn't beyond her to get some kind of normal, ordinary job that paid her and that, with any luck, she wouldn't mess up? Sweeping floors, maybe, or stacking shelves in supermarkets? Emily was too broke to be able to afford the luxury of pride.

And with a job, she thought, *then I'd have spare cash.* And with spare cash, who knew? Maybe, just maybe, she might be able to carve out some kind of life for herself. A better, cleaner, sober life this time, with nothing stronger than fizzy water to fall back on.

'Don't speak too soon,' Susan said. 'Because there's a catch. A very, very big one.'

'Name it,' said Emily, her head buzzing with excitement.

'You haven't met your landlady yet.'

'What's wrong with her?'

'You'll see,' said Susan, pointedly looking dead ahead. 'In fact, I think the less you know about Miss Violet Hardcastle, the better.'

'Susan, I've just got out of rehab,' Emily sighed. 'I've got nothing, *nada, niente, rien.* Any port in a storm, as they say.'

'I'll quote all that back at you,' said Susan. 'After you've met Violet. Or Violent, as the kids around here all call her.'

'How bad can this Violet be?'

Susan thought for a moment before replying. 'Imagine the Wicked Witch of the West,' she said, 'crossed with Cruella de Ville, by way of mid-1980s Margaret Thatcher, with a dash of Mrs Danvers thrown in for good measure.'

'That's what this Violet Hardcastle is like?'

'Oh no. That's her on a very, very good day.'

Violet

It was all the fault of that bloody newspaper delivery man. *Blithering idiot*, Violet thought crossly, as she twitched back the curtains in her hallway and peered out over the square. Ordinarily, that nice Mr Santos, who delivered her newspaper every day come rain, hail or shine, pushed the paper firmly through the letter box, just the way she liked it. Mr Santos was absolutely marvellous like that. Dependable. Reliable. And he never seemed to mind if you were a bit behind on your payments; he just kept on delivering anyway, which was probably just as well.

But today was different. Today, Violet's neat copy of the *Irish Chronicle* – the same paper she'd subscribed to for over forty years – had been unceremoniously dumped at the bottom of her step. It was actually lying on the pavement, waiting to be blown away. This meant of course, that Violet would have to go outside to get it safely back. *Outside.* As in, leave her house. Step out of her front door. Go out onto the square. Away from safety.

Panicking at the very thought, she squinted out the windows, scanning anxiously up and down the square to see if there were any neighbours around who she could call on for help. After all, if this didn't classify as a dire emergency, then she didn't know what would. But it was early, just after 8 a.m., and apart from a few commuters racing past from nearby Pearce Street, the road was completely deserted.

.Then Violet spied him – young Sam Keyes from number twenty-four, with a few of his friends, all in their school uniforms and dawdling on their way to school.

Violet had no great love for any of the Keyes family; they'd been on the receiving end of many of her spidery, scrawled letters over the years – even Sam himself, who'd once dared to park his bicycle up against the railings outside her house. If memory served, she'd threatened to sue him over that, but that useless Free Legal Aid woman she'd engaged to take her case instantly dismissed it, on the grounds that Sam was barely ten years old at the time.

'You there!' she called imperiously out the doorway. 'Sam Keyes! Come here at once. I need help!'

At that, Sam stopped in his tracks and nudged one of his friends.

'Piss off, you mad, aul' bitch!' he yelled back, crossing over to where Violet stood just inside the doorway, clinging for dear life to her dressing gown.

'You mind your language, Sam Keyes!' she barked back. 'Now kindly pick up my newspaper and hand it to me, and we'll say no more about it.'

'Hey lads!' Sam yelled across to two of his mates. 'Come get a look at Violent – the maddest nutjob you'll ever meet.'

'Don't you dare speak to me like that, young man!' Violet retorted – but by then it was too late. Sam's mates had clustered around him, so there were three of them now, picking up her paper and tossing it from one to another, laughing and skitting and generally acting like a bunch of primates.

'Hand that newspaper back to me immediately!' she screeched. 'Or I'll write a strongly worded letter to each of your parents!'

'Fuck off, you mad bitch!' yelled Sam, their laughter getting more and more aggressive as the lads began to shred her paper up and toss the tiny pieces all over her front doorstep, like a grotesque kind of confetti. 'You want your paper? Come outside and get it yourself, you lunatic!'

'Don't you dare use language like that to me!' Violet screamed. 'I'll write to your school about you – I'll get you expelled for this!'

At that, the lads went hysterical.

'Get us expelled, will you?' one of them sneered, a youth who couldn't be more than fourteen. 'You can't even walk down three steps to get your own bloody paper, you whack job!'

'Everyone around here hates you, you know that?' yelled Sam. 'Violent Hardcastle – that's what we all call you!'

'If your house was on fire, we'd all laugh!'

'My da says you should have been locked up years ago, only no nuthouse would take you!'

'Stop it!' Violet said, wincing from their taunts. 'Stop saying those dreadful things right now!'

'Violent Violet, Violent VIOLET!!!' the lads began to chant, pointing and laughing at her as she crumpled against her hall door, her hands clamped against her ears to block out their yelling.

Suddenly she was young again, lost, frightened and far from home. All alone in a yard, crouched low against a wall, while the other girls jeered at her and threw apple butts and loose bits of stones at her.

Then as now, they were all calling out the very same thing.

'VIOLENT VIOLET, VIOLENT VIOLET!!!'

'You're a fucking WEIRDO!'

'If you died, no one could care!'

'Do us all a favour, Violent, and just drop dead!'

'MAKE IT STOP!' Violet yelled, shutting the door against the taunts that grew louder and louder in her ears, their voices harsh, ugly, frightening.

Exactly like they had been, all those long years ago.

Frank

Frank found the place he was looking for, then spent a good twenty minutes more dithering over which was the safest and most legal parking space, making sure he was the optimum six inches from the kerb and taking particular care he wasn't obstructing a clearway.

By rights, I don't even have to keep this appointment at all, he told himself. The resolve that had got him this far was fast evaporating and the thoughts of crawling back to the relative safety of his office were approximately seventy-five per cent more tempting. *I could just cancel,* he thought, as he sat back against the driver's seat. People cancelled appointments all the time, didn't they? Who was even to know?

Everyone, he reminded himself, with a sad reality check. Just about everyone he'd even met in his entire life had been at that dismal, awful party. They all *knew.* Apparently there had been posts on social media, tweets had been retweeted, and God knows how many comments there had been about him on Facebook. His mortification was complete – so why not go ahead with this? The cat was well and truly out of the bag, anyway. What had he got to lose?

Take a chance, he thought, opening the car window and trying his best to concentrate on breathing. Apart from getting married and having kids, this was probably the biggest thing

Frank Woods had ever done in the whole course of his neatly structured, organised life.

But if there was one thing he was certain of, it was this.

He needed to talk to someone non-judgmental – badly. Someone neutral and impartial. He'd make a right balls of trying to explain things to Gracie and the kids. But then, how could he possibly explain what he was going through to them when he'd spent the best part of his life trying – and failing – to explain it to himself? Nothing about going ahead with this appointment could possibly make things any worse.

Be brave, he told himself. *No more Mr Cellophane. For once in your life, take a risk.*

Frank kept a bottle of Rescue Remedy neatly packed away in the glove compartment, for an emergency exactly like this one. With slightly shaky hands, he put three drops into his mouth, took a deep breath and braced himself. Then he got out of his spotlessly clean Toyota Prius and banged the door behind him, so his whole life as he knew it could begin to change.

Beth Taylor saw his type all the time. The ones who were shy, to the point of mortification. The ones who flushed raw red if you dared make eye contact with them. The ones who said: 'Course I'm not here for me, really, I'm only here for a friend.' The ones who'd probably knocked years off their lives in accumulated stress just to keep this appointment on time. Clients who looked like they'd wrestled demons purely to cross the threshold of the clinic where Beth worked.

Here's another one, she thought, spotting a middle-aged guy shuffle uncertainly around reception, before taking a seat and burying his face deep in a copy of that day's *Irish Times*, so no one would recognise him, even though the reception area was empty. This man was so average-looking, you'd have awful trouble describing to the Guards if you had to provide them with a photofit image. Medium height, normal weight, wearing round-rimmed glasses, dressed in a grey suit and tie, with neat brown lace-up shoes. He looked sensible – like a tax inspector or a civil servant or a guy who worked behind the counter at a passport office. Beth would almost have said that he looked normal.

Except that if there was one thing working at the Transformations Clinic had taught her, it was this: no one, absolutely no one, in here or in the outside world, was 'normal', and that was to be celebrated. Normal didn't exist. Period.

Beth's big heart softened because she knew exactly how mortified the poor guy must have felt. How much it cost him just to take this first, brave step into the unknown. She knew that all clients like this needed was a little reassurance and a big warm smile to help them relax. The promise of tea and sticky buns generally helped no end, she found.

As she approached, the man seemed to crumple back into his seat, twiddling anxiously with his glasses, whipping them off and dusting imaginary dust off them.

'I take it,' Beth said gently, 'that you're my eleven o'clock?'

There was a scarily long pause, where he couldn't bring himself to look at her. Instead he just kept wiping at his glasses till they actually squeaked. Beth used the silence to go back to double-check the appointments book behind reception.

'Frank Woods?' she asked respectfully. 'That's you, right?'

Again, silence. Even from where Beth stood, she could see that he was sweating profusely. Calmly, she walked around from the reception desk and this time came right over to him. She'd seen many patients like this before and instinctively knew how to handle them. The way she handled everything – with honesty, compassion and kindness.

'Frank,' Beth began gently, 'believe me, I know.'

'You know what?' he said, nervously folding and unfolding the paper on his lap in front of him.

'I know exactly what it cost you,' she replied, 'just to walk through that door this morning. So, first of all, well done. I want to reassure you, I'm here to help.'

He stopped fidgeting for a minute.

'Because this is huge, isn't it?' Beth said softly. 'Just by making an appointment to come and see me, you're admitting that up until now, you've been living the wrong life. Am I right?'

Again, Frank didn't speak, just focused uncomfortably on the floor. Beth saw the emotion welling up in him and knew this was probably the first time anyone had actually offered this poor man a sympathetic ear.

'How about a nice cup of tea?' she offered. 'We don't have to talk about the clinic or the reason why you're here. How about just you and me have a little talk?'

Frank looked up at her with sad, red-rimmed eyes. 'I'd like that very much,' he said.

'I'll get the kettle on,' she smiled. 'And to hell with the diet – how would you like a few nice Hobnobs on the side?'

Emily

There were house rules here, lots of and lots of stupid, gobshite house rules. That much, at least, Emily could deal with. Ever since she'd been turfed out of her sister's, she'd been couch-surfing with total strangers, thanks to a cheapie website she'd found where hard-up homeowners charged you a few quid to sleep on their sofa overnight. Provided of course that you made yourself scarce the following morning.

For days now, she'd stood in a total stranger's living room and pretended to listen as her house-proud, over-privileged host or hostess outlined all the dos and don'ts of sleeping on their precious IKEA sofa for a single night.

This one, however, really took the biscuit.

'No gentleman callers whatsoever,' Emily's putative landlady told her, while Emily stood in a gloomy, dusty hallway, backpack at her feet, taking in the dilapidated state of a house that looked like it hadn't seen a lick of paint since Old God's time.

Worse still, her new landlady seemed to be a champion hoarder. Everywhere you looked there were mounds of old newspapers and magazines, with royal family memorabilia dotted on every spare surface. Mugs to commemorate the Queen's Golden Jubilee and coasters to celebrate the birth of Prince William – all that kind of tat.

More's the pity, Emily thought. Because you could see the bones of a big Victorian terraced house like this were fundamentally good. If you had all the money in the world to pay builders and architects, then you could really do something special, even with a semi-derelict tip like this. Not that Emily had ever been much of a home-maker. A home-ruiner, that was far more her style.

As she pretended to listen to her landlady, Emily wondered what exactly she was letting herself in for. She'd certainly stayed in some dumps before this – for God's sake, she'd even slept on the streets at one stage – so a kip like this shouldn't faze her. But even if you left aside the gloom and the dust, there was just something spooky about the place. A distinct atmosphere – a feeling that something really seismic had happened here. She could feel it and smell it, just like she could feel and smell the damp.

'Excuse me, are you listening?' her landlady barked, rapping her walking stick on the wooden floor and sending a flurry of dust flying.

'Yeah, yeah, I heard you,' Emily said automatically. 'No gentleman callers,' she repeated dully, thinking: *Ha! Chance would be a fine thing.* The last fella she'd dated had been her husband and just look how that turned out for all concerned.

Just then, Emily's mobile phone rang. Instinctively, she fished it out of her jeans pocket and double-checked the number, mainly because hardly anyone rang her these days.

It was the same number as the missed call she'd had the previous day. Which was weird. And again, whoever was calling left no message either, which was even stranger.

'And that's another thing,' her landlady sniffed. 'I strongly dislike mobile telephones. The end of all civilisation, if you ask me. It's beyond rude,' she added, glowering at Emily, 'how people these days break off in mid-conversation purely to stare at a blank screen.'

'OK, OK.' Emily shrugged, shoving the phone back into her jeans pocket. 'I'm putting it away for you. Happy now?'

'If you absolutely must speak to someone urgently,' her landlady insisted, 'you may use the house telephone, here in the hall.'

At that, her landlady indicated a dust-covered landline on a filthy hall table, which had a tiny metal padlock on the dial pad, so you could only receive calls and not make any.

Oh for Christ's sake, Emily thought. *Come back, St Michael's, all is forgiven.*

'Rent is payable in advance,' her landlady was saying, 'and I expect your bedroom and the communal areas to be kept spotlessly clean at all times.'

'Spotlessly clean?' Emily muttered under her breath, as she trudged upstairs after Mrs Old Lady. 'The place is a fucking health hazard as it is!'

'Did you just say something?' her landlady said, turning sharply around on the stair return to face her.

'Ehh . . . no,' Emily lied.

'Because I could have sworn I heard foul language, and that's something I simply will not tolerate.'

'Whatever you say!' Emily said, throwing her arms up in an 'I surrender' gesture. 'No bad language, I get it!'

'Right. Well, here it is then.' With that, the old lady imperiously threw open a bedroom door on the top floor, as if she were showing the Hall of Mirrors at Versailles, and not just a poky little box room. It barely held a single bed, with cast iron, uncomfortable looking bedposts, and a knackered chest of drawers that looked like something even a charity shop would reject.

The one good thing about this room, Emily thought, as her landlady droned on about the perils of leaving the immersion on, *is the view.*

There was a tiny little Victorian sash window that over-looked Primrose Square, and instinctively Emily drifted over to the windowsill, which was deep enough to sit in, so she could look out over the square properly. From that vantage point, she could see the tips of the cherry blossom trees that lined the street below, all the way over the memorial rose gar-den in the dead heart of the square and out to the opposite side, where lovely Susan lived with her lovely husband and even lovelier daughter.

I could wave to Susan from here, Emily thought. It struck her as funny that such a little thing could make her smile.

'You'll be sharing a bathroom with another lodger, who'll be arriving later this week,' her landlady was harping on. 'So, I expect you to leave the lavatory area spotlessly clean behind you at all times. Excuse me, are you even listening to me?' At that, she banged her walking stick on the dusty wooden floor to get Emily's full attention.

'Who's the other lodger?' Emily asked. 'Just out of interest.'

Please let them be nice, she thought. That's all she wanted. A normal person, so the two of them could get together and have a giggle about this witch of a landlady and the manky state of her dilapidated house.

'A local resident in need of temporary accommodation,' came the sniffy reply. 'Not that it's any concern of yours. In this house, I'll thank you to mind your own business and afford others their privacy.'

'You're the boss,' Emily shrugged, wondering how soon she could throw open the bedroom window and light up a fag. 'So would I be violating your code of privacy to ask what I should call you?'

A wary pause.

'My name is Violet. But you will kindly address me as Miss Hardcastle.' Then, glaring witheringly down at Emily's tattered rucksack, which had been dumped on the floor, she said, 'I'll leave you to unpack now. But before I go, there's a distinct stench of cigarette smoke about your person. Don't even think about indulging your revolting habit in this house. You have been warned.'

With that, Violet swept out of the room, as grandly as a duchess at a state ball.

Finally left alone, Emily slumped down on her rickety little single bed and looked around her. She took in the nauseating flock wallpaper that had long since faded, the pool of droplets on the bare wooden floor where the roof was clearly leaking, and the old-fashioned chest of drawers that stank of mothballs.

I've backpacked around South America, she thought ruefully, *and stayed in mud huts with corrugated tin roofs that were more appealing than this.*

Then her mobile rang, shattering the silence. Jesus Christ, it was that same number yet again.

Whoever this is, Emily thought crossly, *they're certainly not giving up easily.*

'Hello,' she said flatly. 'Who is this and what do you want?'

'Emily?' said a man's voice. 'Is this Emily Dunne?'

'Yes.' Emily sighed. 'Who are you?'

'I'm Leon Ryan and I've been trying to get hold of you.'

Emily racked her brains. Someone she'd worked for? Gone out with? Got pissed with? An old boozing buddy that she'd maybe shagged, back when she was off-her-face drunk? But she drew a blank. The name meant absolutely nothing to her.

'St Michael's Wellness Centre gave me your number,' he explained.

'Did they now?'

'You're not interested in why?'

'Not particularly.'

'Well, as a matter of fact,' said Leon, 'I'll be your sponsor when you're going through the alcohol recovery programme.'

'Oh, will you, now?' Emily said, a bit sneeringly.

Course they'd spoken about recovery programmes to her back in the nuthouse, stressing how important it was to go to meetings and stick with the treatment. Emily had signed all their poxy forms about joining the AA and all that shite, but had taken it all with a big, fat pinch of salt. *Fuck that for a game of soldiers,* she'd thought. *All I need to do is stick to fizzy water and that's it – that's me, recovered. End of.*

'It's probably a good idea if we meet up sooner rather than later,' Leon went on. 'So what do you say?'

'You want to know what I say?' Emily snorted down the phone. 'I say I've had enough fucking nutjobs to deal with today. That's what I say.'

With that, she clicked off her mobile, went over to the window, threw it wide open and lit up a lovely, soothing fag.

Two months, she thought. *I give myself exactly two months of living hand to mouth in a rented room that a novice nun would turn her nose up at, in a manky house owned by the sourest old witch in the northern hemisphere. I'll get a job*, she thought. *It'll be fine, providing I tell them absolutely nothing about my past life. As long as I lie through my teeth, it'll all work out beautifully.*

The phone rang again. Yet again, that tenacious fucker, Leon. But Emily didn't even bother answering this time.

And her AA sponsor could feck right off with himself.

Frank

The gossip at Creative Solutions, the advertising agency where Frank worked, was spreading scarily fast. They'd all been at his birthday party – they all *knew*. Frank heard people talking about him in the corridors; everyone seemed to be staring at him, and every time he walked into a room it would fall silent. Colleagues who he'd worked with for years started acting weirdly around him, turning on their heels if they spotted him in the hallway, or sending him emails rather than speaking to him at his desk.

So he went back to his default position of smiling and nodding and pretending he was absolutely OK, that he didn't mind the non-stop humiliation. He kept his head down and worked as hard as he ever did, praying that the invisibility cloak he wore back when he was the office's Mr Cellophane would soon return, and that everyone would leave him in peace. This had to blow over, didn't it? Surely this was just a nine-day wonder that would pass when they all found something else to gossip about?

Yet day after day, it dragged out. He was the office joke; they were all talking about him behind his back. Whenever he walked into the staff canteen, everyone went silent. Every head would swivel his way, just in case – what? In case he'd walk in wearing a dress with full makeup on?

Didn't they realise how prejudicial they were being? Had they any idea of the hell he was going through? Frank had a wife who was barely speaking to him and a son who pointedly ignored him. If it wasn't for his daughter, he often thought, he might easily have gone and done something very, very foolish long before this.

He was at a crossroads and all his work colleagues could do was suppress muffled sniggers and make him the butt of their jokes. Once he even came back to his desk to find a Post-it note stuck to his desktop screen with just a single word written on it in bold, black handwriting.

FREAK.

⚜

After everything that had gone down at Frank's fiftieth birthday, Gracie had insisted on carting him off to their family GP, 'to see how we can straighten this whole mess out'.

'It's mid-life,' she'd said to Frank, on one of the rare occasions when she'd actually spoken to him. 'I see this all the time in work. Middle-aged men who start acting like complete idiots, just like you. Except their mid-life crises manifest in more usual ways. Like buying a Maserati or thinking that they can still date young girls in their twenties. Morons, in other words.'

'Gracie,' Frank said hesitatingly, taking care to close the kitchen door, so that there was no danger of Ben or Amber overhearing. 'Of course I'll go to see a doctor, if that's what you want me to do. I'll do anything to make this better, you know that. But . . . but . . .'

'But what?' said Gracie briskly, laying out a mound of legal briefs in neat piles on the kitchen table.

'I think I already know what any GP would say to me,' he said, feeling brave for getting that much out.

'Oh, do you, now?' said Gracie crossly. 'You've got a degree in medicine as well, now, do you?'

'It's not mid-life,' Frank said, under his breath. 'There's so much of this I don't understand, but I do know that much at least.'

'So, what is it then? What makes a perfectly normal man start sneaking around dressed up as a woman?'

'I don't know,' was all he could say. 'All I know is . . . that it goes . . . so much deeper than just the clothes. Oh Gracie, love, you have no idea.'

It's frightening, he wanted to tell her. *It's not just dressing up as a woman, it's much more. And I don't even know how it's all going to end. I'm scared and lonely and, more than anything else, I need my family now – in spite of the hurt and all the pain I've caused.*

He never got a single word out, though. Instead, Gracie gave him a disgusted look, turned on her heel and stalked out of the kitchen, banging the door firmly shut behind her.

It seemed like the only person who listened to Frank these days – really listened to him, that is – was Beth Taylor from the Transformations Clinic. Frank had instantly liked Beth the very moment he'd met her. She was a warm, open sort, and she was the one person who'd shown him gentleness and kindness when everyone else treated him like a weirdo or, worse, some class of pervert.

Having been referred by his GP, it took every gram of courage Frank had to cross the threshold of Beth's tiny clinic. But he had yet to regret it.

'Now, first things first,' she'd said at one of their very first meetings, 'how would you like to be addressed? As Frank or as Francesca? I'm anxious for you to be as comfortable as possible.'

He hesitated before answering – no one had ever asked him that before. 'Frank is fine, thanks,' he told her.

'For the moment, at least.'

'You're sure?'

'I think until everyone is comfortable calling me Francesca, then it's easier all around if I just stay known as Frank. It's fine by me,' he added. 'I'm used to pretending.'

'So, when did you first start feeling like this?' Beth asked. 'That you identify more as female than male?'

The sheer relief he felt just at being asked was overwhelming. To be able to talk candidly about how he felt was beyond price. For the first time in his life, Frank began to feel that maybe, just maybe, he could tell the truth. *His* truth.

'Since . . . since . . . always, really.'

Funny thing, but once Frank began to open up to her, it was actually difficult for him to shut up. Decades of feelings he'd taken pains to suppress started to gush out. Beth, meanwhile, sat beside him and listened, asking all the right questions, taking notes and passing the Hobnobs.

'Since I was a small child,' Frank told her. 'Since I discovered I infinitely preferred watching my mother putting on makeup than playing football like my brother.'

Beth nodded, like what he was saying was the most normal thing she'd ever heard.

'It's perfectly common to start that way,' she told him calmly. 'More so than you'd think. Society tells us that gender is binary – but supposing it's not as straightforward as that for some people? Wouldn't be the first time society got it wrong, now would it? So keep talking, Frank. I can't promise you that the process will be painless, but I can at least promise you this: from here on in, things will start to get so much easier for you.'

'Thank you,' Frank managed to say, sounding choked. All the taunts and jibes in work, he could deal with. It was when he was shown kindness and compassion, that's when he began to feel like he might fall apart.

'Tell me everything.'

So that's what Frank did. He spoke about feeling as if he'd always been born into the wrong body, right back from when he was a little kid starting school – how strange it felt to him to be dressed in long pants and a shirt and tie. The girls' uniform – kilt skirt, blouse and jumper – had always looked so much more inviting.

'Why can't I wear a skirt too?' he'd asked innocently, but his mum only told him to stop asking silly questions and to do as he was told.

As a small child, his joy was to lose himself in his mother's wardrobe, where he'd spend hours trying on her dresses and coats, revelling in the freedom of it and then not understanding why he was in such deep trouble when his father found him there one day, in an evening dress that was way too long for him and a faceful of clumsily applied makeup.

There was so much he didn't understand as a child. Why was it that he didn't feel like a boy – not once, not ever? When he pretended to be a girl, he was so much happier and more contented. Why was it that when he was writing out his list for Santa Claus and asked for a pair of bright pink evening gloves with a handbag to match, Santa didn't listen? Instead he and his brother both got Lego, which wasn't the same thing at all.

Frank talked about his parents, how they'd brushed this behaviour under the carpet, thinking he'd grow out of it in time. As a teenager, he was sent to an all-boys boarding school, where you were ruthlessly beaten up for being in any way different. So for years, Frank managed to suppress that whole side of himself. *Maybe it's gone away for good now*, he used to hope, shrinking under the covers in the dorm he shared with a gang of boisterous fifteen-year-old lads. *Maybe I'll never feel that way again.*

But he was wrong. Very wrong.

Frank could have talked to Beth for hours more, but to his astonishment, his first session came to a close before he'd barely even tipped the iceberg.

'It will take many more sessions,' Beth said, 'but for today, you've made a wonderful start. I'm very proud of you. Now just before you go, tell me this, do you know any other trans-women?'

Frank shook his head. 'There's a club I go to sometimes but . . . There's no one I know well there.'

'If and when you'd like to, there are support groups we can put you in touch with. It can help sometimes to talk to other people who have been through what you're doing now.'

Frank nodded. 'That's very kind of you, but I'm not sure if I'm quite ready for that yet. I'm still getting used to talking openly.' Frank had always been quiet and shy at the easiest of times, and the thought of meeting new people in the midst of all this was still scary.

'That's okay.' Beth smiled. 'In the meantime, I'm here for you. Now, remember, honesty in all things. If your kids ask, you tell them quite openly that you're in therapy, that you're dealing with everything and that they shouldn't worry about a thing. Also, if they want to talk, I'm here for them too. OK?'

Frank came out of his first session feeling not quite as if a burden had been lifted, but at least that his life might start to be a little more bearable from here on in.

He badly needed his life to be bearable, because that was the other thing. Gracie had insisted that he seek help, but her other firm, irrevocable demand had been that Frank move out of the family home, as soon as he could find suitable accommodation.

It was kind-hearted Jayne Dawson from across Primrose Square who presented him with the perfect solution.

'You know Violet Hardcastle from down the square is looking for lodgers just now?' she mentioned to Frank one evening. 'I'm just mentioning it to you in case . . . well, in case you ever needed to know.'

Of course Frank knew Violet. She was a neighbourhood legend – although not necessarily in a good way. She was famously sour, bad-tempered and a bit of a joke around Primrose Square. *Not unlike myself,* he thought sadly. But at least renting from Violet would give his family a bit of respite, while still keeping him close to his kids, in case they needed him.

So, the very same evening of his first session with Beth, he trundled home to Primrose Square, packed his bags and shuffled down the road to number eighty-one. Predictably, Amber was the only one of his family who actually helped him, carrying one of his bags and hugging him a tight little goodbye.

'Don't be sad, Daddy,' she told him. 'This is only for a while, just till Mummy is less cross. Then you can come home again. And at least this way, we can wave to each other every single night before we go to sleep.'

'I hope so, pet,' Frank said, standing on the steps that led up to Violet's house, surrounded by stuffed suitcases and black binliners that contained all his earthly goods. He had to take his glasses off and keep his head down, pretending to clean them, so that Amber wouldn't have to see her father tear up.

So this is it, he thought. *This is what rock bottom feels like.*

'Say "okey dokey" Dad!' Amber insisted, tugging at his elbow to grab his attention. 'That's the only way I know you really are OK.'

'Okey dokey.'

Later, Violet – or Miss Hardcastle, as she insisted on being called – outlined a lengthy list of house rules and showed him to an upstairs bedroom, a bit like a prison governor inducting an inmate. Frank politely thanked Violet for letting him stay, agreed a weekly rent, and prayed to God that he wouldn't have to stay there for too long.

'And no funny business while you're staying under my roof,' Violet said pointedly. 'I presume you know what I'm referring to, Mr Woods. There'll be none of that perverted carry-on in my house.'

She knows, Frank thought, looking down at the fussy lacy bed-spread that stank of damp and probably hadn't been changed for years. *But then why should that surprise me? They all know.*

As soon as she'd left him in peace, he sat down on the lumpy mattress and looked around the old-fashioned room.

I'm fifty years old, he thought sadly. For most people, that was a cause for celebration. But for Frank, no matter where he looked, he'd disappointed someone. *I've worked hard all my life*, he thought. *I've tried my best to be a kind, good, responsible person. I've kept my head down and everything I've done has been for the love of my family.*

And now here he was, a half-century old and all alone, renting a room in a run-down, dilapidated house, just so he could keep the peace at home.

There was just one single bright light left in the life of Frank Woods. One other person who gave him a reason to get out of bed in the morning. Someone who made him feel on top of the world, like he could take on any challenge and win.

Someone who knew that there was an awful lot more to him than boring old Mr Cellophane.

Suddenly Frank was up on his feet, rummaging through one of the suitcases he'd packed earlier. A moment later, he found what he was looking for, right at the bottom of his suitcase, carefully wrapped up in tissue paper.

Next thing, he was carefully undressing, then gingerly taking the exquisite fabric out of the tissue and allowing it to slide down over his body.

I've lost weight, he thought. It was true what they said – stress really was a great diet. He walked over to the ugly mahogany cheval mirror in the corner, did a twirl and scrutinised himself in the reflection. Already he was starting to feel better, stronger, more in control.

Next, Frank went back to the overnight bag on the bed, unzipped it and fumbled around in a concealed inner pocket. A moment later, he produced a flowery makeup bag and took a seat at the dressing table by the window. Slowly, carefully, he began to apply a layer of foundation.

God, it felt good to feel the creamy liquid glide over his face. His whole mood instantly lifted. Like putting on a second skin. Like putting on armour to shield him from the world. Next, Frank began to apply eye makeup as painstakingly as any professional MUA, taking great care to flick the liquid eyeliner, just like he'd seen on YouTube. A cat's eye it was called, apparently, and it needed the utmost concentration.

Then Frank unpacked a pair of high heels he'd had the greatest difficulty in sourcing, because his feet were so big, and the only place he could find shoes large enough to fit was some dodgy website in the States. This, of course, led to much mortification when the parcel had arrived at his house all those months ago, and Frank had been forced into a bare-faced lie when the postman he'd known for years checked the customs declaration on the parcel and wanted to know why exactly Frank was buying a pair of high spangly heels?

'It's meant to be a surprise for Gracie,' Frank had blurted out on the doorstep, flushing bright red to his temples. 'For her birthday,' he added, silently cursing himself for embellishing the lie.

'And Gracie takes size eleven, does she?' the postman had asked with a knowing smirk, as Frank thanked him politely and closed the door.

Frank slipped his bare feet into the five-inch stiletto heels and began to walk around the room, feeling invincible, like a goddess. *Worth it*, he thought. It was well worth the hassle and humiliation of getting the shoes in the first place, just so he could feel like this.

There was just one more finishing touch and then he was done. The elegant, brunette wig, which he'd found in London on a work trip some years ago. He kept it hidden away carefully, constantly transferring it from one hiding place to another, lest Gracie or the kids ever stumbled on it. Frank had spent a fortune on it; this was real hair, none of your cheap acrylic rubbish. This was a class act, glossy and thick, just like Kate Middleton's glorious mane of hair, and given that Frank was prematurely bald, the wig instantly took ten years off him.

Only then did he allow himself to really look at his own reflection in the mirror. And he liked what he saw. As Frank Woods, he may have been Mr Cellophane, the biggest joke on Primrose Square and a sad disappointment to his family. Like this, though, he felt he could take on the world and win. Because this was the way he should have been born, no matter what anyone said. This was the person he was meant to be.

Like this, Frank Woods simply didn't exist.

And in his place was Francesca.

Emily

'Good morning. You must be Emily.'

He stood on the upstairs landing in front of her, a wiry little man with a shiny bald head in a neatly cut grey suit and tie. Somehow, he managed to look groomed and immaculate, even at 6.30 a.m.

'Oh. Right. Frank, is it?' Emily said, sleepily stretching out her hand to shake his. She hadn't expected to meet her co-lodger so early in the morning – she'd only got up to use the bathroom down the corridor, knowing she had another few extra hours in bed ahead of her.

'It's good to meet you.'

'And you too.'

A pause, while Frank looked at Emily in polite embarrassment, as if he wasn't sure where to look.

'Well,' he said, flushing red. 'I'd better get going. I'm anxious to beat the traffic. Eleven-minute delays, according to Google Maps. You know how the N11 can be at this hour of the morning.'

Emily didn't, but she nodded along anyway.

'I hope I'll see you for a proper chat later,' Frank said, sounding a bit flustered as he went to leave. 'Maybe at dinner time?'

'Sounds good,' Emily yawned, padding back down the corridor. It was only when she was in the privacy of her own room that she realised.

She'd been wearing her knickers with yesterday's bra and absolutely sod all else.

Later that morning, Emily was starting to get the weirdest feeling that she was being followed. As the day wore on, it became more than a feeling, it became a very deep suspicion. Everywhere she went, she kept noticing a taxi behind her – a silver Audi with tinted windows, so she couldn't see who was behind the wheel.

You're fecking imagining things, she told herself. *Years of boozing have melted your brain and now you're being paranoid.*

Of course it was all in her head. Emily didn't know anyone who drove a taxi for starters. It couldn't be that she'd run up an unpaid fare, because she hadn't taken a cab in years; she couldn't afford to. Who'd take the time to follow her anyway? No one cared about her that much to go to such trouble.

Yet as she strode past Trinity College, weaving her way through the throngs of students and tourists who were permanently congregated there day and night, there it was again. That same bloody cab, but this time, its car horn blared at her.

Fuck's sake, Emily thought crossly, shoving her hands deep into her pockets and marching on. She crossed the busy road at the bottom of College Green and made a point of giving the driver two big fat fingers as she passed by. *Jesus Christ,* she thought. *Haven't I already dealt with enough arseholes for one day?*

Violet – or Miss Hardcastle, as she insisted on being called – had bollocked her out of it earlier for daring to smoke out her bedroom window. Emily had of course told her that what she did in the privacy of her own room was her own business, and the ensuing row had been monumental. Only Violet's threat that she'd turf Emily out on her ear if she didn't obey all the house rules prevented Emily from telling the old witch to fuck off with herself.

So now here she was, pounding the pavement, striding all the way to the dole office on Cork Street, right in the heart of Dublin's Liberties. Annoyingly, the walk took approximately half an hour longer than it should have done, because there was a long list of her old haunts en route, which Emily had to avoid. Neal's Pub on Townsend Street, the Lock In on Thomas Street, Digger Magee's on the Quays.

Emily had drunk in all of them, made a show of herself in all of them, and now had to plan route maps for herself that neatly sidestepped each and every one of a scarily long list. But like it or not, she had to get money from somewhere, and the dole, it seemed, was the only option available if you were a forty-year-old single woman who no employer would touch with a bargepole.

It was busy and bustling when she eventually got to the Liberties, but Emily had no difficulty finding the dole office. There it was, right at the bottom of the street, clearly identifiable by the stragglers outside, looking miserable and sucking on cigarettes.

Emily had never signed on the dole before and it was every bit as depressing as she feared it would be. She had a good hour waiting to be seen and when she eventually worked her way to the top of the queue, (hatch fourteen, new claims), a gaunt-looking guy, with round glasses that made him a dead ringer for Harry Potter, nodded curtly at her.

'So, what exactly was your field of employment?' he asked flatly, as she sat down on the plastic swively seat that was nailed into the floor in front of him.

'Event management,' Emily replied, praying that her claim would be swiftly assessed by this 'community welfare officer', so she could get the feck out of there as quickly as possible. Sitting in the waiting area surrounded by prams full of screaming kids was starting to do her head in.

'And what exactly does an event manager do?' asked Harry Potter, through a glass grill so thick, it looked almost bulletproof.

'It's a fancy name for organiser,' Emily sighed wearily. 'Basically, my job was to arrange all manner of corporate events, from film premieres to big birthday bashes.'

'And the reason why your employment ceased?'

Oh, for fuck's sake, Emily thought crossly. Was it really necessary to make her jump through all these hoops? Couldn't they just see that she'd been a good little taxpayer all her working life and hand over the giro? But Harry Potter just blinked back at her.

'I imagine my employment terminated,' Emily answered evenly, 'because I had a tendency to use events my company organised as a chance to get royally scuttered with the clients. I called it client bonding; they called it alcoholism. But there you go, each to their own.'

Then a memory popped into her head, unbidden and unwelcome.

A hot August night, just over three years ago, when Emily's company had organised a huge corporate shindig for a large overseas tech firm. The drinks reception and dinner had gone off well enough, and the whole event was to culminate in a giant firework display, coordinated by a professional team who'd been hired in especially. Emily had tried to hustle everyone outside to see the fireworks, but apart from a few stragglers, no one budged from their tables.

So what did Emily do about it? What she always did, of course. Made a holy, mortifying show of herself. Without a second thought, she strode up onto the podium, grabbed the microphone and yelled into it: 'OUTSIDE!! NOW, YOU SHOWER OF OVERPRIVILEGED ARSES!!!'

'Of course I wasn't being serious,' she remembered slurring to her boss Dee, when she was yanked outside and royally ticked off. 'It was only a joke, that's all. Fuck them if they can't take a joke, eh?'

'Emily,' Dee had said crossly. 'I'm only going to ask you this once and I'd appreciate an honest answer. Have you been drinking?'

After that, the rest of the night became a blur. She remembered staggering over to the firework stand and grabbing one of the control levers on a giant whizzing rocket. She'd only wanted to help, but no one would let her.

Then faces, voices, confusion, smoke. Voices screaming through the darkness. The rocket almost hit someone in the face, someone said. It grazed his cheek. One of the waiters, someone else said. A young, hard-working Polish kid, who was delighted to get a night's work and hadn't stopped serving food all evening. A lovely young fella, everyone said. A good, conscientious worker. He could have lost an eye, they all said. He could have ended up scarred for life.

After that it was just fuzz and white noise and pain, so, so much pain that all the vodka in the world couldn't numb.

'Miss Dunne?' Harry Potter asked behind the glass grille, hauling Emily's attention back to that dismal, dreary dole office. 'I asked you a question. Before I can process your claim for jobseeker's allowance, I need to know the reason why your last employment ceased.'

Emily thought for a moment. If she wanted to get that precious bank giro at the end of every week, it seemed that only the truth would do. She reminded herself that she badly needed money, because apart from a few paltry quid she got from selling her car, she barely had enough rent money to pay Miss Hatchet-Face Violet.

'Because I was very ill back then,' she told Harry Potter out straight. 'I was a sick woman. But I did what I had to do. I went for treatment and here I am, all cured and back to normal, and in dire need of cash. So come on, when does the state start paying me for a change?'

Soon, it seemed. All the boring paperwork needed to be processed, of course, but in a few weeks at least, Emily hoped she'd be back in clover again.

Well worth the humiliation, she thought, finally getting out of the dole office and wishing she had enough spare cash on her to buy fags.

Not earning money was bad enough, she thought, but even worse than that was the boredom. It was barely 11 a.m. and the whole day stretched out ahead of her, with absolutely shag all way of filling in the time.

Visit her mother? Ha! That was a laugh. The last time Emily and her mum had spoken, they'd had a row so vicious she thought the police would have to be called. Give Alec, her ex-husband, a call? Maybe even ask if he'd lend her a few quid, just to tide her over?

Fat chance, she thought, striding on through the crowds.

'For Christ's sake, Emily, you've got to stop this,' Alec had said the last time they spoke, when Emily had rung him at 5 a.m., drunk out of her head, with a black eye that stung from a date that had gone badly wrong.

'Come on, Alec . . .' she'd slurred down the phone. 'I only want to talk to you, that's all . . .'

'I'm hanging up the phone now, Emily,' came his icy cold reply. 'You can go right ahead and ruin your own life, because you're done ruining mine.'

So, what to do, Emily wondered, with the whole day ahead of her and the whole world against her? Who was left for her to turn to now? She found herself weaving her way around

Trinity College, where a bunch of students had gathered at the railings outside and were handing out leaflets and flyers to the general public, asking them to vote yes in an upcoming referendum election.

I used to be like you guys, Emily thought as she walked on by, taking a flyer that one of them had thrust at her. *I used to be a Trinity student – an honours student at that. I used to be passionate about politics and equality, just like you. I used to be young like you, studying English and History, with nothing to worry about except looming exams and the dilemma of where to spend the long summer holidays that stretched ahead.*

But just take a look at me now, she wanted to stop and warn them. *I'm a living, walking cautionary tale of what happens to you if you skip one too many lectures so you can hang out in the student bar instead.*

Emily vividly remembered wondering why she couldn't have been like the rest of her friends back then. Why was it that everyone else around her could have one or two drinks and leave it at that? Why was it that she seemed to have no pause button? What was this deep need in her to keep on drinking till she could barely stand up? She was barely fourteen when she'd had her first proper drink – a vodka and tonic, filched from her dad's drinks cabinet at home when her parents were out. It had made her sick as a pig, but still she'd kept going and had never looked back since.

Oh, fuck this, she thought, marching past Trinity as quick as she could. As well as having to avoid half the pubs in central Dublin, she'd just have to find a route through town that

CLAUDIA CARROLL | 92

avoided Trinity College. There were far too many horrible memories there, just waiting to jump out at her.

Like her final year exams, for one. Sitting in that packed exam hall with an exam paper in her hand, barely able to focus on it, the words swimming in front of her. She'd gone for 'just the one' the previous night, to steady her nerves, but somehow that had turned into the all-night bender to end all benders. She'd woken up in a strange bed with some randomer, then helped herself to a bottle of brandy in his kitchen on her way out the front door. Breakfast.

Throwing up in the exam hall . . . The disgusting smell of puke on the wooden floors . . . The college medics having to be called . . . The scene, the chaos, the fuss, three hundred horrified students all staring at her as she was carted out of the exam . . . Then hospital . . . A crowded A & E . . . Her stomach being pumped . . . The pain of it, the soreness and then the almighty hangover that followed . . . Her mother coming in to collect her, standing at the foot of her hospital trolley in floods of heartbroken tears.

'You're intelligent and bright,' her mother said, with red-rimmed eyes from crying. 'And that's what makes this harder to bear than anything. Because you should have sailed through your exams. And now look at you. The provost is talking about expulsion, to make an example of you. Why, Emily? With all the wonderful things in your life, with the great future you had ahead of you, why do you have to throw it all away?'

Primrose Square. Suddenly Emily badly had the need to go home, even if it was back to that stultifying, filthy house with that nutter Violet glowering at her. A room of one's own. Peace.

I'll just train myself to nap during the day, she told herself. *That'll kill a few hours, won't it? I'll think of some kind of job I can apply for, where even someone with my employment history is acceptable. Like stacking the shelves in a supermarket, maybe. Or else cleaning loos.*

To her surprise, when Emily turned the corner onto the square and strode down towards Violet's house, there it was yet again. That same bloody taxi that had been trailing around after her for the whole morning.

Weirder still, there was someone sitting on the steps outside Violet's house. An older guy in a leather jacket, with hair more pepper than salt and a greyish beard. He was twiddling car keys in his hands, like he was waiting for someone.

Her, as it happened.

'Emily?' he asked, looking up as he heard her approach. 'Emily Dunne?'

She ripped the earbuds out of her ears and lit into him.

'Who are you, anyway?' she snapped. 'And why are you following me around? If you're someone I owe money to, you're wasting your time, mate. I'm broke, penniless. Just take a look at where I'm living, for fuck's sake,' she added, gesturing towards number eighty-one, with weeds growing in through the windows and decades of grime caked into its redbrick walls.

The guy stood up tall and glared at her.

'Just get in the car, will you?' he said crossly.

'Oh yeah, right. Like that's going to happen.'

'Emily,' he said evenly, 'I'm Leon. Remember me? You've hung the phone up on me? I'm your AA sponsor and I'm not going anywhere till we talk.'

'Suppose I tell you where to go?'

'Suppose I tell you this is something you agreed to, before they let you out of St Michael's? So come on, what's it to be?'

Violet

Personally, Violet thought she had been extraordinarily gracious. She'd permitted not one but two tenants to lodge in her private home, but regrettably, the experience had not been entirely successful.

With Frank Woods, it appeared to be a case of so far, so good. Say what you like about the man – and Violet certainly wasn't one to hold her tongue – but he was at least quiet and polite around the house. He'd already mopped and bleached the kitchen from top to bottom, much to Violet's approval. And he'd offered her a nice cup of tea the previous night. Of course, he hadn't used the correct leaf tea or served her the tea in the china cup she liked – the one she'd purchased via mail order to celebrate Prince William's wedding – but still, the kindness of the gesture wasn't lost, not even on Violet.

His family, however, were proving to be a grave annoyance. Particularly that young daughter of his, the girl with the ridiculous name that sounded like a gemstone. Ruby? No. Amber, that was it. Cheeky scrap of a thing had the nerve to hammer roughly on Violet's front door earlier that day. Where did the girl think she was, anyway – some kind of public boarding house?

'Hi, Violet,' she'd said. 'Will you give my dad a message when he gets home?'

'It's Miss Hardcastle to you,' Violet barked back. 'And no, I will most certainly not pass on a message for you. What do you think I am, a social secretary? Your father is in work and may I point out, young lady, that you should be in school.'

'But I'm on my school holidays!' Amber protested.

'Then I strongly suggest you go and find some sort of gainful summer job for the holidays.'

'Please, Violet – I mean, Miss Hardcastle,' Amber went on, refusing to budge off the front doorstep. 'It's such a lovely day, I thought Dad could take me for a picnic in the square. Will you at least tell him I called?'

'Don't be so ridiculous,' Violet snapped, slamming the door firmly in the girl's face. *What appalling manners,* she thought. Primrose Square used to be gentrified and genteel back in her day. And now? Overrun with youngsters who behaved as if they'd been raised in a barn.

That aside, though, Violet didn't have much else to gripe about when it came to Frank Woods, as a lodger. Of course, were she to discover him kitted out in . . . female clothing – then he'd be out on his ear without a second's notice. She shuddered at the very thought. A grown man who dressed up as a lady for pleasure? Not under her roof, that was for certain.

Her second lodger, however, was proving to be far more challenging. An opinionated, unruly woman was Violet's first impression of Emily Dunne – and her first impressions of people were unwaveringly correct. Madam Emily had barely been under her roof for twenty-four hours when Violet had caught her red-handed smoking a cigarette out of her bedroom window. Needless to say, the ensuing row had been legendary.

Think of the financial reimbursement, she reminded herself, over a nice soothing cup of leaf tea in the privacy of her own drawing room. She'd finally been able to settle her account with those wretched people at the electricity board for one thing. She'd made sure to write them one of her spidery letters along with her cheque, informing them that harassing elderly, infirm ladies such as herself was an utter disgrace, and asking how they'd like it if their own mother had been spoken to in such a manner.

The following morning, Madam Emily was on the receiving end of one of Violet's missives too. She personally deposited a handwritten note on the bed in Emily's room, reminding her of house rules.

NO SMOKING MEANS NO SMOKING!

Violet took particular care to write in bold red ink, and that insufferable madam could take it any way she liked. Then, later that day, she spotted Madam Emily out on the front step consorting with a strange man, who appeared to have been loitering beside his car on the pavement, waiting solely for her.

Violet had watched the incident clearly from the upstairs window, which gave her a most convenient bird's eye view right over the whole square. The man in question had a beard, so clearly he wasn't a gentleman. And, of course, the minute Emily appeared, the two of them whizzed off together in his motorcar. Violet had rapped on the window with her stick and shouted: 'No gentleman callers!' at Emily, who'd responded by raising the middle finger of her left hand.

Honestly, Violet thought. *That woman is rudeness personified. Mind you, that's what happens when you let an alcoholic into the house.*

She'd better check her china collection later on. Alcoholics were notoriously light-fingered and the lovely mug she'd treated herself to, to commemorate the Queen's Golden Jubilee, had already gone missing.

Trying her best to banish thoughts of the wretched Emily from her mind, Violet settled down in front of the television box, planning to enjoy a most pleasant afternoon of racing from Royal Ascot. The Royal Procession down the racetrack cheered her up no end, Her Majesty the Queen looking particularly fetching in a sharp lime green hat with matching coat. Beside her in the carriage was Kate Middleton – now *there* was a young lady who knew how to comport herself with a bit of dignity. Madam Emily could certainly learn a thing about good behaviour from her.

Violet must have dozed off during the last race, though, because next thing she knew, the racing was over and the evening news was on, showing highlights from the day at Ascot.

'Doesn't the Queen look fantastic?'

Violet almost jumped out of her seat. Frank Woods was right behind her, that quiet little mouse of a man, briefcase in hand, having obviously just come in from work.

'You startled me!' she said crossly.

'I'm terribly sorry about that, Miss Hardcastle,' Frank replied politely. 'But I just wondered if you'd like something to eat? I stopped off at the supermarket and bought a roast chicken with garlic stuffing and some new potatoes, if you'd like to join me?'

Violet though for a moment. Her instinct was to tell him that she despised foul-smelling garlicky food in her kitchen, but then she felt her tummy rumble and realised she was starving. She'd been living off tins of beans for so long that the thought of an actual home-cooked dinner suddenly held great appeal.

In the background, Sky News were running highlights of the day's racing.

'The Queen really is an astonishing lady, when you think about it,' said Frank softly, his head tilted sideways as he studied the TV screen. 'Ninety-three years old and look at her, as hale and hearty as ever.'

'Hmmm,' said Violet, still thinking about the roast chicken.

'I mean to say,' Frank went on, 'how many ninety-three-year-olds do you know who can still leap in and out of carriages? And look at Camilla beside her,' he added. 'Doesn't she look lovely in that hat?'

'Philip Treacy,' Violet said, interested in spite of herself. 'That's what the commentator said earlier.'

Then a nasty thought struck her. Why was a man like Frank Woods talking about fancy hats? Surely not because he intended dressing up in one? Disgusted at the thought, she snapped off the TV and an awkward silence fell between them.

'So, what do you say then?' Frank asked after a pause. 'Can I tempt you to a bit of roast chicken? I don't know about you,

Miss Hardcastle, but I'm starving and there's plenty for both of us.'

'Well. . . . I do hate to see perfectly good food go to waste,' she said, hunger getting the better of her. 'So in that case, thank you, yes. Dinner would be most agreeable'

It was too. As well as cooking, Frank did everything else, insisting on setting the table with Violet's good china, before serving up a delicious chicken with garlic stuffing, roast potatoes and fresh garden peas on the side. They had tea afterwards and Violet graciously permitted Frank to drink from the mug she got to commemorate Prince Charles's first wedding. From there, they fell into a very interesting chat about the royal family, both discovering they'd long been admirers of the late Princess Diana.

'More sinned against than sinning, I always felt,' Frank said, sipping from the mug, which read: *Charles and Diana, St Paul's Cathedral, 29 July 1981.*

'My thoughts exactly,' Violet chimed approvingly, greatly enjoying the chat and relishing the chicken, which she'd devoured hungrily. 'And from now on,' she added condescendingly, 'I think you may address me as Violet.'

'Have you ever watched *The Crown* on Netflix, Violet?' Frank asked her.

'Net what?'

'It's a streaming service,' he explained helpfully. '*The Crown* is a truly wonderful series about Queen Elizabeth when she was young and first came to the throne. Would you like to watch an episode? I can get it for you on my iPad, if you like?'

'An iPad?' Violet sniffed dubiously. 'I'm not incontinent, you know.'

But then Frank produced some sort of electronic device, the like of which Violet had never seen before, and introduced her to the very first episode of *The Crown*. Instantly, she was captivated.

Really, Violet thought, looking fondly at Frank and congratulating herself on having secured such a likeable lodger. This evening was turning out to be one of the most enjoyable she'd had in ages.

When the doorbell pealed out later on that evening, it shattered Violet's concentration on *The Crown*, just as the young Elizabeth was about to marry Prince Philip. Frank went to answer it, and when he came back in, his expression had completely changed.

'My daughter Amber is outside,' he said quietly, fiddling with his glasses. 'She mentioned that she'd called earlier and that she'd asked you to tell me.'

'Did she, now?' Violet said flatly, still staring at Prince Philip on the iPad screen.

'Maybe it slipped your mind?' he said kindly.

'Hmmm.'

Frank looked at her, as if he were weighing up whether or not to say any more.

'Actually,' he said, 'as it's such a lovely, sunny evening, Amber and I were going to go for a stroll in the square and then get some ice cream. Maybe you'd care to join us?'

At that, Violet looked up from the iPad, horrified.

'What did you just say?'

'That maybe you'd like to come for a little walk with Amber and I?' Frank repeated. 'She's just outside and she'd love to get to know you.'

'A walk?' Violet snapped. 'Do you mean . . . *outside*?'

'Yes, just around the square.'

'Out of the question.'

'Only for half an hour or so,' Frank said gently. 'We've been having such a lovely evening, but wouldn't it be nice to get some fresh air?'

'I already said no,' she insisted. 'Are you stone deaf?'

'Oh now, come on,' Frank said, 'I'll even buy you a nice ice cream?'

'I don't go out. Not now, not ever.'

'Yes . . . but just this once . . . ?'

'Kindly close the hall door firmly behind you and go. And another thing,' Violet added bitterly, as she picked up the iPad and shoved it away from her. 'You can take that ridiculous contraption with you and as far away from me as possible.'

'But . . . I thought you were enjoying *The Crown*?' Frank said, looking hurt and confused by this sharp about-turn in her manner.

'Then you thought wrong, didn't you?'

'Well . . .' Frank shrugged. 'In that case, I'll wish you a nice evening, Violet.'

'It's Miss Hardcastle to you.'

Gracie

Jesus Christ, Gracie thought, with a biro clamped tightly between her teeth as she gingerly reversed her car into the narrowest space imaginable. Like she had time for this. She was due in court in exactly two hours' time and by rights she should have been in her chambers at King's Inns carefully revising her notes. But instead here she was, in a tiny back-street in the city centre, on her way to a counselling session with Frank.

Actual *couples* counselling. Dear God, did she ever think it would come to this? She and Frank had been together for over twenty years; they had two great kids – or at least, the kids had been doing fine up until all of this ridiculous nonsense started.

Ben and Amber. Just invoking their names in the same sentence as Frank's made Gracie's blood boil. What had either of them done to deserve this? One minute, Ben was a happy-go-lucky, well-adjusted, sporty eighteen-year-old who never gave any trouble, and literally overnight, he'd morphed into a wired, moody ball of tension. And who could blame the kid? He was furious and angry and confused, and Gracie didn't even know what to say to him, because that's exactly how she felt herself.

Then there was Amber. Gracie's heart twisted when she thought of her daughter's pale, worried little face asking why

Daddy had to go to live at Violent Hardcastle's horrible, stinky house? And when would he be coming home?

Gracie successfully parked, leaned back against her seat to let out a deep, exhausted sigh, then massaged her throbbing temples to relieve the dull, pounding headache that seemed to be permanently there these days.

What angered her most was that, by rights, this should have been a happy, contented time for their family. She and Frank had worked their asses off and now, with the two of them approaching mid-life, they should have been reaping the benefits. They lived in their dream home on Primrose Square, and over the years, they'd lovingly renovated the house till it was like something off a Pinterest board. They were both still reasonably young and healthy, and should have been looking forward to a long, relaxing summer ahead with Ben and Amber.

They'd had a good marriage, Gracie thought, rapping her nails off the steering wheel in frustration. Not perfect – but then, what marriage was? They were strong together, though; they made a great team, and false modesty aside, she thought they were pretty good parents too.

That's what killed Gracie more than anything else. This should have been a fantastic, milestone year for them both. But instead, here she was, getting out of the car, on her way to a clinic to sit in a room with Frank and a councillor, and somehow try to fathom what to her was incomprehensible. That her husband, the husband she'd loved and the marriage she'd worked so hard for, was effectively put on pause – at least until they figured out what the hell Frank was going through and why he was acting like this.

Other friends and their husbands, Gracie knew, had gone through the whole mid-life/male menopause thing. But the way those guys acted out was so predictable, it was bordering on cliché. They went out and bought bikes and lycra cycling gear. They got tattoos. They started dying their hair and eyeing up considerably younger women in public.

But Frank's latest hobby? A man who now wanted to identify as a woman, or whatever fecking buzzword you were supposed to use now? It was sickening; it was unthinkable. Worse, far worse than anything else for Gracie was the sense of betrayal. Whether Frank was a transvestite, a transsexual, transgender or had decided out of a clear blue sky that he was gay, one thing was for certain. That the man she loved and trusted more than anything had been leading a whole secret life apart from her for years. Or possibly decades, for all she knew.

You couldn't love someone and do that to them, she thought, as her temper began to flare up again. Did Frank still love her at all, she wondered, as she walked briskly to the door of the clinic and stepped inside.

Or had he ever really loved her in the first place?

Frank was already there ahead of her, waiting in a tiny cramped office that barely held a desk and a few chairs. With him was a younger, smiling woman in a wide cotton floral dress, who introduced herself as Beth as she stood up to shake hands warmly.

'Gracie – may I call you Gracie?' Beth asked. 'It was so good of you to take the time to meet with us today. I understand that you're a very busy woman.'

'Nice to meet you too,' Gracie replied coolly, shaking hands. Frank was sitting on the chair right beside her, twitching the way he always did whenever he was on edge.

It was the first time they'd actually been in a room together since Gracie insisted he move out. The whole set-up felt horribly artificial and uncomfortable to her – so it served Frank bloody well right if he was a bag of nerves.

Frank stood to peck Gracie awkwardly on the cheek, but she instinctively pulled away from him.

'It's good to see you, Gracie,' he said quietly. 'You look well.'

A lie, she knew. She didn't look well at all. She looked stressed and tense and underweight, the way she always did during any court case, never mind with all the crap she had to deal with in her private life on top of that. But she wasn't about to get into semantics; the sooner they got this over with, the better.

'OK if we start right away?' Gracie said to Beth, sitting down without being asked and producing a notepad and pen from her briefcase. 'I'm under a lot of time pressure.'

'Absolutely, let's get going,' Beth said, smiling towards each of them as she took her own seat behind her desk. 'Well, first of all, thank you both for coming here today.'

As Gracie clicked her mobile phone on to silent, she noticed that she had six missed calls from her office. *Six*. In the last five minutes. That's how little time she had for this utter nonsense.

'So,' Beth said, turning to Frank. 'I understand that you've moved out of the family home, till things settle down a little. Why don't we begin there? Why don't you tell me how that's working out for you both?'

Frank was still fidgeting away with his glasses, so Gracie answered for him, as she so often did.

'With Frank gone,' she said crisply, 'it's certainly less tense back at our house, that's for certain.'

Of course there was a big part of Gracie that missed little things about Frank being home, but she certainly wasn't going to let him know that. She missed his calm, even-tempered presence around the house, for one thing. The times when he and only he could reach Ben when he was acting out and generally being a complete teenager. Amber missed her dad too, Gracie knew; it was heartbreaking to see the child sit for hour after hour on the window seat in their hall, 'just so I can watch out for Daddy's car when he gets home'.

Gracie melted for a minute when she thought of her little Amber – but then she disciplined herself to remember the awful night of the party. The image of Frank, standing in the doorway, looking like that, dressed like that. The confusion on the faces of those around her. Friends she and Frank had known for years not having a clue how to react in the moment. Some looked shocked, some giggled and some took photos, which of course were liked and shared on social media to death.

Horrible, tortuous memories, which Gracie could never blank out, no matter how hard she tried to distract herself with work and the kids.

And above all, she remembered her own humiliation, trying to make light of it when people asked her what Frank was playing at, when all the time her own marriage seemed to be crumbling right in front of her. Passing around vol-au-vents and topping up drinks and trying to be a perfect hostess when everything she'd worked so hard for seemed to be collapsing around her in ruins.

Gracie took a deep breath, composed herself, then turned to speak to Beth. 'I think it's absolutely best that Frank lives apart from us,' she said, calmly and coolly, just like the way she spoke in court. 'It's infinitely better he stays away till he comes to his senses.'

'That's an interesting choice of words,' said Beth. 'Why do you say, "till he comes to his senses"?'

Gracie took a moment, before giving her calculated answer. Years in court had taught her that words had import and should only be chosen with great care.

'Well, why do you think?' she said, patiently spelling it out. 'My husband is clearly going through some sort of phase. But being brutally honest, any other manifestation of a mid-life crisis would have been easier to deal with than this. If you'd had an affair, Frank,' she said, turning to look directly at him, 'that, I would have understood. I'd have hated every second of it, but at least I'd have understood. But *this*? Cross-dressing, when you think no one can see you?'

It was torture sitting in that horrible, cramped little office, but Gracie felt a cool satisfaction at the hurt look on Frank's face.

She'd drawn blood. *Good*, she thought. *Now he knows how it feels.*

'I can understand that emotions are running a little high just now,' Beth interjected. 'So why don't we let Frank have the floor for a bit? Frank? Is there anything you'd like to say in return?'

Both women turned to look at him.

'I'd like to say,' he began softly, 'that I love my family very much. Gracie, you're everything to me.'

Gracie didn't know what to say to that, so she said nothing.

'We met almost thirty years ago, you know,' Frank said. 'Back when we were college students. Do you remember, Gracie?'

Of course she remembered, only too well. Back then, Gracie had been something of a college star, auditor of the college history society and a frequently labelled 'one to watch' by her lecturers and class tutors.

The night she and Frank met, Gracie had been speaking at a raucous college debate, and when her team carried the motion, she was surrounded afterwards by backslapping, boisterous teammates and supporters.

But there, in the middle of the melee, was quiet, soft-spoken Frank Woods. Turned out he was in Gracie's class, though she'd never really noticed him before. Somehow Frank wasn't the type that you noticed; he was a blend-in-with-the-wallpaper sort of person. It took time getting to know him, but once you did, his loyalty and kindness were second to none. Where her other boyfriends and admirers had been competitive and high-achieving, Frank was gentle and loving and utterly devoted to her. All those decades ago, the twenty-year-old Gracie thought she knew a good man when she saw one.

She thought very differently now.

'I want you to know how much you mean to me,' Frank was saying to her. 'Because I'd die for you and the kids, and it kills me to think that I've caused you all this pain. But Gracie, love—' he said, shifting around in his seat so he could face her full on.

'Don't call me love,' she said coldly. 'You don't get to call me love anymore.'

'This isn't a phase,' he said. 'This isn't a mid-life crisis. This isn't something that I'm going through that I'll snap out of in time. I know it's hard for you to take and I know it was an awful shock to find out the way you did. But this is me, Gracie. This is who I am.'

Gracie turned to Beth. 'I can't listen to this.'

'If we can just let each other finish—' Beth began to say.

'I know exactly who my husband is,' Gracie interrupted. 'I don't need to come here to be told. The man I married is a warm-hearted, kind, loving husband and father, who works for an advertising agency and who drives a Prius and who you could set your clock by, he's so reliable and dependable. The man I married,' she said, but faltering and failing to keep the raw anger out of her voice, 'isn't someone who sneaks around dressed as a woman whenever he thinks the coast is clear and humiliates me and my children in front of everyone we know.'

'But I'm still all of those things, Gracie,' Frank tried to say. 'You're acting like the man you married is dead, but I'm not,

I'm right here beside you and I always will be. I'm not going anywhere; never could, never would.'

'OK,' Beth interrupted. 'How about if we just take a moment . . .'

'How about if I save us all a whole lot of time,' Gracie said, hating that her voice was starting to sound so choked up, 'and ask when this is all going to end? You're a therapist,' she said, turning her attention sharply back to Beth. 'So why can't you just fix this? When are my family going to get the Frank Woods we all know and love back again?'

There was a silence. Frank shifted in his seat, then coughed as Beth locked eyes with him.

'Come on,' Beth said gently to him. 'Remember what we talked about. Communication is a wonderful thing.'

Frank cleared his throat before he could speak. 'Gracie love, that's what I've been trying to tell you all along,' he said steadily. 'The Frank Woods you all think you know, isn't who I want to be anymore. I've lived a lie for long enough and now it's time for me to live my truth. And my truth is that I'm not Frank Woods at all. I'm Francesca.'

There was a long, stunned silence.

Funny thing, Gracie thought much later on. *Frank seemed to grow about two inches as he said it.*

Emily

'Queen of Tarts?'

'Just sit down and shut up, will you? And what's wrong with Queen of Tarts anyway?'

'Nothing. Just didn't think you'd get away with a name like that these days.'

'This place is famous. Their frangipane has won awards, I'll have you know.'

'I'll have to take your word for it.'

'Now what do you want, coffee?'

'You'll have to pay for it. I'm on the dole. I'm broke.'

'I'm a gentleman. Of course I was going to pay.'

'A gentleman who just kidnapped me from the front steps of my house.'

'Jesus, there's just no pleasing some people, is there?'

Unceremoniously, Leon parked Emily at a vacant seat and went up to order for both of them. So Emily took the chance to sit and have a good look at him from behind.

Chunky. Shorter than her. Jeans too tight and the leather jacket gave him the look of an ageing rock critic. He was older than her, maybe mid-forties at a guess. He walked with a swagger, and on the drive here Emily had noticed how sweaty he smelled, as if he'd been working all night and hadn't been home to shower since his late shift ended. Like her, he'd obviously done a stint in St Michael's and was now in recovery. *An AA sponsor,* she thought, picking up a menu card and fanning her face with it. Christ Almighty, was this what it had come to?

Still, though. It wasn't like she'd anything else to do or anywhere else to go. And a free coffee with a slice of frangipane was probably the best offer she was going to get all day.

'So,' Leon said, when he got back to the table, carrying a loaded tray with two Americanos and two slices of cake. 'You're a tricky woman to get a hold of, Emily Dunne.'

'My mother always told me not to speak to strange men,' she retorted, grabbing the coffee from the tray and taking a lovely, reviving sip. It was strong and bitter. *Not unlike you, Emily,* her mother used say, back when they were still on speaking terms.

'You are aware of the twelve-step programme?' Leon asked.

'Of course I'm aware,' she said, rolling her eyes. 'They banged on about it for long enough back in the nuthouse.'

'Then you're also aware that you should be going to meetings regularly,' he replied. 'You may perhaps remember signing a release form with words to that effect? You promised your shrink you'd follow the steps of the programme, which means being in regular contact with me, as your sponsor. Returning my calls would be a good start.'

'Hang on a minute,' said Emily, 'aren't women supposed to get female sponsors? Not that I particularly care,' she added.

'Only if there are enough people to go around,' said Leon, picking up a fork and horsing hungrily into the frangipane. 'Besides, you got yourself a bit of a reputation back at St Michael's. No one else would have you. So I drew the short straw.'

'Listen to me, Leon,' Emily sighed. 'I think I can save us both a whole lot of time and bother here, OK? I used to drink and now I don't anymore. That's all there is to it. I appreciate you offering to do the whole sponsor thing, but I promise you, there's no need. I don't do meetings. Meetings are for oddballs with issues and over-sharers who love the sound of their own voices, not for people like me. I don't need twelve steps and I certainly don't need someone breathing down my neck every two minutes. All I need is to avoid pubs and stick to fizzy water and I'm good.'

'You don't need help?' he said disbelievingly.

'Just told you, no.'

'You don't need money? Lucky you.'

'Well, yeah,' she said grudgingly, 'course I need money. We all need money, don't we? But getting some kind of a job is next on my list.'

'You're not going to be able to hold down a job,' Leon said, still horsing into his cake, 'unless you stick with the programme.'

'That's bollocks!'

'Oh yeah, because your employment history to date has been so stellar?'

Then with his free hand, he reached into an inside pocket of his jacket and produced a twelve-step handbook.

'Just read it,' he said, shoving it towards her. Emily glared back at him, then started to flick through the booklet, more as a piss-take than anything else.

'"Step one,"' she said, reading aloud as Leon demolished the last of the cake in front of him, '"admit your powerlessness over alcohol." Yup, been there, seen that, done it, have the T-shirt. And what have we here?' she went on. "Step two: come to realise that a power greater than ourselves could restore us to sanity." Ooh, and take a look at step three,' she went on, waving the booklet about theatrically. 'Make a decision to turn our lives over to the will of God.'

Leon stopped eating and looked over at her, an inscrutable expression on his face.

'Now, let me ask you something,' Emily went on, oblivious. 'Do I look like a God-botherer? Do I strike you as a good little Mass-going Catholic? Last time I was in a church was for my father's funeral, and that was about three years ago now.'

'Keep reading,' Leon said quietly.

'"Make a moral inventory of ourselves",' Emily read aloud. 'Yadda, yadda, yadda. "Be entirely ready to have God remove these defects of character." Jesus Christ,' she sneered, 'who wrote this shite?'

Leon continued to look at her, waiting.

'"Humbly ask him to remove all our shortcomings,"' Emily read on, '"which neatly brings us to step eight."'

'There you go,' Leon nodded. 'That's the one.'

'"Make a list of all persons we've harmed and be prepared to make amends to them all."'

Emily looked at Leon and shrugged. There was a tight pause as he sat back, shoved the empty plate away and folded his arms.

'Step eight,' he said, holding her gaze. 'Right there – that's where we all fall down. Is there no one in your life that you'd want to make amends to?'

Emily took another sip of coffee and looked anywhere except at him.

'Jeez, must be hard being a flawlessly perfect human being like you.'

Again, Emily said nothing. Instead she focused on looking out the window in front of her, point-blank refusing to engage.

'Let me be perfectly clear with you from the start,' Leon said, sitting forward, his voice low and gravelly. 'I don't want to be here any more than you. You think I've time to go chasing around the city trying to get a hold of you, Emily Dunne? You think I could be arsed putting up with your rudeness and your attitude? Dream on. But when I first got out of St Michael's, my sponsor kept me sane and kept me sober, and that's why I'm here. Because I believe in paying things forward. If I can help you even a quarter as much as my own sponsor helped me, then I'll have paid my dues.'

'Look, I appreciate you're trying to do your best here,' Emily said, 'but come on. I'm a grown woman. Are you seriously expecting me to buy into all that shite about higher powers having control over me? Get real.'

'Oh no,' he said, 'you're the one who needs to get real.'

'Excuse me?' she said defensively.

'Like a good sponsor,' Leon went on, 'I took the time and trouble to learn a bit about you before we met. I know what you've been through, Emily. I know loads about you. I know that before you went to St Michael's for addiction treatment, you were in and out of other recovery programmes the way other people are in and out of revolving doors. I also know that while you were at St Michael's, you were widely considered to be one of the most troublesome patients ever to cross their threshold.'

'Well, excuse me,' she replied, 'but the reason I went to all those places – that poxy kip of a treatment centre, St Michael's, included – was to dry out and kick the booze. And you know what? Job done. I'm dry, haven't touched a drop in months. I'm one hundred and two days dry now, if you want to be pedantic about it. So I'm good. I'm cured. And if you don't mind, I'll thank you for the free coffee and be on my way.'

She pulled her seat back and was just about to haul her long legs out from under the table when Leon's voice stopped her.

'What about your mother? Your sister?' he asked, swivelling around to face her. 'Your friends? Or don't you have any friends? Common enough with dry alcoholics. Believe me, I know what I'm talking about.'

I bloody do have a friend, Emily was about to reply, thinking of Susan. But then, she reminded herself, she'd only known Susan for a short time – they met when sharing a room together at St Michael's. Susan only knew the sober side of Emily, not the darker side that she worked so hard to keep under wraps. Susan had never once seen Emily drinking, and never would.

Friends, Emily thought, the very word freezing her dead in her tracks. She remembered back to all those long weeks and months in treatment. Sunday was visiting day, but no one came to see Emily. Not once, not ever. Sundays were a killer for her back in treatment. Sundays almost drove her over the edge. Everyone else would sit down in the recreation room or stroll outside in the grounds chatting with loved ones, drinking tea and coffee, stuffing their faces with cakes and treats that visitors had brought.

But Emily would sit alone upstairs, watching daytime crap on telly and trying to convince herself she didn't care.

Leon continued to stick the knife in.

'I know you have an ex-husband too,' he said. 'No reparations to make there – nothing at all? Are you really going to tell me that everything is forgiven and hunky dory in your private life?'

Emily slunk back into her seat, feeling a whole lot smaller.

'That's the thing about alcoholism, isn't it?' Leon said. 'It's not just your own life you piss all over, is it? One person's drinking can drag up to a dozen others down with them.'

'I know,' she said quietly. 'I don't need to be reminded.'

'Good,' he said. 'Then you also know this: your chances of not drinking again increase tenfold, providing you have the right support around you. But you're never going to get that support unless you're prepared to build bridges with everyone you harmed in the past.'

Emily thought of Sadie. How close they used to be, back when they were younger. How much did she miss that closeness now? Far more than she cared to admit.

Then she thought of Jamie, who she'd stolen money from and reduced to tears. Jesus Christ, how could she have done that to an innocent little boy? There was Boring Brien, who she'd once propositioned when fried out of her brain, three years ago now, just as her marriage was breaking up and her drinking had spiralled out of all control. What had possessed her to sabotage her relationship with the only brother-in-law and sister she had?

And towering over them all was her ex-husband, Alec. Alec, who she'd really, truly loved more than any other living person and who now wouldn't even take her calls. For fuck's sake, what the hell was wrong with her anyway? Why was it that whenever she had someone good in her life, someone just like Alec, she had this deep, primal need to challenge their love, to test them to the limit, until she pushed them away?

And of course, there was her mother, who Emily had bitterly rowed with the last time they'd spoken, not long after her father died and when the shit really hit the fan.

To this day her mother's harsh words rang in her ears, loud and clear.

'I can try to forget what you put me through,' her mother had told her, 'but I'll never forgive. From this day on I only have one daughter and that's Sadie. You're dead to me. Do you hear me? Dead.'

Leon rapped a teaspoon off the side of a saucer, pulling her focus back to that cluttered, noisy little coffee shop.

'I'm offering to help you here, Emily,' he said. 'Why won't you just accept a bit of help? There's no shame in it.'

'But . . . but supposing no one from my old life wants to talk to me?' she asked in a very, very small voice.

'Suppose you don't try? Then look at your life now and ask yourself, which is worse?'

Violet

All morning long, Violet had a sickening, nauseous feeling deep in the pit of her stomach. She was pretty sure that she had been thorough and that there was nothing to worry about, but still. There was no harm in double-checking, was there?

It was quiet at number eighty-one Primrose Square and, for once, she had the whole house to herself, lodger-free. Frank was at work and that appalling, unladylike Emily was off with her gentleman caller again, up to God knows what.

The state of that man too, whoever he was. Violet had had a good look at him as he loitered outside her front door earlier. Not only was he far hairier than any grown man had a right to be, but she distinctly saw evidence of a tattoo. A tattoo on any person meant just two things: either that the person sporting it had just been released from prison, or that they were about to burgle you.

For the moment, however, the house was deserted. Not a sound apart from the ticking of the grandfather clock in the hallway and the creaking of the ancient floorboards as Violet padded around in her slippers with her walking stick.

Perfect, she thought. This was the ideal time to slip up to the bedrooms and make sure there was nothing lying around that might possibly come back to incriminate her. Naturally, she'd taken particular care to clear out both of her spare rooms prior to lodgers descending on her, but still. You never could tell, and that Emily one in particular was a case in point. Violet would put nothing past her, including taking the chance to burrow at the back of drawers and cupboards where she'd absolutely no right to be.

With purpose in her step, Violet began her search in Emily's bedroom, at the very top of the house. Without a second thought, she let herself into the room – and let out a gasp when she saw just how untidily it had been left. Items of clothing were strewn all across the bed, and the floor was covered in sweet wrappings, half-drunk water bottles and empty Tayto crisp bags.

I'll give that little rip a right dusting down the minute she gets back here, Violet thought. *Where does she think she's living anyway – the city dump?*

She made straight for the dresser just opposite the window, a heavy, old-fashioned mahogany piece of furniture that had been in the house since her late father's time. The top drawer was stiff and unwieldy, but it gave after a good yank and she stood on tiptoe to peer inside.

Disbelievingly, Violet pulled out what looked like a straggly piece of bright red dental floss – except this article appeared to be made of lace. An undergarment? Surely not. This item was little more than a piece of string. But there was a padded brassiere that came with it in exactly the same colour. Violet fished it out, repulsed. Really. That Emily Dunne had to be forty years old if she was a day. Was this really the kind of thing that she wore under those revoltingly tight jeans that she appeared to live, eat, drink and sleep in?

Aside from that, though, there was nothing. Not a single thing that might give Emily a single scrap of ammunition against her. *All clear*, Violet thought, abandoning the top drawer and moving on to the second one. There, she scooped out a most alarming-looking contraption, a strange, flesh-coloured object of a curiously phallic shape, with all manner of buttons down the side, to operate whatever it was. Violet pressed one, where-upon the item in her hand began to vibrate gently, emitting a low buzzing sound. She had no idea what such an item could possibly be used for – perhaps one of those devices that kept away bluebottles in the heat? There was a tube beside it, which looked every bit like a tube of toothpaste, but had something most peculiar written along the side of it:

DUREX INTENSE LUBE

Goodness me, Violet thought, puzzled. Something you used in the engine of a motor car, perhaps? Which was peculiar, though, given that Madam Emily didn't even own an auto-mobile.

Then her beady eye lit on the very thing she feared most.

There was an old, yellowing newspaper lining the drawer that had doubtless been there since Old God's time. But it was the date that made Violet stop rummaging as her blood ran cold.

18 September 1968.

Violet's eighteenth birthday. Gently, almost tenderly, she took away all of Madam Emily's items of clothing and removed the paper, now almost falling apart and ready to crumble. She held it in her hands, smelling it deeply.

And suddenly she was that girl again. Eighteen years of age and the spoiled darling of the house, about to celebrate her special birthday at Primrose Square. Father had insisted on having a party, 'with no expense spared for my only child,' she could still hear him saying.

1968. It was over fifty years ago but Violet could still remember how excited she'd been, how beautiful the house had looked, with her late mother's good Persian rug rolled up in the drawing room downstairs, all set for dancing after supper. Where there were cobwebs on every surface now, then there were huge bouquets of flowers. But then their house-maid Betty had always been particularly skilled at floristry.

'I want this party to be the talk of Primrose Square,' Father had said. 'All those begrudgers who've spent years looking down their noses at us, invite them all. Invite everyone! Whatever sort of a party you want, Vi, you can have. Just make sure that we're the envy of everyone on the square.'

Violet stood, fingering away at the yellow newspaper, lost in thought and remembering back to those happy days, when she was a spoiled, eighteen-year-old young lady with the whole world at her feet. There was only her and Father in that big house; Violet's mother had died when she was just a baby and she and Father were as close as two peas in a pod. Betty lived in the maid's room at the top of the stairs, because, as Father always said, if a live-in housemaid was good enough for the gentry, it was good enough for him.

Father. Violet could still remember him so vividly. How tall and proud he was, how he'd brag about Violet's musical talents every chance he got. Nowadays, of course, a man like

Father would be described as an entrepreneur, but back then people referred to him as 'self-made'.

Freddie Hardcastle had started out in life as a builder. He was a bricklayer by trade, and he'd slowly and steadily worked his way up, until he had his own contracting business – and a highly successful one too. In the building boom after the war, Violet's father had made his money building houses for Dublin Corporation in the newly formed estates all around Drimnagh and Whitehall. Which meant he could easily afford to buy a gorgeous, two-storey over-basement Victorian terraced house on Primrose Square. The very best house on the square, as everyone said.

Best of all, having money allowed Freddie Hardcastle to do what he really wanted more than anything else: to buy his way into polite society. He may have been born a humble brickie, but he was determined to spend his middle years rubbing shoulders with quality. Doctors and lawyers, that class of person. There was even a judge living on Primrose Square. These, Freddie hoped, would be Violet's new friends; maybe given time she might even marry into that social class.

At eighteen, Violet was her father's pride and joy. Tall, slender, pretty as a peach and talented too; she had a real gift for the piano.

'You'll do great things in this life, Vi,' he used to say to her. 'You'll have everything you ever wanted. And one day you'll make me a very proud grandfather – when you meet the right young man, of course.'

The night of her big birthday party couldn't come quickly enough for Violet. The guest list exceeded well over a hundred;

her own friends from finishing school were included, and Father insisted on inviting a great many of his business acquaintances.

'Do you know, I don't know a single sinner your father's asked,' Betty had grumbled to Violet, shaking her head. 'It's all politicians and judges and priests. There's even a Monsignor in there. Not a single one of his old brickie pals. And your father worked with them all for so many years.'

'Never mind, Betty.' Violet had smiled, not caring who her father had or hadn't invited. 'We'll have a wonderful time, no matter who's here.'

She was beyond excited as the date for the party grew ever closer. Back in 1968, Violet had just completed finishing school, the Hibernian School for Young Ladies, where she'd learned grooming, deportment and how to play the piano to concert level, something she loved to do more than anything else.

She felt so alive when she was playing; it was the single thing that made her most happy. Even more importantly though – according to Father, at least – she'd been taught how to entertain guests properly, so together she and Betty worked tirelessly in the kitchen downstairs, or 'below stairs', as Father insisted on referring to their basement, preparing everything down to the last little detail.

Even Monsieur Jaques Feraud, Violet's culinary tutor at finishing school, would have approved of the menu they were planning for the party. There would be paupiettes de veau à la Marseillaise to begin, because Violet read that's what had been served at Princess Margaret's wedding a few years ago, and if it was good enough for royalty, it was good enough for them.

Then lamb with a minted dressing for mains, followed by an elegant Philadelphia cheesecake for dessert, or 'pudding', as Monsieur Feraud taught her to call it at school.

As a birthday present, Violet had received the wonderful gift of a record player from her aunt Julia, and all of her friends had very kindly given her some vinyl singles and even a few albums to play at the party. She had her beloved Beatles albums too – who didn't back then? Father despised them and said John, Paul, George and Ringo were a bunch of long-haired idiots who wouldn't be heard of in years to come.

'The kind of din you'd only hear on a building site,' he used to sneer.

'It's what's popular now, Father,' Violet would answer, teasing him out of his grumpiness.

'Why can't you play the piano? Something classy that'll impress them all?'

'Because it's not that kind of party,' she'd insisted. 'I want everyone to dance and have fun!'

'But I want this to be a refined affair,' Freddie had said, before he'd harrumphed off to his study. 'Don't you? Sure, what's the point of me buying this fine big house and throwing the party for you in the first place, unless it's going to be something that'll have all the begrudgers talking for a long time to come?'

Violet threw her eyes to the ceiling – message received loud and clear. She knew the secret to a peaceful life was to keep Father happy all at costs, so she took great care to practise a few Mozart piano concertos, just in case she was called on to entertain.

Freddie Hardcastle had insisted on inviting in the Primrose Square neighbours too, 'so that they can all see what houses like these should look like – with a bit of class and a lot of money spent on them.'

So Violet had dutifully dispatched embossed invitation cards to everyone she knew around the square, including one new neighbour, who was already turning into a great friend.

Jayne Dawson and her husband of just a few months, Tom, had moved into a significantly smaller house directly across Primrose Square, and as she was only two or three years older than Violet, they'd bonded almost as soon as they met. Jayne was the perfect neighbour. She was warm and kind, and although she wasn't moneyed and middle class, like most of Violet's friends from finishing school, the two girls quickly became close.

'They're a good enough sort, that Jayne and Tom Dawson,' Father had sniffed. 'But not really the sort of friends I want you to be hanging around with, Violet. Dr Burke's two daughters, now – they're lovely young girls. Far more suitable as companions for you.'

Violet had giggled at him, though. Father was only being snobby, she knew, just because Jayne's husband was a carpenter, and not a more professional class of person. But Jayne Dawson was perfectly agreeable as a chum and Violet was delighted to include her and Tom among the guest list. Jayne had been a fantastic help, too, forever popping around to help Violet and Betty with sponges and fruit cakes down in the kitchen.

Then, just about a week before the party, Jayne arrived at Violet's front door, puffing and breathless, with wisps from her elegant beehive hairdo falling down all over her face.

'Hello Jayne!' Violet greeted her on her way out the door. 'I was just on my way to Woolworths. Will you come with me?'

'Oh Violet,' Jayne panted, 'I'd love to, but you won't believe what's happened. A cousin of Tom's from England has just landed in on top of us. He's got nowhere to stay, so of course Tom offered him our spare room and said we'd put him up while he's staying in Dublin.'

'And is everything all right?' Violet asked, as the two girls clickety-clacked their way in kitten heels down Primrose Square together. 'Is he a difficult guest? Is that what's upsetting you?'

'Oh no!' Jayne said. 'Andy's lovely, a dream visitor! So easy to have around and great fun too. He's a musician, you know; he plays bass guitar in a band.'

'Bass guitar.' Violet laughed. 'Just like Paul McCartney.'

It was well known that Paul was Violet's favourite Beatle, although she did have a bit of a weakness for John too.

'Anyway, Andy will be here for at least another week,' Jayne went on, 'so I was very cheekily wondering . . .'

'If you could bring him along to the party?' Violet grinned. 'Of course! I'd love to meet him. Any friend of yours is always welcome, you know that.'

'Oh, thanks so much, Vi.' Jayne smiled, turning to hug her tightly. 'You're just the best neighbour anyone could ask for! I'll tell Tom and Andy – I know they'll be so pleased. I was worried, you know, because I know your father wants this to be a very high-class affair, and folk like us mightn't be fancy enough for him . . .'

'You and Tom are coming,' Violet said firmly, 'with your guest too, and Father will just have to get used to the idea. Besides, half of the guest list are boring lawyers and barristers and people I never even heard of.'

Violet sat on the rickety little bed, clutching the newspaper tightly in her fist, staring out the window over the treetops on the square.

Miss Violet Hardcastle, who celebrates her eighteenth birthday party today, the paper's caption read, along with a faded black and white photo of a tall, reed-thin, pretty young woman clutching a bunch of gardenias and beaming happily at the camera.

Was that young girl really me? Violet wondered. *Was I ever that happy?*

All Freddie Hardcastle had wanted was for his daughter to be the talk of Primrose Square. Turned out that he got what he wanted, except not quite in the way he'd envisaged.

Abruptly, Violet stood up and left the room, taking great care to shred the newspaper into a thousand pieces in the kitchen waste bin, where no one would ever find it.

Frank

'This is a huge decision,' Beth had warned Frank, during one of their long therapy sessions. 'It's like crossing a Rubicon. Once you make up your mind, there quite literally is no going back.'

'I know,' Frank replied quietly.

'It's going to affect not just your own life, but those around you too. Gracie, Ben and Amber, and that's just for starters. Then there's all your friends and work colleagues, not to mention your extended family too. It's quite a long list.'

'I'm in blood stepped in so far . . .' Frank said thoughtfully. 'It's a quote from *Macbeth*,' he explained, seeing the puzzled look on Beth's face. 'Because I'm already halfway there, aren't I? No one can understand why I'm doing this. Already they're writing me off as a weirdo. Or else, like Gracie, they think I'm going through some sort of mid-life thing. In fact, if it wasn't for our sessions here, I don't know what I'd do.'

'My door is always open,' Beth said. 'That goes without saying.'

'And while I'm deeply grateful for that,' Frank said, 'as far as everyone else is concerned, I've become an embarrassment. I'm someone they all want to brush under the carpet. But this is *me*, Beth. This is who I am. I've denied myself ever since I was a small child and kept it up for almost fifty years. The truth will out and it's time for the truth.'

Then he thought of Francesca. How free and honest and strong it felt to inhabit her skin. How *right* it felt. But Frank had kept a lid on Francesca for the longest time; back when the kids were small, he made it a firm, hard rule never to become her, ever. His family came first and last; nothing mattered to him more.

What Frank hadn't counted on, though, was how much this would eat at him. The huge, unbearable toll it would take on his mental health. How much he missed the female side of him and how, for year after year, it almost felt like he was playing the part of a straight, upright married man and father, good little employee and all around conscientious, upstanding member of the community.

So a few years ago, Francesca began to come back. Secretly, to begin with – late at work after everyone had gone home. In the privacy of his office, Frank would become Francesca – and oh, the sheer joy of it sustained him, nourished him, fed his soul. With that outlet, Frank could go home and be the perfect husband and father that he was expected to be.

Soon, however, even that wasn't enough. As his confidence grew, so did his desire to go out as Francesca, to be her in public, to take her out for a test drive, as it were, to see how that felt. Cautious as ever, he ran a discreet online check and discovered various hotels and bars in town where like-minded souls went to hang out safely. Nowhere seedy – that was out of the question. No, these were classy places, where just being with others and interacting as Francesca soon became as necessary to Frank as breathing. This was who he was.

Was it so selfish and awful, he wondered, after five decades on this planet, to want to live the rest of your life as yourself? In this age of honesty and equality and tolerance, was it a bridge too far to hope that, in time, they might come to understand how he was feeling?

There was a long pause as Beth sat back at her desk and weighed up what Frank was saying to her.

'In that case,' she said kindly, 'if you really are determined to proceed . . .'

'I don't think I have a choice,' he said simply. Like it or not, the part of him that was Francesca wouldn't be denied anymore.

'Then I can help. I can set you up with a family support group. You only get to do it once. So let's get it right. Just know I'm behind you a hundred per cent of the way.'

'Okey dokey,' Frank said, with a shy little smile.

❧

'You have got to be kidding me,' Gracie said, when Frank called to their home on Primrose Square later that evening, so he could break the news face-to-face. 'Please, for the love of God, tell me that this is some kind of sick joke.'

She'd been standing at the kitchen island chopping onions for dinner, but abandoned it to process what she'd just been told.

'As if I'd ever joke about something like this, love,' Frank replied calmly.

'Don't you *dare* call me love. You don't ever get to say that to me again. You forfeited that right the night of your birthday, remember?'

'Sorry, sorry,' Frank said hesitantly, wiping his glasses.

'Jesus Christ, Frank,' Gracie snapped. 'Things have been bad enough, but now you want to go and make things a hundred times worse? And for God's sake, will you stop fidgeting?'

'Sorry,' he said automatically, as Gracie went back to chopping onions in angry, cold silence. He sighed, then reminded himself: he had absolutely no right to expect any reaction other than this. This was possibly the biggest step he was ever going to take in his life. Of course his nearest and dearest would see him as being monumentally selfish and very likely insane.

'The thing is, Gracie,' he said tentatively, 'the kids have a right to know how this is going to play out. As Beth always says, communication is a wonderful thing.'

'Beth this, Beth that,' Gracie said sarcastically. 'Well, if Beth said to go ahead and do this, then I suppose you'd better do it. Never mind about this family, never mind what it's doing to the rest of us. You just focus on keeping your precious Beth happy, because that's all that matters, isn't it?'

'Please, just hear me out,' Frank replied. 'Beth is helping me. You know that. Hormonal therapy is a huge part of this process and she's there to guide me through it.'

He badly wanted to tell her how terrifying this all was for him. There were so many different stages to come and each one would come with its own set of fears and terrors. Frank wanted to say it felt like he was standing on top of a towering skyscraper, about to jump off. More than anything, all he craved was a bit of support and kindness, and maybe even understanding from the woman who'd been his best friend for all these decades.

But with Gracie in the mood she was in, he didn't dare to. She'd been chopping the onions with a lot more vigour than usual, and now she was wielding the sharp kitchen knife almost like it was a weapon.

'So, you're determined then?' she said, sounding scarily calm. 'You're putting yourself ahead of your family? You don't care how this is already tearing us apart? You're not bothered about Ben and Amber and how this is going to affect them? You really are that selfish?'

'I'm not going anywhere, Gracie,' he said quietly. 'If I take this first step, I want to be open and honest with the kids. I want them to know how much I love them and that nothing in their lives will change. Absolutely nothing.'

'Except that everything has already changed, hasn't it?' she said. 'The man I loved vanished into thin air overnight.'

Frank stood there and took it, trying to understand how he'd feel in her shoes. *I deserve this,* he thought. *I've no right to expect any more.*

'Did you ever even love me in the first place, Frank? That's what I want to know.'

That hurt. That stabbed him deep.

'Oh Gracie, of course I love you . . . You're everything to me. Being Francesca, it doesn't change that. Not for a single minute.'

'So from now on, you'll be . . . what exactly? A lesbian trans-woman? Is that what you're telling me?'

Frank nodded, looking guiltily down at the floor.

'Let me get this straight,' Gracie persisted. 'You're telling me you're attracted to women – but the thing is, I'm not. Never was, never will be. So where exactly does that leave me, Frank? Did you ever stop to think that I might have feelings too?'

'Gracie love,' he said gently, 'my feelings for you are the same as they always were. I wish I could make you understand that you and the kids . . . you're everything to me . . . you must know that . . .'

But she quickly silenced him.

'Oh, spare me this patronising crap,' she snapped, going back to her chopping and dicing. 'You had this whole secret life on the side for years and years behind my back. You can't love someone and do that to them, Frank. Don't you realise that?'

'Please . . . If you'd just listen . . .'

'You betrayed me,' she said. 'And you betrayed us. Worst part of it is I still don't even understand *why*.'

'Gracie, please . . . if you'd just let me explain—'

'Go on then,' she interrupted furiously. 'Go ahead and talk to the kids, if your mind is made up. But if you hurt a single hair on their heads,' she added, 'God help me, I won't be held responsible.' She brandished her sharp chopping knife threateningly as she said it.

'Now get out of my sight before I make your surgeon's job a helluva lot easier for him.'

'Jesus, Dad, will you just PISS OFF?'

This was the blunt response Frank got on his first attempt to speak to Ben, just the two of them, father and son, alone.

'For fuck's sake, what part of "leave me alone" don't you understand?'

That was the second attempt.

By Frank's third attempt, Ben wasn't even bothering to be obnoxiously rude, instead he just pointedly shoved in earbuds whenever his dad was at the house, blanking him out completely.

He's hurting, Frank took pains to remind himself. His son might be over six feet tall and eighteen years of age, he might look and sound and act like a man, but inside, Frank knew only too well, there was a little boy whose whole perception of the world around him had just been blown apart.

I've done this, Frank told himself. *And only I can make it better.*

He thought back to Ben's childhood – how incredibly close they'd been, how much simpler life had felt back then. He thought back to all the weekend days that he'd spent in the icy cold on the sidelines of a soccer match, cheering his son on, always so ridiculously proud, no matter how badly the team fared. Frank didn't follow soccer or rugby, but made a pretty good fist of pretending to, purely so he could bond with Ben on the way to or from a match.

He'd tried to interest Ben in theatre and the arts over the years, but without success. So Frank did what any good father would: developed an interest in Arsenal FC, took his son to away games as often as money would allow and pretended to have an informed opinion when Arsène Wenger finally stepped down.

If there was one thing Frank Woods was particularly good at, it was pretending.

On Frank's fourth attempt to speak to his son, he fared a bit better. Ben had been out late celebrating the end of his Leaving Cert exams and called his dad at 5 a.m. to say he hadn't any money left for a taxi home, and was there any chance of a lift?

'Believe me,' he'd slurred down the phone, his voice sounding groggy after the night's celebrations, 'you're the last person I want to call, Dad. But I've no choice. Besides, you're not really in a position to give me a bollocking after what you did, now are you?'

Frank sprang out of bed, wide awake. Never mind that Ben sounded utterly wasted. This was a golden opportunity to spend time alone with his son and one he wasn't about to let pass.

Half an hour later, Frank waited outside the house party as his eldest child grudgingly clambered into the passenger seat, looking wrecked and smelling like a brewery. Quickly, Frank realised all that was wrong was that Ben had had a few too many tins of Heineken and that a good sleep would soon set him to rights. He'd drunk enough to celebrate the night, but hopefully not so much that he'd forget this conversation.

So now's as good a chance as I'll ever get, Frank thought.

'I'd really like to talk to you, son. It's important.'

'Not now, Dad. I'm not in the mood, OK?' Ben growled back at him, putting his feet up on the dashboard, even though he knew Frank hated it.

'But you're never in the mood to listen, are you?' Frank said, as they drove through the dawn to Primrose Square. 'You've been avoiding me every chance you get.'

'Oh, here we go again,' Ben said theatrically, rolling his eyes. 'Look Dad, I'm already ahead of you on this, OK? So let me just save us both all the bother and mortification of this conversation. Yes, I already know what cisgender means. And I know that you've been doing a great impression of a cisgender man up until all this shite started. I know what trans is, and I know the difference between a cross-dresser, a transvestite and a transgender person. And I hope you know how bloody mortifying it is for me to even have to use these words when I'm trying to talk to my own father. When are you going to drop this so we can get back to how it was before?'

'But Ben, that's what I need you to understand—'

'Have you any idea how upset Mum is?' Ben interrupted him, sounding more and more sober. 'She's stressed out of her mind with this court case she's working on – and now this?'

'I know. I never meant to hurt her—'

'And Amber?' Ben insisted. 'Did you ever stop to think about her? She's only eleven, Dad. She feels she's being punished over something that she doesn't even understand. We all hate this.' He kicked at the dashboard in frustration. 'You're putting us all through hell! And to lie to us all that time, to let us find out *like that* – do you realise what a selfish prick that makes you? Or do you even care?'

Frank winced. Bit his tongue. Reminded himself that he was dealing with a hurt child, then tempered his response as best he could.

'Everything that I did or have ever done,' he said gently, 'was for you and Amber, and for your mum too. Every hour I've worked was for you. Every cent I ever earned was to make your lives better.'

'Whatever,' Ben said dismissively.

'No, I'd really like you to listen to me,' said Frank more firmly. He looked over at Ben, who was lying stretched out on the passenger seat by then, with that expression of boredom mixed with deep mortification that only teenagers can really pull off.

Be truthful in all things.

That's what Beth kept saying. *You'd be amazed how much human beings can deal with, if you're completely honest and upfront with them.* That was her mantra.

All his life Frank had lived a lie. So now, wasn't it time for the truth?

'I know you feel I'm being selfish,' Frank said, 'but if I could just make you see this through my eyes—'

'And if I could just make you see this through mine, Dad,' said Ben, sounding scarily grown-up. 'Because nothing will ever be normal again. Do you get that? You and Mum will never be you and Mum again and you'll never be my dad – what am I even supposed to call you now? And you've just fecked off and left us and decided you want to be a woman, and moved out to your new life and left us all behind. I see what you've done to Mum and Amber and I hate you for it. Do you hear me? I *hate* you.'

Frank sat back, focused on the road ahead and bit his lip.

Frank Woods mightn't be able to say or do the right thing around his son.

But Francesca certainly would.

❦

The only thing that cheered him up was seeing Amber later on that evening. She'd just got her music test results, scored top marks and wanted to go out with her parents to celebrate.

Gracie, however, quickly put the kibosh on it.

'Oh honey, you know I'd love to,' she said to Amber, 'but I'm flat out with this case and I really need to catch up. Why don't you go with your dad and I'll take you shopping at the weekend to celebrate?'

Point made, albeit subtly. No way in hell was Gracie going to play happy families with Frank around, not if she could help it.

'So where would you like to eat, pet?' Frank asked his youngest and dearest as the two of them strapped themselves into the car. 'Wherever you want, the sky is the limit.'

Amber, however, had gone unusually quiet.

'Honey?' Frank prompted. 'You OK?'

'It's not about spending money in a fancy restaurant, Dad,' she said so softly, he almost had to strain to hear her. 'All I wanted was for you, me and Mum to be together. But that's not going to happen now, is it?'

'Well, maybe not right now,' Frank conceded reluctantly.

'Dad?' she asked, as they stopped at traffic lights.

'Yes, pet?'

'When will all this be over? I mean, I know you and Mum are fighting and that she and Ben are so angry with you, but . . . Dad . . . why don't you just say sorry and then we can all be happy again?'

'Because . . . because it's not quite that simple, love.'

At that, Amber let out an exhausted, grown-up sigh and sat back against the car seat.

'Whenever I ask Mum what's going on, she says you're having some problems and that you just need a bit of time out, that's all. And now when I ask you, you keep saying that it's not that simple and that I wouldn't understand. But all I want to know is this, Dad. When are you coming home?'

Frank's heart cracked as he looked over at her. *I'm quite literally the worst father in the world*, he thought, *for putting her through this*. But then, what could he possibly say? Being open and honest and transparent with Ben was one thing, but with an eleven-year-old girl, it was something else entirely.

Living the lie might have been a long, slow death sentence. But it was so much easier than living the truth.

Emily

Emily had always been a great believer in not doing things by half measures. When it came to boozing, she wasn't your common or garden unhappy alcoholic, she was an all-guns-blazing, go-down-in-flames drinker, the kind who took whole families down with her. And now, when it came to trying to rebuild her life, she figured she might as well start at the top and work downwards from there.

Her mother.

It took her two buses and a very long walk to get there, but eventually she found herself standing outside the gated entrance to sheltered housing for the elderly – or 'independent living' as the sign outside referred to it. It was called Ambrosia Independent Living, it was located quite literally in the back arse of nowhere, and it was every bit as vile as it sounded.

'Ambrosia has a lovely view overlooking the mountains,' her sister Sadie told her, not long after their father's funeral. 'Mummy will be very happy there.'

'She's used to living in the suburbs,' Emily had retorted. 'Mum is used to her good neighbours and her lovely home and the garden she's spent her whole life tending. Look at this place – it's a bloody shoebox!'

'Well, whose fault is that? Bit late for you to start developing a conscience now, isn't it, Emily? Always remember that Mum's only here in the first place because of you.'

It was a cruel remark, Emily thought now, but probably about ninety per cent true.

She strode through the main gates, sucked on her last and final fag for comfort, stubbed it out on the gravel, then followed the signs to the reception building. It was light, airy and modern inside, with everything painted in a shade of primrose yellow that would have sent her running for the hills had she been hungover. Every available sofa and cushion was covered in bright floral fabrics, which was doubtless meant to be cheery and uplifting for the residents, but which actually looked like Cath Kidston had vomited on it.

Two elderly men sitting in wheelchairs, staring vacantly into space, perked up considerably the minute Emily walked past them. She nodded a curt hello, then made her way through another set of doors to the reception desk, where a woman in her twenties was completely absorbed by the computer in front of her. Emily caught a sneaky glimpse of her screen: she was updating her holiday posts on Facebook.

'Hi there,' Emily said. 'I'm here to see Mrs Beryl Dunne. Can you tell me where to find her?'

Without even looking up from the screen, the receptionist muttered, 'What's the name?'

'I'm her daughter. Can you just tell her I'm here?'

Heaving a long, exhausted sigh, the receptionist pulled herself away from her computer, checked a stuffed file in front of her and dialled a phone number.

'Mrs Dunne? I've a visitor at reception for you. Says she's your daughter.'

A muffled sound of a response down the phone, then the receptionist turned back to Emily.

'She says it's not your day for visiting.'

'Tell her I'm not that daughter. I'm Emily. Tell her the prodigal one is here.'

This time, Emily heard a muted, hushed conversation, even though the receptionist took care to cover the phone with her hand.

'Sorry,' she said a moment later, hanging up the phone. 'I made a mistake. Wrong number. Your mother's not there. No one home. It's probably best if you leave now. Pointless you waiting here.'

'Oh yeah, is that right?' said Emily. 'So, who were you talking to just now? The butler from *Downton Abbey*?'

But the receptionist just shrugged and went back to her Facebook page.

'What number is her house?' Emily persisted.

'I'm hardly going to tell you that, now am I?' came the cheeky response. 'I just told you there's no one home. In your shoes I'd just take the hint and leave.'

Realising she was going to get nowhere, Emily held her temper and resisted giving two fat fingers to the receptionist, then stomped off back through the doors she'd come in. Not that she was all that surprised at her mother's reaction. But she'd come such a long way, it was a right kick in the teeth having to leave without doing what she'd set out to do.

Then, just as she was about to haul the heavy outer glass door open, one of the elderly men in wheelchairs stopped her in her tracks.

'So you're the famous Emily Dunne,' he said, in a voice that sounded more like a tubercular wheeze.

Emily turned to look at him. 'You know who I am?'

'Emily Dunne, as I live and breathe,' his companion hissed. 'Your mother always said hell would freeze over before you ever came to visit her, and now lo and behold, here you are.'

'Oh dear,' the other man wheezed, 'I hope this doesn't mean one of us dies tonight.'

'For God's sake, she's a middle-aged woman in a fleece jumper and trainers, not the angel of death.'

'Do you know where I can find my mother?' Emily asked, chancing her luck.

'Flat sixty-one. Five doors down, on your left. You didn't hear it from us, though.'

Emily thanked them warmly, then stepped back outside into the warm, summery sunshine. *It's like Butlins for the elderly here*, she thought, taking in the surreal neatness of the gravelled pathways and the overriding smell of boiling cauliflower. Make no mistake about it: this place really was God's waiting room.

Picking up her pace, Emily strode to the little flat she'd been directed to, as a few residents who were sitting under the shade of a tree playing cards all stopped to watch her go by. One braver inmate – *sorry, resident*, she corrected herself – was on a motorised mobility scooter and looked like he fancied himself as one of Hells Angels, even though he was wearing pyjamas and doing about four miles per hour tops, down a gentle garden path. He stopped to wave at Emily, curiosity getting the better of him, and she gave a quick little wave back.

Two minutes later, she was standing outside the flat she was looking for, neat as a new pin, with a gleaming front door and well-tended pots full of geraniums dotted outside. All so very *her*, Emily thought, bracing herself as she rapped on the front door.

There was a pause. So she knocked again. Another pause. Then the sound of an inner door opening, and a TV on full volume. Even from the far side of the door, Emily could hear the theme tune to *Agatha Christie's Marple* blasting out at full volume.

'Cathy, lovely, is that you?' came her mother's unmistakable voice, her Cork accent as singsong and musical as ever. 'Is it time for my medications already? One minute there, lovie, till I unlock the door!'

Seconds later, the hall door was opened and there she was, her mother, the same woman who'd told her that she was dead to her. The same mother who'd tried to bar her from her own father's funeral. Ordinarily she was a smiling, cheery woman, but she certainly wasn't smiling now.

There was a throbbing moment as both women stared at each other.

I've missed you, Mum, Emily wanted to say so badly. *I know I've fucked up, but I'm here and I'm asking for a second chance.*

Her mum registered shock – but then her face went a funny colour. Red first, then scarily snow white. Emily took the chance to really have a good look at her, and the good news was that her mum looked healthy and robust, dressed in a floral twinset and a sensible pair of slacks that doubtlessly came from M&S, like just about every other stitch in her mother's wardrobe.

Then snippets of their last, horrific conversation came back to her.

'You as good as put your poor father in his grave, you know that?' her mother had said to her, through near-hysterical tears. 'You broke his heart first, then you broke mine. And now you have the barefaced cheek to turn up at his funeral, like nothing happened? Go to hell, Emily Dunne. You're no daughter of mine, and you're not welcome here.'

Every word was like a stab to the heart. Worst of all? Emily knew she deserved every single word. That, if anything, she deserved far worse.

And now here she was, face to face with the woman she'd wronged more than anyone else, with the impossible task of trying to make amends.

'Hi Mum,' she said, forcing herself to smile and sound cheery. 'Surprise!'

Her mother just stared numbly at her, gaping now, slack-jawed in shock.

Emily grabbed the chance to fill in the silence. 'Here,' she said, fumbling around in her huge, overstuffed handbag and producing a paper bag with *The Sweet Emporium* written on the side of it. 'I brought you a present. Nougat. You see? I remembered how you always used to like nougat.'

Look at me, Mum – I've changed, I'm better now and all I'm asking for is a chance.

From the corner of her eye, she was aware that the other residents who'd been playing cards close by had abandoned their game, so they wouldn't miss a minute of the unfolding drama. She could feel their eyes boring into her back as her mother composed herself enough to speak.

'I thought I told you,' her mum said, low and clear, 'that under no circumstances were you ever to come near me again.'

'Please,' Emily said, acutely aware that they had an audience, 'can I just come inside? For a minute? There's something I need to say to you and it's really important. I only ask that you hear me out and then I'll be on my way. I faithfully promise.'

But her mum ignored her, and instead waved across the garden to where the card players were sitting, riveted.

'Ladies?' she called, her voice panicky and shrill. 'Can you call security? Tell them it's an emergency and to come as fast as they can!'

At that, one of the card-playing old ladies hobbled off on a zimmer frame, so Emily took her chance. Audience or no audience, she'd come to say her piece, and it was too late now to back out.

'Please, just listen to me, Mum,' she tried to say. 'I know I'm the last person you want to see, but I've come a very long way and I only want to talk to you for a second.'

Her mum yelled, 'Don't you think about saying another word. Just go!'

'For Christ's sake!' Emily said, stepping inside the doorway, trying to get even a modicum of privacy. 'All I want is to say sorry. That's it. That's all. That's the only reason I've come here.'

She'd rehearsed a great speech on the way to Ambrosia Independent Living, but quickly realised that she hadn't a chance of getting a word of it out. Not now.

'Just leave,' her mother said, borderline hysterical. 'You can't do this to me – I have a heart condition, you know! You can't threaten me in my own home like this. Haven't you done enough to me? Security are on their way and they'll turf you out any second now!'

'Please, just look at me,' Emily said, making a 'calm down' gesture. 'Just take a good, long look at me.'

She was about to say: *because I'm dry now.*

She was about to say that she'd always be an alcoholic, because it wasn't something that could magically be cured, but that she was a sober alcoholic now.

She wanted to tell her mother that it had been months since she'd last had a drink. She wanted to say that the Emily of old was long gone.

But not a single word would come out. Because just then, Emily spotted the family photos that lined the walls in her mother's doorway. Photos from decades ago, Christmases that they'd had as a family – Emily, Sadie and both of her parents, back when her dad was still alive. Photos of Sadie's Communion, confirmation, her wedding pictures, and then in pride of place, recent photos of Sadie with her husband, Boring Brien, and Jamie, their son.

But Emily herself had been cut out of every single one. Decapitated, deleted, erased. Most hurtful of all was a particularly old photo of her and Sadie as kids, playing with their dad, who was dressed up as Santa Claus. Emily had only been about seven when the photo was taken; she remembered it vividly. Now though, the photo had been completely torn in two, so only Sadie remained.

If a picture spoke a thousand words, then these spoke millions. Slowly, silently, Emily scanned the hallway, taking it all in.

Wow, she thought. Her mother certainly didn't do things in half measures. Emily had been entirely airbrushed out of her own family. Dead Girl Walking.

'Now, will you leave quietly?' her mother asked in a softer voice, 'or do you want to cause another scene?'

Emily needed no persuasion. She felt like she'd been smacked right across the face – the exact same sensation. So without another word, she turned on her heel and stumbled her way out, aware that the pensioner card players were watching her every move. She left, walked across the grass you weren't supposed to walk on, then out through the main gates.

She wasn't a crier. Not even when her dad died could she shed a single tear. Course, everyone said that was a guilty conscience on her part, but that was only part of it. Tears didn't come naturally to Emily; she'd almost forgotten how to be emotive. For years she numbed all emotion with booze – but she didn't have that security blanket anymore.

It was a good half hour and two buses later before she could think clearly again. Then she rang the one person she knew had to listen to her.

'Hey, there you are,' Leon said, as soon as he answered. 'How goes the day?'

'I can't do this,' Emily said shakily. 'This Step Eight lark. It's too painful. I tried and it was vile and awful and a huge mistake, so that's it, I'm over and out.'

'Then try again. Try harder. Fail better.'

'Jesus, Leon, I've never needed a drink so badly in my whole life. I need vodka and I need it now. Just a small one. And I'll stop after that, I promise.'

'Stay exactly where you are,' he said. 'I'm on my way.'

Violet

In spite of herself, Violet was beginning to develop an irritated fondness for Frank Woods. If one discarded the fact that he was clearly unhinged – because what man in his sane mind would possibly wish to dress up in ladies' clothing? That consideration aside though, Mr Frank Woods was proving to be perfectly acceptable as a paying guest. Considerate. Tidy. And regularly including Violet in his dinner plans whenever he cooked at home, which thankfully was frequently.

A frightening amount of her new-found rental income had been swallowed up by outstanding bills, workmen to come and reconnect her boiler, an electrician to fix her faulty fuse box, and suchlike. *Tradespeople,* Violet's father Freddie would have sniffed, she thought with a harrumph. Back in the day, such callers wouldn't even have been permitted to enter the house through the front door.

'That's what the basement door is for,' Father used to say. Even builders who her father had started out with, even his own cousins who all worked as painters and decorators, weren't allowed in through the grand front door that looked out over Primrose Square.

If Violet concentrated and focused her mind hard enough, she could still see her father's tall, proud outline standing in the downstairs hallway, dressed in the good three-piece suit he wore for Sunday Mass, checking his pocket fob watch against the grandfather clock in the hall, to make sure both were perfectly synchronised.

What would you make of this, Father? she often wondered. The house he was so proud of and had put so much money into, now a crumbling, decaying wreck with rising damp on the walls and most of his good furniture auctioned off years ago for cash. Freddie Hardcastle would have spun in his grave at the thought of paying guests lodging at his house. Back in his time, the likes of Madam Emily Dunne wouldn't have been permitted to cross the threshold – either through the front door or the tradesman's entrance.

Frank Woods, however, was at least proving to be a gentleman. Night after night, he would gently rap on the drawing room door to ask Violet if she'd care for some chicken casserole, perhaps, or a delightful lasagne he often rustled up. Violet was invariably starving but would feign lack of appetite until Frank gently asked a second and even a third time.

'Well, if you insist,' she'd say, and minutes later, she'd be sitting down to a proper, nourishing home-cooked meal – every single one delicious. No one had cooked for her like this in years. Not since she was a young girl.

'So, Emily seems nice,' he said to her over a particularly good dinner one evening. 'Although, I think very possibly not a morning person.'

'Emily Dunne?' Violet said, her fork frozen in mid-air.

'She's out just now,' Frank went on, dishing up lamb chops and mint sauce, 'so should I leave some dinner in the fridge for her? Then she can have it later when she gets back.'

'Don't dream of doing any such thing,' Violet said sternly.

'I just thought it might be nice . . .'

'Out of the question,' Violet said crisply. 'Emily Dunne is a rude, malicious little madam and she certainly doesn't deserve lamb chops. Did you know that's she's actually just been released from—'

'Probably kinder not to judge,' Frank gently interrupted.

For the life of her, Violet completely failed to comprehend why. She infinitely preferred people who judged just a little bit.

That blip aside, though, Violet thought later, as she tucked herself up under her patchwork eiderdown quilt for the night, Frank Woods was proving to be perfectly satisfactory as a house lodger. She'd treated him to one of Bach's preludes on the pianoforte after dinner that evening, and he'd nodded along most enthusiastically. Best of all, Emily Dunne stayed out of the way for most of the evening, though God alone knew where she was. Doubtlessly off with that gentleman caller of hers. The one with the array of tattoos. Well, good riddance to her. The last thing Violet would have wanted was the likes of Emily Dunne shattering the peace of her lovely evening with Frank.

Violet heard the little rip coming home at well after 11 p.m., slamming the hall door behind her, then thudding up the stairs loudly enough to wake the dead.

Miss Emily Dunne, she thought crossly, would most certainly be receiving one of her handwritten missives the following morning. And if Violet ever caught her using one of her royal family mugs, there'd be merry hell to pay.

Trust that interfering do-gooder to go and ruin everything. Jayne Dawson, Primrose Square's very own resident bleeding-heart liberal.

'It's so wonderful to see you and Frank bonding so well,' Jayne said, cutting two slices of chocolate biscuit cake and handing over a generous piece to Violet. She'd come round to run a few errands and had brought the cake with her, knowing it was Violet's favourite. The two ladies were sitting down to tea at the kitchen table, with the cake neatly laid out on the special plates Violet had bought to celebrate the late Queen Mother's one hundredth birthday.

'Eric was just saying it's heartening when two souls from different generations connect so beautifully,' Jayne chatted away. 'It's often a past life thing, Eric was telling me.'

Ordinarily Violet would have gobbled up the chocolate biscuit cake in a single helping, but this time she paused, wondering where exactly Jayne was going with this. Violet was no great fan of Jayne's second husband – a new age hippy from Florida, if you could believe that. Ever since they'd got married the previous year, it was all 'Eric this' and 'Eric that'. But if you saw the state of this Eric fella, Violet thought, you'd run a country mile. Honestly, the man dressed head to toe in snow white. In Dublin. Even in winter. He looked like one of those idiots who ought to shave his head and bang a tambourine up and down Grafton Street, instead of irritating Violet with his second-hand opinions on her new lodger.

Past lives indeed.

'I don't see how this is any of your fancy man's concern,' Violet said, taking a sip of her tea. That was how Violet signified her strong disapproval of Eric; whenever she was in Jayne's company, she constantly referred to him as 'your fancy man'. Never, ever as 'your husband' or, Lord forbid, by his Christian name.

Not that Jayne even seemed to notice, she was so away with the fairies these days.

Just look at her sitting at my kitchen table, Violet thought, *in her baby pink tracksuit with a pair of rubber-soled shoes in a shade of neon pink no one over the age of three had a right to be seen in.* 'Trainers', as Jayne referred to them. Trying to look and act like a teenager when she was well over seventy years of age.

'It's so lovely for you to have company, Vi.' Jayne smiled. 'I often used to worry about you here on your own. I know before I met Eric, I hated rattling about a house this size, all on my lonesome.'

'That's because, unlike me, you didn't grow up in a fine house like this,' Violet said haughtily. 'It's hardly my fault if your family came from a Corporation estate, now is it?'

Jayne took a sip of tea and let the insult whizz over her head. There was a long, measured pause before she spoke again, as if she was choosing her words very, very carefully.

'Frank has just turned fifty,' she eventually said.

'And what's that got to do with anything?' Violet said imperiously.

'Well, it's just that he'd be exactly the same age as . . .'

Violet glared back at her over her teacup. 'As whom?' she said, sounding deadly calm. 'To whom can you possibly be referring, Jayne Dawson?'

'Oh come on, love,' Jayne said gently. 'You know exactly who I mean. We're old friends, Vi. We have no secrets.'

Violet took her time before she deigned to answer. 'I have absolutely no idea whom you can possibly be alluding to. And if you had the slightest bit of breeding in you, you'd appreciate that now would be an appropriate time for a change of subject.'

Jayne sighed, then reached across the kitchen table and took Violet's thin, bony hand in hers.

'Honesty in all things,' she said. 'That's what Eric always advises.'

'Do you have to keep droning on about your fancy man?' said Violet sourly. 'It's terribly boring.'

'Eric says that when we miss out on a part of our life,' Jayne went on, 'we often go back to reclaim it.'

'And what exactly is that supposed to mean?'

'All I meant,' Jayne replied, 'is that if you ever felt like you missed out on . . . well, you know . . . on a whole lot of things over the years, well . . . then there's no need to anymore, is there? Because you're having a special relationship with Frank now. Which is wonderful,' she added, seeing Violet's face slowly turn a furious shade of crimson.

'And what, according to you,' Violet said, drawing herself up tall, even though she was sitting stock still, 'is it that I missed out on throughout the course of my life?'

'Oh Violet, come on, don't be like this. You know right well what I'm talking about.'

'I most certainly do not.'

'Vi, please. You don't need to pretend with me of all people. I was there. I *know*.'

Violet stood up as if she'd been electrocuted. There was a scarily long pause before she could answer. Instead, she fumbled around for her walking stick in stony silence, as Jayne bit her lip.

'I'll thank you to get out of my house right now, Jayne Dawson,' Violet said, in a low, calm voice, her arthritic hands shaking with anger.

'Please don't be angry,' Jayne said. 'You know the last thing I'd ever want to do is upset you.'

'Just leave,' Violet said coldly.

'Times have changed, you know,' Jayne tried to say, as Violet stood at the kitchen door, rapping her walking stick impatiently off the floor. 'People are so much more open about the past now. It's OK to talk about these things, Vi. Everyone understands.'

'I already asked you to go,' was Violet's icy response. 'Are you stone deaf as well? And you can take that revolting cake with you.'

Emily

Emily had known some long nights of the soul in her time, but nothing, absolutely nothing, compared with this.

The following day, she stayed holed up in her room with her head under the duvet for as long as she possibly could, ignoring her hatchet-faced landlady hammering on the door. It was only when Violet threatened to have the door broken down unless she made herself scarce, that Emily eventually hauled herself out of bed and out of the house. Then she managed to kill most of the afternoon on a park bench in Primrose Square, until her pal Susan got back from work later that evening. The sheer sense of relief she got when she saw Susan's slim, petite outline coming around the corner of Pearce Street on her way home was overwhelming.

The two women saw each other most evenings, talking, gossiping, going for long, relaxing strolls through the square in the cool evening air, then maybe slipping back to Susan's for a barbeque dinner.

But that particular night, Emily needed her friend more than anything.

They sat side by side on a rattan sofa in Susan's south-facing back garden as the sun set. For once, they didn't bother going out onto Primrose Square. Here, they had peace and real privacy to talk.

'You poor thing,' Susan said, when Emily told the sorry tale of her visit to her mother the previous day. 'I can't imagine how that must have felt for you.'

'Worst part of all, though,' said Emily, 'was that my first, instantaneous response was to reach for a drink. Literally the only thing I could think about was knocking back a very large vodka. All those months of being sober, all that time I spent trying to get sober – I'd have undone it all in five minutes, for the sake of getting my hands on one, single drink.'

'But you didn't, did you?' said Susan, horrified.

'No,' Emily said, shaking her head. 'No thanks to me, though. Full credit to Leon, my sponsor, for that.'

'What did he do?'

Emily sat back and squinted up at the dying sun. 'He dropped everything,' she said, pulling her fleece jumper tighter around her, almost as if to comfort herself. 'He'd been out in his taxi and zipped straight over to meet me. He even stayed on the phone the whole time until he picked me up. Then he took me to McDonald's in town, bought me a strong coffee and let me rant at him till I got it all off my chest.'

And boy, had Emily ranted. All the pain and humiliation she'd felt at her mother's outright rejection of her came tumbling out.

'I know I deserve no less,' she'd kept saying to Leon, 'but Jesus Christ, this *hurts*. It really fucking hurts. I've only got one parent left on this earth and all I tried to do was make amends to her and I can't even do that much right.'

Emily hadn't cried in front of Leon, but she'd been bloody close to tears. And all the while, he sat patiently and listened.

'I want a drink,' she told him honestly. 'Just one. And that'll be it. I promise. I just need to steady my nerves and I'll never drink again. I swear.'

At that, Leon had sat forward and gently took her hand.

'You don't,' he said quietly. 'Trust me, a drink is the very last thing you want at this moment in time. This is just the craving, and this too will pass.'

'If it wasn't for Leon,' Emily said now, turning back to Susan, 'I honestly don't know what I'd have done. He dropped me home afterwards and called me first thing this morning and . . . he's turning out to be such a rock. You have no idea.'

There was a long, thoughtful pause.

'I know it's none of my business,' Susan eventually said. 'But if it's not too personal, can I ask you something?'

'You and me have no secrets,' Emily said, savouring the quiet and stillness of Susan's back yard. The calm after the storm.

'Why drink?' Susan asked. 'I mean, what started you off drinking in the first place? I know you were just a teenager, but . . .'

'But . . . I have the bad luck to have been born with an addictive personality,' Emily finished the sentence for her. 'I know, some people are lucky enough to be able to drink in moderation, but a very long time in therapy has taught me that I'm not one of those people. It's all or nothing with me, and not just when it comes to drinking, either. It's not enough for me to have just one vodka and tonic – I want the whole bottle. Then, of course, the more you drink, the more it takes to get properly drunk, so without knowing it, *bam*! You're trapped in a vicious circle. That's me, that's my pattern. And somehow, I have to learn to live with that.

'My dad drank too, you know,' she said. 'It was perfectly normal in our house to have bottles of wine on the table at meals and to see Dad passed out in an armchair with an empty bottle of whiskey beside him at night. I'm not making excuses,' she added. 'It's just that they say a lot of it can be genetic. There is alcoholism in my family, and I was unlucky enough to inherit the gene. Dad was a functioning alcoholic, though; he was able to drink heavily, and yet sustain a family and hold down a job. I couldn't do either.

'I started drinking young too,' she said, as Susan listened intently. 'Filching booze from my dad's drinks cabinet when I was a teenager, that sort of thing. Mind you, I was always the wild child at home; my sister Sadie was the perfect one and I could tell even at that age that both my parents infinitely preferred her to me. So, what did I do? I drank to make the pain of that go away. I had it under control for a while when I met Alec, and when we first got married, but once he and I broke up, that was it, I couldn't control it anymore. Tried and failed. So, from here on in begins a lifetime of vigilance. And that, my friend, is the price of sobriety.'

Hours later, Primrose Square was dark and deserted as Emily strode through it in almost pitch darkness. But it was peaceful and soothing to hear the gentle breeze blowing through the sycamore trees that lined the square, and it made a welcome change to have the whole place to herself. It was past 11 p.m. and apart from one lone woman walking two very yappy dogs, she was all alone with her thoughts.

Had she been on the drink, she thought, she'd doubtless have climbed the fence into the kid's playground area, screaming and yelling her head off as she whizzed around on the roundabout and high-kicked it on the swings. Old Emily wouldn't have given a shite if she'd woken every single neighbour within a two-mile radius – but the new, sober her was very different. More respectful. Considerate. And even though she couldn't stand Miss Violet Hardcastle, the last thing Emily would have wanted was to disturb that quiet, mousey fella, Frank what's-his-name, the guy who looked a bit like a frightened gerbil.

Even with all the crap I'm dealing with right now, she thought, striding around the square, heading for home, *I much prefer being sober Emily.* And sober Emily was very much how she wanted to stay.

Whipping out her phone, she texted Leon.

No words to thank you for last night. You talked me in off the ledge. I owe you, big time.

He texted her back straightaway.

Go on out of that, would you?

Emily smiled. Then, to take her thoughts off boozing more than anything else, she distracted herself by taking a really good look at number eighty-one as she approached the house from the opposite side of the square.

Funny thing, she thought, but she'd always been interested in architecture and design. Not that she'd ever really had a chance to indulge her passion – the one and only time she'd been a homeowner was back when she was still married to Alec, and just look how that turned out.

But number eighty-one had something about it that made you stop in your tracks and take a second look. It was slightly bigger and more imposing than a lot of the neighbouring houses. It had a balcony to the front, for one thing, and grand twin pillars on either side of the entrance hall. A house that was clearly designed to put manners on people, Emily thought, although it was beyond sad to see how wretched and decayed it looked now.

Give me a few tins of paint, she thought, *and I could have that place spruced up in no time.* A house like that could be truly magnificent, something very special, instead of what it was like now – which was essentially Grey Gardens, without either the cats or the Bouviers. Given free rein, she'd sand down the bare wooden floors, then lash a coat of varnish on them, which instinctively she knew would look fabulous.

Emily tripped up the stone steps, part of her itching to give them a decent scrub, so that the granite would really shine. Letting herself quietly through the heavy oak door, she thought about how a good decluttering could really transform the place.

Get rid of all that bloody royal family tat, for one thing, not to mention the stacks of royalty magazines that were piled high on the hall floor, so you almost tripped over them as you came in. The bones of a fine house were already there, she thought, taking in the high ceilings in the hallway, its intricate plasterwork now all covered in cobwebs and stinking of damp. It really was beyond heartbreaking to see the place fall into rack and ruin.

If Violet were halfway normal, Emily thought, taking off her shoes before tiptoeing up the main staircase, she'd offer to clean the place for her and give it a good lick of paint. Who knows? She might even get paid for it, or at least get a discount in rent.

If Violet were a kinder person, she sighed, padding across the upstairs landing towards her own room, *I might even do it for free.*

The landing at the top of the house was gloomy and pitch dark, but from under Frank's doorway, Emily could see that there was still a light on. So he was still up, then. She stood outside his door for a second, wavering. Part of her didn't want to disturb him, especially when he was the type who got up at 6 a.m. to beat the traffic to work. But then part of her really wanted to get to know him a bit better. What was he like? Was he nice? Was he someone she might even be able to have a good laugh with about Violet, and how bloody off her head barking bonkers the old witch was?

'Frank Woods is quiet and unassuming,' was all Susan would tell her on the subject. He was apparently going through some marital troubles, which was why he'd moved into Violet's House of Pain in the first place. Apart from that, though,

Susan refused to be drawn any further. 'Let's just mind our own business and let him get on with it.'

I'll just say a quick hello, Emily thought, tapping quietly on Frank's bedroom door.

No response. So she tried again. Straining at the door for a reply, she thought she heard a rustling sound, so she gingerly opened the bedroom door and peeked inside.

But Frank wasn't there. Sitting at the dressing table, utterly absorbed in putting on fake eyelashes and concentrating deeply, was probably the most beautiful woman Emily had ever seen in the whole course of her life.

Francesca

'Jesus, you look stunning!'

Francesca was concentrating hard on her eyelashes, which were always tricky at the best of times.

'Shh!' she said, spotting Emily in the mirror in front of her.

'I'm so sorry,' Emily said, shaking her head in confusion. 'I thought this was Frank's room.'

'So it is, darling,' said Francesca, 'so it is.'

'Oh,' said Emily, staring. 'Are you a friend of his?'

'I said hush!' said Francesca. 'I might make these eyelashes look easy, honey, but trust me, they're far from it.'

A pause as a whole rainbow of confusion washed over Emily's face.

'It's just that . . .' she faltered. 'I thought Frank and I were the only lodgers in the house . . . so . . .'

'So?' was Francesca's smirking response, almost like she was enjoying Emily's discomfort.

'Are you a friend of Frank's, by any chance?' Emily asked, still staring at her in the dressing table mirror. 'Like . . . a girlfriend, maybe? Not that it's any of my business,' she added hastily.

'Well, that's good to know, honey,' said Francesca, still absorbed in the mirror. She was lashing on mascara now and taking great care to slick it thoroughly from underneath, just like she'd learned to via some random video on YouTube.

'Right, then . . .' Emily said, making to leave the room. 'Well, maybe you'd tell Frank that I dropped by? Just for a chat, that's all.'

'Don't you find a smoky eye just the most difficult thing to do?' Francesca said, apropos of nothing. 'It takes so much effort. I've calculated it takes exactly eleven minutes to apply and half a pack of baby wipes to remove. I mean, honestly, is it really worth all the bother?'

'Ehh . . . yeah,' said Emily, looking more and more baffled the longer this strange conversation went on. 'Smoky eye. Yeah. It's a disaster. Anyway, I'd better leave you to it, I suppose . . .' she trailed off. 'Nightie night.'

'Oh now Emily,' said Francesca, abandoning her mascara and slowly swivelling around to face her full on. 'Aren't you just dying with curiosity to know what a total stranger is doing in Frank's bedroom? Take a closer look, honey.'

So Emily did just that. Francesca couldn't help smiling as her expression went from bewilderment to disbelief and finally . . . eventually . . . to full recognition.

'I do not fucking believe this,' Emily said. 'Frank? Frank, is that actually you under all that glamour?'

'It's Francesca, actually.'

'Jesus . . . I need to sit down . . .' Emily gestured towards the bed and slumped down onto it, the very picture of shock.

At that, Francesca began to giggle. 'Oh sweetie,' she said, 'if you could see your face! I expected a reaction, but this is beyond anything!'

Then Emily surprised Francesca by throwing her head back and bursting out laughing.

'You're utterly fabulous, Frank, do you know that? Really, truly unrecognisable! You know, I really thought that I'd seen it all in this world, but Christ Almighty!'

Francesca gave her a half wink, then picked up a makeup brush to contour that beautiful, angular face.

'But I'm not Frank anymore, honey,' she said with a smile. 'I'm Francesca. And it's so lovely to meet you properly.'

She turned around to shake Emily's hand, resisting the masculine habit of squeezing her hand too tight.

'Enchanted, my dear. Oh now, don't look so shocked,' she added, taking in Emily's stunned expression. 'Surely you've seen someone transgender before?'

'Not like this,' Emily said, slumping back on the bed. 'Not up close and personal. I mean to say, as Frank, you're . . . like . . . well, you're sort of . . .'

Francesca smirked, greatly enjoying herself as Emily grappled around for the right word.

'The thing is,' Emily was flailing about, 'as Frank, you're . . . well, I got the impression that you were sort of conservative. Quiet. That you keep yourself to yourself. But like this,' she said, gesturing up and down at Francesca, 'well, I mean to say . . . like this, look at you! You're breathtaking. You're a goddess. I want to *be* you!'

'Well, aren't you just a doll,' said Francesca, brimming over with confidence now and feeling on top of the world. She'd always loved it when strangers got to meet Francesca for the first time; seeing their reactions was so empowering. But up till now, Francesca had really only met other trans men and women in a safe club in town, where rule one was that you never, ever talked about who or what you'd seen there. Just like in the movie *Fight Club*. Francesca had always held back, and never let herself make friends with anyone there, knowing she'd have to go home at the end of the night and go back to being Frank Woods again.

This was different for Francesca, though. This was meeting someone who actually knew her other incarnation as Mr Cellophane himself, Frank Woods. And to have such an appreciative audience as Emily really was the icing on the cake.

'So how long have you . . . ?' Emily asked. 'And don't worry,' she added, 'you can tell me anything. I'm unshockable.'

'Oh, since forever, honey,' said Francesca, uncrossing her long legs and showing off fabulously elegant silvery evening shoes – smart high, but not tart high. 'Since the age of six, when I was the only boy in my class who actually *wanted* to play Mary in the school Nativity play, just so I got to wear a long white dress.'

Then she stood up to her full height, which, given the heels, was considerably taller than Frank Woods ever was. She didn't so much walk, as glide over to the mirror on the wardrobe, and then took off her dressing gown to reveal an almost girlish figure in a long, clingy slip.

'My God,' said Emily. 'Look at the figure on you! You're like . . . a perfect size ten.'

'All down to a half decent pair of Spanx,' Francesca replied, pulling open the heavy mahogany wardrobe door and scanning around inside, till she found exactly what she was looking for. Concealed right at the very back, so no prying eyes could have found it, was a beautifully elegant wrap-over dress, in a deep, emerald green. She stepped into it, before twirling around in the mirror to see the final effect.

'Wow,' said Emily, mesmerised. 'Just wow. You look so tasteful and sophisticated.'

'Works, doesn't it?' said Francesca, flicking back her mane of long, chestnut brown hair and brushing away an imaginary fleck of dust.

'I mean, I've been to drag clubs before,' said Emily, 'but there the guys dressed as women always end up looking garish and OTT. But you, though,' she said, 'just look at you! Amal Clooney, eat your heart out!'

'You know what I think?' said Francesca, playfully swatting Emily with the silk belt of her dress, absolutely glowing from all her encouragement. 'I think this could be the beginning of a beautiful friendship.'

'And you've been dressing up like this . . . ever since you were little?' Emily asked tentatively.

Francesca was well prepped with her answer. 'Tell me this, honey,' she said. 'Did you ever walk around in the wrong pair of shoes that didn't fit properly and that pinched your feet till they bled?'

Emily looked down at the same battered pair of Converse trainers she'd been living, eating, drinking and occasionally sleeping in for months now.

'Not really,' she answered, 'but I can sympathise.'

'Well, that'll give you a small idea of what it's like to spend your whole life in the wrong body,' Francesca went on. 'But you know, I'm so glad you're here, because now comes the hard part.'

At that, she went over to the windowsill and rummaged through a paper pharmacy bag for a neatly labelled box of pills, along with several other metallic strips of tablets.

'Oh,' said Emily. 'So this is more than just . . .'

'Believe me, this goes a whole lot deeper than just playing at dress-up,' said Francesca, taking two of the pill bottles, then sitting down on the bed beside Emily.

'And you don't just do this . . . like, for the fun of it?' Emily asked. 'For a bit of escapism?'

'Fun?' Francesca said, raising a beautifully pencilled eyebrow. 'Are you kidding me?'

'Sorry,' Emily backpedalled quickly. 'Stupid of me. Insensitive.'

At that, the whole mood in the room seemed to shift. Where they'd been having light-hearted fun a moment ago, now it was more serious.

'What you have to understand is that this,' Francesca explained, waving her hands up and down that enviably lean figure, 'by which I mean being me – the real me, the me you see here beside you – has quite literally cost me everything. My home, my marriage, my kids – and given that I'm now a laughing stock in work, very possibly my job too. I've hurt people. I've brought a whole world of pain into my family's lives, and all because I wanted to live an honest life. Fun doesn't even come into it.'

Emily said nothing but looked suitably chastened as Francesca twiddled with one of the pill bottles, so it rattled in her hands.

'Let me guess,' Emily said after a pause. 'Oestrogen pills?'

Francesca nodded.

'How long have you been taking them for?'

'First time,' Francesca said. 'Right here, right now. And these aren't the only ones, by the way. You see those?' she said, nodding towards a stuffed pharmacy bag on the dressing table. 'You name it, that's what I've been prescribed. To lower testosterone levels, decrease erectile function and, you know, to start developing secondary female characteristics.'

'What are secondary female characteristics?' Emily asked, puzzled.

'I might start getting boobs,' Francesca said, with a wry little smile. 'It's all to do with female fat distribution. Women carry fat differently and that's what this first course of treatment is about.'

'Will it be painful?'

'Not physically – but emotionally, yes,' Francesca replied. 'But then, as I said to my therapist, I've come this far. I've lived a half-life for so long, and now here I am, fifty years old. It's time for truth. Everyone knows about me anyway, so why live a lie for much longer?'

'Fucking hell,' was all Emily could say, over and over. 'I mean, this is *huge*. I came in here thinking you and me might have a good aul' bitch about our nutty landlady.'

'This is just phase one,' Francesca said, with a shrug of her shoulders. 'The easy part, according to my therapist. It's when I get to phase two that my life as I know it will really begin to change.'

'Dare I ask what phase two involves?'

'Oh, so much, honey. It's a long, long process. There's all the social changes to deal with, for starters; people are going to react to me differently, aren't they? And I have to be prepped for that. In work, for instance, everyone will have to call me by a new name and start using a different pronoun when they refer to me.'

'And then?' Emily asked.

'Then the real body modification begins,' said Francesca. 'All triggered off by these little pills. That can take years, but then, all being well, the end goal is full gender reassignment surgery.'

'Wow,' said Emily.

'Wow is right.' Francesca nodded. 'It's scary and it's frightening – and the part of me that's still cautious, timid little Frank Woods, who never took a risk in the whole course of his life, is terrified. Because once I swallow this,' she said, indicating one of the silver tin foil strips in her still-mannish hands, 'then that's it. I'll have begun the process. It'll be goodbye to Frank for good.'

'How do your family feel about this?' Emily asked gently.

Francesca just looked at her wryly. 'Well, what do you think, honey? I had to move out and now I'm living in a shoebox. I'm two hundred metres from the son I love, a daughter I'd die for and a wife who can't accept that I still actually do love her. That, my dear,' she said, 'is how my family feel about this.'

'Sorry,' Emily said. 'Dozy question. What about everyone else, though? Your friends?'

'They're all acting like I'm dead and gone – but the thing is, I'm not. I'm still very much here. I'm not going anywhere, and I want to be in their lives just as much as I always did. But as Francesca from here on in. That's all. Otherwise, I'm still here. Still me.'

'But you're nervous about taking the pills?'

'Terrified,' Francesca nodded, for the first time sounding unsure of herself. 'I was prescribed them days ago, but somehow I can't bring myself to actually swallow this very first one. Once I do, I'll have decided that this is it. It's letting go of the old part of my life and stepping into the new.'

'And it's scary for you and overwhelming,' Emily said. 'Believe me, I can sympathise. I know all about what it's like to let go of the old you and move towards the newer, better version of yourself. For what it's worth, though, there is one piece of wisdom I can share.'

'What's that?' said Francesca.

Emily sat back against the bedpost and chose her words carefully before replying. 'You and me, my friend,' she eventually said, 'seem to have one thing in common. Frank 1.0 didn't work in this world, any more than the first version of Emily did. So, here's to Frank mark two. Here's to Francesca. This is the part where we both have to trust that the shiny, new rebooted version of ourselves can only be better.'

'Thank you, honey,' Francesca said, looking back at her with shining eyes.

'For better or for worse,' said Emily. 'Shall I get you a glass of water, so you can wash down those pills?'

'Down in one?' Francesca asked.

Emily grinned. 'Down in one.'

Gracie

If there's one thing that Ben had never been to his mother, it was an enigma. Every thought that went through her son's head, Gracie could predict; every emotion he was feeling, she was able to second-guess, purely by looking at the food he was shovelling into his body. For years now, food had been an emotional barometer with Ben, and Gracie could almost gauge what he was feeling in direct proportion to what he ate.

From his early teens, Ben had always been something of a clean eater. Food was a big passion of his, and although he occasionally allowed himself white meat and fish, chips, carbs and anything too sugary or starchy was right out. Gracie had always been prouder than proud that she had a son who'd turn his nose up at McDonalds, who she'd regularly come home to find chopping onions and garlic to make a Thai green curry from scratch, frequently teaching Amber as he went along.

When Ben was in good form, he lived off the cleanest food going, wolfing his way through whole bunches of kale, forever at his mother to stock up on fresh smoked salmon, organic veg and spelt bread. Whenever he was stressed out, though, it was the total opposite. For instance, when he'd been in the throes of the Leaving Cert exams, he tucked into the carbs like someone on death row. No matter how much food Gracie stuffed the fridge with, Ben would get at it, and two minutes later, there'd be nothing but an empty tub of Häagen-Dazs and the remains of a few sad oven chips staring back at her.

When Ben broke up with his first girlfriend, Gracie had known just how upset he was about it when she noticed empty Tayto packets lying all around his computer screen.

'Comfort eating,' she'd said to Frank, back when he was still living at home. A very bad sign. She'd only realised that Ben was over said girlfriend and getting back to himself when blueberries and ripe avocados started disappearing from her fridge again.

Ever since Frank had moved out though, he'd been living off nothing but pizza and chips, to the extent that Gracie was starting to get seriously concerned. Officially, Ben had finished school and had a part-time summer job in a vegetarian restaurant. Officially, this should have been a happy, carefree summer for Ben, having worked so hard in school the previous year.

Not now, though. Not anymore. Since Frank had left, Ben had become more and more withdrawn. *Yet another reason,* Gracie thought, *to wring Frank's selfish, gobshite neck for visiting all of this on his blameless family.*

Time and again she and Frank had tried in their own clumsy ways, to reach out to the kids, to somehow find a way to parent them through this. Gracie grudgingly had to at least give Frank that much; he probably spent more time with Amber now than he ever did when he was living at home.

But Ben was a totally different kettle of fish; he'd shut himself down emotionally and was refusing to engage with anyone. At the very least, though, Frank did appear to be making a big effort with him, constantly driving him places, always there for his son at the drop of a hat, if and when needed.

That therapist they were seeing, Beth what's-her-name, had talked to both Frank and Gracie about having a 'healthy transition'– if you could even believe such a thing existed. Gracie certainly didn't, but she did very much want to protect her kids with every last breath in her. She tried her level best to talk to each of them in turn, to broach the tender subject, to try to gauge how they felt about Frank's transitioning.

With Amber, it was impossibly difficult to find the right words, and harder still not to feel resentful and angry that she was reduced to having these mortifying conversations in the first place. Invariably, Amber would look up at her mum, puzzled and confused, and say, 'But all I want to know is . . . when is Daddy is coming home?'

What kind of a mother am I, Gracie thought sadly, *that I can't protect my child through this?* Frank was the one who'd put her in this position – why the hell couldn't he clean up his own mess and explain it to the kids himself? Why did she have to do his dirty work for him?

Ben was the toughest of all. He was eighteen years old, a grown man now, and the strong, silent treatment was about as much as Gracie could get out of him.

'You never have your friends over anymore, love,' she tried saying to him one night, after Amber had gone to bed and it was just the two of them on their own in the kitchen.

Ben grunted, but kept his head buried in the fridge, where he was picking at a family-sized tub of potato salad, which ordinarily he'd have lectured Gracie for buying in the first place. A very, very bad sign.

'I can't remember the last time your pal Hugo was here,' she added. 'All you ever seem to want to do is hang out at his house these days.'

'Whatever,' he said, without even turning around.

'So . . . would you like to ask him around this weekend?' she offered. 'I'm taking Amber to Granny's, so you'll have the whole house to yourself?'

Ordinarily, Ben's eyes would have lit up at the thought of a free house. Not now, though. Instead, he took out a big bowl of leftover cheesy pasta, unpeeled the cling film from it, then sat down at the kitchen table with a giant serving spoon and tucked in, like this was his last meal on earth.

'You could have some of your mates from school around?' Gracie said gently. 'Dare I say it, you could even have a party?'

Again, silence.

'Ben?' she persisted. 'Did you hear me, love? You've been at me all year to have a party here in the house, and now I'm say-ing it's OK. Go ahead. Just stay the hell out of my bedroom,' she added, trying to lighten the mood, 'and you and me have a deal, buddy.'

At that, Ben lowered an overstuffed spoonful of penne pasta and looked at her for the first time.

'Thanks, but no thanks,' he said.

'You sure? This is my final offer, kiddo. I'll even sweeten the deal by tossing a few quid your way, so you can go shopping and cook for your pals?'

'Mum, I already said no.'

'But Ben,' she said, 'you love cooking for the guys. You always say it relaxes you. Come on love, I'll even take you to the farmer's market at the weekend so we can shop for ingredients together, if you like?'

He sighed, put his spoon down, wiped a blob of creamy sauce off his mouth and sat back.

'Look, I know you mean well,' he said. 'I know you're just trying to keep the show on the road for Amber and me. But you have to remember – my mates were here that night. They all *know*. They all *saw*. And now I'm the guy whose dad goes around in high heels and dresses. So if you think I'll ever have any of my friends round to this house again after that night, after what that selfish bastard put us through—'

'Ben, that's your dad you're talking about,' Gracie said loyally, although she had absolutely no idea why she was bothering to be loyal. Force of habit, she figured. 'Whatever he's done, he's still your dad and we're still a family. I know you and Amber didn't ask for any of this, and I know you're angry. Believe me, love, you're not as angry as I am. But somehow we have to find a way to work through this, and I know the only way we can is if we stick together.'

'Mum,' Ben said, sitting forward, looking like he wanted to stab someone with his spoon. 'He's not my dad anymore. He's not the same person. And the dad I've always known, it's not – it's not really him, is it? And after all that, after all the lies he told us and what he's put you and Amber and me through, I never want to see him again. He's ruined us.'

'I know, sweetheart,' Gracie said, wincing a little at his disparaging choice of words. 'But I need to protect you and Amber, and make sure that your lives go on as normal. That's my job. That's what I need to do.'

'No, Mum,' Ben replied. 'It's the other way around. I'm the one who wants to protect you. If he ever hurts you or Amber like that again, I'll never, ever forgive him. As it is, I don't want to see him or speak to him or have anything more to do with him. And that's not negotiable.'

Gracie sat back and bit her lip, and when she thought of what lay ahead, was suddenly very, very worried.

Violet

Hmph, Violet thought crossly. It was nigh on ten o'clock in the morning on a gloriously sunny July day and that lazy lump upstairs, Madam Emily, was yet to rise from bed and vacate the house. Violet liked to have her peace and privacy during daytime hours and made it perfectly clear to both her paying guests that immediately after breakfast, they were expected to clear off till dinner time at least. Not an unreasonable request, surely?

Frank was no trouble. He was up at the crack of dawn, quiet as a mouse, and rarely came back to the house till he'd seen his children in the evening – or at least the daughter, the one with the housemaid's name. The sole member of his family who was still speaking to him, apparently. Frank, as far as Violet was concerned, was a delightful guest and a model lodger.

Madam Emily, however, was an entirely different story. Ten a.m. came and went, and there still wasn't as much as a stirring from inside her bedroom – Violet had already had a good listen at the door. She'd then taken particular care to walk loudly up and down the corridor outside, banging her walking stick as noisily as she could, but no, still nothing.

Eventually, after twenty minutes of thudding noisily around the bare boards of the house, Violet reached breaking point.

Hammering on Emily's door with her walking stick, she yelled, 'Kindly leave the property at once! This is not a house where you can loll about in bed all day, you know.'

There was rustling from behind the closed door, then a moment later, a dishevelled, sleepy Emily stuck her head around the bedroom door, her hair a complete disgrace, with the remnants of some class of sooty black maquillage streaked down her face. Not only that, but Madam Emily appeared to have slept in some class of white long-sleeved night attire with *Your Worst Nightmare* written across it in lurid pink.

How appropriate, Violet thought.

'Jesus wept,' Emily groaned. 'Where's the fire?'

'Out!' Violet barked back at her. 'I'm giving you exactly five minutes to get out of this house. This is not the Ritz Carlton, you know.'

'You can say that again,' Emily yawned.

'You needn't think you can laze about in bed at my expense all day.'

'Oh, keep your hair on. You think I want to be here all day under the same roof as you? Get real.'

'Then I strongly suggest you find some class of gainful employment,' was Violet's crisp retort. 'What sort of person just hangs around the house all day anyway?'

'I dunno,' Emily said. 'Someone just like you, I imagine.'

'Out of here in exactly five minutes!' Violet said. 'Or be warned, I shall come in there and take particular pleasure in escorting you out the hall door myself. Somehow, I doubt that this would be the first establishment you've been thrown out of, Madam Emily Dunne!'

'Don't suppose there's any chance of a strong coffee before I go?' Emily added cheekily, before banging her bedroom door right in Violet's face.

That's her seen off, Violet thought half an hour later, twitching at the curtains in her drawing room and watching Emily finally leave. Insolent little rip. *Looking like a homeless person too,* she thought sniffily.

Suddenly, she had the need to hear something soothing, restful. An antidote to that awful madam and her rudeness. Instinctively, she gravitated towards the upright pianoforte in her drawing room, the one item of furniture she'd categorically refused to pawn when times were rough and money tight. Violet would starve before she could be without her music, and besides, always hovering at her shoulder, in this of all rooms particularly, was the absent ghost of Freddie Hardcastle, tall and proud, standing at the bay window and surveying the comings and goings up and down Primrose Square.

Bach, she wondered, as she stretched out her fingers, expertly skimming over the keys. No. It was far too sunny and pleasant outside for Bach. Mendelssohn. The very man for a summer's day. Letting her subconscious take control, Violet began to play the opening bars of his wonderful piano concerto in G minor, and without knowing how, she found herself thinking back to a beautiful summer's evening in that very drawing room, with her father standing proudly at the same window she was now playing at.

She'd played Mendelssohn that particular evening too, before any of their guests started to arrive.

'It relaxes me,' Father had said. 'And besides, it sets the right tone for the evening ahead. Ladies of class and culture play the piano at parties. Let them all see how beautifully you can play, Vi.'

But oh, how very differently the drawing room had looked that night. The whole room had gleamed for her party – Betty, their housemaid, had seen to that. Giant floral arrangements donned every surface, and everywhere you looked, you were left in no doubt that a wealthy, prosperous family lived at number eighty-one, Primrose Square. Extra staff had been hired for the night to help with the catering, and Father had even allowed a makeshift bar to be set up in the dining room, where a bow-tied barman was on duty for the whole night, with the strict order to keep the drinks free-flowing.

Not only that, but Father had generously given Violet money to go shopping. 'Remember, that's to buy yourself something classy, Violet, love,' Betty had warned her. 'None of those mini-skirts, now, or any of that plastic stuff that you see all the young ones parading around in. Your father will have a fit.'

'You don't need to remind me, Betty.' Violet had laughed, but then she and Betty were only a few years apart and had become friends as much as housemaid and the spoiled, privileged daughter of the house. 'Stay as far away from Mary Quant as possible, and all will be well.'

'Laugh all you like,' Betty had replied briskly, as she ran wet sheets through the wringer downstairs in what was then the laundry room, and which was now a decaying outdoor shed. 'But you know what Mr Hardcastle is like. For God's sake, Violet, just keep him happy and everything will be grand.'

For her eighteenth birthday party, Violet had struck a wonderful compromise regarding her wardrobe. With the money that her father had given her, she treated herself to a brand-new evening dress from Arnotts – white satin, and tight-fitting, so it showed off her tall, elegant figure to perfection, yet high-necked and long-sleeved, so even Father couldn't object. Besides, Violet had thought, handing over the unheard of sum of five pounds and ten shillings for the dress, if he did give her a hard time over it, she'd just tell him that she saw exactly the same one on Princess Margaret in a magazine, and that would surely keep him quiet.

Father had wanted everyone to come, and indeed, everyone had. Neighbours from Primrose Square, family, most of Violet's old school friends and a few of Freddie's former work colleagues – the very few who he deemed swanky enough to be invited to such a glitzy celebration.

The drawing room had been packed to the rafters and everywhere you looked the waiting staff where dashing about, topping up champagne flutes and taking care of the glamorous guests, who'd turned out in force for Violet.

Every single one of her friends from finishing school had shown up, 'looking like a beautiful bunch of Tralee Roses,' as Father had said proudly. 'Nice, well brought-up young ladies from good families. Perfect company for you, Violet.'

Just then, Violet's long, slim piano fingers reached the tricky bit in the concerto, the part where you really had to concentrate or else the 4/4 staccato beat would run away with you.

Funny, she thought. She'd been at exactly the same point in the music when he'd walked in through the drawing room door, with his old friends Jayne and Tom Dawson from number nineteen Primrose Square.

Not many people could divide their lives neatly in two, like slicing an orange right down the centre. But Violet could. There was before that night, before the party – before everything that had led to this point.

And after.

After Andy McKim had casually strolled into her father's drawing room and into her life.

Emily

'Can't do it,' Emily said. 'Can't and won't.'
    'You have to.'

'It's a total fucking waste of time. Theirs and mine.'

'So how else are you going to fill in your day? It's not like you're rushing off to a job, now is it?'

'Gimme a break. As a matter of fact, getting a job is next on my list. If I have to spend a minute longer under the same roof as my landlady, I will actually throttle her.'

'She can't be that bad. I've seen her glaring out the front window of your house loads of times. She's a little old lady on a walking stick. You're honestly telling me you're afraid of a little old lady on a walking stick?'

At that description of Violet, Emily had to resist the urge to guffaw into her coffee. She was with Leon in a greasy spoon café, just off Dublin's Capel Street. Leon's taxi was parked close by and, given that he was about to do a ten-hour shift, he said he needed at least three eggs, two rashers and a clatter of white toast to kick-start the day.

Emily meanwhile, sipped at a coffee and pretended she wasn't hungry, although the truth was she barely had enough cash on her to pay for the coffee, let alone breakfast. Her stomach rumbled at the smell of the fry-up Leon was horsing into. Did she know him well enough to stretch out and help herself to a bit of leftover toast he wasn't eating?

But then she thought of what the day ahead held for her and her appetite instantly turned to ash.

'You know what?' she said. 'Today's not a great day to do this. I think I'll leave it till tomorrow. Weekends are always better.'

Leon looked up at her, with a fat sausage in one hand and a mug of milky tea in the other.

'You don't put off until tomorrow,' he growled in his twenty-fags-a-day voice, 'what you can easily do today.'

Emily winced. 'You haven't met my sister.'

'Get over yourself, would you? I'll even drive you there myself.'

'No need,' she said, a bit too fast. 'I'll grab a bus.'

'Taxi's right outside,' Leon grunted, as he went back to his breakfast. 'That way, at least I know you'll go through with this.'

'Oh, come on, what do you take me for – a child?'

'For fuck's sake, stop arguing and just drink your coffee. Now, do you want some toast with that?'

'No thanks.'

'I'm paying.'

'Then in that case, yes please. Thought you'd never ask. I'm bloody starving.'

Leon was as good as his word. Without any small talk, just the over-bright tones of a highly caffeinated presenter on the radio in the background, he deposited Emily outside her sister's neat suburban house, in her neat tree-lined road, surrounded by other neat two-bedroomed semi-detacheds just like it.

Sadie worked from home in a converted office upstairs, so her car was parked in the driveway, where not so much as a stray leaf seemed to sully the atmosphere of calm tranquillity.

Well, I'm certainly about to shatter the peace in this house, Emily thought, unstrapping herself from the passenger seat of Leon's taxi and clambering out.

'Wish me luck,' she said to Leon.

'Luck has nothing to do with it,' he replied. 'Just remember this is about one thing and one thing only: atonement.'

'Jesus, you're fun in the mornings, aren't you?' she said, banging the car door shut and striding up the driveway, dying to get this over with.

It was a God-awful, horrible feeling, she thought, having to retrace her footsteps back up that driveway, Sadie's words still ringing crystal clear in her ears from the last time the two had spoken: 'From now on, I have no sister.'

Ouch.

She rang the doorbell and waited. Rang again, waited some more. Sadie's immaculately organised office was directly overhead, so if her sister was indeed working from home, then all she had to do was throw open the window to look down and see who it was.

Still nothing, though – not a whisper from inside the house. Emily shoved her hands in her coat pockets and took a moment to look around the pristine front garden, with her sister's gleaming new BMW hybrid in the driveway, proudly bearing 19-D number plates which might as well have screamed: 'We're so affluent and comfortable here!'

Jesus, she thought. *I'm three years older than Sadie and I've got absolutely nothing to my name.* A few fast-dwindling savings and that was it. Yet here was her younger sister, living prosperously with her gorgeous little boy, happily married to Boring Brien, although how anyone in their sane mind could be happy with someone like him was beyond Emily.

But then, you could have had all of this, she reminded herself. *Showroom home, nice car, great lifestyle, even a husband. And you threw it all away. You ran screaming from suburbia the minute you got the chance.* So if none of this would ever make Emily happy, then what would? *That,* she thought, *is the million-dollar question.*

She knocked a third time, louder this time, starting to get impatient. God Almighty, all she'd come to do was apologise and then she'd be on her way. She was only asking for approximately three minutes of her sister's time – would it really kill her to answer the bloody door?

She started to yell through the letterbox. 'Sadie,' she said loudly, 'I know you're in there and I know you can hear me. I faithfully promise I'm not here to cause trouble. I only came to say that I was sorry for everything. For all the horrible things I did and for all the hurt I caused you and Mum.'

Eerie silence as her voice trailed off into thin air.

'Anyway,' she added, feeling like an eejit as her voice echoed down the hallway inside. 'That's it, I suppose. So I'll be on my way now. I doubt we'll ever see each other again, so this is goodbye. Have a nice life and . . . remember that I did at least try to say sorry. I get that you don't want to see me any more than Mum does, but please remember that I did try.'

Could this whole 'Step Eight' crap-ology possibly go any worse? Emily wondered, as she stomped back down the gravelled driveway, finally admitting defeat. Just as she reached the garden gate, she spotted a wheelie bin with an actual neon pink cover over it. *Typical Sadie*, she thought. Even the wheelie bin was spotless, and doubtless Boring Brien was out there every other day with a garden hose cleaning it down.

The old her would probably have kicked it over, purely out of badness. The old her would probably have had to be dragged kicking and screaming from the house. The old her would doubtless have smashed windows and given Sadie's car tyres a right good kicking. But this was Emily 2.0 and Emily 2.0 wasn't that person anymore.

Then, turning over her shoulder, she caught a glimpse of Sadie peeking out from behind her gleaming white plantation shutters on the first floor. There was no mistaking it; Emily saw her shadowy figure hiding behind the window, with her phone in her hand, double-checking that Emily had really gone, and probably ready to call the cops at a moment's notice.

So Emily didn't cause a scene. Instead she went quietly, without a fuss. She even gave a little half wave in the direction of Sadie's office.

You see, Sadie? I told you I'd changed. You don't believe me? Just keep on looking.

The worst thing about being unemployed, she was learning, was the sheer, unrelenting, mind-numbing boredom.

Emily used the last spare change she had in her jeans pocket to go into town, but with the whole day stretching ahead of her, was at a complete loss what to do. Catch an afternoon movie, maybe? Out of the question on her budget. Window shopping? Boring – and given how broke she was, annoying too, when she started seeing all the things she could ill afford.

Feeling utterly out of place among the busy families wheeling prams down Henry Street, she wandered aimlessly until she found herself close to the Ilac shopping centre. There was a library there, she remembered. Perfect. The ideal place to kill time cheaply when you were on the scratch and still had a good seven hours to fill before she could even think about going back to Primrose Square for the evening.

She texted Leon to thank him for the lift to Sadie's earlier, stressing that it had all turned out to be a colossal waste of time. Then she loitered outside a coffee shop in case he replied, secretly hoping he might even be free between taxi fares for a quick cuppa and a chat.

Be good to talk to someone who actually got it, she thought. But her luck was out – no response from him at all, which meant he must have had a fare and couldn't get back to her.

Jesus Christ, I have GOT to get work, Emily thought, striding up the stairs that led to the Ilac centre library. When was the last time she'd even been inside a library? When was the last time she had all these long hours stretching out ahead of her, not having the first clue how to fill them?

There was a time when she'd have gone straight to the nearest boozer and happily spent the day there, propped up on a bar stool, talking shite to whoever would listen – or better yet, to whoever would pay to keep the drinks flowing.

She shuddered, thinking back to all those long, boozy days when she'd been fired from her job, but somehow still had the cash to go drinking in the daytime. Day regularly turned into night, then turned into morning, and Emily would find herself passed out on some random stranger's sofa – or worse yet, in their bed. Hard to believe now, but nakedness, mortification and killer hangovers were often how she used to start her days.

Once, she even came to lying in a pool of her own blood on the floor of a dingy apartment, with her right arm bleeding profusely, as she lay semi-conscious in the middle of a mound of broken glass. There were shards everywhere, even in her hair and mouth.

It was only when the fire brigade broke down the door to let her out that she managed to put two and two together. Apparently she'd gone back to some randomer's flat, then panicked when they'd gone to work the next morning and she realised she was locked in. So what do you do when you're trying to get out of a strange flat, still numb from the two bottles of vodka you drank the previous night? Put your right hand through a plate glass of an emergency exit, of course, and try to get out that way. To this day, Emily still had scars from the twenty-seven stitches she'd been given in A & E. It was what had propelled her into treatment – her first bout of treatment, that is, before she fell off the wagon and went back on the sauce again.

Oh fuck this, she thought, as she slunk into a cool, quiet seat in the library near a bank of computers, where unemployed and very possibly homeless people like her were all availing themselves of the free facilities to go online.

It's all well and good apologising to people I've wronged in the past, she thought. But it seemed the main person she needed to apologise to was herself.

Emily managed to fill in a good chunk of the day at the library, honing her CV, which, as Lena, a Polish girl half her age at the computer next to her, said, essentially meant lying. Then she emailed off her embellished, over-inflated CV to every online employment agency that she could find.

'Turns out there's not that much out there,' she said to Lena wryly, 'if your only experience is in event management and you haven't worked in a couple of years.'

'Try being a nail technician,' Lena replied. 'My last job offered twenty euro.'

'An hour?' Emily asked.

'A day.'

'Are you serious? How are you supposed to live off that?'

'Oh no,' Lena said, shaking her head. 'That's not what you earn. That's what I was expected to pay the owner of the nail bar for the first month. A training fee, she called it.'

'Sweet God,' said Emily, shaking her head. 'So you pay to work? Now I've heard it all.'

They closed up the library at 6 p.m. on the dot, and after saying her goodbyes to Lena, Emily made her way back outside the shopping centre and onto the now semi-deserted Henry Street.

Christ Almighty, she thought, glancing down at the time on her phone. It was still way too early to head back to nutty Violet's House of Pain. Frank, or rather Francesca, still wouldn't be home from work yet, which of course meant Emily wouldn't even be able to have a good moan about her utterly soul-destroying, pointless day.

Then, as she paced down Henry Street, a fresh thought struck her. Given that she appeared to be stuck in Dante's Ninth Circle of Hell, why not go the whole hog? Why not do a job lot of apologising to everyone she'd wronged?

Emily had already accepted that none of them, her own family included, would probably ever speak to her again, so what was to stop her getting this one last obstacle out of her way? There certainly was a lot to be said for getting all this crawling in the dirt lark over with in one go. At least then she could abandon the whole twelve-step programme for the useless, self-indulgent twaddle that it was. This way, she reasoned, she could go back to Leon, say she'd done her level best, but claim that the whole thing was a colossal waste of time, both his and hers.

Which brought her neatly to the Big One. The trickiest one of all. The one she'd been putting off for as long as she possibly could. The one person who Emily could look in the eye and say, *actually, it wasn't entirely one hundred per cent my fault*. Seventy-five per cent her fault maybe, but definitely no more than that.

He didn't live too far away, either. Only about twenty minutes' walk. With her feet leading the way, Emily found herself striding in the direction of Manor Street in Stoneybatter – or Bitter Batter, as it was known, as so many unemployed actors and artists lived there.

Not him, though. Not Alec, Mr Workaholic Success Story. After he and Emily had divorced, he'd invested in a bang-on-trend, two-up two-down redbrick cottage in a row of houses just like it. Alec was a software designer and worked from home several days a week. Fingers crossed he'd be at the house now – probably still working, knowing him.

Emily knew the address from countless post-divorce letters she'd been served with and didn't have much difficulty finding it. But what she wasn't prepared for was for how bloody fabulous it all was. A small house – a fraction of the size of what you'd see on Primrose Square, but still. The houses all along Manor Street were well maintained and 'bijou', in estate-agent speak.

Typical Alec, she thought ruefully, walking down the street till she found the right number. Always a wise, cautious investor, always with his eye on how to make money long-term. The only bad investment he'd ever made in his life was marrying her.

From the outside, number eleven was your typical two-up two-down *Coronation Street*-type home – but this being Alec, doubtless it was a stunning architect's dream on the inside. A quick glimpse through a sash window that overlooked Manor Street confirmed this; all Emily could see were minimalist exposed wooden floors and a lot of sexy, expensive-looking chrome furniture going on.

This time, she hesitated at the door. With her mother and Sadie, she had no doubt in her mind what she was going to say. A grovelling apology and she'd be on her way.

But with Alec, it was very, very different. How, Emily wondered, did she even begin to put into words what needed to be said? She thought back to how different it had been when they'd first met and fallen in love – how magical it had all been. How happy she used to be – so happy, she didn't even feel the need to drink. Being with Alec was joy enough and no amount of booze had made her feel as high as she did with him.

Everyone loved Alec, but then it was impossible not to. A good-looking, charming guy with a fantastic job at a global tech firm – what was not to like? They'd met in a bar in town about twelve years ago now, when Alec was out celebrating a pal's stag night and Emily had been out on the piss with a few random stragglers from work. Back then, she was an indiscriminate drinker; at the end of the day in the office, she'd loudly proclaim: 'I'm going for just the one, anyone coming?'

But her pals had long since abandoned her that particular night and Emily was three sheets to the wind and drinking alone when she found herself standing beside this tall, good-looking guy about her own age, jostling for position at the bar.

'When they call last orders in here,' she'd said cheekily to him, 'it's a bit like the bull run in Pamplona.'

He'd laughed. To this day, Emily still remembered how warm his smile was. A proper, crinkly smile that reached his eyes.

'If I get served first, I'll shout your order in for you, if you like?' he'd very kindly offered. Music to Emily's ears.

Booze, she thought, wavering outside his front door. Booze had been right there from the very start of their relationship and was with them to the very end. *Well, if nothing else*, she thought, drawing herself up tall and strengthening her resolve, *let Alec see me sober. Let him at least see that. If nothing else, he'll see me dry and maybe, just maybe, this journey won't be a wasted one.*

She rang the doorbell – one of those expensive ones that chimed elegantly inside the house. Moments later, the door was opened by a much younger woman – petite, pretty and blonde.

So you're her, then, Emily thought. *You're Poppy.* That was her name: Poppy. This one suited her name too; she was all bright-eyed and bushy-tailed, standing in front of Emily with a big smile on that pretty, clear-skinned, annoyingly unlined face.

She was clearly living with Alec now, utterly clueless that this was his ex-wife standing mutely in the doorway, staring back at her like the wicked queen from a panto.

Fuck's sake, Emily thought. *All I need is a puff of green smoke and the sound of thunderclaps going off in the background to complete the picture.*

'Hi, you're here at last,' Poppy said, giving Emily a lightning-quick up-and-down look. But before Emily could answer, she was yelling up the stairs.

'Alec love?' she called out. 'The babysitter is here. Are you ready to go?'

Babysitter? Emily had to take a second to process what she was hearing. *Did she just say babysitter?*

At that, Poppy threw the hall door open wide to reveal a gorgeous little baby dozing placidly in a pram, a beautiful, bouncing boy, dressed in blue and looking so like Alec, it took Emily's breath away.

'Thank God you're finally here,' the younger woman said, smiling at Emily. 'Alec and I need this date night so badly! So the baby is fed and changed, and I think he should go down for you fairly easily—'

'I'm so sorry,' was all Emily could stammer, as she stepped backwards in shock. 'I think I must have the wrong address.'

Frank

'Now you know that here at Creative Solutions, we pride ourselves on being an inclusive organisation.'

'Yes,' Frank said quietly. 'Yes, I do know that.'

'And of course, by inclusive, we mean . . . we like to think that we support staff. In everything. In every aspect of their lives. Whatever their . . . orientation.'

Frank cringed in his chair as he sat opposite the company's HR manager, Hannah. Ordinarily, Hannah was a generous, hard-working colleague, who had only the best of intentions at heart. She did, however, suffer from a tendency to tie herself up in knots when it came to corporate-speak. So anxious was she not to come across as being politically incorrect, she'd now strayed deep into the territory of acute mortification.

Carefully, Hannah glanced down at her notes in case there was any other bang-on point she might have forgotten to raise, something that might land her in trouble on social media afterwards. 'I'm transitioning gender and I got no help or support from my heartless, prejudiced bosses!' was exactly the sort of post she was clearly hoping to avoid.

'So, moving forward,' she said, looking earnestly across her desk at Frank, 'is there anything that we can do to help you with what you're going through? Professionally, I mean,' she added hastily. 'You know what a valued team member you are here at Creative Solutions. We're anxious to do all we can to make this as seamless as possible for you. We want you to be comfortable here – at Creative Solutions.'

By then, she'd repeated the company name so many times, Frank half wondered if the conversation was secretly being filmed and he was a heartbeat away from appearing on a YouTube video, entitled: 'The correct way to deal with an employee suffering from gender dysmorphia.'

'What I'm trying to say –' Hannah blushed – 'is that if you were to present at work as your transitioning self, we'd be one hundred per cent supportive.'

She means if I came to work as Francesca, Frank thought. Which was more than kind of her, and while he greatly appreciated the offer, it was entirely out of the question for him.

Because how could he possibly? Frank was struggling with so much as it was. He couldn't even begin to articulate what he really felt. He'd started hormone therapy now, and it was as if he was standing quietly terrified, at the edge of a precipice. It was keeping him awake at night as he lay in that dismal little bedroom in Violet's house, staring at the ceiling as the hours ticked by, torturing himself with thoughts that no matter where he turned, he was causing pain to someone.

The deep, never-ending fear of hurting Gracie and the kids was almost impossible for him to put into words. If a miracle ever happened and if he ever reached a point where his family were OK with him as Francesca in public, that would be one thing. But until then, doing as Hannah suggested and coming to work as Francesca would just be plain wrong. As far as Frank's professional life was concerned, all he really wanted was to keep his head down. To go back to being Mr Cellophane.

'It's very good of you,' he said, taking off his glasses and cleaning them fastidiously. 'But really, there's no need for concern. None at all. So, if that'll be everything, Hannah,' he said, dying to end this mortifying conversation, 'I have a meeting with a client shortly and I just need to brush up my notes on their account.'

'Oh . . . just one thing before you leave . . .' Hannah said, as he got up to go.

'Yes?' he asked politely.

'Well, can I just ask . . . if it's OK with you . . .' She flailed about, searching for the most PC phrase to hand. 'And this is in a purely professional capacity, of course, you understand. But the thing is . . . well . . . how would you prefer to be addressed in work?'

Frank had to give it a bit of thought, never really having considered the question before.

'Frank is just fine for the moment, thanks,' he said.

Until Gracie and the kids are comfortable with me as Francesca, he thought, *then the kindest, simplest thing I can do is to stay known to everyone around me as Frank.*

'Pronouns?' Hannah offered hopefully.

'Excuse me?'

'I mean, how would you like us to refer to you? As him, or her? Or them?'

'Him is just fine, thanks.'

'What about non-binary bathrooms?' Hannah threw after him, as he was almost halfway out the door. 'Would that help? Because you know, here in the creative field, we pride ourselves on being gender blind.'

'I know,' he replied softly. 'But really, it's OK.'

It wasn't, as it happened, but it was something that Frank was far too embarrassed to be drawn any further on. He'd actually had to stop using the communal men's room on the third floor after one too many weird looks.

And there'd been an incident a few days ago with Jake, a considerably younger colleague who'd just graduated from college and whose gut-thirsty ambition knew no bounds.

'You in here, Frankie?' he'd said jokingly one day – of course when the men's bathroom was reasonably full, to maximise his audience. 'Because there's no Tampax machines in here, you know. Time of the month, is it? Yeah, I thought you were getting a bit over-emotional in that last meeting all right. You're covered in zits and you're starting to get bigger tits than some of the real women around here.'

The part of Frank that was Francesca wouldn't have stood for bullying like that, not for one second. It gave Frank great heart to think of how the real him would have made mincemeat out of the likes of Jake and all his snide little insults.

But the bad news was that he was still a very long way off being Francesca openly. So instead, he did what Frank Woods always did. Blushed red, beat a hasty retreat, then crawled back to the safety of his desk, utterly mortified and aware of the titters from all around him.

'So, everyone is being supportive to you here at work?' Hannah persisted, bringing Frank's concentration back to that gloomy little HR office. 'You sure there's nothing more we can do for you?'

'Certain, thanks,' was Frank's quiet reply. All he really needed was to put back on the invisibility cloak he'd been wearing very successfully for the last twenty-five years and get on with his job.

Just leave me alone, he wanted to yell all around the office. *You've all ignored me for years. Is it too much to ask that you continue treating me like I don't exist?*

He just wanted normality. Not to be the centre of unwanted attention every single time he walked into an office meeting. Not to be stared at and pointed at behind his back as he stepped in and out of the lifts. 'That's him,' he could imagine them all saying. 'That's the tranny. That's the man who's about to turn into a woman. He probably has a bra and a G-string on underneath his work suit. There goes Frank Woods, the office joke.'

I've only just started treatment, Frank fretted to himself. What would the office make of him once the hormones really began to kick in?

The very thought of it made him feel nauseous.

But then, just when he needed a gram of hope most, Francesca's voice came to him, strong, clear and confident. *Oh, fuck the lot of them anyway, babes. What do they know? Eyes up, big smile – and when they go low, we go high.*

Frank had been to see an endocrinologist, Dr Roberts, to discuss the hormone therapy he'd been taking, so they could monitor his dosage carefully. Dr Roberts had been perfectly polite and informative, but he had a packed waiting room outside and precious little time to talk through the emotional impact of the therapy.

So Frank was given a fresh prescription, but this time was almost taken aback by the whole cocktail of drugs he was expected to take: antiandrogens to decrease testosterone and estradiol cypionate to start boosting female hormones. There were over eleven pills in total, Frank could barely pronounce the names of any of them, and at no point in the process did his harassed-looking consultant take the time to talk through the side effects.

'You're having some kind of therapy on top of this, I hope?' was all Dr Roberts had said on the subject. 'Because some patients find the whole process more challenging to deal with than others. Remember, so far all you're doing is taking hormones. But once we perform a penectomy, there really is no going back.'

Subtext read, point taken. *Get as much help as you can, Frank Woods, because your whole world is about to shift on its axis and, when push comes to shove, will you really have the emotional reserve to deal with it?*

If it wasn't for Beth Taylor at the clinic, Frank honestly didn't know what he'd do. Sweet-natured, understanding Beth – the one person in his life who'd listen to him compassionately, without judgment. She'd also helped him get in touch with others who were transitioning or already had, and though he hadn't got together the courage yet to attend a support group or gathering in person, he'd spent hours on trans forums and websites, reminding himself again and again that he was not alone.

With Beth, you were never made to feel like another patient in a long line of them, to be shoved a prescription, charged through the nose and then dismissed. Instead, it felt almost like coming to visit a friend. And just then, Frank needed all the non-judgmental friends he could get.

'The thing about the hormone therapy you're on,' Beth patiently explained to Frank during one of their twice-weekly sessions, 'is that often patients are prepared for the physical changes, like fat in your body redistributing, or breasts starting to feel heavier and maybe even lumpy. But you'll find it's the emotional changes that'll trip you up. Getting teary at the wrong time and for all the wrong reasons. Emotional changes can be subtle for some patients, and more pronounced for others. Some MTF's – that's male to female, by the way – have reported feeling almost euphoric on oestrogen and progesterone. Whereas for others, mood swings can be a major issue. Everyone's body chemistry is different, and that's why it's so important that we monitor your response very carefully.'

'My facial hair seems to be lessening, which is something,' Frank told her, over the tea and Hobnobs they seemed to have at every session.

'How are things with your family now?' she asked.

'All the more reason to get teary.'

'Still that bad?' Beth asked sympathetically.

Frank just nodded in reply – all he was good for, when he thought of Gracie, Ben and Amber.

Gracie was still so understandably angry with him that it was difficult to have any kind of normal conversation with her at all. In front of the kids, she was always tolerant and even-tempered – but when it was just her and Frank alone, she could barely look at him.

One day, in a fit of remorse, Frank had sent her a huge bouquet of flowers to the house, with a little note that read: *I'm so sorry for putting you through this. I love you now and I'll love you always.* He'd even asked for pink peony roses, her favourite. But when he'd come to visit the kids that evening, he's seen them deadheaded and shoved upside down into the brown bin outside the house on Primrose Square.

Message received, loud and clear.

With Ben, Frank was just trying to be there for him every chance he got. Teenagers, he knew of old, really just wanted money and Wi-Fi, but Frank knew he had to do so, so much more here. Time was the best currency he could possibly give his son, in the hopes that if they spent enough time together, Ben would one day start to thaw.

If he sees I'm here for him day in and day out, Frank reasoned, *surely then he'll know how much I love him?*

There was never a single word out of Ben, though; every lift Frank gave him, every time he drove him to meet his friends, every time he dropped him off at rugby practice, he barely got a grunt of acknowledgement.

But I'll persevere, Frank thought. *I'll keep turning up. I'll be here for him, day in and day out, till the day he's ready to talk. One day,* he hoped. *One day soon.*

Amber continued to be the only bright light in his life and Frank thanked God for her smiling face every time he called to the house to see her. The simple things made her so happy, like eating Cornettos together in Primrose Square in the evening sunshine, or going to a blockbuster movie together, then allowing her far too many sugary treats afterwards.

'Nothing has changed between you and me, pet,' Frank kept reassuring her over and over. 'Your old dad loves you more than ever.'

'That's what you keep saying,' Amber said to him one evening, looking puzzled. 'But if everything is the same, then why can't you come home?'

What could Frank possibly say to that? How were you supposed to explain to an eleven-year-old girl that you were coping with gender identity disorder and that now you wanted to transition sex? Grown adults had difficulty wrapping their heads around it – what chance had he of explaining it to a child? He had tried his very best and was always left floundering.

'Just come home, Dad,' was all Amber would say. 'I miss you so much. And I promise I'll be so good. And if you want to dress up like a lady sometimes, that's OK with me, if you'll only come home.'

❧

'When it comes to your family,' Beth said, interrupting Frank's thoughts, 'keep taking it back to first principles. Keep reminding yourself why you're doing this in the first place.'

Frank sighed and sat back against the comfy, deep sofa in Beth's consultation room. 'Why am I doing this?' he repeated softly. 'I'm doing this because for the longest time, I was living a lie. I'm doing this because for most of my adult life, I thought there was something fundamentally wrong with me. If it hadn't been for the night of my fiftieth birthday, then absolutely nothing would have changed. I had all this foisted on me, whether I liked it or not.

'So I'm doing this,' he said, his voice slowly growing in confidence the more he spoke, 'because I was given a choice: either to live my truth or to continue to live the shadowy half-life I was used to. I'm doing this because I choose to live in truth. I only wish my family didn't have to suffer because of it.'

'You're in a transitory phrase right now,' Beth said wisely. 'But this too will pass. So, you know what? This is the part where you have to trust in the process. You have to believe that living just a single day as the real you, as the woman you were born to be, as Francesca, is going to be worth a whole year of living a lie as Frank Woods.'

'I hope so,' he said, his voice cracking. 'I really hope to God what you're saying is true.'

'Here,' she said, thoughtfully handing over a tissue, which he gratefully took to wipe his eyes with. 'And it's OK to cry. That's the hormones doing their job, that's all.'

'At least they're working.'

'Just let the tears out,' Beth said, looking at him sympathetically. 'You know, I wish there was a magic wand I could wave to make all this easier for you and for your family, but there isn't. There's no shortcut. You just have to go through what you're going through. And my job is to be there with you, every single step of the way.'

Just one day later, back at Creative Solutions' trendy, chrome and glass open-plan office, Frank had very deep cause to regret everything.

It was an ordinary Wednesday afternoon and the pressure was really piling on. One of his biggest client accounts wasn't happy with their latest ad campaign and it fell to Frank to try to fix the problem – but then, working quietly behind the scenes to keep everyone happy had always been his forte in work.

He was beavering away at his desk when Jake swaggered past, pausing at Frank's desk and perching at the edge of it, as if they were the best of buddies.

'How's it going, Frankie?' Jake asked casually.

'Busy,' Frank said, glancing up, dimly aware that a few other colleagues seemed to be looking over this way.

'I was just nipping out to the coffee shop across the road,' Jake said as half the office stared over. 'Fancy an Americano?'

He's being nice to me, Frank thought, an alarm bell instantly sounding in his head. Anxiously, he looked around for a bit of back-up. Where was Florence when he needed her? Or Tracey, who was always so good at diffusing tense situations?

Just then, Jake's eye landed on some family photos sitting neatly on top of Frank's desk. Photos of him taken over the years, with Gracie and the kids. Precious, happy memories that never failed to put a smile on Frank's face, no matter how stressed out or upset he was.

'Well, well, well,' Jake said, picking up one of them and taking a closer look at it. 'What have we here?'

It was a photo of Frank with Amber, taken at Disney World in Florida on a family holiday about four years ago. She was sitting high on her dad's shoulders in the shot, with a giant pink candy floss in one hand as she laughed her head off. A gorgeous photo. A happy memory of a very happy day.

'This your daughter?' Jake asked, and Frank could have sworn that the office around them went silent.

'Yes,' he stammered. 'Yes, it is. Now would you mind putting that back down, please?'

'She must be so proud of her daddy,' Jake went on, waving the photo high in the air as Frank tried to take it back. 'So tell me, how does she feel about her father dressing up like a freak in his spare time?'

'Jake,' Frank tried to say, 'please, I'm up to my eyes here, just give it back to me and let me get on with my work.'

Jake wasn't done, though.

'So, how's this going to work in your house, then, mate?' Jake sneered. 'Is your little princess going to have two mummies from now on? "Daddy, why are you wearing girlie clothes?"' he said, doing a crude impression of a little girl. '"Daddy, why do you have ladies' bras and frilly knickers hanging up in the utility room? Dad, are you getting periods now?"'

'Drop it, Jake,' Frank said, aware that a few other colleagues had started to look over their way, curious to know what was going on. 'You can stop it right there.'

'And what about this fella here?' Jake asked, hitting on a photo of Ben taken with his rugby team. '"Hey Dad,"' Jake went on, this time dropping his voice in an exaggerated impression of a teenage boy, '"do me a favour and stop hitting on my pals, OK? You're, like . . . *seriously* embarrassing me."'

'Hey, come on, cool off, will you?' said Joe from sales, coming along at the perfect moment and diffusing the situation. 'Give Frankie a break, OK?' he barked at Jake, who instantly backed down and scuttled back to his own desk when faced with an Alpha male.

'You OK, man?' Joe asked, but Frank was too upset to do anything more than nod back. He hated himself for not having the guts to stand up to the likes of Jake, and was mortified that someone like Joe had to come along and intervene, like they were kids in a school yard.

If he could only have been seen as Francesca in work, that would never have happened in the first place. She would have throttled Jake with her bare hands and not even considered the consequences. But instead, Frank just slumped back in his office chair, waited till he was alone again, then hid his face in his hands and let the tears flow unchecked.

Rock bottom, he thought. *This is it. It cannot get any worse.*

Violet

She spotted him almost the minute he came into the room.

Back then, it was hard to miss Andy McKim. He was tall and pale and so terribly good-looking. He also looked slightly out of place; all of the other gentlemen, Jayne's husband Tom included, were wearing suits. Neat, respectful, sober jackets with ties. It was that sort of party – make no mistake, this was strictly a formal occasion, heightened by the presence of bow-tied waiters who were hovering around discreetly topping up champagne glasses, while a small army of caterers served canapés to guests from heavy silver platters. All of Freddie Hardcastle's friends and business associates had turned out in force for such a fancy 'do'; there was even a chief justice present.

If Violet was being truthful, it was all a tad intimidating too.

In the middle of all this, Andy drifted in looking like a beatnik, dressed head to toe in black, with a slightly scruffy turtleneck jumper and black leather boots with Cuban heels that were all the rage, smoking a cigarette. Every eye in the room seemed to gravitate his way – Violet's included. Two thoughts struck her. How much this stranger resembled Richard Burton, and how utterly out of his depth he looked.

Suddenly, she found herself looking at her own party from an outsider's point of view. How stiff it all must have seemed, with her playing piano concertos and with half the guest list on the wrong side of fifty.

This is not a fun scene, she thought. Even she had to admit that not a single guest seemed to be enjoying themselves. She'd even overheard two of her close friends from school planning to slip away to a nightclub in town when the coast was clear.

Violet would dearly love to have slipped off with them to dance and have fun – exactly the memorable birthday celebration she wanted. But she knew it was out of the question. Her father expected her to be hostess for the night, so if that meant playing Mendelssohn concertos and making small talk with boring judges and lawyers and politicians, then that was the price she had to pay.

Jayne had arrived with Andy, of course, as well as her husband Tom, and the minute they arrived, Jayne bounced over to do the introductions. Jayne, it had to be said, was looking pretty wonderful herself in a copy of a scarlet red minidress that Twiggy had once worn, which she'd run up on her Singer sewing machine. Jayne was creative about saving money like that and was a dab hand at replicating outfits she'd seen in fashion magazines with her own needle and thread. So unlike Violet, who just bought everything from Switzer's and charged it to her father's account without a second thought.

Ordinarily, Violet couldn't help feeling just a little smug beside Jayne, knowing how much more expensive and shop-bought her own wardrobe was compared with her friend. Not tonight though; on this of all nights, even Violet grudgingly had to admit that Jayne really did look beautiful, with her freshly washed long fair hair swept up into a beehive, and with the bright red lipstick that she'd bought in Woolworths, which matched her dress perfectly. Beside her, Violet felt old-fashioned and a little dowdy, in spite of the fact that her own dress had cost almost an unheard-of sum for a simple white party dress, ballerina-style. She'd dearly have loved to look as sexy and stylish as Jayne did, but her father liked to have a say in what she wore and would have gone ballistic if her skirts had been inappropriately short. When it came to her father, she knew of old, some things just weren't worth the argument.

'Happy birthday!' Jayne squealed excitedly, hugging her friend tight, as Tom handed over a beautifully wrapped birthday gift.

'This is a surprise now,' he cautioned, wagging his finger playfully. 'Not to be opened till long after we're gone.'

'If you say so,' Violet laughed. She'd always been terribly fond of Tom, who was a big, tall bear of a man with a good heart. Even if he was just a carpenter, as father was never tired of reminding her. 'A carpenter who lives on the wrong side of Primrose Square,' he used to say. 'Can't you find a nicer class of friend to pal around with, Vi? After all the money I've spent on your education, are Jayne and Tom Dawson really suitable companions for you?'

Violet banished her father's barbed comments out of her mind, as Tom offered to get drinks for everyone. As soon as he'd drifted off, Jayne introduced Andy with a happy smile.

'How do you do?' Violet said politely.

Andy beamed broadly, looking right at her with big, soulful brown eyes.

'So you're the birthday girl, then?' he said with a little smile, speaking in a Liverpool accent that somehow made everything he said sound funny. 'You're looking fab tonight, love. Just gorgeous. The dress suits you. You're like a model; like Jean Shrimpton.'

Violet smiled, utterly charmed by this tall, good-looking stranger. Even if he did refer to her as 'love', and even if he didn't shake her hand like most other young gentlemen of her acquaintance would have done.

'And you play piano too, yeah?' Andy asked, genuinely interested. Which again made a welcome change for Violet; she dearly loved to play and was so seldom asked about it.

'Oh, she plays so well!' Jayne enthused. 'Violet studied piano at a really fancy finishing school, you know. She might even teach one day.'

'You're musical, then?' he said, with a smile that made his eyes crinkle.

'Well, one tries one's best,' Violet said demurely.

But this time, Andy seemed to be teasing her when he said: 'Oh, one does, does one?' he twinkled down at her. 'Might one give us another turn on the piano then? Maybe a bit of rock and roll? Jerry Lee Lewis? Or how about a bit of Mr Berry?'

'Mr Berry?' Violet said, puzzled, but then she thought she knew every composer going.

'Well now, you've heard of Chuck Berry, haven't you?' He grinned. 'If not, then I might just have to introduce you.'

'Andy's in a band over in Liverpool,' Jayne said helpfully. 'The Moptops. Tom and I heard them at a concert they gave in Manchester once and they were magic. Oh,' she added with a beam, 'and guess what? They once worked with the same record producer as The Beatles – George Martin. Isn't that so cool?'

'Well, now.' Violet smiled, impressed in spite of herself. Merseybeat was all the rage and everyone knew that if the mighty George Martin deigned to work with an act, then they were surely destined for stardom. 'In that case, I can say I knew you before you were famous, Andy. Maybe you'd play for us later on?'

Andy looked down at her, as if he was being challenged. 'If the birthday girl would like me to play right now,' he said, 'then yeah, of course, your wish is my command. So how about we kick-start this party properly, then?'

Violet smiled back delightedly. Then, with a confident stride, Andy went over to the very piano that still stood in pride of place in Violet's drawing room, slid onto the chair, shoved a clumpful of his thick, jet-black hair out of his eyes and looked into the crowd for a moment, almost as if he was assessing them before deciding what to play. A minute later, he was playing and singing along to 'Having a Party' by Sam Cooke in a rasping, husky voice. It was the perfect choice of song and was the first bit of fun at a party that up till then, had been staid and deadly boring. The music caught everyone's attention, and in no time the whole room seemed to be clapping and singing along.

'He's really good, isn't he?' Violet said to Jayne, who was singing away at the top of her lungs.

'He's magic!' Jayne laughed back. 'Wait till you see, he'll be on the Hit Parade before the year is out!'

In no time, Andy had the whole room eating out of his hand. He launched into a medley of well-known pop tunes, including 'It's My Party', and with a nod towards the crushed blue velvet dress that Violet's pal Annabel was wearing, he even sang 'Blue Velvet'. Guests were whooping and cheering by then, as Andy cheekily called into the crowd: 'Any requests, folks?'

'Givvus "The Twist"!' someone from the back of the room shouted.

So he did. And it was raw and raucous and lively and fun, and suddenly it was as if the whole party had really kicked off properly for everyone.

For everyone apart from Freddie Hardcastle. Hearing the noise from the drawing room, he strode in to see what all the commotion was, which was particularly annoying for him, as he'd been deep in conversation with Cheif Justice Laffoy in the front parlour room.

And what a sight greeted him, the minute he thundered into the room, all guns blazing. Younger guests were up dancing, jiving and generally twisting the night away, yelling, clapping and singing along to 'Let's Twist Again' by Chubby Checker. Jayne and Tom were already bopping away, and Violet was swaying and clapping along with a few schoolfriends when her father abruptly rapped her on the shoulder, demanding her attention.

One look at his face and her blood turned cold.

'What the hell is this racket?' Freddie demanded, having to shout to be heard over the noise. 'And who is that idiot at the piano?'

'His name is Andy – he came with Jayne and Tom,' she told him, instinct telling her all father needed was to be soothed and calmed down. 'Isn't he wonderful?'

'He's got long hair,' Freddie snapped. 'He's a bloody gate-crasher with long hair, who's in my house and who's ruining this party.'

'He's not ruining it, Father,' Violet said stoutly, the two glasses of Babycham she'd had emboldening her. 'He's entertaining everyone – look, they're all up dancing now! Everyone is having a wonderful time, so you don't need to worry.'

'Chief Justice Laffoy is here with his son Eugene,' Freddie growled back. 'They've been here for over half an hour now and you haven't even bothered to come and say hello to them. Instead, I find you in here making a show of yourself while some uninvited blow-in seems to be taking over.'

Just then, Andy slowed the music down and launched into 'Love Me Tender' by Elvis Presley. It was a softer, quieter song and the whole mood of the room seemed to mellow a little. A few couples started to slow dance. Freddie gripped his daughter tightly by the arm and took her aside, so no one could overhear the rest of their conversation.

'Get him out of here,' he said in a low, threatening voice that she knew only too well meant trouble. 'Either you get that beatnik out of my home right now, or by Christ, I will.'

At that moment Jayne bounced over, with a fresh drink for herself and Violet.

'Oh Mr Hardcastle,' she gushed, seeing Freddie standing there and completely misinterpreting his mood, 'isn't the music brilliant? What a fantastic party. I can't thank you enough for asking us, and of course Andy too.'

'Except that I didn't ask him, did I?' Freddie sniped back at her. 'Who do you think you are, Jayne Dawson, dragging this lowlife into my private home? The barefaced cheek of you!'

Jayne opened and closed her mouth in total shock, but no sound came out. Meanwhile Violet just stared at the floor, praying he wouldn't lose his temper.

'Do I go dragging total strangers into your house without permission?' Freddie Hardcastle demanded, as Jayne looked utterly mortified. 'Of course, I should have known you hadn't an ounce of breeding in you, treating my home as if it's some kind of freebie nightclub. And as for you, Violet? I'm utterly ashamed of you.'

At that, Freddie turned on his heel and stormed back to the front parlour. Violet bit her lip and turned to Jayne, who looked as if she'd been slapped right across the face.

'I'm so sorry,' Violet began to say. 'You know what's he's like when he gets into these moods.'

'Now don't you worry a bit,' Jayne said, though she looked like she was close to tears. 'I totally understand. Of course your father wasn't going to like us bringing Andy along. I know that we're not fancy enough for him and that's OK with me, honestly. But when your dad's calmed down a little, maybe you'd tell him that Andy meant no harm by playing a few tunes. That's just what he does. He's really sweet when you get to know him.'

Then Jayne's voice wobbled, and a moment later, Tom and Andy had sauntered over to see what the fuss was. Seeing his wife upset, Tom slipped his arm supportively around her waist.

'Come on, love,' he said fondly to her. 'Chin up. What's the matter, then?'

'Mr Hardcastle is very angry with us, Tom,' Jayne told him. 'I think it's probably best if we leave. Now. You too, I'm afraid, Andy.'

'I'm so sorry about this,' Violet spluttered, the awful atmosphere her father had created casting a pall over the whole evening. 'I don't know what to say – this is so embarrassing.'

'Hey, not your fault,' said Tom kindly. 'Don't you worry a bit about us. We'll be on our way now, so you can enjoy the rest of your night.'

'No! Please don't leave,' Violet said. She'd wanted to tell them that the whole night had only really kicked off when they'd arrived with Andy, but she felt so choked up with humiliation, somehow she couldn't find the right words.

Andy was having none of it, though. 'Hey, come on, everyone,' he said in that laid-back, easy way he had that instantly seemed to lighten the tension. 'We can't go home yet – the night is but a pup. I'm not letting anyone go anywhere, not when we're all done up like kippers and ready for a proper night out. How about we go on to a club in town? Check out the scene?'

'A nightclub?' Jayne said, instantly brightening at the thought. 'An actual, proper nightclub? Oh, that sounds lovely! I've never been to a nightclub before and I've always wanted to.'

'Oh,' Violet said flatly.

So they were all heading off to have a night of real, proper fun. Without her. She'd have to stay here and make small talk with the judge's boring son, while they all had a rare old time of it in a nightclub.

'Don't suppose the beautiful birthday girl fancies coming with us, then?' Andy said, with a wink in Violet's direction. Violet flushed, but Jayne was having none of it.

'Don't be silly, Andy,' Jayne chided him. 'She's the hostess; she can't just disappear off like that! Besides, there's a judge's son inside and her father expects her to entertain him.'

This time Andy looked at Violet almost as if he was challenging her.

'So, what's it to be then, love?' he asked. 'The judge's son, or a night of fun? Come on, it'll be a good laugh – I promise.'

Violet froze for a moment. This party had been months in the planning and it had cost her father an absolute fortune. If she were to slip away, she'd surely be crucified, no ifs, ands or buts. But then . . . it was her birthday, wasn't it? She's only just met Andy and already he was by far the funniest and most entertaining guest there. She longed to go to a nightclub with him, Jayne and Tom. She couldn't bear the thought of them having all the fun without her. Just this once, couldn't she do what she wanted? If she were to be very careful and just disappear for an hour or so, she might be able to get away with it.

Without another thought, she locked eyes with Andy and gave him his answer. Quickly, before she lost her nerve.

'You know, if I were to slip out the side gate,' she said, lowering her voice so no one would overhear, 'I don't think they'd even notice I was gone.'

By the time she'd grabbed her coat and slipped out of the side door to her house, leaving the party in full swing, Tom had hailed a passing taxi. A moment later, Jayne, Tom, herself and Andy were zooming off on their way to town, full of giggles and high spirits.

'Have you ever been to a beat club before?' Andy asked her, as they sat side by side, squished together into the back seat of the car. 'Because a mate of mine who I play with says there's a really cool one here in Dublin. The Cave, do you know it?'

'No,' Violet giggled, 'but I've heard of it, of course.' She didn't like to say, but the main reason she knew the name was because The Cave was always in the papers as the kind of place where mods and rockers hung out, and where the police were inevitably called to at all hours of the night to sort out the fights that regularly broke out. It was dangerous and out of bounds, and more than anything, she wanted to see it for herself.

'I can't believe I'm actually doing this. I've never done anything wild like this before in my life!'

Jayne laughed as Violet grinned back happily at her friend. This, she thought, was amazing. This was going to be the best night of her whole life. This felt wild and fun and reckless and all the things that you were supposed to be when you were young. Then Andy's thigh lightly grazed against the tulle of her ballerina gown, making her skin tingle in a most agreeable way.

This, Violet thought, really felt like living.

❧

After Andy walked her home at dawn the next day, the row with her father was legendary. Epic. He was biblical in his anger. He roared and shouted the most vile, abusive obscenities at Violet, just the way he used to at builders who worked for him. Freddie Hardcastle's temper was lethal and both Violet and poor, blameless Betty had no choice but to lie low downstairs in the kitchen, out of the line of fire. The upshot was that Violet was effectively declared housebound for the rest of the year, her allowance was cut drastically and the atmosphere of cold silence at the house lasted for a full month.

'I've seen him lose his temper before,' Betty hissed to Violet one evening, 'but nothing like this. This is terrifying.'

Oddly, though, Violet didn't seem nearly as concerned as she should have been. She'd wanted her eighteenth birthday party to be the happiest, most memorable night of her life, and in spite of the heavy price she paid, it was.

It most certainly was.

Emily

As was her habit now, Emily had spent most of her evening across Primrose Square at Susan's, all the better to decompress after the day she'd just had.

'I went in there all guns blazing,' she said to Susan, who listened as patiently as she always did. 'I even had it worked out in my head what I'd say to Alec. But then his woman opened the door . . . Poppy, that's her name, if you can believe that there's someone over the age of seven in Dublin actually called Poppy . . . Anyway, she just stared at me, not having a clue who I was . . . with a gorgeous little boy in a stroller beside her. And you should have seen the baby – he was Alec's doppelganger.'

'So you didn't get to see Alec at all?' Susan asked, dishing up a helping of pasta for her friend.

'Not a glimmer,' Emily said, shaking her head. 'I got such a shock, I was out of there like a scalded cat.'

'Shit,' Susan said, sitting down at the kitchen table opposite her. 'Shit, shit, shit.'

'I know,' Emily said flatly, picking at the food and feigning an appetite.

'I mean, I've seen you after you went to see your mum and sister,' Susan said, 'and you were in bits. In absolute flitters. Yet Alec was the one person . . .'

'You don't need to remind me,' Emily said.

'You didn't have to go crawling back to him . . .' Susan said, trailing off.

'I know.'

'I mean, this is *Alec* we're talking about.'

'I know,' Emily repeated.

'You could have held your head up high there. And Alec should have had plenty to apologise about as well.'

'But life isn't like that, is it?' Emily said. 'And now he's off on his romantic date night with Poppy and I have to go back to the House of Pain, probably to be bollocked out of it by Violet for daring to use her Diamond Jubilee toilet-roll holder.'

'What was she like, anyway?' Susan asked.

'Who do you mean?'

'Who do you think? Poppy.'

Emily sighed. 'Young. Pretty. She probably hasn't slept since she gave birth, she didn't have a scrap of makeup on and she still looked well.'

'I hate her,' Susan said loyally.

'I don't,' Emily said, after a thoughtful little pause. 'After all, she's not to blame really, is she? If anyone is at fault, it's him. It's Alec.'

Strange, Emily thought hours later, as she tiptoed in through the front door of number eighty-one Primrose Square. It was well past 11 p.m., yet there was still a light on in the front room – or the drawing room, as Hatchet-Face Violet constantly referred to it.

Which was weird. The house was usually pitch-black by then. Emily had stayed in Susan's as late as she could on purpose, so she could just slip back home in darkness and not run into anyone. If Frank – or rather, Francesca – was still up and about, that was one thing, but the thought of having to deal with Violet after the hellish day she'd just had was another matter entirely.

Emily took her shoes off, padded noiselessly through the dusty hallway, then stuck her head around the drawing room door. A side table lamp was still brightly lit, and lo and behold, there was Violet, Cruella de Vil herself, stretched out on the knackered-looking chaise longue, out for the count and snoring lightly.

Funny thing was, Emily thought, stopping in her tracks to take a really good look at Violet, the old she-devil actually looked nicer when she was asleep. Younger too. Softer around the edges. For a moment, Emily wondered what she would have been like when she was young. Was she ever young in the first place? Had she ever had a boyfriend, ever been in love?

At that thought, Emily wanted to giggle. Not a chance in hell. When Violet was young, back when dinosaurs roamed the earth, she was probably the exact same as she was now. People like Violet Hardcastle, Emily knew, only ever soured with age. She was born a black-hearted aul' witch and would doubtlessly stay like that till the day she died, unmourned and unloved by anyone.

Strange thing though – whatever thoughts Violet was dreaming, they seemed to be particularly happy ones, because, shock horror, her mouth was curved up into a small little smile.

Before Emily went upstairs to the safety of her bedroom, she took up a worn, woollen throw that had been gathering dust on an armchair, and very gently wrapped it around Violet, so she wouldn't get chilly in the night. Then she slipped off Violet's shoes and placed a soft cushion under her head, like a makeshift pillow.

What the hell, she thought, switching the light off and leaving her to snooze on in peace. *Just because the woman is a complete horror story, doesn't mean that I can't turn the other cheek every now and then, does it?*

The phone on Emily's bedside table woke her the following morning, sharply pealing through the early dawn silence. *6.45 a.m.,* she thought, glancing at the time displayed on the phone before answering. *Fuck's sake.* Who the hell was calling her at 6.45 in the morning? Was the building on fire?

'Emily?' said a deeply familiar voice when she groggily answered the phone – and in an instant, shock had jolted her wide awake.

'Alec?' she said. 'Is that really you?'

'Were you at my house yesterday evening?' was his brusque reply.

'What did you say?'

'Jesus, Emily, it's a very simple question. Did you or did you not call to my house in Stoneybatter last night, about seven in the evening?'

Now that Emily had the chance to tune into the phone call properly, he sounded like he was on a bus or train with all the background noise.

'I might have, yeah,' she said.

'I knew it,' he sighed down the phone. 'I knew it had to be you. Poppy was in bits about it afterwards – it took me ages to calm her down. For God's sake, Em, what did you think you were playing at?'

'So that's her then,' Emily said, at the exact same time. 'That's the famous Poppy.'

Alec paused for a moment, as if choosing his words to spare her feelings before answering.

'You know I had never intended for the two of you to meet like that,' he said wearily. 'That's the very last thing I would have wanted. But yes, in answer to your question, that's Poppy. She's my fiancée now. And we have a seven-week-old son, as you probably realised.'

'I know,' Emily said flatly. 'I saw. He's a lovely little boy too. Congratulations.'

She'd fully expected Alec to move on after the divorce. He had every right to and guys like him were never single for long. But now he was a family man too.

Wow, she thought, slumping back against the pillows. *Alec had always wanted to be a dad and now he is. Yet another person*

*from my past whose life is one hundred per cent better off without
me.*

Was that the life she could have had, she wondered? If
she'd been a better wife to Alec, if he'd been a better husband
to her, could that be the two of them now, blissfully happy
and living in a cute little townhouse with a gorgeous baby of
their own?

'I'm really happy for you,' was all she could say out loud,
but she knew it sounded forced and fake.

'Thank you,' Alec said curtly. 'And I'll thank you even more
if you leave us in peace from now on.'

'But. . . . just one more thing,' Emily said, as a fresh thought
struck her. 'How did Poppy know it was me at the door last
night?'

'Not hard to figure,' Alec replied. 'She came into the kitchen
and said that a tall, middle-aged woman with long brown hair
in jeans and trainers had called, asking if I was home. She was
puzzled and confused when you ran off on her, so I put two
and two together. For God's sake, Em, what possessed you?
What good could you possibly think would have come out of
hammering on my door out of the blue like that?'

'I'm sorry,' she said, curling up into a tight little ball and hugging her knees to her chest. 'And I'll never bother you again,
I promise. It's just that I'm dry now, and in AA, they make you
write a list of everyone you've wronged when you were drinking, so you can say you're sorry to them and make amends.
And that's it, Alec, honestly. I was a horrible wife to you and
all I wanted was to apologise.'

'Oh,' he said, taken aback. 'Right then.'

There was a long, awkward pause before he spoke again.

'I thought you were probably on the scrounge for money to go drinking with,' he said.

'Been there, done that, got the T-shirt,' she said. 'Never again.'

'Well, you can take it as read that you've apologised to me,' he said, clearly wanting to end this excruciating phone call.

Emily wasn't finished, though. *Fuck it,* she thought. She had him on the phone; if she didn't say this now, she never would.

'And while we're doing apologies, Alec,' she said, 'is there anything you'd like to say to me?'

'How do you mean?' he said defensively. The background noise around him swelled, as if he'd just stepped off a packed bus or a busy Luas stuffed full of commuters on their way to work.

'I've said I'm sorry for everything I put you through,' Emily said, her voice growing stronger the more she spoke. 'I was mostly to blame. But I wasn't entirely in the wrong, was I? I've taken the lion's share of the blame, but don't you think I'm owed an apology here too?'

'What are you referring to?' Alec muttered down the phone.

'I dunno.' She shrugged. 'Maybe the fact that you were seeing Poppy behind my back for the last year of our marriage had something to do with our break up?'

This time there was silence from the other end of the phone. Just the background noise of the early morning traffic and car horns blaring.

'You remember when I found out?' Emily persisted. 'Because I do. It's very hard for me to forget. Mainly because that's what propelled me into the worst drinking binge I'd ever gone on. I ended up hospitalised, Alec. And you didn't even come to see me – not once. Have you nothing to say to me about that?'

There was a long pause before he answered. All Emily heard was the siren of an ambulance blaring, deafening her, even down the other end of the phone.

'I have a meeting now,' he said curtly, cutting her dead. 'I really have to go.'

Before she'd even had the chance to say goodbye, he'd hung up on her. He was gone.

Later that morning, Emily texted Leon and as ever, he suggested meeting up in a café.

So I can have breakfast and you can sip coffee and pretend not to be starving.

She texted back immediately:

Fine. Just need to talk. Badly.

And his response:

I was joking. Of course I'll stand you breakfast, you eejit. Humble pie not v filling, is it?

Thank God for you, you grouchy fuck, she thought, hauling herself out of bed and into her jeans, with the same battered pair of trainers she'd been wearing for months. How had she been so dismissive of Leon when they first met? How could she have been so thick? Had she really been arrogant enough to think she could just sail through recovery without any help at all?

'Did you ever meet a greasy spoon café that you didn't like?' she said to him, arriving into a run-down snack bar off Pearce Street in the dead middle of the city centre.

'Gimme a break, would you?' came Leon's growled reply. 'In the first place, I got parking here, and in the second, I'm buying you breakfast. Now sit down and order. Then tell me what the feck is wrong with you.'

They ordered – a coffee and a bowl of porridge for her, the usual full heart attack on a plate for him.

'Not bothered about your cholesterol at all?' she said, as their food arrived and Leon lashed butter onto a slice of toast that came with fried eggs, sausages and rashers, all swimming in what looked to be a big puddle of grease.

'When you've just done an all-night shift ferrying drunks on stag nights from one watering hole to another,' he quipped back, 'then trust me, high cholesterol is the least of your worries. Right, come on then, fill me in on why you wanted to talk. How bad are things with you?'

'Oh God, *so* bad,' she groaned, slumping back against the cheap bright red plastic seat. 'But the good news is that at the very least I did it. I went to my mother, my sister and my ex-husband, and I told all three of them that I was very sorry.'

'And?'

'And in two cases out of three, I practically had doors slammed into my face.'

'Two out of three?'

'Mum and Sadie, my sister.'

'And what about your ex?'

'Another story,' Emily sighed deeply, 'for another day.'

'I see,' he said, wolfing into a sausage dribbling with ketchup.

'So,' Emily went on, 'I suppose I just wanted to meet you this morning to say thanks for all the time and trouble you went to with me. Not to mention the free breakfasts.'

'All part of the service.'

'And I hope the next ex-drinker you get to sponsor is an easier case than me.'

'So you're just giving up, then?' Leon asked, wiping sauce off his mouth with the back of his hand.

'Well, what choice do I have?' She shrugged, trying not to feel too sorry for herself. 'My ex has moved on and my family have made it pretty clear to me that they all have far better lives without me. So that's it. Clean, sober Emily will just have to navigate life from here on in all on my lonesome.'

It hurt, though, just articulating it out loud. Emily had been alone for so long, she thought she was immune to feeling isolated and lost by now. But maybe she wasn't after all. Then there was a pause while Leon stopped eating, sat back and looked across the table at her.

'There's something I have to ask you,' he said.

'Ask away.'

'What the hell happened with your family in the first place?' he said. 'Sorry, Emily, but I *have* to know. For your own mother to turn her back on you, it must have been something pretty spectacular. Usually with recovering alcoholics, it's the reverse. There's always at least one family member who welcomes you back to the fold like the prodigal child.'

There was a long, measured moment before she could answer.

'I'd rather not talk about it,' was all she could say.

'If I took you to an AA meeting,' Leon persisted, 'would you talk about it there?'

'My private life in front of a roomful of strangers?' she said, shooting a warning look at him. 'Are you kidding me?'

'Lots of recovering drinkers find meetings helpful.'

'And the best of luck to them.'

'Then tell me and consider it an act of penance,' Leon insisted. 'It won't be easy getting it off your chest, but at least I'll understand why your own family want nothing to do with you. Start with what happened between you and your mother. Go on, then – you talk and I'll listen, while enjoying my high-cholesterol breakfast in peace.'

Emily sighed. *This is it*, she thought. *Leon is absolutely right. This is what real repentance feels like.*

'I may have drunk her house,' she eventually said.

'Jesus Christ,' he said, with his mouth stuffed full with a rasher. 'Go on, tell me more.'

'Well,' she said, fortifying herself with a sip of coffee before she could go on. 'Before my dad died, my parents were very comfortably off.'

'Figured as much,' he said as she raised an eyebrow back at him. 'You may dress like a homeless person, but you sound very posh.'

'I'm a waste of a perfectly good education,' Emily told him. 'At least, that's what my mother always said about me.'

'Go on, then – the house. What happened?'

'When my dad was still around, I was – believe it or not – happily married to a very nice guy called Alec. Or at least I thought he was a very nice guy back then. Anyway, we lived a perfectly ordinary, middle-class suburban life, thanks very much.'

'Except that you were hitting the bottle.'

'Yeah, but I was a secret drinker back then,' Emily qualified. 'I was a functioning alcoholic for a long time before it all started to fall apart. Anyway, a few years before Dad passed away, he developed dementia, so my sister Sadie and I took power of attorney over all his financial affairs, because Mum didn't want any of the responsibility. Sadie already had a house of her own, so Dad had willed the family home to me, knowing I'd never live in it and that my mother could stay there for the rest of her days. On paper, at least. That was it in theory.'

'Oh good Jaysus,' Leon groaned. 'Don't tell me you sold the house from under the woman's nose?'

'Not quite,' she said, 'but almost as bad. Equity release, so I could get cash to go drinking with. Then, of course, when I couldn't make the repayments anymore . . .'

'They repossessed. Course they did.'

'The same month that my father died. It all happened at the exact same time – the shit hit the fan and Mum realised she'd have to move out. So she was widowed and made homeless within weeks. She said she'd never forgive me for it – and so far, the woman has certainly stuck to her guns.'

Emily's voice cracked as snippets from that awful time began to come back to her.

Standing outside the family home – a gorgeous Edwardian house in the poshest part of Sandymount – all the neighbours had clustered together, gathering around a hearse that had come to take her dad to his final resting place. His coffin was just being carried out of the house, followed by her mother and Sadie, both dressed in neat black coats. The front garden was thronged with neighbours, distant cousins and well-wishers, who were all there to support the family through their trouble.

Yet when Emily appeared, the respectful hush seemed to shift, and now distinct mutterings could be heard. Mrs Kennedy, the biggest gossip on the road, and Mrs Bergin, her mother's bridge partner, began to nudge each other.

'The cheek of her, turning up after what she's put her mother through . . .'

'Some people just have a brass neck . . .'

Then someone whose face Emily couldn't see actually stuck up for her. 'Come on, it's her father's funeral . . . She has every right to be here, doesn't she?'

'You mean you didn't hear what Emily Dunne went and did?' Mrs Kennedy said disgustedly. 'Turns out she remortgaged the house and never kept up the repayments . . . So now, on top of all her troubles, her poor mother is being turfed out of her own home . . . Utterly unthinkable . . . Such a disgrace . . . Her own father must be spinning in his grave.'

'She didn't even have the decency to turn up sober . . . Look at the state of her! Falling over drunk. That poor husband of hers, how did he put up with her? No wonder he's divorcing her. Would you blame him?'

Emily saw pallbearers gently guiding the heavy oak coffin out through the front doors of the family home, as she tried to shove her way through the other mourners so she could get up close. But for some reason her feet wouldn't work properly, she kept stumbling, and her vision was blurry, so she couldn't even see where her mother had got to.

Next thing, she felt a bony arm grasp hers from behind, then her mum's voice hissing in her ear. 'Get out of my sight, Emily Dunne. You're not welcome here. Haven't you done enough damage to this family? I want you gone – and I want you gone now.' Her mother's raw anger was palpable. Frightening.

Then Sadie's husband, Boring Brien, stepped forward, looking weirdly ghoulish in a long, black coat that only emphasised his sunken, hollow face. He looked like the angel of death as he gripped Emily around her shoulders and steered her away, through the crowd and back out onto the street.

'I know you want to be here for your dad,' he said kindly, 'but believe me, Em, you're only making things worse.'

Emily struggled against him, insisting that she had a right to be at her own father's funeral. 'Who the fuck do you think you are, anyway, to tell me where I can and can't go?' She wished she hadn't yelled at him, but she had.

'Tell you what,' Brien had offered as a compromise. 'If you stand quietly at the back of the church, you can say your goodbye that way and not upset anyone. But then you have to promise me something,' he added.

'What more do you want?' she slurred back at him, her mouth rasping by then.

'You get the help you need,' he insisted. 'You check in somewhere and you don't come out until you're clean. Until then, you can take it as read that none of us will ever have a single thing to do with you. Sadie is still in shock, but that'll wear off pretty soon, and believe me, she'll be so angry with you, you'll wish you were in the ground along with your father. And you know what your mother is like. She'll never forget this, and she'll certainly never forgive. Have you any idea the toll this has taken on her? If she survives this, it'll be a miracle.

'Get help, Emily. You have got to get help.'

'You've only got the one mammy in this life,' Leon said, pulling Emily's attention back to the greasy spoon café. 'And she's not getting any younger.'

'I know,' Emily said.

It was hard for her to say much else. How were you supposed to explain to a relative stranger how it felt when the one person who was supposed to love you and stick by you through thick and thin, didn't want to know you anymore? And that you'd brought it all on yourself? Emily felt the guilt wash over her yet again, as agonisingly awful as it ever was – except this time without the anaesthetic of vodka to numb the pain.

'It's not enough,' Leon said simply.

'What isn't?'

'To say you're sorry to her and hope for the best. Not after what you've put your mother through. You have to show it too.'

'Yeah,' Emily sighed, 'but show her how?'

'Jesus Christ, you're a grown adult – use your imagination, will you? You were a horrible drunk, and if you're going to rebuild your life, you need to start being a lot nicer to people. Your mother being a case in point. You lost her house from under the poor woman's feet. Surely she's worth a lousy bunch of petunias?'

Gracie

'I can't stress how important it is to keep talking to the children about what's going on,' Beth was saying, up in the Transformations Clinic one sunny afternoon, when Gracie had a thousand other places to be and far, far better things to do. 'So how are you both getting on with this at the moment?'

Well, duh, Gracie thought impatiently. As if talking to the kids honestly had never occurred to her before now. *Well worth the trip here*, she thought, rapping her biro off the notepad on her knee. *Well worth taking a full hour out of an incredibly hectic schedule to sit here and be patronised, like I'm a complete idiot.*

But talking to Ben and Amber was so much harder than she ever thought it would be. She was trying her very best and getting it all wrong, and so was Frank. Both of them seemed to be stuck in a cycle of failing and flailing, and she knew her children were suffering, and she didn't stop worrying about it, not for one single moment, each and every day. She couldn't eat, couldn't sleep – all she could do was stress and fret herself to the point of exhaustion.

She and Frank were sitting side by side in their counselling session. *For all the good it's doing us*, Gracie had wanted to bark at Beth. But she didn't, of course – if nothing else, because Beth seemed like a perfectly nice young woman, who was only doing her best.

So outwardly, Gracie remained perfectly polite and composed. She diligently took notes. She even turned to acknowledge Frank and tried not to cringe when his voice cracked, as it did repeatedly. All because of whatever cocktail of hormones he was pumping through his body. It reminded her of Ben a few years ago when his voice was breaking, and she almost couldn't bear it.

'Also,' Beth was saying, 'it's a good idea to remind Ben and Amber that it's the entire family that transitions, not just you, Frank.'

Actually, that's bollocks, Gracie felt like saying. *It's just Frank who's going to inject himself with God knows what, then have his willy cut off, so he can prance around dressed like a woman for the rest of his life. It's just Frank who's dragging our family through hell and who's done nothing except heap pile after pile of humiliation on us ever since this nonsense started.*

But yet again, she didn't. Instead she nodded, looked intent and scribbled down a few notes. Gracie had always been the perfect student, even at a time like this.

'To explain it another way,' Beth went on, 'the family comes first, and your transition second. This can be hugely traumatic for children, so Ben and Amber need to know that you still love them, no matter what. When it comes to dealing with children, a united front is probably the greatest gift you can give them. When they see you both getting on with things, they will too.'

But I'm not getting on with things, Gracie thought. *I want to kill Frank for putting us through this. The only reason I'm here in the first place is because I want my kids to come out of this unscathed. If it's possible for anyone to come out of a situation like this unscathed, that is.*

'As we discussed, there's lots of tips and advice I can give you to help when you're both talking to the kids,' Beth said. 'Although obviously, the way you'll speak to Ben will be very different from the way you talk to Amber, who I know is only eleven years old. But using and explaining the correct terminology is a great start, I find. Normalising terms such as transgender and transwoman, which is what you're presenting as,' she said, with a respectful little nod in Frank's direction. 'That's when you were born biologically male, but you identify as female. Kids are much more gender diverse now, they're more tuned into gender fluidity and that's a very welcome development. Plus, there are a lot of resources out there that can help.'

'Such as?' Gracie asked. *This'll be good,* she thought. *Tips on how to talk to your kids on probably the most mortifying subject imaginable.*

'I have a list of very useful books I can give you,' Beth said, with an encouraging smile. 'There are some podcasts too, which Ben in particular might find helpful.'

Books, Gracie thought. *Podcasts.* Jesus, how much was Frank shelling out for these therapy sessions anyway? Money down the toilet as far as she was concerned.

'I do appreciate that this whole process can seem very long and laborious,' Beth said, seeming to read Gracie's mind as the session came to a natural end. 'But believe me, you will begin to see real progress soon. And in the meantime, I'll see you both at the same time next week?'

'Yes, of course,' Frank chimed automatically.

Gracie shot him a hot glare. 'Absolutely,' she said out loud, taking care to write an entry in her diary, then underline it in red biro. *Counselling session – absolutely do not attend. Phone to cancel that morning.*

They said their goodbyes and Frank escorted her back out onto the street, where her car was parked. He was silent and twitchy and fiddly, which Gracie knew of old, inevitably presaged that there was something he wanted to get off his chest. She let him suffer till she got to her car, unlocked it, then turned to face him.

'Well, that's it, then,' she said briskly. 'Amber will expect you to pick her up at lunchtime on Saturday, and as it's the day before she goes off to Irish College, I suppose she can stay out till nine p.m. and no later. OK?'

'Yes, yes, thank you,' Frank stammered, 'that's perfect.'

'Goodbye then,' she said curtly, slipping into the driver's seat and not even bothering to offer him a lift.

'There's just one more thing, Gracie, if you have a second,' Frank said, just as she'd started the engine.

'Can you make it quick?' she said, sticking her head out of the car window, already indicating to pull out.

'Well . . . I know how tough this must be on you, Gracie,' Frank said hesitantly. 'So I just wanted to say thank you. That is to say, I'm grateful to you. Very grateful. You're a busy woman, I know, and this means a great deal to me. I mean, that you're making the time to come to therapy sessions with me.'

He was starting to stammer, and normally when he stammered, Gracie reached a comforting hand out to him and told him to take a nice, deep breath and relax. But not this time.

A pause, while Frank just looked helplessly at her, like a bespectacled little vole. His words hung there as Gracie locked eyes with him.

'I'm not doing this for you,' she eventually said, her voice steely calm. 'None of this is for you. Not a bit of it. I'm only here because of the kids. They're my only concern. As far as I'm concerned, you, Frank Woods, or Francesca, or whatever you're calling yourself these days, can rot in hell.'

'Oh,' she distinctly heard him say as she pulled off. 'Rightio.'

Ever since the moment Frank had been outed at his birthday party, word had spread like wildfire around Gracie's office and beyond. Mistakenly, she had thought this would be a nine-day wonder that would blow over, but she'd been quite wrong. Even now, months later, a few well-intentioned friends and work colleagues would still talk about what happened.

It was beyond humiliating.

'How are things at home, Gracie? I mean, between you and Frank?'

Gracie's response was unchanging. She held her head high and replied that they were working through things and even having counselling together. *Now piss off with yourself and go and find something else to gossip about, thanks very much,* she often wanted to add, but never did. Good manners and professionalism always prevailed.

'It's, like, seriously banging to identify as non-binary now, you know,' Jess, one of Gracie's junior office interns, had said to her in passing, with a swish of her Instagram-glossy locks. 'You and your husband and kids are going to be the coolest family going, once you've got all this sorted. You could even go on YouTube and record all your experiences. I bet it would go viral in no time.'

Gracie knew the girl only meant well. Still though, worry about the kids had effectively taken over her whole life. She was hugely anxious about Ben, who at eighteen years old, was a man now, a strapping, six-foot-tall school-leaver, who was old enough to vote. Ben was bright and robust and had an active social life and a great summer job, working in a raw food bar, for a respectable wage, plus tips. This should have been a wonderfully carefree time in Ben's life, with the whole summer ahead of him to enjoy, before hopefully starting college in the autumn.

But instead, he had all of this drama to deal with at home. Before all of this blew up, Frank and Ben had been close, but now Ben could barely be in the same room as his dad. *God,* Gracie thought, *would this living nightmare ever come to an end?*

Then there was Amber, who'd always been such a happy, normal, outgoing child. Never once in her almost twelve years of life had she ever given Gracie a day's concern or worry – no matter where Amber was, she just blossomed and thrived. A great kid, everyone said. Good in school, with lovely friends too. A happy, well-adjusted little girl, who should have been enjoying the long summer holidays before starting secondary school in September.

But all that had changed now, and even other parents had started to comment.

'Is Amber OK? She seems so quiet and withdrawn,' one mother had said to Gracie when she collected her after a play date.

'She's fine,' Gracie had said defensively. 'I'm sure she's just a bit tired, that's all.'

'And of course, your husband transitioning must be a huge stress to you all as well,' came the overly nosey reply.

'We're dealing with things as a family,' Gracie replied, putting up a perfect shop front as usual. 'But thanks so much for your concern,' she added briskly. 'I'm sure Amber had a wonderful time.'

Then she turned on her heel at the doorstep and went back to her car, where Amber was patiently waiting for her.

Amber hadn't had a wonderful time at all though, she seemed to hate being away from the safety of Primrose Square these days, and now worry about her consumed Gracie day and night. Time and again, Gracie gently broached the subject of Frank with her.

'Sweetheart,' she asked one evening when the time felt right. 'How would you feel if Dad began to look a little different? That would be OK with you, wouldn't it? Imagine if Dad began to look and dress a bit more . . . well, a bit more like a lady . . .'

'But why would he do that, Mum?' Amber asked innocently.

'Because he's more comfortable like that, pet. Just like you're more comfortable in your jeans than you are in your school uniform.'

'I don't mind, Mum,' Amber sighed. 'I don't really care what Dad looks like. All I really want is for him to come home again.'

But that would mean all is forgiven, Gracie thought. That would signify to Frank that he could just do this to all of them, rip their marriage apart, shit all over their lives, then bounce back home as if nothing had happened. That would mean that they were a couple again, and that was clearly out of the question. She loved Amber more than life itself, but knew in her heart that she couldn't live her life with Frank again. How could she?

Gracie was still processing the fact that her relationship had ground to a shuddering halt, and in that much at least, she knew herself to be entirely blameless. She'd once thought her marriage was as solid and secure as they came, yet this felt like such a deep rejection, not only of her, but of their whole shared history together too. So how could she possibly let Frank back into the house again, even if he were to sleep in the spare room, as if she were OK with it all? *I'm barely holding it together as it is*, she told herself. *But this would really be the straw that broke the camel's back.*

There was Ben to consider, too. He had right to say how he felt about Frank coming back home and he had long since made his feelings on the subject perfectly clear.

'It's him or me, Mum,' Ben had said, firmly and decisively. But then that was Ben all over; once his mind was made up, there was no turning back. None. 'I just – I can't even look at him right now. I don't know him anymore.'

Which of course meant even more sleepless nights for Gracie, torn between each of her kids, trying desperately to hold her little family together and knowing that she was failing at every turn.

Then, out of nowhere, came a huge warning sign. Amber had spent most of the school year begging and pleading with her parents to be allowed go to an Irish College in Waterford; it was just a two-week summer school and all her school friends were going.

Gracie had agreed, thinking that the two-week breather away from home and all its inherent stresses would do her the world of good. So she packed Amber's bags for her and got her all organised for the trip; she'd even taken her shopping for some new clothes to wear while she was away. Then, one sunny morning, she dropped Amber off at the school coach and watched her clamber aboard, surrounded by all her over-excited friends and classmates.

'Have fun, sweetheart!' Gracie called out through the coach window. Amber had smiled back at her and given a big thumbs-up sign.

But after just two days, Gracie had a phone call from one of the Irish teachers at the college – the call every parent dreaded.

'I'm afraid Amber doesn't seem to have settled here at all,' Gracie was told matter-of-factly. 'She's desperately upset and crying and keeps saying she wants to come home.'

Gracie ran out of her office, cancelled no fewer than three meetings, jumped in her car and hotfooted it for the three-hour journey to Coláiste na Rinne in Waterford.

The sight of her daughter, pale and withdrawn as she sat in the passenger seat beside her, ready for the long drive home, cracked at her heart.

'Sweetheart, are you really sure you want to leave?' Gracie asked her gently. 'It's only been a few days and you were so looking forward to the trip. Did you really give yourself a proper chance to settle in?'

'Don't be angry with me Mum,' Amber said, looking white as a ghost. 'All I want is to go home.'

'But Amber, you've got the whole rest of the summer to be at home.'

'I need to be there, Mum.'

'Why, love? It's the summer holidays and you're meant to be off enjoying yourself.'

'Just in case.'

'In case of what?'

'In case Dad comes home and I'm not there.'

Gracie's hands tightened around the steering wheel as she navigated the motorway back to Dublin. *Jesus*, she thought furiously. *I could wring Frank's selfish, self-absorbed neck for this.*

She was a big girl and she could handle the myriad of humiliations she had to deal with herself on a daily basis. It was only when she looked across the car seat to Amber that she felt like a mother tiger defending one of her cubs. *I could gladly commit murder*, she thought, *and it would serve Frank right for putting us all through this.*

'Are you OK, Mum?' Amber said in a worried little voice, a few more miles down the motorway. 'You've gone all quiet.'

'I'm fine, pet,' Gracie said tensely, hating herself for the lie. 'Mummy's absolutely fine.'

Violet

Violet must have fallen asleep on the chaise longue in the drawing room – fully clothed too, which was most unlike her. Even more curiously, she'd woken up with a woolly blanket neatly tucked around her, a cushion at her head and her shoes carefully placed beside her.

Well, it must have been Frank who'd been so kind while she slumbered, she thought. Madam Emily Dunne certainly wasn't capable of anything thoughtful. Violet had shuddered awake just as the grandfather clock in the hall chimed four in the morning, whereupon she gathered herself up and inched stiffly upstairs to her own bed.

Then, there was an even more bizarre occurrence. When she finally roused herself, at exactly nine the following morning, she heard a distinct noise coming from the kitchen directly beneath her. Loud clattering and the sound of pots being banged together. Frank would long since have vacated the premises to get to work, Violet knew, so what on earth could possibly be going on? Alarmed, she wrapped herself in her tattered quilted dressing gown and slowly made her way downstairs, armed with nothing more than her heavy mahogany walking stick.

Burglars? she wondered. She readied herself to call the police as a surge of anger swept over her. This house was her safe place, her respite and her Fort Knox all rolled into one.

How dare any burglar intrude on her? Violet felt no fear as she braced herself to open the kitchen door – just the bittersweet thought that any criminal who'd broken into her home had far more to fear from this particular elderly lady than they could possibly have reckoned with.

But then the unlikely smell of rashers and sausages wafted up to her. Followed by a sight that utterly knocked Violet for six – none other than Madam Emily Dunne herself, standing at the cooker and flipping sausages on a frying pan. She was dressed in some class of undergarment that read: *I will not keep calm and you can f**k right off.* Delightful.

'There you are,' Emily said casually, turning around to acknowledge Violet as she heard her come into the kitchen, as if the two of them met for breakfast every day of the week.

'What on earth do you think you're doing?' Violet demanded.

'What does it look like?' Madam Emily shrugged back. 'I'm making breakfast, aren't I? Now, do you want a rasher and a few sausages or not?'

Violet just glared at her, as if she couldn't quite take in what she was seeing.

'You needn't worry,' Emily said, second-guessing what Violet was thinking, 'I paid for all the food myself out of my dole money. None of this is costing you a penny. Now sit and eat, would you? You're making me nervous standing there, glaring at me.'

Violet didn't have a single iota what had brought about this volte-face in Madam Emily, but out of curiosity more than anything else, she did as she was bid, taking her usual seat at the head of the dining table. The smell of the fry-up was too divine to resist and, although she was loath to admit it, her stomach was already rumbling.

'Tea?' Emily asked.

'Thank you,' Violet said crisply. 'Served in my good china cup, please. The one with the picture of the late Queen Mother on it.'

'You could easily get a few quid for all the royal family shite on eBay, you know,' Emily said, boiling the kettle and making a big pot of tea.

'Must you use such foul language at this hour of the day?' Violet retorted. 'If you persist in swearing, I shall have no choice but to introduce a swear box.'

'Oh for fuck's sake,' Emily said, 'I'm trying to do a nice thing here, OK? Now just sit and eat and quit nagging me for two seconds, that's all I'm asking.'

At that, she plonked a plate of bacon and sausages in front of Violet, along with some hot toast, fresh out of the grill. Violet demurred for a bit, as all ladies should correctly do when presented with food – but then hunger got the better of her and she began to nibble delicately at a corner of a piece of toast.

'Grub OK?' Emily asked, sitting down across from her and horsing into her own fry-up. 'Happy I'm not trying to poison you?'

'Such a thought never crossed my mind,' Violet replied, taking a sip of tea from her favourite Queen Mother cup. 'My curiosity was piqued, that's all. What on earth has caused this sea change in your behaviour, Miss Dunne?'

'It's Emily, as you know right well. And aren't I allowed to do a random act of kindness every now and then?'

'It just seems grossly out of character for you,' said Violet. 'You've been here for weeks now and I've barely had a civil word out of you. If you think this is going to get you a reduction in rent, then you'd best think again.'

'Oh, come on,' said Emily. 'Why can't you all just give me a chance? Why is it that people get the wrong idea about me?'

'How should I know?' said Violet, taking a delicate mouthful of a particularly juicy, well-cooked sausage.

'It's been happening to me my whole life,' Emily said. 'Everyone seems to have me down as a total waster, but I'm not. At least, I'm trying my best not to be. I'm trying to rebuild my life and all I'm asking is that people stop treating me like a terrorist. That's all.'

'If you're serious about rebuilding your life, as you put it,' said Violet snippily, 'then you might start by pursuing some class of gainful employment.'

'Do you always talk like that?' Emily asked, genuinely puzzled.

'Like what?'

'Like a Victorian. There's characters in Edith Wharton novels less formal than you. All you're short of is a hoop skirt and a penny-farthing parked at the railings outside.'

'Hmph,' Violet snorted. 'Well, at least now I'm beginning to see the reason why society has deemed you unemployable. Rudeness gets you nowhere, young lady.'

Emily sat back, cradling the hot mug of tea in her hands. 'A job,' she sighed, 'would be the answer to my prayers. And I'm searching high and low for one, I really am. But the problem is that when any prospective employer sees the long gap on my CV and asks about it, I have to tell them the truth, which is that I was having treatment. Interviewers are always very polite and supportive about it, but I can practically hear them going: "next!"'

'What is it that you're trained to do?' Violet asked, curiosity getting the better of her. Some lowly class of menial job in a secluded office, she assumed, where someone as rude as Emily Dunne didn't have to interact with anyone.

'Event management,' Emily said flatly. 'Although I was never really much good at it. I looked after corporate events – swanky work dos in posh hotels, that sort of thing. It's a very social gig, you see, and towards the end, when my boozing went out of control, I ended up drinking a chunk of the profits at every event I ever organised. And I might have rubbed a few gold standard clients up the wrong way too. I can't remember a lot of it. So there you go; not what you might call an ideal employee.'

'And you have no other source of income?' Violet asked. 'No rental properties? No savings to speak of?'

'Ha! Are you having a laugh? No offence or anything, Violet, but do you think I'd be living upstairs in your box room if I had any dosh of my own?'

'We are not yet on terms,' Violet said witheringly, 'where you may address me by my Christian name.'

'Sorry, your Royal Highness.'

Violet went back to her sausages and toast. Then another thought struck her. 'May I ask,' she said, 'what it is that you *want* to work at?'

She had a particular reason for asking, too. Oftentimes, if there was nothing else on the telly box, Violet found herself watching some inane television show where hordes of young persons would sing, most of them excruciatingly badly, in front of a panel of judges, headed by a person whom all the others seemed to defer to and who they referred to as 'Simon'. Not a single one of the contestants appeared to have a musical bone in their bodies and Violet often found herself wincing at off-key crotchets and tuneless half quavers they'd come to pollute the air with. This particular programme was supposed to be a musical contest, yet not one of the contestants appeared to know an Aeolian cadence from a strong bar of carbolic soap.

In spite of their ignorance, though, contestants frequently spoke about 'their dream'. 'But this is my dream!' they'd often protest, usually when about to be eliminated from the competition. It was a bizarre concept to someone like Violet, that one could indeed 'live one's dream'. Yet that's what all young persons seemed to think was their absolute birthright nowadays.

'What is your dream?' Violet said out loud.

Emily almost guffawed into her mug of tea. 'Where d'you learn to talk like that? That doesn't sound like you at all.'

'Nonetheless, I should very much like to know,' said Violet. 'Surely you have some type of ambition? Some goals in life to which you aspire?'

'Architecture,' Emily replied, without even having to think about it. 'I always loved design and buildings and structure. I was actually studying it at one time, before I dropped out of college.'

That took Violet completely by surprise. But then she was remembering her father's words. 'A good architect is manna from heaven for a developer like me. Most of them don't know a handsaw from a beer mat.'

'You know, if you had a decent budget and the will to do it,' Emily said, looking around the kitchen, 'then this house here could be something very special. The bones are all there: the high ceilings, the pine floors, the statement staircase. Gimme a good building crew and a half decent designer and this house could be the envy of Primrose Square.'

'It used to be once,' Violet said thoughtfully. 'A very long time ago now. This house used to be the most beautiful home for miles. Everyone said so.'

Abruptly, Emily got up, clattering cups and plates and taking them to the big Belfast sink to wash them.

'Anyway,' she said to Violet, 'architecture was only ever a pipe dream for me. The fact is, I'd be doing very well to get a job scrubbing public toilets, with my track record. You done eating yet? Hurry up, will you? I want to get the washing-up done before I go.'

Violet wasn't done eating at all, as it happened. She was far hungrier than she let on and was greatly enjoying the fried collation on her plate. Even if it was common-as-muck trucker food, the sort one might expect to find in a cheap roadside café.

'Where are you off to?' she asked Emily, still munching on toast, reluctant to let go of her plate.

Emily rolled her eyes as she put on a pair of Marigolds and started to fill the sink.

'To go and see another elderly lady who can't stand the sight of me.'

'To whom can you possibly be referring?'

'None other than my mother,' said Emily. 'Who's effectively disowned me. I'm going to try to make my peace with her and show her that I'm a nicer person now, even though the woman will probably call security as soon as she sees me coming. If what happened the last time is anything to go by.'

Violet didn't answer. It wasn't too great a stretch of the imagination to imagine Madam Emily with a mother who couldn't abide her.

'You could come with me, if you want?' Emily offered, running her plate under the hot tap. 'You and Mum would get on great. You could form a little "we hate Emily" club.'

'Was that comment intended to be sarcastic? Because sarcasm is the lowest form of wit.'

'Any other tips for me?' Emily said. 'Put yourself in the position of a mother who'd prefer to dance on her offspring's grave singing alleluia, rather than have a conversation. You don't have kids, I know, but what would you do if you had?'

There was a long pause, as the whole atmosphere in the room seemed to shift. Violet glared hotly back at her, too indignant to even speak.

'What now?' Emily said. 'Did I say the wrong thing? Yet again? Wow, that makes about twenty times I've offended you in a single morning. Must be some kind of record.'

At that, Violet stood up, taking care to give her walking stick a right good thud off the floor to really indicate her displeasure.

'While I enjoyed this morning's collation,' she said icily, 'I must inform you, Miss Dunne, that on this occasion, you go too far.'

Normally, Violet found that this was perfectly sufficient to silence all around her. Normally, when she adopted her imperious manner, she sent all and sundry scuttling for the hills. It appeared that Madam Emily was not your normal person, however.

'Oh, get over yourself, would you?' Emily said. 'Your Margaret Thatcher act doesn't wash with me. Now come on, I asked you a straightforward question – how do I handle another cranky old lady who can't stand the sight of me? You're not my mother, but just imagine for a second if you were.'

'Stop it!' Violet snapped. 'Stop it right now.'

'What's got into you?' said Emily, bewildered. 'I'm only asking for a simple bit of advice. There's no need to bite the face off me.'

'It's rudeness of the highest order,' Violet said, 'to make presumptions on matters about which you know nothing. Now kindly vacate the premises. I've had quite enough of you for one morning. I'm a busy woman and I have important work to do.'

'And what important work would that be?'

'None of your business.'

'Because as far as I can see,' Emily said, 'you spend all day sitting around the house, picking fights with people you barely know.'

'How dare you!' Violet spluttered.

'Or else you just sit around the place wondering what colour Prince Philip's arse is today.'

Violet didn't even lower her dignity to reply to such a crass comment. Instead she pounded her way to the kitchen door on her walking stick, then paused in the doorway, determined to get the last word in.

'If it is indeed your intention to show that you're attempting to become a nicer person,' she said frostily, 'then I strongly suggest you try doing the one thing you clearly have never once done in your life.'

'Which is?'

'Instead of being rude to me, you might instead try being kind to your mother.'

Emily

'You're always bitching about that landlady of yours,' Leon said to Emily, when he picked her up in his taxi from Primrose Square that morning. 'But from what you've been saying, she does actually come out with the odd pearl of wisdom every now and then.'

'Oh piss off, don't you start.' Emily clambered into the passenger seat beside him and handed over a sausage sambo she'd made and carefully wrapped in tin foil earlier. Leon was forever driving her around all over the place and part of her was mortified he never once let her pay for any trip. So the very least she could do, she figured, was feed him brekkie.

'"Try being kind to your mother for a change,"' Leon said, gratefully taking the sandwich. 'Yeah, I like it. There's worse things you could do on a sunny morning like this.'

'Let me tell you something,' Emily said. 'This is like the Matterhorn of all this step eight malarkey for me; this is the K2 of atonement. Because I don't think I was ever nice to Mum throughout my whole adult life – certainly not when I was drinking.'

'Ahh, you're being very hard on yourself there,' Leon said. 'It can't all have been bad. I'm sure you even made her proud when you were younger, pre-drink.'

At that, Emily threw her head back and laughed bitterly. 'My mother,' she said, 'has never been proud of me once, in the whole course of my life. My sister Sadie is the only one who gave her bragging rights, even when we were kids. There's one in every family, you know – the good kid, the one who never puts a foot wrong. Anyway, with us, it's Sadie. She gets to have her photo plastered all over the house and she's the one Mum will chat about to her pals. The absolute best that a nobody like me can hope for is to try and make her less ashamed.'

'You're not nobody,' Leon said. 'You're never nobody.'

To her surprise, Emily was genuinely touched at that.

'Thank you,' she said simply.

Twenty minutes later, they pulled up outside the gates of Ambrosia Independent Living and Leon hopped out to help Emily with the canvas bag she'd stuffed into the boot of his car.

'Jaysus,' he said, feeling the weight of it. 'What have you got in here – a dead body?'

'The contents of this bag,' she said, 'are the price of penance.' Then, taking the bag, she leaned over to give him a quick little half-hug.

Leon blushed, told her to feck off with herself and a moment later was gone.

Why did I just do that? she asked herself. She was most definitely not a touchy-feely, huggy-type person, and couldn't explain it to herself, other than Leon was just being so out-of-the-ordinary kind to her. And kindness had always been in short supply in the life of Emily Dunne.

Right then, she thought, steeling her nerve and walking through the heavy iron gates. *Showtime.*

She found her mother's little house straightaway but didn't even bother to ring the doorbell. Waste of time, she figured. Her mother would just slam the door straight back in her face again, so she might as well save them both the aggro. Instead, she unzipped the canvas bag she'd brought with her, rolled up her sleeves, got down on her hands and knees, and started to tidy up the garden, weeding and deadheading roses.

A few of the Zimmer frame brigade threw curious glances her way, as they shuffled past her down the gravelled pathway outside. More than once she heard the odd hissed whisper as she diligently worked away.

'That's the daughter. No, not that one, the other one. The one who . . . well, we all know what she did.'

'She has a right nerve showing her face here, I can tell you. Her poor father must be spinning in his grave.'

This particular beaut was delivered in such a clear, ringing tone, Emily couldn't but hear it loud and clear. She schooled herself not to let it get to her, though. Nor did she stop working, not once. Instead, for the next hour, she tackled her mother's overgrown garden, cutting it back with secateurs she'd borrowed from Susan, and trimming everywhere she looked.

With the very first payment from her dole money, Emily had bought a few packets of seeds from a garden centre in town. Sunflowers, which had always been such a favourite of her mother's, back in the day.

You see, Mum? I remembered. And I'm doing this for you, so I can't be all bad.

She'd done more than that, too. She'd put by a few quid for her nephew Jamie, determined to repay him what she'd 'borrowed' from his piggy bank, no matter how long it took. Plus, it was Sadie and Boring Brien's wedding anniversary the following week, so she'd texted and offered babysitting services for free, just in case the two of them fancied a night out together. No response back, of course, but still. Slowly and painstakingly, Emily was doing her own little bit to make amends. She was planning to send them an anniversary present too – nothing fancy, given her lack of funds, but still. She'd make the gesture anyway. In for a penny, etc.

Very carefully, she planted a row of sunflowers just under the front window of her mother's house, so that every time her mum glanced out, she'd have something pretty to look at. She'd even brought a few tough bin liners and filled two of them up to the brim with garden waste, then hauled them back to the reception area, where there was a neat row of compost bins she could fill.

'You're wasting your time, you know,' one elderly man, who'd been playing chess at a table outside, yelled across at her. 'Your mother's out.'

'Saw her leave with my own two eyes,' wheezed his companion, another old man in a wheelchair who looked about a hundred and ten. Emily remembered the pair of them vaguely from the last time she'd been there and silently nicknamed them Waldorf and Statler.

'That daughter of hers called earlier to take her out for the day,' the first one said. 'The nice daughter, the one she likes.'

For a moment Emily felt a bit deflated, but still. At least this was a little surprise her mother could come home to later.

'You're definitely the other one, then, are you? I have to check – my cataracts are at me.'

She shrugged. 'That's me.'

'You're not going to mug us or anything like that, are you?'

'Don't be ridiculous,' Emily called back, putting down the heavy bin liners she'd been struggling with and wiping sweat from her forehead. 'Why would I do that?'

'Well, if the rumours about you are anything to go by . . .'

At that, a sprightly elderly lady, who'd been strolling through the rose garden at the back of the park, came over on her walking stick to interrupt.

'Oh, listen to yourselves,' she said to the two aul' fellas. 'Have you nothing else to do except harass this young woman? Get back to your game of chess, you gossipy pair of old codgers. Pay absolutely no attention,' she added, turning her attention to Emily. 'Emily, isn't it?'

Emily nodded.

'I saw you working away in your mum's garden just there and I thought: what a lovely gesture. I imagine you're thirsty after all that – fancy a cup of tea?'

'I'd murder one.' Emily smiled, delighted to meet one person who didn't automatically presume she was the spawn of the devil.

'I'm Norma,' the elderly lady smiled kindly. She had huge cornflower blue eyes that twinkled, and that ageless quality where she could have been any age between seventy and ninety.

Norma linked Emily's arm as they walked back towards reception and on into a sort of recreation room, with sofas, coffee tables and armchairs dotted about the place. There was a sideboard with makeshift tea- and coffee-making facilities, and a crumbly looking half-eaten packet of plain digestives on a side plate, but that was about it as far as refreshments went. The whole place seemed dead and depressing to Emily, with an atmosphere a bit like a funeral home.

There were a couple of other elderly people in the room, with some of the care home assistants buzzing about. Did Emily imagine it, or did more than a few heads swivel her way when she came in? It made her doubly grateful to have someone like Norma with her, who at least seemed to be on her side.

The two sat in wicker chairs by the window overlooking the park and Emily made tea for them both.

'Boring as arse in here, isn't it?' Norma said, as Emily looked back in shock at her. 'What?' Norma replied, reading the look on her face. 'You think just because I'm old, I've forgotten how to swear?'

'Just surprised, that's all.' Emily grinned, very glad now that she'd come in for the cuppa.

'That's the worst of being in a place like this,' Norma said. 'The sheer boredom is what gets you in the end. Do you know what passes for entertainment around here?'

'What?'

'Take a look at the noticeboard. Read it and weep. Come here and I'll show you.'

Emily did as she was told and walked over to an ancient-looking tiled wall with a clutter of posters on it. Flower arranging was one class advertised. The evening rosary was another. But the biggest, showiest poster of all was reserved for an Elvis impersonator who was: *playing live at 5 p.m. on Saturday night – don't be late!*

'Did you ever see such a pile of shite?' Norma said, as she stood beside Emily, surveying the 'entertainments' on offer. 'Flower arranging? Can you think of anything more boring? The evening rosary is all well and good if you're devout, but what about those of us who aren't? And as for the Elvis impersonator? My back side is more like Elvis than he is.'

Emily couldn't help snorting.

'Honestly,' Norma went on, 'a concert that starts at five in the afternoon? Did you ever? I was a bit of a Rolling Stones fan back in the day, you know,' she added. 'And nothing – *nothing* – good ever started at five on a Saturday evening, believe me.'

'Well, well, well,' Emily said, impressed. 'A real live rock chick. As I live and breathe.'

'Here, it's not cancer or a stroke or a heart attack that gets us, you know, love,' Norma said wisely. 'It's boredom. The sheer, unadulterated boredom. Do you know how it feels to have a diet of afternoon telly and soap operas on a constant loop?'

Emily didn't want to tell her that, actually, she did. Having spent the guts of the last year in and out of treatment, she knew exactly how mind-numbingly tedious it could all get, day in, day out. She said nothing, though. Just nodded in agreement.

'I hope you never have to,' Norma said. 'And another thing – I don't suppose you have a cigarette on you, do you? You look like the kind of girl who smokes.'

'Do I?' Emily said, surprised.

'Takes one to know one. I haven't had a fag in twenty years, and if you could smuggle me in a gin and tonic next time you're here, I'd die a very happy woman.'

Emily smiled and led her outside for a cigarette.

And in a moment, she knew exactly what she needed to do to really, properly make amends to her mum.

Violet

When Violet had the whole house to herself and nothing but her own thoughts to occupy her, she could still hear Emily's sharp rebuke ringing in her ears, clear as crystal.

As far as I can see, you spend all day sitting around the house, picking fights with people you barely know.

Violet eked her way through the day, expert by now at filling in the hours, yet she couldn't stop thinking about Madam Emily. It would certainly take more than a rasher and a few sausages to change Violet's ill opinion of her, that was for certain. When it came to being in her bad graces, this lady was categorically not for turning.

When Emily finally vacated the premises, Violet did what she always did every morning: took up her armchair seat in the front bay window with her notepad and pen in hand, ready to scribble off missives to anyone whose behaviour she deemed inappropriate or unruly. It was high summertime, so there were rich pickings, and her view from the front window commanded the whole square.

Yesterday alone, she saw young Hugo Kearns freewheeling on his bike through the grass on the square, in spite of a notice gargantuan in size with the simple instruction: *Keep off the grass.* And as for that sulky Monica Miller from number seventeen? Violet had seen her swinging on the roundabout in the playground area, which was intended for children only, and Monica had to be sixteen if she was a day.

If it wasn't for me, Violet thought, *there would be anarchy on Primrose Square.* Yet did she get any thanks for it? Not a bit of it.

She sipped on her morning coffee, this time served out of her china mug with Prince Harry and Meghan Markle on it, which she'd purchased via a most reputable mail order service provided by *Majesty* magazine, her favourite periodical. She wasn't enjoying her tea at all, though; Madam Emily's words had given her heartburn. So instead, she sat back and surveyed the square outside, remembering back to a far happier time, when nobody would have dared to speak to her so cruelly.

'It's just a night out at the pictures,' Jayne had said, as the two girls sat together up in Violet's bedroom, scheming how best to get Violet out of there so she could see Andy without her father finding out. Freddie Hardcastle was at work just then, thankfully, because otherwise even the sight of Jayne Dawson in his house would have sent him over the edge.

'I'm sure if you're honest with your father, he'd understand,' Jayne added hopefully.

'He'd never understand!' Violet wailed, throwing herself down onto the bed and lying prostrate. 'You've no idea how bad it is! I've seen him in black moods before.'

'I'm sure,' Jayne said, rolling her eyes.

'But never anything to compare with this. Oh Jayne, the morning after the party he almost crucified me! I'm not allowed to go outside the front door for months, probably, and by then – wait till you see – Andy will have forgotten all about me and met some other girl. Some lovely Liverpool girl who doesn't have a complete tyrant for a father.'

She was almost hysterical by then, but Jayne knew how to soothe troubled waters.

'Don't upset yourself,' Jayne said calmly. 'It's nothing. Andy just asked you to the cinema, that's all. It's not that big a deal. Not really.'

Actually, Andy had done considerably more than that. He'd called to Violet's house earlier that day, knocked on the front door, bold as brass, and it was only by the grace of God that her father had been out. Betty had been busy in the kitchen, so Violet had quickly ushered him away from the doorstep and across into the square, so they could talk in peace, far away from prying eyes.

'You know I go home to Liverpool tomorrow?' Andy said to her, looking at her with those gorgeous, soulful brown eyes and reaching out to hold her hand. He'd been in Dublin for five whole days by then, and in spite of the horrible tensions at home, Violet was still on top of the world. The memories of that wonderful night, when she and Andy first met, sustained her. Every time her father shouted at her or threatened her, all she had to do was remember dancing with Andy in the nightclub, how tightly he'd held her, how thrilling it all was, and how completely alive she'd felt.

They'd chatted the whole night away, as if there had been no one else present. Then after they'd left the club, Andy had insisted on walking her back to Primrose Square. Dawn was just breaking as they strolled home arm in arm, with Andy's coat draped around Violet's thin shoulders to keep her warm. Her birthday party had ended hours and hours before. She knew she'd taken a huge risk, sneaking out, and there'd be merry hell to pay – but she didn't care. Because something had changed in her tonight. She had to see Andy again before he left. She'd absolutely die if she didn't and that was all there was to it.

'Anyway,' he said, 'I'd love to take you out before I leave. Just you and me, this time, with no need for Jayne and Tom to chaperone us. It's not like we're a pair of twelve-year-olds, now is it, Vi, love?'

There. Andy had called her Vi. Her pet name, that only close family and friends ever called her. It felt so lovely. She let him chat away, adoring his accent, his sense of humour, not to mention the warm, clammy feel of his hand tightly gripped around hers.

'*2001: A Space Odyssey* is on at the Carlton cinema,' Andy said, 'so if you're up for it, I'll get tickets for us. Even buy you a bag of chips on the way home. Can't say fairer than that, now can I?' he added cheekily.

'I'd love nothing more,' Violet said. 'But the problem is my father. He's still so angry over what happened the night of the party . . .'

Andy was ahead of her, though. 'So how about if we do this right, then?' he said. 'The real old-fashioned way?'

'What do you mean?' she asked, confused.

'Your old man wants his daughter to be with a gentleman, so let me show him that I can be just that,' Andy said, looking intently at her. 'In spite of the long hair and the fact that I play in a band, let me show him that I know how to treat you right. We got off on the wrong foot, and I did things all wrong by taking you away from your party, but I can always apologise to him and start again, can't I?'

The idea of her father giving anyone a second chance almost made Violet splutter. She was eighteen years old and never once in the whole course of her life had she ever seen that happen.

'I know he wants the best for you,' Andy went on, as Violet wavered, 'but come on, love, I'm only in Dublin for one last night. Why don't I call to your house tonight, with flowers for you and a bottle of whiskey for your old man, and let's start afresh. What do you say?'

Violet stayed silent, afraid to say what she really thought. Which was that if she even dared mention the name Andy McKim to her father, she'd be in real danger of being locked up in her room for the night, like a 1960s Lady of Shalott. She knew Andy only meant well, but she also knew her father would go through him for a shortcut if he as much as thought about crossing the threshold of the house again.

So she took matters into her own hands. An alibi, she thought. That was the solution to all her problems. And she had the perfect one in the form of Miss Adele Lanagan O'Keefe, the most boring girl in her whole year at the Hibernian finishing school, but who her father was forever encouraging her to be pals with, mainly because Adele's family were terribly grand, living in a mansion out in Foxrock, with its own tennis court and everything. Not only that, but Adele's grandfather was a senior politician, and the newly minted Minister for Agriculture to boot.

Later that day, and for the first time in her whole life, Violet looked her father in the eye and lied to his face.

'I know you said I couldn't go out for months,' she told him, forcing herself to make the fib sound convincing, 'but you see, Adele's invited me to a piano recital in the RDS and all her family will be there, including the minister.'

'I see,' said Freddie thoughtfully, sitting in his wing-back armchair by the fire, a copy of the *Irish Chronicle* in his hands – always, Violet knew of old, the best time to catch him in a good mood. 'Well, don't think this means you're forgiven for how you behaved the night of the party, Vi. Far from it. But I suppose just this once you can go. Only because it's the Lanagan O'Keefes, though. And you'll be back here on the stroke of eleven or else there'll be hell to pay.'

Bingo. As Violet got dressed that night, into a sensible tweed two-piece suit, just like one she'd seen Princess Margaret wearing in a magazine, she was brimming over with excitement. Her plan was all set. She'd warned Andy not to come near the house, and instead had arranged to meet him outside the Carlton cinema at 7 p.m., giving her plenty of time to dash into Clerys department store across the road before they closed. Once there, she could slip up to the powder room and change into the mini dress she'd stuffed into the depths of her handbag, which was far sexier and showed off her long, skinny legs, just like Twiggy's. Infinitely more suitable for a night out with a possible future boyfriend.

'I'm off now, Father!' she said cheerily, sticking her head around the door into his study, where he was still sat pouring over that day's newspaper. 'There's no need to wait up for me, but don't worry, I won't be late!'

'Be sure to invite Adele in on your way home,' her father said. 'And the minister too, of course.'

Violet didn't dare answer that one, though. Instead, she just gave a light-hearted little wave and dashed out of the house as fast as she could.

The best I can hope for, she thought, tripping down the steps and walking the short distance towards O'Connell Street, *is that Adele doesn't blow my cover by telephoning the house and ruining everything.* As she ran breathlessly down Westmorland Street, Violet offered up a silent prayer to her mother that all would be well. After all, Adele rarely rang her or called to the house impromptu, so what were the odds?

Well worth all the stress and the web of lies, she thought, when she saw Andy's tall, slim outline waiting for her outside the cinema. He looked unbearably handsome too, wearing a dark navy jacket and tight trousers, as he pulled on a cigarette and shivered against the autumn breeze. She picked up her pace to meet him and he grinned broadly when he saw her coming.

'Well, now, aren't you a sight for sore eyes?' He beamed, slipping his arm around her shoulder as he guided her inside. Andy hadn't a bean to his name, but still insisted on paying for everything, even the Wimpy burger that he treated Violet to in the café beside the cinema afterwards.

At the finishing school Violet had been to, they were always given dire warnings about boys and how to behave around them. Never go out with a boy on your own, never let him touch you – and above all, never allow yourself to be alone with any boy, without another friend around, or better yet, a parent.

Yet in a single night, Violet had broken all their stupid rules, but she was having far too much fun to care. She had so little experience of boyfriends – the young men she did know tended to be her friends' brothers or neighbours. All good, middle-class, well-educated gentlemen, who bored her to sobs.

Andy wasn't like any of them, though. He was fun and passionate about his band, ambitious and determined to take on the world and win. He and Violet chatted like they'd known each other for years, and when they got back to Primrose Square, he even suggested a little moonlight walk together through the park.

'But it's almost eleven p.m.,' Violet said. It was late September by then, and the square always closed early in the autumn months.

'So?' said Andy, totally unfazed. 'That's what railings are for – climbing over.'

Gamely, he helped Violet up, as the fabric of her mini dress caught in one of the railings and tore slightly. She felt a bit exposed, with her bare legs dangling over the railings, one arm clinging to the branch of a tree, the other onto Andy for support.

'Well, now, there's a pretty sight,' he wolf-whistled as she blushed and giggled, trying to cover herself up a bit. Together they found a secluded bench in the moonlight, facing towards the south side of the square, where Jayne and Tom lived.

As they sat side by side, Violet shivered.

'Cold?' Andy said. 'Here, love, take my jacket.'

In a moment, he'd whisked it off and tenderly placed it around her shoulders. Violet snuggled into it, loving the feel of the warm wool and, most of all, the musky, sweaty smell of Andy from it.

'I leave first thing in the morning, you know,' he said. 'This is my last night in Dublin.'

'Oh, don't remind me!' Violet said. 'Not when we're having such a nice time.'

'You could always come back to Jayne and Tom's for a nightcap?' he offered.

Violet glanced at her watch and, to her horror, realised that it was well past her curfew.

'I can't. Just can't. I have to go, Andy,' she said, panicking. 'Now, quick, before my father misses me.'

'Come on, then,' he said, as relaxed as you like. 'There's no need to panic. I'll walk you home and you'll be there in two minutes.'

'No!' she said, far louder than she meant to. 'I mean, there's no need. Honestly.'

'What kind of a guy leaves his date in the middle of a deserted park at this hour?' Andy smiled. 'I'll come with you, love, it's no bother.'

'Please, no,' Violet said, as Andy helped her back over the railings again. Sheer, blind panic made her climb the iron railings far faster this time. 'You don't know my father . . .'

She hadn't the stomach to tell Andy the truth, which was that she'd lied through her teeth about her alibi, so it would be fatal to let herself be seen with him this close to the finish line.

'OK,' he said reluctantly, climbing the railings after her, then standing toe to toe with her on the corner of the square, exactly equidistant between Jayne's house and the Hardcastle's. 'But can I at least say goodnight to you properly?'

Next thing, he bent down to kiss her, and suddenly Violet didn't care whether anyone saw her or not. Andy's arms slid around her waist and she melted into him, lips locked, as he tenderly, gently kissed her once, twice, then so many times she lost count and wasn't particularly bothered how late she got home or who the hell was watching.

Her luck was in. As she let herself into the pitch-black hallway, only Betty the housemaid was still up and awake. Her light was on in the downstairs kitchen and as Violet tiptoed up the stairs to bed, Betty loomed out of the darkness, almost scaring the wits out of her.

'Well, now, missy,' said Betty, crossly for her. 'What hour of the night do you call this?'

'I'm so sorry, Betty,' Violet said in a little voice. 'I didn't mean for you to wait up.'

'Lucky for you your father is asleep,' Betty said, pulling the heavy bolts on the huge front door behind her, 'otherwise there'd be merry hell to pay. So how was your concert, then?'

Violet didn't know if she was imagining things, but she could have sworn she heard a sarcastic tone in Betty's voice that hadn't been there before.

'Fine,' she said, not wanting to embellish the lie.

'Adele in good form, then? Did the Lanagan O'Keefes' car drop you home?'

'Umm . . . yes,' Violet muttered, turning her face away and climbing the stairs, so she wouldn't have to look Betty in the eye.

'She's changed quite a bit, Adele, hasn't she?'

'Sorry?'

'That certainly didn't look like Adele you were kissing goodnight to on the street outside, not five minutes ago, did it?'

Gracie

Nicole Wilson was a thirty-something lawyer who worked in Gracie's office and who Gracie had personally hired all of a decade ago now. Which, in retrospect, she reckoned, was probably one of the soundest decisions she'd ever made.

Nicole was cool and vibrant, bright as a button and a great addition to any team, as well as being Gracie's right hand at work. The two women had a wonderful working relationship and it was Gracie's secret hope that other workmates in the office would look at someone as efficient and well-adjusted as Nicole and treat her as a sort of role model.

In happier, less stressful times, the professional side of their friendship had frequently spilled over into socialising in the evenings, in spite of an age gap of almost fifteen years between the two. Mind you, it had been an age since Gracie had indulged herself in a night out.

'You're, like, seriously working your ass off,' Nicole was forever saying to Gracie whenever the two had a snatched moment to talk about something other than case work. 'And it's not good for you. You're putting in twelve-hour days and that's before you factor in everything you're going through in your private life too. You know what you need, Gracie Woods? A night out. Fun. A laugh, a giggle. You need to get drunk, blow off some steam and roll home at five a.m. And to hell with anyone who has a problem with it.'

'You have got to be kidding,' Gracie laughed bitterly. 'Me? Go out and enjoy myself? I can't even remember how you go about doing that.'

The concept of time out hadn't occurred to her in so long, it was as if Nicole was suggesting they take a trip to the space station.

'Come on, just one night out,' Nicole persisted. 'The world won't grind to an end if you come with us for one lousy gin and tonic on a Friday night.'

'It's lovely of you to ask me,' Gracie said, as Nicole looked expectantly across the desk at her, 'but you have to understand it's out of the question just now, with the way things are at home. I need to be with the kids as much as I can. Whenever I'm not here, then they're my top priority.'

'Now you just listen to me,' Nicole said. 'I love my own kids dearly too. But I know that taking a bit of me time makes me a better parent, because I need to get offside every now and then. As do you, Gracie. Urgently.'

'With respect,' Gracie said dryly, 'the last time I looked, your husband hadn't moved out of the family home and announced he was transitioning to a woman.'

'All the more reason why you need time out – for you,' Nicole insisted. 'Come on, Gracie, one night, that's all I'm asking! We're kicking ass on the McLaren case and the chances are good that we'll have a fantastic settlement by the end of the week.'

'Let's not take that for granted,' Gracie said, turning back to the computer in front of her and tapping away.

'Nonetheless,' Nicole said, 'if the case does settle in our favour, then I insist on you coming out with us all on Friday night to celebrate. Just for the one, OK? And then I faithfully promise to leave you in peace.'

Gracie sighed and said yes, even though she didn't really mean it. Then she went back to work, plodding on with her day, her night and the whole week ahead, with stress everywhere she turned. Honestly, there were times when she felt like an elastic band stretched to break point. At work, she felt guilty for skulking away at a reasonable hour, even though she'd been slaving away at her desk since 6 a.m. Then at home, she had all the worry of the kids to deal with. Every parent worried, she knew that, but how many of them had to deal with what her family were going through?

Amber was at least eating and sleeping normally – no alarm bells there. But the problem was that she was now point-blank refusing to go out with anyone other than her dad. These days, the child lived for the evenings when Frank would call to see her and take her out for a movie or else hang around the house, doing nothing in particular, just being together, watching Netflix more often than not.

Gracie herself was hurting too, far, far more than she could ever show in front of the kids. However, she was at least grateful that Frank was as reliable as the mail, always turning up when he said he would, punctual to the dot. Plus, it gladdened her heart when she saw Amber's whole face light up at the sight of her dad. These days, it was the only time when Amber actually laughed and giggled and seemed like her old self again.

'Dad should be thankful for small mercies,' Ben had quipped to Gracie one night, when it was just the two of them in the kitchen alone. 'At least one person in this house is glad to see him.'

God help me, Gracie had thought, during another sleepless night spent tossing, turning and worrying – in that order. Was this to be her life from here on in? Amber desperately missing her dad and not understanding why he wasn't living at home anymore, and Ben barely able to be in the same room as him?

And what of her own feelings? She felt betrayed and utterly abandoned by the one person she thought she could rely upon most in the world until this. All her life, Gracie had excelled at juggling and keeping multiple parties happy – but this? This would have defeated an entire UN peacekeeping force.

Then, in work at least, some good news. The McLaren case, the one Gracie and her team had sweating over day and night for almost two years, settled for a hefty seven-figure sum, as accurately predicted by Nicole. The clients were happy, the team were overjoyed, and even Gracie allowed herself the luxury of a small smile, before kicking off the high-heeled shoes she wore for the office and changing into the neat, practical flats she kept under her desk. After an exhaustive week and a marathon slog on The Case That Wouldn't Settle, suddenly there was a relaxed air of jubilation in the office.

'Right, that's it,' Nicole said, bouncing over to Gracie's desk and handing her a glass of fizz. 'Grab your coat. We're all going to the Liquor Rooms to celebrate in style.'

'Nice try,' Gracie said, packing up her briefcase, 'but I need to be home with the kids. It's not one of Frank's nights for taking Amber, so I really have to get back as quick as I can.'

'So call and tell the kids you'll be half an hour late getting home,' Nicole said firmly. 'Ben's all grown-up now. Will the world come to an end if you're one lousy hour behind schedule? This is HUGE for us, Gracie. Days like today come along so rarely, we need to mark this properly. Now will you call your kids, or will I?'

Sighing, Gracie did as she was told, but to her surprise, when Ben answered his phone, he was all on for it.

'Stay out as late as you like, Mum,' he told her. 'I'm home with Amber and we're both good, I promise. All we were planning on doing was having a bite to eat then crashing out in front of the TV.'

'Are you sure?' Gracie asked worriedly. But then these days, her natural default setting was worry. She didn't know what to do with any emotion other than that.

'I'm here, Mum. I'm a grown adult and I'm taking care of Amber for the night and that's final. Now go and have fun, would you?'

So Gracie allowed herself to be dragged to the Liquor Rooms, where her team ordered bottle after bottle of champagne and charged it to the company, and she didn't even bat an eye. She wasn't sure how much she'd drunk, as Nicole was constantly topping up her glass. All she knew was that by 10 p.m., she felt no pain, just a lovely, woozy sensation as she finally relaxed and started to let her guard down a little. Just a little.

Yet again, she called Ben's phone, to double-check that all was quiet on the Western Front.

'We're cool here, Mum,' he reassured her. 'Now for fuck's sake, will you stop worrying?'

'You said the f-word!' Amber was tittering in the background.

'Let me talk to her,' Gracie said, as Ben passed the phone over.

'Hi Mum,' Amber said, sounding delighted with herself and chatting away with her mouth full. 'Guess what? Ben made sweet and sour popcorn and it's really lovely.'

'Pet, are you OK? I know I'm out much later than normal – it's just a work thing that Mummy has to go to.'

'You sound funny,' Amber giggled. 'Your words are all slurred.'

'She's pissed,' Gracie heard Ben saying.

'I'm not!' she said defensively. 'I'm just . . . tired and emotional, that's all.'

'Have a good one,' Ben said. 'And the next time I'm dying with a hangover, remember that I'll hold this as ammunition against you.'

Gracie smiled and hung up, feeling something she never allowed herself to. Deepest, heartfelt gratitude that Ben and Amber got on so well, in spite of the age gap. So close, they were happy enough to spend a Friday night in together. Amber adored her big brother, and for his part, she knew that Ben would physically harm anyone who as much as looked at her crossways. Frank included.

Then Adam, one of the office interns who seemed to know every hotspot in town, piped up: 'Come on, everyone, grab your coats and let's go to Wilde. Wilde is cool. I know the manager there, so we should even get a table.'

'This is where I say goodbye to all you mad young things,' Gracie began to say – but her team were having none of it.

'Twist her arm!'

'Don't let her leave!'

'Shove her into the back of the taxi!'

'Feels good to be out and about, doesn't it?' Nicole slurred in Gracie's ear, as the taxi weaved through the packed streets of Temple Bar, thronged with after-work revellers. 'Just forget all your domestic shite for one night only. It'll all still be waiting for you tomorrow morning, don't you worry.'

Wilde turned out to be just that – wild, loud, noisy and, even Gracie had to admit, fun. As more drinks floated around, she really started to let her guard down and enjoy herself. All her work team were in high spirits and she was having a ball, talking to a lot of them for the first time ever about non-work-related subjects.

Over the next few hours, one drink led to two, and then two to three, and before Gracie knew what was going on, she was being bundled out of Wilde and on to somewhere else.

'I want to dance!' Nicole and a few of the other girls were squealing in agreement. 'Proper dance around your handbag, dancing to songs that I actually know, and none of this techno shite!'

'Say no more,' said Adam. 'I know the perfect spot for a late-night boogie and a nightcap. This place is a bit out there, but I think you might just like it.'

'Jesus, is it really one a.m.?' Gracie said, stunned when she looked at her watch. 'I can't, guys. I really have to go. I've already stayed out so late. The kids will be worried—'

'For feck's sake, if I hear another word about your kids, I'll disown you!' Nicole laughed. 'Ben's in charge, so you're going absolutely nowhere, missy. Besides, they'll be asleep now, so just shut up and come for a nightcap!'

This time, Gracie hadn't a clue where she was being taken to. All she knew was that it had been at least twenty years since she'd last set foot in a nightclub, and in her memory, they were all seedy and dingy and airless and crowded and sweaty.

Not this place, though. The club was seriously high-end, with a 1920s art deco-style cocktail bar at one end and a fabulous dance floor at the other, where a DJ was belting out dance hits from the 1970s, 1980s and 1990s. 'Vogue' by Madonna was playing as they came in, and a moment later, Gracie found herself front stage and centre with Nicole and the gang, all bopping away, not caring that she was still in her formal, navy work suit that she'd put on at five-thirty that morning. Not even caring that she dragged up the average age of the club-goers by about a decade just by being there. Not caring about anything except living in the moment and having good, clean, tipsy *fun*.

'This place is amazing!' she yelled at Nicole over the music. 'I feel like a teenager again!'

'I know,' Nicole laughed. 'This club is probably the nearest I'll ever come to being in Studio 54 in the 1970s!'

They danced till their feet were raw, and then they danced some more. Then a Sister Sledge song came on, one that Gracie had never really liked, even when she was a young one, so she told Nicole that she was going up to the bar.

'Need water!' she mouthed over the music, miming drinking from a glass. 'Back in a minute.'

The bar was thronged, and as she patiently waited her turn in the queue, she took the first moment she'd had alone all evening to really look around her. It was as if a siren call had gone out among the beautiful people in Dublin, who'd all congregated at this particular club for no other purpose than to pose and look utterly fabulous. One guy was better-looking than the next – these were definitely the kind of men who moisturised – every last one of them dressed in cool shirts that were probably Hugo Boss, all suited and booted for the night ahead.

And as for the women? Just looking at their wide smiles and their trendy outfits, proudly adorning stunning gym-honed figures, made Gracie feel like the greatest frump on the face of the planet.

The greatest, most *loveless* frump, she corrected herself. She caught a glimpse of herself in the mirror behind the bar and almost got a shock when she realised how haggard and careworn she looked, surrounded by all the pretty young things.

I might as well be their granny, she thought sadly. *I haven't gone out and got pissed and had fun like this in decades, and it shows on every corner of my face. I'm a middle-aged, exhausted, separated mother of two who's pushing fifty.*

Suddenly Gracie felt very, very alone. And the worst thought of all: this was doubtless the way her love life would stay for her from here on in – because what man in his sane mind would ever look at someone like her again?

It certainly wasn't what Gracie had signed up for; not at all. She'd married a good man who she loved deeply, and now that she had a few drinks in her, she could admit to herself in all honesty that she hadn't stopped loving Frank, not really, not deep down, in spite of everything. She'd signed up for a happy family life; she had thought she and Frank would grow old together, as each other's best friend and closest companion.

Now, though, and through no fault of her own, her marriage had ground to a shuddering halt. Frank had mortgaged their whole future, without consulting her, without talking to her, without even thinking about her, more likely than not. Gracie could be as angry about it as she liked, but it didn't change a single thing; whether she liked it or not, she was alone for the rest of her days, end of story.

She had many a time and oft overheard some of the girls in work bemoaning the lack of decent single guys out there – and they were all perky, pretty twenty- and thirty-somethings who came without baggage. So what chance had someone like Gracie of ever striking it lucky again? Received wisdom had it that over the age of fifty, women just became invisible. Even if she were ever to try online dating, who'd take a second glance at the profile of a separated mother of two with a transgender ex-husband, now facing into her fiftieth year? How could she even begin to explain the mess her family was in to someone else?

By then, the queue at the bar was unbearable and Gracie was just about to give up and go home, when out of the corner of her eye, she became aware of another, younger-looking woman glancing her way, as if she knew Gracie from somewhere, but couldn't quite place her. Gracie felt the eyes on her, but when she looked back to see who was staring over at her so intently, she almost gasped.

Because this woman was truly breathtaking. She was tall, lean and long-legged, with a cascade of glossy chestnut brown hair, immaculately made up and wearing a stunning mid-length primrose yellow dress that clung to her perfectly. All around her, people were stumbling around the worse for wear, yet she still looked demure and graceful. Whoever this woman was, Gracie thought, in a sea of girls dressed in club wear, she seemed like a swan surrounded by cygnets.

She continued to stare over at Gracie. To the point where it became almost disconcerting. Gracie decided she could take no more, curiosity having totally got the better of her. Inching her way through the crowd, she wound her way closer to where this glamazon was sitting on a barstool like a queen on a throne.

'Excuse me, do we know each other?' Gracie asked, racking her brains to think of from where. School? College? Work? Not a chance. This woman was a stunner; there was no way she'd ever have forgotten someone as striking as her.

'Gracie?' the woman said, sounding surprised. 'What the hell are you doing here?'

'You know who I am?' Gracie said, sounding tipsier than she thought she was.

'Of course I do, honey. Don't you recognise me?'

'Should I?'

'Take a closer look. It's me. It's Francesca. Frank. Don't you know your own husband?'

Amber

Earlier that evening, Amber was stretched out on the sofa at home, a bucket of popcorn balanced precariously on her tummy.

'Ben?' she said, deep in thought.

'Shut up, will you? I'm trying to watch this,' Ben said, glued to Netflix.

'Why does popcorn taste different when you make it? It's much nicer the way you do it.'

'Because I don't slather it in butter, like they do at the Odeon. It's better for you this way. Less saturated fat.'

'Ben?'

'Shh! I'm trying to watch this.'

'Why don't you ever come to the movies with me and Dad anymore?'

Ben sighed and pressed the pause button on the remote control.

'I thought you wanted to watch this movie?' he said, folding his arms wearily. 'You haven't stopped yakking since I put it on. You're the one who picked this film, kiddo, not me.'

'Is it because you're still angry with Dad?' Amber asked her big brother innocently. It was rare for the two of them to have the house to themselves at night-time, without either of their parents present, and she was determined to make the most of it. They could watch a stupid old movie anytime. This conversation was far more interesting.

'Am I angry?' Ben sniffed. 'Yeah, right. That's putting it mildly.'

'Why, though?' Amber said, not letting it drop. 'Dad keeps saying he's sorry if he upset us, so why can't you just forgive him?'

'Because it's not that easy,' Ben said tightly, drumming the remote control off his knees, itching to get back to the TV.

'But . . . why not?' said Amber. 'You and Dad always used to be friends. And if you just went back to being friends again, then we could all go back to normal and we could go to the movies together, like we used to. Back when we used to be a proper family. I miss being a proper family,' she sighed wistfully.

Ben said nothing.

'And I really hate the way Dad has to live with that horrible witch Violent Hardcastle,' Amber went on. 'Phil from next door says she shaves her throat with a razor and turns into a werewolf every first Friday.'

Ben took a fistful of popcorn before answering. 'Serves him right,' he said.

'Now you're just being mean,' said Amber defensively. 'Why are you being so mean about Dad?'

'It's complicated,' he said.

'Complicated how?'

'Complicated because it's not just a case of Dad saying sorry and me saying, "Oh, OK then, that's the end of that".

This crap he's going through is going to change his whole life – and ours.'

'But that's not true,' Amber persisted. 'Dad keeps saying that nothing will change, and I believe him. Dad never lies to us, ever, and neither does Mum.'

'But he did lie to us, kiddo,' Ben said carefully. 'This has been going on for years. And he's wrong when he says everything is going to be the same. Sure, look around you – it's already different. And that's why I'm angry and that's what I can't forgive. Do you understand?'

Amber wrinkled her face. 'My religion teacher says forgiveness is the hardest thing of all,' she said, after a thoughtful pause. 'But if I can forgive Dad, then why can't you?'

'Amber,' Ben sighed, switching off the TV, knowing he'd never get to see the end of the movie now. 'I know Mum and Dad have tried to talk to you about what's going on here, but how much exactly do you know?'

Amber went silent, deep in thought. 'They both keep talking about change,' she said, 'and how it's nothing to be afraid of, and how Dad might look a bit different on the outside in future, but that he's still the very same on the inside.'

'Except . . .' Ben said hesitantly, 'that it's going to be a bit more than that. Do you know what I mean, kiddo?'

'Do you mean . . . that he's going to dress more like the way Mum does?' she replied gravely. 'Like he did the night of his birthday party?'

'More than that,' said Ben. 'Dad's not just playing at dress-up here; this is going to be a permanent thing. He's actually going to change into a woman. Do you understand? It's a pretty big deal, actually, and he kept it secret and humiliated us. He didn't even think about us at all and that's why Mum and I are so angry with him.'

'But . . . he'll still be the same on the inside?' Amber asked thoughtfully. 'He'll still love us the same and drive us everywhere and play with us and bring us on holidays and talk to us over dinner and make all our problems go away? Like he's done always, all our lives?'

'Well, yeah,' Ben said reluctantly. 'I suppose . . . yeah, he'll still do all those things with us.'

'You know what? I think we're lucky,' said Amber. 'There's a girl in my class and her dad died last year of leuka . . . leyke . . .'

'Leukaemia?'

'Yeah, that's it. So she doesn't have a dad at all and that's so sad. But we're really lucky, Ben. We have a great dad.'

Ben thought about this for a minute.

'But he's not going to be our dad anymore, is he?' he said. 'He's going to start looking completely different and people will talk about us and it's just . . . weird.'

'Actually,' said Amber, sounding by far the more grown-up of the two now, 'it's not a bit weird at all. There's a girl in my school whose brother is a lady. And she's so cool. Whenever she comes to the school, everyone says how brilliant and brave she is. Our teacher told us something about how Ireland is changing and we all need to embrace change and be kind to each other and then something about tol . . . toler . . . I can't remember the right word.'

'Tolerance,' Ben finished the sentence for her. 'I bet she meant tolerance.'

'Yeah,' Amber smiled. 'That's it – tolerance. So I don't care what Dad looks like on the outside, and I don't care what anyone says. It's what's inside that really counts. Isn't it, Ben?'

Violet

Violet rarely allowed herself to think of her past, but the date she dreaded every single year was growing ever closer and some memories wouldn't be denied.

For weeks they wrote to each other, she and Andy. Hard to believe now, but back in the 1960s, that was what you did. His letters were long and interesting and always, always bitingly funny. So what if he did make more than a few spelling mistakes, and if his grammar was slightly less then flawless? Andy always used to say Violet's lengthy replies never failed to make him laugh. *I can almost hear your posh accent coming through the pages,* he wrote to her once, in a letter she cherished. *I'll have to write a song for you one of these days, my classy Irish lady.*

My classy Irish lady, Violet thought, rereading the letter time and again, till the paper frayed at the edges. *He means me.* It was hard to put into words how very happy that made her.

Then, out of the blue, an invitation came. Andy wrote to say that his band were going out on the road and would be playing a concert at the Odeon cinema in Hammersmith, London. *It's a huge deal for us to play London*, he wrote to Violet in his scribbled handwriting, *and an A&R man from*

Decca Records has promised to come and see us. It would be great if you were here to bring me luck. Come on, Vi, what do you say?

He gave her the date and the name of the hotel the band would be staying in, asking her to let him know her answer as soon as possible. Violet, of course, went off into a tailspin of panic, desperately wanting to see Andy, but feeling as trapped as if there were chains, bars and bolts on every window and door in her house at Primrose Square. It was one thing to sneak out in Dublin, but London was so very far away.

Yet she had to see Andy. She just had to. It had been almost two months since they'd been to the pictures together and she was aching to be with him again. It tortured her to see images of The Beatles out on tour, surrounded by hordes of gorgeous young girls just like her, screaming their heads off and even climbing up fire escapes to break into their idols' hotel suites. Beatlemania, they called it; the papers were full of it every day. It was often something Freddie would snort at over his *Evening Herald*.

'Bunch of over-loud, overpaid louts,' he used to mutter. 'They won't be heard of in years to come, mark my words.'

Violet adored their music, though, and even Betty was often heard singing along to 'When I'm Sixty-Four' when it came on the radio in the kitchen, which was several times a day back then. But whenever Violet thought of Andy, and all the girls who must be throwing themselves at him and his band mates, just like they did with The Beatles, she felt sick to her stomach.

'I don't even know what an A&R man is!' she wailed hysterically to Jayne, as the two of them spent an afternoon together in Arnotts department store on Henry Street. 'All I know is that Andy says this is a huge break for him and I'm not even there to support him!'

'I believe it stands for artists and repertoire,' Jayne nodded wisely. 'Basically, it's like a talent scout. Tom says Decca Records turned down The Beatles, so of course now they're trying to find the next big thing. When are they going to see Andy play?'

'Oh . . . I'm not too sure,' Violet said lightly.

'Really?'

'Soon, I suppose . . .' Violet trailed off. She didn't dare tell Jayne the truth: that she was now racking her brains to find a plausible way to get to London to see Andy in concert. Jayne could be so goody-goody two-shoes about being honest with people. Doubtless Violet would only end up getting a lecture about how she should really tell her father the truth.

'Well, I think it's lovely that you two are still in touch,' Jayne said, steering them both towards Arnotts' linen department. 'We'll have to get Andy back here again for another visit. If he's not too famous to come and see ordinary folk like us again, that is.'

'Hmm,' said Violet distractedly, as Jayne sifted through a pile of tea towels on special offer, at two and six for three of them. 'Can we go now, please? I want to go to the ladies' fashion department to buy something new to wear. Come on, my father gave me my allowance this week and I want to spend it now. This is so boring.'

If Violet sounded a bit like a spoilt princess, she knew her friend was far too kind to say so. Instead, Jayne picked up a neat white tea towel and jokingly waved it in Violet's face.

'This, my dear,' she said, 'is what married life is really about. Tea towels and bedlinen and all the things that you think are so boring now.'

'Well, when I get married,' said Violet, 'I'm never going to be one of those housewives who goes trawling through lovely shops like this, looking for rubbishy old household stuff. I want to shop in the fashion department, and wear fabulous clothes all the time, like Jackie Kennedy.'

'And suppose you marry a man with no money? Like Andy, for instance? What then?'

But Violet ignored her, and when Jayne was at the till queuing to pay with all the other boring housewives, looking like complete frights with their headscarves on over rollers, she slipped off to the second floor all by herself. There, she spent a full five shillings and sixpence on a beautiful pair of capri pants, with a tight black polo neck to go with it, just like Diana Rigg wore on *The Avengers*.

Fabulous, Violet thought, surveying her long, slim figure in the changing-room mirror. She looked sexy and thin, and if she got her hair set the night before, she'd look perfect for her trip to London to see Andy take the city by storm.

Wait till you see, she thought happily, delighted with herself as she peeled off a wad of notes from the generous monthly allowance her father gave her to pay for her new outfit. Andy would become just as famous as Paul McCartney, and she'd be famous too, because the girlfriends always were, weren't they? She'd go to all his concerts and the two of them would go to film premiers and big West End opening nights together, and Violet would be the envy of everyone she knew in Dublin. Who knows? She might even get to meet royalty.

One thing was for certain, though, Violet thought. She'd have the most fabulous, glittering life, and hell would freeze over before she'd be caught dead queuing up to buy tea towels in Arnotts ever again.

Gracie

She'd had a lorry-load to drink that night at the club, but the minute she got home, Gracie began to feel stone-cold sober.

Francesca. Right there, in all her glory. Just sitting on a barstool, enjoying the evening like everyone else. Make no mistake – this wasn't Frank, the husband that Gracie thought she knew inside out and upside down. This was Francesca, and trying to reconcile the two in her head was nigh-on impossible. Gracie had been there and seen it for herself with her own two eyes, and yet she still couldn't really take it in.

Because Francesca, this new, rebooted version of Frank Woods, bore absolutely no resemblance to her creator. Where Frank was shy, Francesca was brimming over with confidence. Where Frank was diffident in manner, forever apologising till you wanted to yell at him to shut up and get over himself, Francesca was utterly self-assured and in control. This woman was effortlessly cool – and 'cool' was the one thing that poor Frank could never have been accused of in the whole course of his life.

Everyone in the club noticed Francesca. She was the type of woman who half the room fancied, and the other half of the room wanted to be. Hell, there was a sizeable part of Gracie that wished even she could be a bit more Francesca-like herself.

Once she'd got over the initial shock, the two of them had begun to talk, stilted and formal at first, mainly because Gracie kept repeating over and over: 'What are *you* doing here?'

'And what's wrong with a night out on a Friday after work?' was Francesca's innocent response.

When Gracie probed further, it seemed that for some time now, Francesca had initially gone to the odd 'safe' club in town, where she could meet other like-minded souls, quietly and privately. She was finally getting to properly know more people like herself, to talk to people with similar experiences. These outings were rare enough in the early days, but as her confidence grew, the time came when she felt comfortable going out and about a bit more.

'But it's never about fun,' she explained. 'Going out in public for me is really just about being accepted. You've no idea what it means, to be able to sit on a barstool and chat as the real me, to new friends. Friends who take me as I am and who don't judge me, or scorn me, or laugh at me. It's wonderful. It's liberating. Cisgender people take something as simple as that for granted. But for people like me, it's a sort of miracle.'

It was the first time Gracie and her husband had talked, properly talked, since the awful night of the party. Strange thing; it felt like a huge relief, and yet it broke Gracie's heart all the same.

When she eventually got home, Gracie thrashed about in bed half the night, unable to sleep, then eventually gave it up as a bad job and hauled herself up. All her life, she thought, she prided herself on not being prejudiced, racist, or biased.

It was how she'd brought up her kids and it was her baseline ethics code in work. Equality, fairness and tolerance in all things. Always listen to the other side of the story, she'd drummed into Ben and Amber. Never, ever rush to judge.

Yet here, under her own roof, had she denounced Frank for what, after all, wasn't really his fault at all? She'd been so fixated on the kids and on her own anger towards him, never once did Gracie actually pause to think what it must have been like for Frank himself. All this time she'd been utterly focused on losing the man she'd loved in the worst way imaginable. She'd been completely wrapped up in her own pain, grieving the end of her marriage and somehow trying to protect her kids. *Poor me, poor me* was all she could think, morning, noon and night.

But what about Frank? This, Gracie was finally beginning to realise, was a man who'd basically denied who he was for most of his life, and all for the love of his family.

Am I one of those vile people who bangs on about tolerance, but is abusive to anyone who doesn't conform to the norm? she wondered. *Jesus Christ, I'll be voting Trump next.*

Wearily, she pulled on her dressing gown and made her way downstairs. Ben was already up and awake, even though it was barely eight on a Saturday morning. He was bright as a button and sitting at the kitchen table having avocado toast and a glass of the kale juice he'd insisted the whole family convert to. So he was back to eating healthy food again, Gracie thought. A very good sign. A definite shift in the right direction.

'Hey, Mum.' He grinned at her. 'You look like total shit.'

'Thanks, love,' she grimaced. 'Any chance you'd make your old mother a very strong coffee?'

'So how was your night?' he asked, getting up to put a pod of coffee into the Nespresso machine. Then he turned to face her as a fresh thought struck him. 'Actually, isn't this a bit weird?' he said. 'Isn't this, like, total role reversal? Shouldn't you be the one giving out to me for crawling in at all hours stinking of booze? You're the parent, not me. I was tucked up in bed by eleven last night, I'll have you know.'

'Very funny,' Gracie said groggily, sitting up at the kitchen island and massaging her throbbing temples.

'Want some eggs with your coffee?' Ben asked. 'Great for a hangover. Not that I've ever been wasted drunk,' he added, a bit too quickly.

Gracie smiled and nodded yes. Then there was silence, while Ben expertly whipped about the kitchen, and she looked on, filled with pride at the sight of her son.

He's in his right and proper place, she thought. *Right here and right now.* The slick, professional way Ben glided about between the island, the hob and the fridge was a bit like watching poetry in motion.

There's no doubt about it, she thought. *Ben belongs in a real chef's kitchen, doing what he loves best. He's his best self here. Just like Frank was his very best self last night.* Two men who she loved very much – both alive and well and very much living their truth. And who was she to stop them, Gracie wondered? She may as well try to hold back the tide.

Later that same morning, Gracie Woods did the one thing she vowed she'd never, ever do on pain of death. She walked out of her own house and down Primrose Square to knock on Violet Hardcastle's front door.

The last time she'd banged on that same door, she reflected, had been all of about ten years ago, when Violet had sent her a particularly stinking letter complaining about Ben. And his crime? To knock on Violet's door at Halloween when he was out trick-or-treating with a gang of his pals. They hammered with such ferocity, according to Violet, that they'd damaged her paintwork, so the entire door would have to be repainted and paid for in full by Gracie and Frank.

Ben at the time was all of eight years of age.

Gracie had wanted to fight back with the full weight of the law behind her. 'This is bullying, plain and simple,' she'd said at the time, adding that a good, strongly worded cease and desist letter would put an end to Violet Hardcastle, and the way she terrorised the neighbourhood once and for all.

Frank, of course, had made her see differently. 'Just because she treats us like this,' he'd said at the time, 'doesn't mean that we should respond in kind. Where's the neighbourliness in that? Turn the other cheek and just try to remember, we know so little about Violet or why she is the way she is.'

Over time, everything did indeed settle down, and Gracie grudgingly had to admit that Frank had been right. But then, that was Frank to a T – always seeing the other person's point of view, always choosing kindness. Tolerance was his natural, default factory setting.

The front door of number eighty-one Primrose Square creaked open, and there was Violet Hardcastle herself, standing tall and proud, even on her walking stick. She was a legend around the square; people almost loved to be insulted by her, trying to top each other with stories about her rudeness. In the local supermarket on Pearce Street, you could always hear neighbours swapping tales from the coalface.

'That Violet Hardcastle!' Gracie overheard one middle-aged woman chatting away to another just a few weeks ago, as they stood in the middle of the vegetable aisle. 'She was sitting at her front room window today, with the window wide open because it's so hot, yelling insults at anyone who passed her by. She told me I was mutton dressed as lamb and that I should be locked up for going out in a mini skirt at my age!'

'That's nothing,' her companion replied. 'Last autumn, she threatened me with a letter to our local county councilor unless I took down my Halloween decorations punctually on the first of November. She said I was lowering the tone of Primrose Square and that blow-ins like me needed to be taught manners.'

Yet the folk figure of legend definitely wasn't the same Violet Hardcastle who opened the door that sunny Saturday morning, though Gracie found it hard to put her finger on what exactly was different. Violet seemed subdued, for one thing. Wrapped up in her own thoughts to such an extent, she didn't even bother having a go at Gracie for wearing flip-flops, as she ordinarily would have.

'Oh, it's you,' she said, when she saw who it was.

'Good morning, Miss Hardcastle,' Gracie said politely. 'Sorry to bother you, but can I have a word with Frank, if he's home?'

The Violet of old would doubtlessly have barked at Gracie to wait on the doorstep outside – but not today.

'You'd better come in then,' Violet said in a very downcast voice, before leading Gracie into the drawing room at the front of the house. 'I'll just go upstairs and let him know you're here.'

What's going on with her? Gracie wondered, as she gingerly picked her way into the dusty, gloomy room, which felt damp and dank, even on a warm summer's day like this. Violet was almost – God forbid – *civil*. Could the woman possibly be on medication?

Then Frank came downstairs, doing a double take when he saw that it was actually his wife standing at the fireplace waiting for him.

'Gracie!' he said in surprise. 'I was expecting Amber. We were planning on having brunch and then maybe going for a walk on the beach.'

Gracie looked at him for a long time, formulating exactly what it was she wanted to say. Frank must have sensed something was coming, because he automatically closed the door behind him for a bit of extra privacy.

'Seeing you like that last night . . .' she began, picking her words very, very carefully.

'Was a terrible shock, I'm sure,' Frank said, taking off his glasses and wiping them distractedly. 'Of course it must have been. I really am so sorry if I upset you in any way.'

'No, Frank, don't apologise,' she said. 'I'm not here to read you the riot act. I only wanted to say that Francesca was . . . I mean . . . *you* were . . . *glorious*. Like a butterfly. That's what you came across as, Frank – like a beautiful butterfly emerging from out of a chrysalis.'

'Oh,' he said, in total surprise. 'I wasn't expecting that.'

A throbbing moment while they each looked at the other.

'So, that's it,' Gracie said, walking back into the hall and getting ready to leave.

'You're leaving already?' Frank said, confused.

'Of course I'm leaving,' she said, opening up the heavy hall door. 'This doesn't mean that you're forgiven or that any of this is OK, Frank. Because I'm still angry that you never told me what was going on inside your head, and hurt that you didn't share this with me. That aside though,' she added, 'I just came here to say . . . well, that I understand a little bit better, that's all. I came away last night feeling like the worst person in the world.'

'But why, love?' Frank asked. 'Why would you feel like that?'

Gracie sighed exhaustedly. 'Because I try to be tolerant,' she said. 'I think of myself as being so liberal and left-leaning and open-minded. But seeing you made me realise . . . maybe I haven't been practising what I preach after all. I may still be angry with you . . . and so sad for what I've lost, but at least now I'm beginning to see your reasons why. And that's it.'

'Okey dokey,' he said gently.

Just then, Amber's coppery head of curls popped around the door. Seeing both her parents standing there together in the drawing room, she burst into a wide, open smile.

'Mum *and* Dad! You're here – together! This is amazing! This is going to be the best day ever! Dad and I are going for brunch and then for a big, long walk down the beach, so why don't you come with us, Mum? Please?'

Violet

Frank and his wife seemed to be deep in conversation downstairs in the drawing room, so Violet left them to themselves and retreated back to the privacy of her bedroom.

Solitude suited her, as it happened, so she could indulge her memories in peace.

Lies, lies and more lies. Violet had told so many, she was an expert by now. After all, she'd got away with it once before, and even though this was to be a two-night weekend stay, she thought her story was pretty fool-proof.

As far as her father was concerned, she was travelling up to County Monaghan for a birthday party at Castle Leslie hosted by one of her school friends, a cousin of the titled, aristocratic Leslie family. Violet had exhausted herself trying to think of the perfect alibi, and this was the best one that she could come up with. In one fell swoop, she could account for a weekend away, and yet appeal to her father's sense of snobbery at the same time.

The Leslie family were proper aristocracy and her father puffed up with pride when Violet told him where she was going. He even slipped her the astonishing sum of ten pounds:

'to buy yourself something nice to wear for the party. You never know who you might meet at Castle Leslie.'

Violet felt a twinge of guilt lying to him, particularly when she saw how pleased he was. But it didn't stop her from taking the ten-pound note and going straight to a hair salon on Grafton Street, where she had her hair cut, washed and blow-dried, before hitting Clerys department store and spending the rest on sexy black underthings.

If this was to be the night she and Andy 'did it', then by God, she was determined to look her very best. Out with her old-fashioned garter belts and the girdles all young ladies were told made for good, solid foundation garments. Instead, she treated herself to Maidenform chemises and lacy brassieres, with underpants that were so sheer and light, they may as well have been made of gossamer.

It made Violet feel dizzy with anticipation when she thought of Andy, seeing her parade around in her brand-new underwear for the very first time. But then, why should she not lose her virginity to him if that's what she wanted? This was the Swinging Sixties, after all, or so all the magazines kept saying. Everyone seemed to be sexually free and easy – except for Violet.

The night before she travelled to London, she took particular care in packing her little overnight bag, tucking the black underwear discreetly into a corner, just in case a chambermaid at the hotel unpacked for her. Then she slipped out of the house to a telephone box around the corner from Primrose Square on Pearce Street, so she could place a call to Andy's hotel confirming all the arrangements, and making sure he knew exactly where and when to collect her.

In his last letter, Andy had said the band would be staying at the Adelphi Hotel, which Violet had no doubt was somewhere fabulous and swish, just like the Shelbourne Hotel on Stephen's Green. After all, his band was trying out for Decca records, and only the best would do.

It took an age to put in a long-distance call through to London, and the operator had to ring her back, but as good luck would have it, there was no one else standing behind her queuing to use the telephone, so at least she had some privacy.

'Adelphi Hotel,' said a lady with a London accent Violet recognised. It wasn't a posh accent, though, like you heard on the BBC radio news at 9 p.m. that her father liked to listen to. This was more like the kind of accent you heard on Radio Caroline.

'Hi, there. Can I speak to Andy McKim, please?' Violet asked. 'He's staying with you at the moment, with his band.'

'Who did you say, dearie?' came the bored reply, as Violet fed shilling after shilling into the coin slot at the side of the phone box.

'Andy McKim, who's with The Moptops,' she said, just in case the name of the band carried any extra weight.

'I'm sorry,' the woman said, 'but I can't tell you who is or isn't here. How am I supposed to know that, then?'

'Well, can I at least leave a message for him?' Violet asked, surprised at her rudeness. 'Can you please tell Mr McKim that Miss Violet Hardcastle will be at London airport tomorrow at twelve noon and to kindly collect me there, please. If you'd be so kind.'

'La-di-da, listen to you,' came the reply. 'What do you think I am then, love, a bleedin' noticeboard?'

Violet couldn't be certain whether she was cut off or whether the receptionist had hung up on her. Which was odd, she thought. But no matter. What she knew for certain was that come hell or high water, she was going to London tomorrow, and wild horses wouldn't hold her back.

Never one to cut corners when it came to spending her father's cash, Violet had splashed out on an airline ticket with Aer Lingus and was flying from Dublin Airport directly to London Heathrow.

She couldn't have felt more excited and grown-up as she tripped through Dublin Airport, aware of more than one appreciative male gaze following her as she strode through the concourse. The sight of the glamorous air hostesses in their neat green uniforms and tricorn hats filled Violet with a mixture of pride and envy – pride that she was a young lady who'd officially joined the jet set, at a time when no one, absolutely no one she knew, ever flew anywhere. And envy that the air hostesses, who were every bit as well made-up and glamorous as she was, got to travel like this every day of the week.

The only pity of this whole trip, she thought, happily settling back into her seat on the aircraft and sucking on a boiled sweet she'd been offered, was that she could never brag about this to anyone, ever. Andy was the only person who'd ever know the truth, and that was the way it had to stay.

There was a gentleman sitting beside Violet in a heavy wool overcoat, who looked a bit green about the gills with airsickness as the place thundered down the runway, but Violet felt nothing except exhilaration. Every moment brought her closer to Andy – and all of this, the expense, the lies, the risk, everything was for him.

Arriving into London Heathrow airport was both exciting and terrifying.

'Got a lovely holiday weekend planned?' one of the chatty air hostesses asked her.

'My boyfriend is collecting me,' Violet told her proudly. 'And I'm seeing him perform in concert tonight. At the Odeon,' she added, to really impress.

But when Violet clipped through the draughty, icy cold arrivals hall, Andy wasn't there to meet her at all. She checked her watch and waited for a good hour before finally admitting defeat.

Obviously there has to be a terrible mix-up, she thought. An innocent mistake. There's no way Andy would let her make a journey like this all on her own, then not have the decency to be there to meet her. Doubtless it was the fault of that dimwit receptionist who'd been so rude on the phone the previous day. Clearly she'd never given poor Andy the message about Violet's arrival time and he was probably back at the hotel now, not knowing where she was or when she was coming – or if she was coming at all.

Panic seized Violet. She was more than grateful she was travelling with wads of money, so taking a cab directly into the hotel in the centre of London wasn't an issue. Somehow, she found an empty taxi outside the terminal building, gave the hotel address, then sat back and tried to ignore the knot of worry in the pit of her stomach.

To distract herself, she looked out the window. Never having been abroad before, driving from the airport into the centre of such a sprawling, vibrant city was a huge adventure. Violet loved Dublin, but the noise, the crowds, the impatience and the urgency of London really were overwhelming.

Wait till you see, she told herself, trying to calm down. *The Adelphi Hotel will be out of this world for luxury and Andy will probably be up in his room waiting for me, maybe even with a bunch of roses and a bottle of champagne to toast my safe arrival.* She was beside herself with excitement to see him and, once they'd caught up properly, Violet hoped that he'd have enough time to show her some of the amazing sights and sounds of London.

There was so much she desperately wanted to see: Buckingham Palace, for a start, then Piccadilly Circus, Trafalgar Square, the famous shops on Oxford Street, and of course the Royal Albert Hall, where she knew the Philharmonic often gave afternoon recitals. She couldn't think of anything more romantic than exploring the city with Andy, and so what if there had been this one little misunderstanding about when and where he was supposed to collect her when she arrived? It was something they'd probably giggle at later on.

'Here you go then, love,' the taxi driver said through the glass grille. 'Adelphi Hotel.'

Violet looked out the car window and recoiled in shock.

'There must be some mistake,' she said, horrified. 'This can't possibly be the right address. Kindly check again, please. I want the Adelphi Hotel in Hammersmith.'

'And this is it, love. That's six shillings and thruppence, please.'

Violet paid, took her little overnight bag, and looked aghast at the Adelphi Hotel. For starters, even referring to it as a hotel was a stretch. This place was more of a cheap, grubby board-ing house – the type of place where a young lady like Violet would never dream of entering, never mind actually staying. In disbelief, she walked up the steps to the entrance door and on through the poky little reception area, where a lad of about sixteen was behind the desk, smoking and reading the paper. The whole appearance of the place was filthy, and the stench of greasy food mixed with damp was almost sick-making.

'I'm here to see Mr Andy McKim,' she told him.

The kid never even looked up at her. 'He's that bloke with the band, yeah?'

'Correct,' said Violet, relieved that at least she was on the right track. 'Can you kindly tell him I'm here, please. I've come a very long way to see him. And then I'd like a strong cup of tea, please. You can serve it to me in your dining room. If indeed, you have one.'

At that, the kid looked up from his paper. 'Where do you think you are anyway, love? Windsor Castle? If you want tea, there's a café down the road. And if you're looking for that bloke from the band, what's his name . . .'

'Andy McKim,' Violet snapped.

'Chances are they're rehearsing at the Odeon. From what I heard, those tossers need all the rehearsal they can get.'

Violet was astonished and didn't reward his rudeness by even thanking him. Instead she went straight back onto the street outside and asked directions to the Odeon theatre. Thankfully, a kindly nanny wheeling a pram happened to be walking in the same direction and explained to her where to go. The first person in London, Violet thought, who'd actually been polite to her.

As it happened, the Odeon was just a short walk away, and at the sight of it, her spirits began to lift. This was a proper theatre, with ushers and a box office and lovely red carpet and a gorgeous gilt bar area just inside the doors. Outside there were huge posters advertising Gerry and the Pacemakers, the lead act for the night, with The Moptops featured as supporting artists in very, very small print underneath them. There was a comedy double act on before them, then a ventriloquist and then, last but not least, Andy and his band.

A smiling lady at the box office told Violet they were carrying out sound checks onstage, but that she was welcome to go backstage if she liked, to try and find Andy. Violet was then shown through a green baize door that said: *Stage Personnel Only.* She went through, still clutching her overnight bag and feeling like a complete bag of nerves.

This was most definitely not the romantic reunion she'd planned with Andy. Still though, she thought, steeling her nerve as she made her way down a cold, concrete corridor, this was showbiz, and if she wanted to be the girlfriend of a famous musician, then this was the price you paid. Tonight was a huge break for the band, with the A&R man from Decca coming to see them, she reminded herself. Was it any wonder if Andy was a bit distracted?

He certainly appeared more than distracted when she finally found the right dressing-room door, deep in the bowels of the theatre, following the sound of guitars tuning up and the huge clouds of cigarette smoke wafting from under the door.

She knocked, waited for a response and, when there was none, just walked in unannounced. And there he was – Andy. With three other lads about his own age, who she assumed were his fellow bandmates, surrounded by a cluster of incredibly louche-looking girls, none of whom seemed the slightest bit interested to see this exhausted-looking Irish girl, overnight bag in hand, standing in the doorway and wondering what the hell was going on.

'Hey Vi,' Andy said lazily, as every eye swivelled her way. 'What are you doing here?'

What are you doing here? she thought furiously. Did he really just say that? As if she lived down the road; as if her being there was absolutely no big deal?

'Who's the chick in the suit?' one of his bandmates said. 'She looks like a nun!'

'Did someone let a nun in here? How are you doing, Sister Mary Margaret? Come to try and make us all say a decade of the rosary, then?'

Violet wanted to snap the faces off the lot of them – most of all, Andy.

I'm here because of you, she wanted to bark at him. *Why else would I be here? And what kind of a welcome do you suppose this is? What sort of a gentleman dares to treat his girlfriend like this?*

But Andy correctly read the shock on her face, because a minute later, he was up on his feet and hugging her tightly, just like he should have done more than two hours ago at the airport. He smelled most peculiar, though, Violet thought. There was a pungent stink from his clothes, his words were slurred, and his eyes were glassy and very strange-looking.

'Come here to me, love,' he said in that adorable Scouse accent, as she dropped her suitcase and fell into his chest. 'Good to see you. I'm a bit surprised to see you, but it's a nice surprise. Come on and meet the band.'

He introduced her as a 'friend' from Dublin to the lead singer, the drummer and the bass guitarist, and Violet heard them snigger as she shook each hand formally, just like she'd been trained to do. Not one of them stood to greet her, which she thought unfathomably rude.

'Posh bird, isn't she?' said the drummer, who had ginger hair and who was called Dave, speaking about Violet as if she weren't even present.

It wasn't just his rudeness that bothered her, though. Lounging around the dressing room in various states of undress and bare feet were three other girls, who completely ignored Violet. Not only that, but they all seemed to be smoking the same cigarette, passing it around, inhaling deeply and only taking one puff each. *Such bizarre behaviour*, she thought.

Violet was never one to be easily intimidated, but suddenly she felt like a middle-aged frump in her high-buttoned tweed suit, which had seemed so elegant at the airport earlier. Now it felt overly stiff and formal and rigid beside these girls in their Mary Quant mini dresses. One of them looked a bit like a tousle-haired Brigitte Bardot as she paraded around in a black lace slip and introduced herself as Melody, which struck Violet as quite the most ridiculous name she'd ever heard.

Melody seemed particularly proprietorial over Andy, who flopped back down onto the sofa beside her and took a drag from the same single cigarette the others were all sharing. Violet most definitely did not like the intimate way that this ridiculous, half-dressed Melody was behaving around Andy. She was giggling stupidly at something inane he'd said and even had her hand on his knee at one point.

'Shouldn't you all be rehearsing?' Violet piped up, unable to take another second in this grotty, smoky room with everyone ignoring her. 'Tonight is meant to be a big break for the band. Surely you ought to be practising?'

'Yeah, lads,' Dave, the ginger-haired drummer said, in a put-on, high falsetto, wagging his finger mockingly. 'Listen to Sister Mary Margaret. Do what she says or you'll all get detention.'

'Bit strict, your bird, isn't she, Andy? Where'd you meet her, then – prison?'

'Just chill, Vi,' Andy slurred at her, as Melody snuggled even closer to him. 'It's groovy here. Plenty of time for that later.'

'Well, seeing as how I'm not interrupting rehearsals,' Violet said crisply, 'in that case I should very much like a cup of tea, please. And then, Andy, perhaps we might do some sightseeing?'

At that, the others all fell around laughing, but for the life of her, Violet entirely failed to see the joke.

The concert was awful.

Violet went to watch on her own, as none of the other girls showed the remotest interest in the fact that there was an actual performance happening. She had to pay for her own ticket and sat at the back, where there were a frightening number of empty seats. There was one solitary gentleman in a suit in the same row as her, who could well have been the A&R man from Decca that the band had been out to impress. However, this particular gentleman left after The Moptops played about three songs and didn't look impressed at all.

Even Violet had to admit, with her classical training, that their sheer lack of musicianship was woeful. Andy could at least sing and play, but the others were shockingly untalented. Had any one of them ever had a music lesson in their life, she wondered? They were out of tune, off-key and the only time the audience perked up a little was when the band performed a cover version of 'She Loves You' by The Beatles. Even the ventriloquist received a warmer response than The Moptops did.

The show perked up considerably in the second half when Gerry and the Pacemakers came on and belted out hit after hit, starting with 'Ferry Across the Mersey', a song Violet loved. This, it was painfully clear to see, was a well-rehearsed, slick, professional band, who took a show like this in their stride. A world away from the lazy amateurism of The Moptops.

After the concert, the band all drifted off to a Hammersmith pub close by called the Old City Arms. The bad news was that those awful, clinging girls who'd been in their dressing room earlier were still very much present. Melody was hovering like a limpet around Andy, and Violet was starting to lose her patience.

How dare these awful people write me off as some kind of nun, who's just a 'friend' of Andy's, she thought crossly. She'd show them – and when she finally had Andy on her own, then he'd get a right piece of her mind for treating her like this. Andy, however, seemed to have finally found his manners by the time they arrived at the pub, and even slipped his arm around Violet's waist as she queued to buy drinks for them both.

'Thanks for coming to the show, Vi,' he said appreciatively. 'And thanks for the drink, love. I could murder a pint.'

There was no question of him paying: it was as if the thought never even crossed his mind.

'You didn't seem particularly pleased to see me in the dressing room earlier,' Violet retorted. 'And I've travelled such a long way, you know.'

'Oh, that was just the dope talking, that's all.' He shrugged, although Violet hadn't a clue what he meant.

'Did you enjoy the show, Sister Mary Margaret?' Dave asked her cheekily, sidling up beside them. 'And I'll have a pint too, if you're buying.'

Violet had never had to buy a round of drinks in the whole course of her life, but she gamely peeled off a pound note from the wad she had in her purse and handed it over.

'Don't mind him, Vi,' Andy said, giving her an affectionate peck on the cheek. 'He's only jealous because I've pulled such a posh bird.'

There were so many presumptions in that sentence, Violet didn't know where to start. No young lady would ever allow herself to be referred to as a 'bird', for starters, but somehow, as the drinks went in and as the night went on, Andy seemed to grow more and more affectionate towards her.

'So, did you enjoy our set then?' he asked her much later on in the night, when Violet had had a total of three Babychams and was feeling a little more relaxed and calm, especially now that Andy was beginning to pay her a bit of attention. The only annoyance was that ridiculous Melody and her cohorts were still clustered around the table with them – absolutely no budging them.

'Very much so,' Violet lied. 'But if you don't mind, Andy, I've had an exhaustive day and I should very much like to go back to the hotel now.'

'You've pulled then, Andy,' the lead singer jeered as Violet got her coat and Andy stood up to take her to the hotel. 'Or is Sister Mary one of those edge-of-the-bed virgins?'

'She looks like a bit of a tease, Andy,' Melody said drunkenly. 'Wouldn't waste my time if I were you.'

Violet flushed red, utterly mortified, but she didn't lower herself to respond. Instead, with a determined glance down at Melody, she linked Andy's arm, went back to that stinking hovel of a hotel, tripped up the ragged carpet with him and slammed the bedroom door firmly shut behind the two of them.

Edge-of-the-bed virgin indeed.

Emily

Finally, after the longest drought on record, an unexpected bit of good fortune entered the life of Emily Dunne of number eighty-one Primrose Square. Leon called her bright and early the following morning with news.

'I'd a passenger in the back of me cab there last night,' he told her, as the sound of an early morning DJ on his car radio blared away in the background.

'And that's the news?' Emily said groggily, half asleep and still in bed. Unsurprisingly, given that it was still only eight in the morning. 'That's what you rang to tell me? You're a taxi driver, Leon. No offence or anything, but it would probably be more newsworthy if you woke me to say you had no one in the taxi all night.'

'Shut up and listen, will you?' came the gruff reply. 'I was out at the airport, and this one gets into the back of me cab, real businesswoman type, well dressed, with a posh accent, just like you. Mind you, she'd a bit more manners than you, but otherwise, you know what I'm getting at.'

'Go on,' said Emily, still too half asleep to take offence.

'Anyway, your woman was well pissed off because she'd just flown back from London, only her flight was delayed till about eleven last night, and she needed to get back to her husband and kids. "Work trip, was it?" I said to her, and she says yes.

Turns out she's the chief buyer for Flynn's Stores. That's every Flynn shop throughout the country. All twenty-nine of them.'

'Great,' Emily yawned. 'Fantastic. Well worth you waking me up for. Can I go back to sleep now?'

'Jesus, have you no patience?' said Leon. 'So she tells me they're seriously understaffed, and that if she had more reliable ground staff to lean on, she wouldn't have to do so much travelling away from her family. "Well you know, that's very interesting," I says to her. "Because I've a friend who's job-hunting at the minute and she might be just what you're looking for."'

At that, Emily woke up properly.

'So, the upshot of it is,' Leon went on, 'is that this manager one, she's like the vice head of knickers or some shite like that—'

'I'm quite sure that's not her real title,' Emily interrupted.

'Anyway, she says you're to be at their head office this morning at ten a.m. for an interview. Nothing special, now, this is probably only a job on the shop floor, but . . .'

He didn't even have to finish the sentence. In a heartbeat, Emily had sprung up out of bed and was already on her way to the shower.

'Leon?' she said cheekily, grabbing a towel on her way. 'Did I ever tell you that I really do love you? In spite of the fact that you're a grumpy old fuck?'

There was no sign of Violet up and about before she left the house, so Emily left a quick, scribbled note on the kitchen table for her.

You know the way you're always telling me to find gainful employment? Guess what? Am halfway there!

❧

Flynn's Stores were a huge, family-owned homeware department store with branches like tentacles that spread over locations everywhere. They were known for mid-priced quality home furnishings, drapery and clothes, and even though Emily knew she'd be lucky to end up cleaning loos for them, she still gave the interview her very best shot.

Turned out the lady Leon had driven home the previous night was called Julie Flynn, executive chairwoman at Flynn's, and in yet another miracle, she and Emily actually clicked during the interview. Emily talked about the designers the company were using for their kitchenware and how wildly popular they were. She spoke knowledgeably, referencing the influence of the Bauhaus Movement and a few art deco designers she was a fan of – and for her part, Julie seemed impressed.

'I'm particularly glad you like the Karen Jones designs we're working with,' she told Emily, 'because we plan on expanding that range considerably in the near future.'

'The sky's the limit,' Emily chatted away, thinking that this was not just the easiest, but also one of the nicest interviews she'd ever sat through. 'Tea towels, bathroom mats – I'd start low-budget, if I were you, then gradually introduce a higher spec in your soft furnishings range – maybe even in the same design.'

Julie nodded along, and when the interview came to an end, offered Emily a job on the spot.

'Now, it's nothing special,' she stressed. 'You'd start on the shop floor, and that's tough work, let me tell you. But I will keep an eye on you, and maybe down the line, you and me can talk. Can't say fairer than that, now can I?'

'Thank you,' Emily said, trying to hide the huge wave of relief and shock that washed over her at Julie's words. She shook her hand warmly. 'I won't let you down.'

'You've got a real friend in Leon,' Julie said.

'He's been very good to me,' Emily replied. Then, in the interests of truth and honesty, she put all her cards out on the table. 'He's my AA sponsor,' she added. 'I was a patient at—'

'At St Michael's,' Julie replied, nodding. 'Yes. Yes, he told me. So was my sister, just a few years ago. I know first-hand how tough it is trying to rebuild your life after something like that, and I'm glad that at least I can give you a leg up on the first rung of the ladder. After all, if we women can't look out for each other, then who can?'

'Thank you,' Emily said, tearing up a little with gratitude. 'I hope your sister is OK now?'

'She's doing amazingly well, thanks,' Julie said. 'And I know you will too. Good luck, Emily. And remember, my door is always open.'

❀

Emily began to work harder than she'd ever done in her life before. She started the very next morning and was particularly touched to see a little Post-it note left for her in the upstairs bathroom she shared with Francesca.

Best of luck in your new job! Now, remember to be punctual and don't go via Pearce Street, as Google Maps is saying there's a nine-minute delay due to an earlier accident. Just go in there, babes, give 'em hell and knock 'em dead!

Huge love and luck on your very first day. F xxxx

Emily smiled and thanked her lucky stars for such a gem of a housemate.

When she got to Flynn's flagship store on George's Street, right in the heart of town, she was quickly inducted by her line manager, then put straight to work on the shop floor – and left to sink or swim. As it happened though, she spent a surprisingly enjoyable shift chatting and helping customers, and if she didn't know the answer to anything, just saying, 'Sorry, bear with me, this is my very first day.'

At the end of her shift, her line manager thanked her and told her to keep up the good work, and that from now on, she was officially one of the 'Flynn's Stores Team'.

Emily walked home, as it wasn't far from the department store to Primrose Square. On the way there, her mobile rang. Leon, she guessed, fishing the phone from the bottom of her bag, doubtless ringing to see how she got on.

But it wasn't. To her astonishment, it was Alec. Ex-husband Alec. Who practically called the cops the last time she'd attempted to contact him.

'Alec, is that really you?' Emily said, wondering if he had butt-dialled her number by accident.

'Emily, yeah, it's me, hi,' he said wearily, to the sound of a baby gurgling and beginning to cry in the background. 'Sorry to disturb, it's just . . .'

'Just what?' Emily said, genuinely baffled and half wondering if he was calling to threaten her with a barring order this time.

'The thing is,' he said, raising his voice to be heard over the baby, 'I felt really shit after the last time we spoke. You were only trying to say sorry and I was a complete bastard to you.'

'You were entitled to be,' Emily replied. 'Given everything that had gone down between us.'

'So I just wanted to say that I'm sorry too, Em. I'm sorry for being a bollocks of a husband and I'm particularly sorry for cheating. I was a total arse to you back then and you deserved better.'

Wow, Emily thought. She almost had to double-check her phone to make sure this really was Alec, and not some crank caller taking the piss. Alec famously never apologised, ever, for anything.

'You deserved better than me too,' was all she could find words to say.

There was a long, awkward pause as the baby's cries grew louder in the background. Alec hushed and shushed the baby down, and that seemed to work, for a moment at least.

'So,' he said. 'All I really want to say is that I hope you and me are cool. That's all.'

'Of course,' she said, still stunned. 'Absolutely.'

'I mean, you're just trying to pick up the pieces of your life. I get it. And I'm in a happy place now, what with my new family and everything. So good luck with it all, Emily, and if there's ever anything that I can do . . .'

'Right back at you,' she said, surprising herself by actually smiling. 'And if you ever want to avail of my babysitting services . . .'

'Don't even joke about something like that,' he sighed wearily, as the baby's cries rose to a crescendo. 'I may just take you up on it.'

When Emily finally put her key in the lock of number eighty-one, she was greeted by the most delicious smell of garlic and cumin wafting towards her from the kitchen. Following her nose, she tripped down the stairs that led to the basement and there was Francesca . . . or should she say Frank . . . with a frilly apron tied around his good work suit, standing over by the oven with about five different saucepans all on the go at once, expertly juggling them all.

Strange to think of him as Francesca, Emily thought, when Frank in all his Frank gear, and she still wasn't quite certain how he'd prefer to be thought of when he was transitioning. *I'll ask him,* she decided. But only when the time felt right. Emily was the least judgemental person alive and all she really wanted for her housemate was to be happy.

'Well, there you are!' Frank said, coming over to give her a warm hug as he saw her standing there. 'Thought you'd never get home.'

'What's all this?' Emily asked, as she peeled off her jacket, intrigued.

'Well, honey, it's not every day that you start a new job, now is it? So I thought we'd celebrate. Just you, me and Violet. Three housemates together, enjoying a convivial evening meal. What's not to like?'

Was Emily imagining it, or was Frank starting to sound more and more like Francesca? Even when dressed like Frank? His voice was certainly more high-pitched, that was for certain. And his mannerisms were a lot more Francesca-like. Emily said nothing, though, just smiled and was very, very glad for him.

'Anyway,' Frank went on, 'I made an Indian korma, with garlic naan bread and basmati rice on the side. Not too spicy, mind you, because I know anything too strong gives Violet terrible wind. Or so she's always saying, anyway.'

'Wow,' Emily said, staggered. 'This is such a treat – thank you! I'm bloody starving and korma sounds great to me.'

'Fab-u-lous, darling,' Frank said, again sounding so like Francesca that Emily grinned.

'What are you smirking at?' Frank asked her, but then Frank missed absolutely nothing.

'You, dearest,' Emily said.

'What about me?' said Frank, turning to face her with a tea towel in one hand and a spatula in the other.

'Well, I was just thinking how wonderful it is, that you can look like Frank, but sound so like Francesca.'

'Well, thank you, sweetie. I do aim to please.'

'Although . . . can I ask you something?' Emily said tentatively.

'Anything.'

'You never dress as Francesca at home,' Emily said. 'I mean, I've seen Francesca up in your bedroom, but never when there's other people around. Bloody hell, that makes you like an Irish Clark Kent that morphs into Superman. You'll be fighting crime next.'

Frank patted her playfully with the spatula and put his hand on his hip.

'Because . . . because of lots of reasons,' he said.

'Is it that you don't feel comfortable as Francesca?' Emily probed, wondering if she was pushing things a bit too far, but dying to know all the same.

'Are you kidding me?' said Frank. 'If anything, I feel far too comfortable as Francesca. When I'm dressed like this,' he said, waving his hands up and down over the sensible black work trousers he was wearing with a shirt and tie, 'it feels fake to me. But when I'm Francesca, what can I say? It's like my second skin. Of course I'm bursting to dress that way when I'm out and about, and in work too.'

'So why don't you?' Emily asked.

'Because my family come first, second and last with me,' Frank said firmly. 'And they know me as Frank, not Francesca. That's what they know, that's their normality. So until my kids are happy and at peace with me as . . . if that day ever comes, that is . . .' But he broke off there, unable to say more.

'I get it,' Emily said, instinctively standing up to give him a warm hug. 'You don't need to say another word.'

'Thank you,' Frank said. 'Really, thank you.'

'Are we done with the PDAs now? 'Cause I'm bloody starving and that grub smells divine.'

'In that case,' said Frank, 'will you call our esteemed landlady and tell her dinner is served? I haven't seen her since I came in, so I'm guessing she's up in her room.'

Emily did as she was told, even though a sizeable part of her would have infinitely preferred it if it had just been her and Frank for dinner on their own. She checked the drawing room, where Violet was often to be found in front of the TV, but no sign of her. Then she padded upstairs and knocked on the heavy oak door that led to her bedroom. Or boudoir, as Violet probably referred to it.

'Violet?' she said quietly, rapping again on the door. 'You awake?'

Nothing. Not a single sound.

'Frank's made us some dinner,' Emily said. 'Do you fancy eating with us?'

Again, nothing.

'If I promise not to curse and swear too much, would you come downstairs?' Emily said coaxingly. 'Come on, it's free food, Violet. We both know you love free food.'

Not a single sound from the other side of the door.

'I'll use your good royal family china if you don't come out,' Emily said, really testing the water. 'The ones that the Queen Mother probably farted on.'

If Violet was awake, there was no way in hell she'd have let Emily get away with a remark like that. So Emily gave it up as a bad job and came back downstairs to Frank and the warmth of the kitchen.

'No answer?' Frank said, as he carried over a bowl of creamy curry to the table.

'Not a peep.'

'She's probably napping, then,' Frank said. 'Best not to disturb her.'

'Definitely best to let sleeping dogs lie.'

Gracie

The previous Saturday had been unexpectedly enjoyable, Gracie thought, as she strode down Wicklow Street in the city centre, hot and sticky even in the light summery dress she was wearing. Just seeing Frank with Amber, and remembering how their little girl's face had been lit from within to see her parents getting on so well, did her heart good.

'I'm so happy the three of us are together again!' Amber kept saying. 'All we need is for Ben to join us, and then we're all back to normal. Aren't we?'

Neither Gracie nor Frank had the guts to answer that one – at least, not just yet. Instead, they allowed Amber to dictate the day, which she did with gusto. That was the one thing about Amber: no matter what was going on she never failed to know her own mind.

'Zip lining!' she yelled, when Frank asked her where she wanted to go. 'There's a zip line place not far from here and all my friends have already been and they say it's really cool!'

So the three of them trooped off to Grand Canal Dock, beside the CHQ museum, just across the Rosie Hackett Bridge and only a twenty-minute stroll from Primrose Square. The sun was blazing and as they queued for their turn, Gracie freely lashed sunblock on herself and Amber, hesitating a bit when she came to Frank. The intimacy of the gesture gave her pause for thought, but in the end there was no need – he took the sunblock himself and lashed it on almost professionally, to the extent that Gracie had to smile. He even patted the thick, gloopy cream under his eyes, like trained beauticians were always saying you should do, to minimise fine lines. All deeply impressive, Gracie had to admit.

There were other tiny changes about Frank that she'd noticed too. His voice seemed to be on a higher register, for one thing. And was she imagining it, or was there something about his weight that seemed to be shifting slightly? As if some of his body fat was redistributing itself? His face looked a bit fuller and there was a definite curvature around the chest. Subtle, but still, there all the same.

Hormones, she knew were the root cause of it, yet it was surprising to see how quickly they were having an effect – albeit a very gentle, understated one. It wasn't as if Frank was suddenly parading around with a full set of boobs and a hairless face. This transition was delicate and easy to get used to. Just like Beth had promised it would be.

After a half hour queuing, eventually it was Amber's turn to zip line, and both her parents cheered and waved her off and took photos on their phones as she was harnessed into safety straps, then hoisted off for a few hours' fun.

There was an outdoor coffee shop nearby, and Frank and Gracie found themselves drifting towards it. Gracie nabbed two free seats on a wooden bench, where they had a great view of Amber suspended a few feet away from them, as Frank went off to get an Americano for each of them. Meanwhile, Gracie sat back, enjoying the feel of the warm sunshine on her face, enjoying the day and particularly enjoying how happy Amber was.

'It was so good of you to come with us today,' Frank said, returning with the coffees and passing her one over. Just the way she liked it, too – extra hot, flat white, no sugar. He remembered – but then Frank forgot nothing.

'It's wonderful to see her back to her old self again, isn't it?' Gracie said, waving at Amber and taking yet more pictures on her phone. 'I mean, she's just so delighted to see you and me together on a fun day out. Not fighting or bickering or sniping at each other. Like a real, proper family, as she keeps on saying.'

'But that's exactly what I want too, Gracie, love,' Frank said simply. 'A real, proper family. I haven't gone anywhere and I never will. I'll always be here. I'm still here. Still me. I still love you and Ben and Amber more than I ever did, and that will never change.'

'Could you imagine, though?' Gracie said, after a thoughtful little pause. 'Down the line, I mean. You and me sitting here watching Amber, except with you as Francesca and not Frank?'

'I'm exactly the same person,' Frank insisted. 'I may be changing on the outside, but that's it. Remember what we used to tell the kids when they were small? We used to say that at the end of the day, appearances don't really matter. Isn't it what's inside that really counts?'

Another pause, as Gracie put on sunglasses and took a moment to really digest this. 'You need to talk to Amber,' she said. 'You need to explain it to her in such a way that an eleven-year-old will understand.'

'I know,' he said softly. 'I've been meaning to. I'm just waiting for the right time.'

'No time like the present,' Gracie suggested. A warm, sunny day like this, where Amber was so happy and secure, seeing her parents getting on well and being so cool with everything. *Why not now?* she thought.

'If you think the time is right,' Frank said, 'then of course I will.'

Gracie paused to take stock for a moment.

'This is pretty huge,' she said, 'because this is it. Once you talk to, Amber, there really is no taking it back. I don't want her lying on psychiatrists' couches in years to come recounting this as the moment her whole childhood ended.'

'That's the last thing I want too,' said Frank. 'But as Beth says, let's be open and honest with her. If we act like it's no big deal for us, then it'll be no big deal for her either. And the thing is, Gracie love, it really *is* no big deal. I'll look a bit different in the future, but that's as far as it goes.'

'I'll be right here beside you,' she said.

'Thank you,' said Frank sincerely. 'You really have no idea how much that means to me.'

'Course I may also be a tiny bit jealous,' Gracie added wryly, 'because Francesca has far better legs than I do.'

'Your problem, baby; yours to deal with,' said Frank with a wink.

This time, he sounded so utterly like Francesca that Gracie had to smile.

Now for the hard part, Gracie thought, spotting the restaurant she'd been looking for on the other side of the busy street and crossing over. Then she reminded herself of her little pre-prepared speech and opened the door of Raw, the vegan bar on Wicklow Street, where all the cool, young hipster brigade were to be found day and night, around the clock, almost like it was their office.

'I had a feeling you were going to ask me something like this,' Ben said, as the two of them sat in a quiet little booth, well out of earshot. He was working the day shift at Raw and was wearing kitchen whites with an incongruous-looking hairnet that held his thick, tufty hair well off his face and made him look about twelve years of age.

Adorable, Gracie thought. *Just like when he was a little boy.*

'I suppose there's no chance you're joking?' he asked.

'It's not a joke, love,' she said quietly.

'I'd do anything for you and Amber, Mum, you know that,' Ben said. 'But for fuck's sake, does it have to be now? Just when I've got this great job and I've left school and I'm beginning to get my own shit together?'

'I know I'm asking a lot of you,' Gracie replied. 'But this is happening whether we like it or not. This way, it's easier on us as a family, that's all I'm saying.'

Ben sat back and folded his arms, looking like he was caught between a rock and a hard place.

'I already ask so much of you,' Gracie said, gently pressing her case. 'I know that. And this is the biggest ask yet.'

'And I'd . . . like . . . have to be there?'

'Yes.'

'And . . . like . . . act all normal and everything?'

'You just be yourself, Ben. You're amazing as you are.'

'Fuck's sake,' he muttered, twitching at the hairnet in frustration.

'Ben,' Gracie said, leaning across the little plastic table towards him. 'I'm not asking you to do this for me. I'm not even asking you to do this for your dad. I'm asking you to do this for Amber.'

Violet

Your 'friend'. That's how young ladies discreetly referred to their menstruations back then. Back at the Hibernian School for Young Ladies, with alarming regularity, one of Violet's classmates would cry off whatever hockey match or outing the girls were due to take part in, 'because my friend's come to visit'.

Violet herself had never had any truck with such euphemistic nonsense. If she had stomach cramps, she told no one and said nothing and got on with it. That was very decisively the end of that.

This, however, was very different. It had been a full six weeks now since her monthly 'friend' had come to visit and she was worried sick. But who to confide in? Her family doctor? That was a joke. Dr Patterson was an elderly man who regularly went to the races with her father – how could she possibly open up to him about something as terrifying this?

Betty? A very firm no to that, thank you very much. Violet and Betty were close; Betty had always been a sort of cross between a housemaid and, on occasion, even a friend. But yet again, there was always the threat that Betty might, just might, feel it was her Christian duty to tell Violet's father – so that ruled her out.

In utter desperation and out of her mind with worry, Violet found herself sitting at Jayne's kitchen table one weekday morning, when she knew Jayne's husband Tom would be at work and they could talk confidentially. There was something comforting about being in Jayne's warm, cosy kitchen; it always smelled of delicious home-baking and Violet found it far easier than she thought to pour out her troubles.

Even if she hated seeing the look of pure shock that slowly crossed her friend's face.

'Oh Vi,' Jayne said, looking horrified. 'You should have told me! You went all the way to London on your own without saying a single word? What if your father had found out?'

'He didn't and he won't either,' Violet said firmly, 'so that's one less thing to worry about.'

In fact, that was the single good thing about this whole sorry mess. Her father was still under the impression that Violet had spent a happy weekend all those weeks ago up in Castle Leslie, swanning around in a whole new wardrobe and meeting suitable young gentlemen of her own age. She'd got away with it and that, at least, was something to be grateful for.

'I don't know what to do, Jayne,' Violet said, white-faced and almost ready to throw up with worry. 'I've had this pressing on me for weeks now and I've nowhere to turn. I've tried writing to Andy at the address I have for him in Liverpool, in the hopes my letters will be forwarded on, but he never seems to get any of them. My last three letters have all just bounced back to me, unopened.'

'And you think you might be . . . you know?'

Violet nodded. This was unthinkable; this was every girl's worst nightmare. How could she, of all people, have done something so utterly stupid? She and Andy had taken precautionary measures; everyone knew you couldn't get pregnant using the Billings method. Violet had eagerly read up on it in a copy of *Cosmopolitan* magazine she'd smuggled into the house. Mind you, the Billings method was also nicknamed Vatican roulette, and now she could plainly see why.

'Oh dear God,' Jayne said plaintively. 'Violet, this is so unlike you! What on earth possessed you?'

'I love him,' Violet said, beginning to cry. 'And he said he loved me too. And there were all these other girls hanging around him and I knew if he didn't end up with me, he'd have gone off with one of them.'

Even as Violet said the words aloud, she could see Jayne thinking: *But that's not real love at all, is it?*

'Let's try to be calm here,' Jayne said. 'Panicking is going to get us nowhere. Worst-case scenario, suppose you were . . . expecting. You could always go away for a year or so? Maybe to your Aunt Julia's down in the country? You could have the baby quietly and privately, then put it up for adoption?'

'You have got to be insane!' Violet said, looking aghast. 'This would . . . it would ruin my whole life! Auntie Julia would tell my father immediately, and you know what he's like. He'd disown me. And what man would ever want me again after something like this?'

Jayne bit her lip, deep in thought. She passed over a tissue to Violet, who had burst into hysterical tears by then.

'What am I going to do, Jayne? I can't get hold of Andy and I've never been so frightened! You have to help me. You're the only one I can trust.'

At least Jayne had a good answer for that one.

'I'll tell you exactly what we're going to do,' she said firmly. 'We're going to make an appointment to see my GP, who's a wonderful lady you'll really love. She's discreet and professional and she'll help us. Wait and see, Vi – this is probably just a false alarm.'

'Do you really think so?' Violet asked her, between big gulping tears.

'Definitely.'

But Jayne didn't look one bit convinced as she said it.

Dr Maguire was kind and understanding and gave Violet a thorough examination, inside and out. She took blood and urine samples and promised that she'd have the results in a few days.

Exactly one week to the day, the results arrived.

In a letter addressed to Miss Violet Hardcastle of number eighty-one Primrose Square, her very worst nightmares were confirmed.

16 August.

It was that date that Violet dreaded. Every year it rolled around and Violet quietly 'took to her bed', blocking out the world, ignoring the telephone and the post and even Jayne when she called in, which she never failed to do on this awful day.

Somehow, exactly fifty years on, this year was worse than ever. Fifty years. Fifty long years and she could still vividly remember that dull, aching torture that went on for hours, followed by the most agonising sharp pains Violet had ever felt, before or since.

From the heavy mahogany four-poster bed upstairs in her room, she could clearly overhear Frank and Emily having what sounded like a most convivial evening down in the kitchen together. They were chatting away gaily and even laughing at some shared joke.

How anyone could laugh on a black day like this was utterly beyond Violet. So she pulled the heavy bedspread over her head and tried to block out the noise.

Tortuous thoughts still wouldn't stop spinning through her head though, as she thrashed around the bed, desperate for this to end.

Dear God, she thought, it had been five decades to the day. When would her penance finally come to an end?

Worry. Sick-making worry was her constant companion. What to tell her father? Need she even tell him at all? Maybe he wouldn't notice, Violet thought in her more cowardly moments. If she got Jayne to run her up some particularly baggy clothing, maybe she'd get away with it. Maybe he'd even be happy at the idea of a little grandchild, she thought in her wilder flights of fancy – though deep, deep down, she knew that was never going to happen.

Jayne was the only living soul who she could unburden herself to, but even she foresaw trouble ahead.

'I can come with you when you tell him, if you want, Vi?' she'd offered supportively. 'He mightn't be as angry as you think, if there's two of us there to break the news.'

In the end, though, Violet could have been spared the trouble of worrying herself sick over how to tell her father, or whether to tell him at all. Unbeknownst to her, a simple medical bill for three shillings and sixpence had arrived from the doctor's surgery, addressed to: Mr Hardcastle, 81 Primrose Square.

Violet had been out walking, pacing restlessly around the square because she'd read somewhere that meant you have a higher chance of losing it. Be a dream come true if she could lose it naturally, she thought. No matter what the health consequences were for her and to hell with what the Catholic Church taught about your soul being damned to hell for having 'relations' outside of marriage. At least that way she'd get away with it with minimal fuss, and without her father ever having to know.

Suddenly, Betty came rushing out across the square to find Violet.

And the white-faced, horrified look on her face said it all.

Violet thrashed about upstairs in her bed, trying to block out her memories and the vile, horrible words her father had used. How violent he'd been, even slapping her across the face as he trembled with rage.

'All that money for your education and this is what I've reared?' he spat at her, his face roaring red as sweat poured down his forehead. 'A useless slut? A slattern? You've disgraced me in front of everyone and you're no daughter of mine!'

Violet remembered something Emily told her: that her own mother had said something similar to her too. Disowned by a parent. It was something the two had in common.

And throughout the whole of her living nightmare, there wasn't a single word from Andy. Even Jayne and Tom were frantically writing to him and trying to telephone – but at every corner, it seemed to be a dead end. He was away on tour, Germany this time, and message after message went unreturned and unacknowledged.

Today, Violet thought bleakly, women had babies out of wedlock all the time and no one batted an eyelid.

But this was holy Catholic Ireland in early 1969. Times were different and she was treated very differently. For an unwedded, pregnant woman, make no mistake: this was where your old life as you knew it ground to a shuddering halt.

Frank

It was exactly 7.59 p.m. when Frank's neat little Prius pulled up into his usual parking space on Primrose Square, punctual to the dot. But then he'd taken care to avoid exit seven off the motorway, as there was a seven-minute tailback, according to a handy app on his phone that kept him fully up to speed on all traffic delays.

He was just taking his briefcase and a few shopping bags from Tesco out of the car when he spotted Jayne from across the square waving over at him. Such a fabulous neighbour and all-round human being, Frank thought, as he walked down the square to say a fond hello to her.

'I was watching out for you, Frank,' Jayne said, coming up to him with a warm smile. 'I knew you'd be here on the dot, as always. Sure I could set my watch by you.'

'It's wonderful to see you,' Frank said. 'Will you come into Violet's with me? I'm sure she'd love to see you.'

At the mention of Violet's name, however, Jayne's face fell a little.

'It's actually Violet that I wanted to talk to you about,' she said, as her tone shifted.

'Oh really?' Frank said. 'Is everything OK? I was just about to make her some dinner. She often comes to eat with me in the evening and we always have great old chats. Maybe you'd like to join us? Plenty of food for us all,' he added, holding up the grocery bags.

'That's very kind of you,' Jayne said, 'but I'm afraid I'm a little worried about Violet just now. She's a bit . . .' She broke off though, as if she wasn't sure what more to say.

'Yes?'

'The thing is,' Jayne went on, 'I went to see her earlier. That is, I tried to get in to see her, but . . . well, I couldn't. She wouldn't even let me into the house.'

'Maybe she's not feeling too well?' Frank asked tactfully. Maybe it was some sort of nervous condition, he wondered. Maybe the poor lady suffered from panic attacks. Maybe that was why she was . . . well, like Violet Hardcastle.

'Violet is fine physically,' Jayne said. 'It's just that around this particular date is always very hard for her, you see. Now, of course I know she's not the easiest to live with, but, well, Violet has been through a great deal and right now, just needs a lot of TLC.'

'I understand,' Frank nodded. 'In fact, now that you mention it, I did notice that she seemed a little withdrawn over the past few days. Not like herself at all.'

He wanted to say that Violet wasn't thudding around on her walking stick, grumping about the neighbours, scribbling off missives to anyone who dared annoy her, and in between all that, still finding the time to chat to Frank about the Duchess of Cambridge and some new hat she was wearing. Definitely not like herself at all.

'I'll mention it to our housemate Emily as well,' Frank added. 'We'll both be sure to be extra-mindful of Violet just now.'

'Thank you, love,' Jayne said. 'I knew you'd be great about it.'

'Would it be cheeky of me to ask one more thing?' Frank said, as they fell into step together and drifted back towards number eighty-one. 'Why is this particular time of the year hard for Violet?'

Was it her birthday, he wondered? Or an anniversary, perhaps of her father Freddie's passing, who she often spoke about and whose photo dominated every surface in her drawing room?

Jayne sighed before she spoke. 'Frank, love,' she said, 'there's so much you don't know about the past. But it's Violet's story to tell and not mine. Ask yourself this, though – do you ever wonder why the poor woman never goes outside of her own front door?'

'Oh,' Frank said, caught off guard. 'I always assumed it was because she was afraid of falling? She struggles to walk even with her stick.'

'It's not because she can't, Frank. It's because she's terrified.'

Violet

The awful, chilling silence at number eighty-one Primrose Square was so much worse than any name-calling or abuse her father might have hurled at her. She wasn't even permitted to go to Mass with him and Betty. But then, no words needed to be spoken – her father's bloodshot glare spoke volumes. So Violet stayed up in her bedroom, safely out of harm's way.

That was, until one day the key turned in the front door downstairs and voices were heard in the hall below. It sounded like two men this time. Her father and . . . Violet couldn't place the other voice. Yet he sounded vaguely familiar, whoever he was.

'Your father wants to see you right away,' Betty said to her, cold and detached. 'He's downstairs in the study with Monsignor Bell. Hurry up, now, don't keep them waiting.'

The Monsignor was here, in the house? Violet had never liked the Monsignor; he always smelled of brandy and had a greasy, oiled-back comb-over, as if someone had melted half a pound of butter on top of his head.

She had a horrible, ominous feeling, as if whatever was brewing certainly wouldn't end well for her.

'Get into the car,' was all her father grunted, unable to even look her in the eye.

No one told her where they were going or where she was being taken to.

'But, why?' she asked him, with panic in her voice. 'Where are we going? And why aren't you coming with me? What's going on?'

'Ignore her,' her father said to the Monsignor, as he squeezed his portly girth into the driver's seat and started up the engine. 'And don't even think you have to be nice to her on the way there. Idiotic little slut deserves no more.'

Hours crawled by on that awful car journey, passing through town after town. Violet badly needed a wee but was too embarrassed to ask the Monsignor to pull over at a hotel so she could use the facilities. Wherever they were headed to, he clearly wanted to get there before nightfall.

Then, just as it was getting dusky, the car finally pulled into the gates of what looked like a huge parkland estate with a long driveway that led to an imposing gothic-looking building, with stone walls and crucifixes everywhere you looked. A third-rate hotel, perhaps, Violet thought wildly.

No, she thought, as the car crunched up on the gravelled driveway and the Monsignor barked at her to get out, which were the only two words he'd spoken to her on the entire journey. This place was most certainly not a hotel.

It seemed to be some sort of a convent, Violet realised, as a surly-looking novice nun opened the hall door and led her and the Monsignor down a long, polished oak corridor towards a little office that was more like a den. She'd been sent to a convent in the middle of nowhere, and yet that made no sense either.

'Monsignor,' she tried to say as the door was opened and an older, stony-faced nun stood waiting, 'what are we doing here? I've already left school; I'm hardly in need of full-time education. Surely there must be some kind of mistake?'

'This is her, then?' the nun asked coldly. She was a large woman with a black wimple that covered her entire head and the most appalling teeth Violet had ever seen.

'This is her,' the Monsignor repeated, handing Violet over as if he wanted nothing more to do with her. Violet was beginning to feel panicky now, but she willed herself to stay strong.

'Are you in charge here?' Violet said to this nun, who-ever she was. 'If so, can you kindly telephone my father in Dublin and tell him that I really do need to come home right away? There appears to have been a dreadful misun-derstanding.'

True, Violet's father could barely look at her, never mind speak to her. Surely, though, when he realised the awfulness of what had happened, he'd relent? He couldn't possibly be cruel enough to leave her in this dreadful place. Could he?

'Listen to the little madam now,' said the nun, mockingly. 'Did you ever? A dirty, fallen woman, daring to speak to me like this?'

Violet looked at her, shocked.

'My name is Sister Helga,' the nun told Violet. 'I'm Mother Superior here and if you ever speak to me like that again, my girl, you'll feel the back of my hand. Understand?'

'That's the stuff, Sister,' said the Monsignor approvingly. 'Needs a firm hand, this one. She's been completely spoiled at home, I'm afraid.'

'Didn't stop her from making a disgrace of herself, though, did it?' Sister Helga said. 'Didn't stop her from fornicating and getting herself into this state in the first place. Now you just listen to me, Violet Hardcastle. You're here for one purpose and one purpose only. You will work like you've never worked before in your life, and through hard work, you will purge your sins before God. Outside of these four walls, you may be daddy's little princess, but here you will be known as Mary, after Mary Magdalene, as a daily reminder of the filthy sinner that you are. Do you understand?'

Violet may have been shocked and frightened, but it would take more than a hatchet-faced nun in a wimple to crush her spirit.

'No, I do not understand,' she answered crisply. 'I don't know where I am or why I've been brought here. I need a cup of tea and the ladies' powder room. Then, if you won't take me back home with you, Monsignor, you'll have to leave me at the nearest train station or else a hotel for the night—'

A series of hard, sharp slaps across her face from Sister Helga immediately silenced her.

'From now on, your name is Mary,' she said icily. 'And I have a feeling this won't be the first time you'll need to be subordinated in the strongest way possible. We'll beat that snobbery and haughtiness out of you if it's the last thing we do, Mary Magdalene.'

Prison can't be this bad, Violet thought, as another younger nun led her down an interminable length of corridor after corridor, then up four flights of stairs and on into what appeared to be a dormitory filled with at least a dozen other girls, who all looked blankly back at Violet as she was led inside.

'Give me your clothes,' the nun barked, thrusting a horrific-looking blue serge uniform at her, made from the roughest fabric Violet had ever seen.

'Prayers are at five a.m., and after that, you'll work in the laundry for the rest of the day. Get a good sleep now because tomorrow, you'll be working hard; you'll fast and pray and you'll offer it all up to God as penance for your sins.'

'You mean I'm expected to share this room?' Violet asked, looking aghast as a dozen pairs of eyes watched her closely. 'But it's so cold! And there's only one blanket on the bed. You can't possibly expect me to sleep here.'

'None of your nonsense now, Mary,' the nun said, before swishing off and locking the heavy door behind her.

Then there was a chorus of titters from the other girls as soon as the door was banged shut.

Violet started to get upset now. Why the hell had her father sent her here? So none of his fancy Dublin businessmen friends would see her pregnant? There's no way he'd have done something like that, had he known what a nightmare this place was. This was no better than a prison.

Tomorrow, she thought, rubbing her face where it stung from the walloping Sister Helga had given her. *I'll find a telephone and throw myself at his mercy. I'll do anything and go anywhere else Father sends me, if it'll just get me out of here.*

For tonight she may have been stuck there, but tomorrow she'd break out, if needs be. Sharing a freezing cold dormitory with twelve strangers all watching her undress? Not on her life. Before this, whenever Violet had been away from her own beautiful bedroom at Primrose Square – apart from those few fateful nights in London – she'd always stayed in the finest hotels. But this place was certainly no hotel.

'So what's your real name, Mary?' one of the girls asked her in no accent Violet recognised. This girl was about her own age and sported a black eye and a garish-looking laceration right down her face.

'I am Miss Violet Hardcastle,' she replied, her face still stinging like it was on fire 'Who are you?'

'Concepta.'

'In that case, Concepta,' she said, 'can you please direct me to the ladies' powder room? And I haven't eaten. Where can I go to get a cup of tea, please?'

Guffaws from around the room, loud and raucous.

'Listen to Lady Muck, would you?'

'The powder room? Go on up and ask Sister Helga for the powder room, I dare you!'

Then a low growl from a bed just opposite Violet's.

'We're going to have a bit of fun with Lady Muck here,' a girl with acne on her face and a shaved head said. She must have been the dorm alpha, because the minute she spoke, the others went silent.

Violet got into the rough, scratchy uniform, climbed into bed and realised that she was feeling real fear now, like an ice-cold clutch on her heart. Something she'd never felt before, not once, not in the whole course of her life.

Emily

On her second morning at work, and with a spring in her step, Emily bounced away from Primrose Square and strode towards Flynn's department store on George's Street.

She'd good reason to be in top form; finally, finally, finally things really seemed to be turning a corner for her. She'd had a fantastic evening with Frank – or rather Francesca – the previous night and had spilled out all her plans for the Ambrosia Independent Living and the special surprise she was plotting for her mother and her friends.

It was a huge undertaking and she needed all the help she could get.

'It sounds fantastic,' Francesca had said, as she served up a sweet and salty caramel trifle she'd bought for dessert. 'And you know I'll help you out in any way I can. I'll rope in my daughter Amber too – she loves a good party.'

'Supposing we go to all this trouble,' Emily said a bit worriedly, 'and Mum hates what I'm doing?'

'And supposing you do nothing?' she replied calmly. 'Then you'll never know, will you? This way, at least your mother will see all the time and trouble you're going to, to give them a wonderful treat, won't she? Who wouldn't be proud of that?'

You haven't met my mother, Emily thought to herself, although she said nothing out loud. It wasn't that kind of night. She and Francesca were having too much fun chatting and plotting and planning late into the night.

Mind you, it was a bit strange that Violet hadn't joined them, Emily thought the next day, as she weaved her way through all the early morning commuters. She would have enjoyed all the chats and the laughs they were having. Of course, she would probably have bossed Emily around and insisted Francesca use the correct china for dinner, but in spite of that, she might actually have had a good night.

Was she feeling all right, Emily wondered? She knew Francesca was being extra mindful of her too, because she'd insisted on leaving a tray of cold meats for her outside her bedroom door, 'just in case she gets hungry in the night'.

Then, just as Emily was passing a newsagent, she saw a glossy magazine with Meghan Markle's beautiful, glowing face on the cover. *Sod it*, she thought. *I'll buy her the shagging magazine. Anything to have the old curmudgeon back to normal, and giving out to me once again.*

That wasn't the only bit of shopping Emily did. With Alec and his new little baby at the forefront of her mind, she nipped into the kid's department at Flynn's Stores and bought a few dotey little Babygros – fluffy blue for a boy – thinking she'd post them to Alec and his new partner, now that they were at peace with each other again.

It was early evening when she got back to Primrose Square, so she left her shopping on the kitchen table, then zipped straight back out again to meet Susan across the square for a hot yoga class that they'd both been threatening to go to for the longest time.

The house was quiet when Emily finally got home – almost 10 p.m. There was no sign of Francesca either, but she remembered her saying something about working late that night and not to wait up for her.

'Violet?' she called from the darkness of the hallway. 'You still awake? I've got a surprise for you – come and get it! I'll give you a hint: it's not unconnected with Meghan Markle.'

Silence, though, nothing but stone-cold silence and the sound of the grandfather clock ticking away in the hallway. Slowly, Emily came downstairs to the kitchen, switching on lights as she went and wondering where in hell Violet had gone to. She couldn't have gone out – the woman never went anywhere. And she was hardly still upstairs in her bedroom, holed away from the world yet again, was she?

Turning on the light in the kitchen, though, there was a sight that made her blood run cold. The Babygros that Emily had bought earlier were still on the kitchen table, but this time they'd all been ripped and shredded into a hundred pieces, scattered everywhere in a big blue cotton puffy ball of mush.

But that wasn't the worst of it. Sitting at the top of the table, bent double and sobbing silent tears, was Violet, fingering the shredded Babygros and looking for all the world like her heart would shatter in two.

Violet

Bells. This place was dominated by the sound of bells ringing. When the bells rang at 5 a.m. punctually each morning, that meant you got up out of bed, got dressed, then went straight downstairs to the freezing cold chapel for morning matins.

'But where am I supposed to wash?' Violet asked in vain, to sniggers around the dormitory and a dig in the ribs from the alpha female, who all the others seemed to kowtow to and who everyone referred to as Moluag. A suitably ugly name, Violet thought bitterly, for such an ugly person.

They were made to dress in that horrific starchy blue uniform, then after prayers, they were all marched down to the refectory for breakfast. Food, Violet thought ravenously. Well, at least that was something. She'd eaten nothing the previous day and was starving. Besides, she had a busy day ahead; she planned on getting to a telephone so she could reach her father and explain to him that there had been some horrific kind of mistake. She'd howl, she'd cry, she'd crawl on her hands and knees to apologise to him, if he'd only just arrange to have her collected as quickly as possible.

Breakfast, however, turned out to be nothing of the sort. A tiny glass of milk and a piece of stale bread – that was it?

'But I'm still hungry!' Violet whispered to Concepta, who was beside her. But you weren't supposed to speak at meals, so even her hushed whisper carried down the long hall, and a moment later, that terrifying Sister Helga was beside her, brandishing a wooden cane.

'You again, Mary?' she said, glowering down at Violet. 'I might have known you'd be trouble. Do you all hear that, girls?' she said loudly to the room. 'Little princess here seems to have been expecting a meal from the Royal Hibernian Hotel.'

Suppressed titters from around the room, but Violet held her head high.

'Do you know what we do here with filthy sinners like you,' Sister Helga demanded, 'who are riddled with arrogance and pride?'

The room fell silent at that and Violet knew something very, very bad was about to happen. Then the crack of a loud clatter, as Sister Helga walloped the cane sharply across Violet's back. She cried out in shock and pain, and the more she cried, the more the blows kept raining down on her, till she could feel the blood seeping through her thin blue uniform and she could take no more.

'And that's not the only punishment we keep for sinners like you,' Sister Helga said coldly. 'Stand up at the top of the room beside the head table and read passages from the Bible aloud to us. Every single day for the rest of the month, until I decide that you've done enough to purge the pride out of you.'

Violet could barely stand, let alone walk, but somehow she got to her feet and managed to stand shakily where she was told and read aloud from the Book of Psalms.

That particular punishment lasted for the best part of two months, by which time Violet had learned to keep her mouth shut. Worst of all though, was having to read aloud when she was weak with hunger, forced to watch the nuns feasting on scrambled eggs and proper toast, as her own stomach rumbled.

To her absolute horror, her waistline had begun to thicken by then, and in the mornings, she was particularly nauseous. The sickness was worse than anything; Violet had never been ill a single day in her whole life and now she could barely stand without needing to throw up. As the weeks wore on, the stench of the greasy fry-up as the nuns gorged themselves was more than she could take.

But even that was nothing compared with the backbreaking work the girls were made to do to fill in the long days. They were sent to a laundry in the basement of the convent, and were forced to wash, scrub, launder, hang out, dry and iron sheets and shirts, some of them covered in the most unimaginable human filth.

Throughout her first few weeks there, Violet thought she'd die from exhaustion, and plenty of times she actually did pray for death as a form of release. The work was gruelling and some of the girls were in advanced stages of very visible pregnancies. Surely they shouldn't have been working like dogs every hour that God sent? Violet had never done any kind of manual labour before in the whole course of her life and said so loudly on her first day.

'But at home I have a housemaid who does all our laundry for us!' she said. 'You can't expect me to work like this. Ladies don't work inside a laundry room!'

That particular beating was so bad, her face swelled out like a balloon and she was fairly certain that the nun in charge of the laundry had broken a few ribs. Yet again, that night Violet was made to stand starving by the nun's dining table in the convent refectory and read aloud to them, as the blood dripped from her swollen eye down onto the page below. Most tortuous of all, she could smell the roast chicken and gravy the nuns were gorging themselves on, just a few feet away from her.

That night, as Violet eased her aching, battered body into bed, Concepta slipped up beside her and, unseen, slipped an orange into Violet's pocket. The kindness was something that stabbed at Violet's heart and made her cry worse than any beating any nun could give her.

At night, after lights out, the taunting would start, generally led by Moluag and her cohorts.

'Oh, at home we've got a housemaid who does all our manual labour for us!' Moluag would say, doing a high-pitched, crude impression of Violet's well-spoken accent.

'I'm so hungry, can't you drive me to a hotel nearby for dinner?' another would chip in.

'My uniform is scratching at my skin; can't you take me shopping for nice new clothes?'

'And my hands are all red from washing laundry! You can always tell a lady by her hands and mine are ruined!'

'And my favourite of all?' Moluag sneered. 'This is all a horrible mistake! My father will be here to collect me any day now!'

At that, Violet snapped. Unable to take any more, she leaped on Moluag and walloped her hard across her face. But the beating she was given in return was far more savage than anything any nun inflicted on her. The whole dorm seemed to join in, viciously punching Violet time and again till she howled out in pain, begging them to stop, afraid for her baby, even though this pregnancy had been the ruination of her.

Two things happened after that savage attack. She never picked a fight with Moluag again and she earned herself the nickname Violent.

'Violent Violet, Violent Violet, VIOLENT VIOLET.'

Night after night, the taunts would grow louder and louder, and Violet would turn into her pillow on that stiff, freezing cold bed with just a single blanket to cover her face, so she could really let the tears flow.

'Hey, hey, hey, come on, missus,' Emily said now, cradling Violet's frail, bony shoulders in her arms and handing her a lump of kitchen roll to mop her eyes as best she could. 'What's all this, then? What's brought this on?'

But Violet couldn't answer, she was still too choked up with tears and with the depth of her own pain.

'Is it your father?' Emily asked, as her eyes fell on the old black and white photo of him that dominated the kitchen sideboard. 'Some kind of anniversary, maybe?'

'No,' Violet wept – big, gulping, uncontrollable sobs. 'You don't understand.'

'What?' Emily persisted gently. 'What don't I understand?'

'I'm not crying for my father at all,' Violet said, wiping her nose in the lump of kitchen roll Emily handed her. 'I'm crying for my little boy.'

Gracie

Gracie felt very guilty when she thought back to how crassly she'd written off Beth Taylor and her therapy sessions as a load of useless twaddle. Boy, she really had cause to eat her words now.

Because Beth was actually proving herself to be invaluable.

'Frank and I have finally spoken to Amber – together,' Gracie told her, during a one-on-one appointment she'd requested at the last minute. 'Mainly because . . . well, it just seemed like the right thing to do on the day in question. You know, natural and unforced.'

'And how did she take it?' Beth asked.

'Amber was . . . oh, she was amazing,' Gracie said, unable to stop herself from smiling. 'She knew things hadn't been quite right between Frank and I for some time, of course . . .'

She broke off there, remembering back to the previous Saturday, when they'd all gone zip lining. How serious Amber's face had been at first when both parents had sat her down and said: 'There's something we'd really like to talk to you about, pet.'

'Are you and Dad getting a divorce?' was her first question.

'Nothing like that at all,' Frank rushed to reassure her. 'It's just that . . . well . . .'

'It's just what?' Amber had said, abandoning the dregs of a 99 ice cream and looking from her mother to her father, not having a clue what was coming next. 'Is it something even worse? Because you look so worried, Dad. Are you sick? Is that it? Are you sick and do you have to go into hospital? Do you have cancer, like Mrs Dolan on the square, who had to take medicine that made all her hair fall out?'

'Oh n-no, love,' Frank stammered, fiddling with his glasses. 'I promise you, I'm as healthy as a horse.'

'Here's the thing, honey,' Gracie said, picking up the reins, seeing as, for the life of him, Frank couldn't manage to find the right words. Her years of summing up in court helped her, as she knew of old the best and clearest way to communicate anything important was to be short, concise and to the point.

'How would you feel, Amber,' she asked calmly, 'if Dad was to make some changes to himself from now on?'

'Oh, I already know about this,' Amber said brightly. 'Me and Ben talked about it for ages. You mean, like . . . Dad's going to wear the kind of outfits you and me wear? Like girls' clothes?'

Frank nodded. 'Yes pet, that's the idea.'

'And would you wear makeup too?'

'Maybe,' he said, 'but only if it was OK with you, of course.'

'Course it's OK,' Amber said. 'Like I told Ben, if you're the same inside, that's all that matters.'

'And there's a bit more too,' Gracie said, with an encouraging little nod towards Frank.

'My voice and body would be different too,' Frank explained. 'More like . . .'

'Like a lady's, you mean,' Amber finished the sentence for him. 'Because if you're going to dress like a lady, then you really are a proper lady, aren't you?'

'Well, one day, I hope,' Frank said. 'But only if that was OK with you. You know I'd never do anything you didn't want me to.'

'But the main thing I want to know is . . . will you and Mum still be married?'

A look passed between Gracie and Frank that seemed to telegraph so much in a heartbeat of time.

'Your dad and I will always be each other's best friend,' Gracie said truthfully. 'And of course, your dad can move home again. Because we miss him, don't we, sweetheart?'

Frank mouthed a silent 'thank you' and seemed choked into silence.

Meanwhile, Amber stunned them both by putting her hand over her mouth and giggling.

'Dad's coming home again!' she squealed happily. 'This is the best news ever!'

'And you're OK with what Dad wants to do?' Gracie asked.

'Of course I am. It's like, no big deal, really,' she grinned, as Gracie and Frank turned to each other in confusion. Could she really be taking it this well?

'In fact, I think it's really cool!' Amber said. 'We can all go dress and clothes shopping together from now on, can't we? That would be amazing!'

Gracie looked to Frank, who caught her eye and the two of them smiled. Maybe now, after all these long weeks of stress and worry, Gracie could begin to see the light at the end of the tunnel. Maybe now she could relax again. Maybe now she could finally start to breathe.

'You know I'm only changing on the outside, pet, that's all,' Frank said to Amber. 'Inside, I'm the same as I always was and always will be.'

'I know,' said Amber. 'So can we start clothes shopping now, Dad? Mum? Can we go to Zara and buy new outfits for all of us?'

'It's wonderful Amber took the news so well,' Beth said, interrupting Gracie's thoughts and pulling her focus back to that cramped little clinic in town. 'But for today, let's talk about you. So tell me Gracie, how are you feeling now?'

Gracie had to carefully formulate the words in her own head before she could answer.

'Of two things, I'm certain,' she said.

'Tell me,' said Beth.

'I know that Frank still loves me. And I know that my life is so much happier with him a part of it, in whatever guise he takes.'

'And the second thing?'

'And . . .' she forced herself to say, 'I'm finally coming to terms with the fact that the sexual side of my marriage is over. Frank . . . or Francesca, I suppose I should say, is attracted to women. But I'm not – I'm straight. So that changes things for me, doesn't it? Physically I mean.'

'You know I'm here to help you in any way I can,' Beth said supportively.

'And while I appreciate that,' Gracie said, 'the funny thing is that I'm beginning to be OK with it. My relationship with Frank was always about so much more than the physical side of it. It's about companionship and friendship and being there for the kids and all the things that make up family life. My family have always had such a happy life together.'

'And you always will,' said Beth. 'It's wonderful that you can see this now. That you know how committed Frank, or rather Francesca, is to you, and to the kids, and how nothing on earth will change that.'

'Maybe years down the line, I'll go on to meet someone else,' Gracie said, thinking aloud more than anything. 'Who knows? Certainly stranger things have happened.'

'You're an attractive woman, Gracie. That window is always open for you, if that's what you choose.'

'That's as maybe,' Gracie said, 'but for the moment, at least, what I love more than anything is family life. And Frank is pivotal to that – either as Frank or Francesca. We're a unit – and a bloody strong one at that. After all, if we can get through this, we can get through anything, can't we?'

A pause, while Beth put down her pen and notepad. Then she astonished Gracie by giving her a little round of applause.

'Good for you, Gracie,' she said warmly. 'I want you to remember this moment, because this is what we call a breakthrough.'

Gracie flushed and batted it aside.

'Speaking to Amber together was a huge turning point for me – for us both, in fact,' she said.

'Do you feel better for having done it?'

Gracie had to think before she could answer.

'It's a funny thing,' she said, pulling her thoughts into focus, 'just how enlightened that younger generation are. People complain about Generation Z and dismiss them as snowflakes, but we have no idea how open-minded they are and how tolerant too.'

'So, what about Ben?' Beth asked.

'Well, I've asked him to meet Frank as Francesca with Amber and me,' Gracie said, 'and he's agreed to do it, but there may have been a lot of heavy emotional blackmail involved on my part. I guilt-tripped him into it, I'm afraid, and I'm not proud of it. But at least Ben did say he'd go through with it. So now my prayer is that he'll be as accepting as his little sister.'

'We can't force these things,' Beth nodded sagely. 'All we can know for certain is that it's time for your kids to see the real Frank. Or Francesca, I should say, by rights.'

'Which is why I'm here at such short notice,' Gracie said. 'Any tips or bits of advice you might have would be very gratefully received.'

'For what it's worth, then,' Beth smiled, 'this is exactly how I'd advise you move forward. For one thing, I'd suggest meeting in a public place – we tend to be more social and well behaved when there are other people around. It normalises things for us. Give the kids time to get used to Francesca and to using new pronouns around her. Just remember, there's never a right way to do this. But if the kids see you being supportive and not having an issue, then they won't either.'

'Duly noted,' Gracie said.

'Because you're doing brilliantly, Gracie, and now it's time. Don't you think that it's time?'

Violet

After a time, Violet learned. She learned to keep her eyes open and her mouth shut. She learned that when Sister Helga approached you, you kept your head down and avoided all eye contact. If addressed directly, you said, 'Yes, Sister, sorry, Sister,' and prayed that you'd be left alone. She learned that the beatings and bullying seldom had anything to do with a specific misdemeanour on her part; it was just that everyone seemed to hate her in this place. The nuns and the other girls despised her; they had done since day one and that was all there was to it.

There was just one forlorn hope that kept Violet going. Which was that as soon as she had this wretched baby, this unwanted child, this thing growing inside her that had cost her not just her old life, but her home and her sanity too – then and only then, maybe she'd be allowed to go home again. Back to Primrose Square, back to her beautiful house, back to her father and all her old friends, back to her moneyed life of leisure and shopping and fun. She might not have appreciated how good she had it back then, but by God, she did now.

I'll be nicer to everyone, she thought. *I'll be more like Jayne Dawson, who's always so considerate and kind. I'll do absolutely anything, if I can just get out of here.*

Assuming her father forgave her and allowed her back home, of course.

He certainly never came to visit, that was for certain. The physical pain Violet dealt with on a daily basis, she'd grown used to, but nothing, absolutely nothing compared to the emotional pain of being abandoned like this. Of course she knew she had broken her father's heart. Of course she knew how angry and disappointed he was with her. But her fervent hope had been that eventually he'd forgive her. Violet had always been his pride and joy; they'd adored each other. Surely, she thought, as the months slowly dragged on, surely he'd come to realise he missed her? Maybe in time, she hoped, he might even allow her to come home again?

As for Andy? Violet had all but given up on him. What, she sometimes wondered, would he do if he knew she was being detained here, no better than a prisoner? Violet could daydream all she wanted about him finding her, rescuing her and getting her out of this hellhole. She could fantasise about him being overjoyed about becoming a father. In all those useless daydreams, he always insisted on marrying her and 'doing things properly', she could almost hear him saying in that accent she'd once loved so much.

But deep down, she knew these were nothing more than flighty daydreams. The hard, cold reality was that Andy had ignored her long before she came to this place. Even if he knew what had happened to her, the chances were high that he'd continue to ignore her and get on with his own selfish, self-absorbed life.

Besides, even if she'd wanted to contact anyone from her old life, she couldn't. None of the girls were even allowed to write letters here, and Violet had earned herself another merciless beating for protesting about it.

'But even in prison you're allowed to write letters!' she'd said aloud one day. Sister Helga had overheard her, though, and hit Violet so hard across her face for insubordination, she feared that her nose had been broken.

So, Violet learned. *I'll do my time here like a prisoner, if that's what they want*, she thought, *but the very minute this baby comes, I'll find a way out of here.* She'd tunnel a way out if she had to. Like prisoners did during the war.

Her stomach swelled and grew larger, but she paid as little heed to it as possible. Who would have listened to her anyway? She was one of about a dozen other girls who were in various stages of pregnancy and it made absolutely no difference; you still had to work in the laundry just as hard as everyone else. If you got dizzy or tired or showed any sign of weakness at all, you were either beaten or else denied food. Or in Violet's case, both.

Occasionally, she'd wake in the middle of the night to the sound of screams, as one of the other girls went into labour. A day or two would pass before they'd return, hobbling, bleeding, sick and heart-sore.

'What was it like?' Violet would hiss, curiosity consuming her.

But the girls were strictly forbidden from talking about it, under threat of even further punishments. Which, of course, only added to the horrible, all-consuming worry about what childbirth would actually turn out to be like. Never mind what would actually happen to all these babies, when they did eventually arrive.

Then, early one sunny August morning, not far off her due date, Violet was woken by cramps so acute, she thought she was dying. She was physically strong, with a high pain threshold, but this was way beyond anything she'd ever experienced before.

'It's your baby,' Concepta said urgently. 'I think your baby is coming. Stay in bed and I'll get one of the nuns to help. And whatever you do, don't dirty up the sheets – they'll murder you!'

'I need a hospital. I need a proper midwife to take care of me!' Violet yelled in agony, but to no avail. She was taken to a room no bigger than a cell, with bars on the windows; she was even made to walk there herself in spite of the fact that she was doubled over in howling agony. Then she was laid down in a tiny single bed with just a novice nun in charge of the birth, who didn't seem to have a clue what she was doing. Sister Ruth was this particular nun's name and she seemed, if not exactly kind, then at least slightly less savage than the rest of her order.

The birth was long and excruciating, and took almost the whole day. Violet blacked out more than once with the pain. Throughout it all, Sister Ruth seemed as terrified as Violet herself was, and her sole contribution was to peal off into gabbled Hail Marys every time Violet screamed out for help.

Eleven hours of undiluted agony later, with one final push, Violet's baby was delivered into the world with a loud, raucous cry that would have woken the dead.

'It's a boy!' Sister Ruth said. 'And he's perfect, thanks be to the good Lord!'

Violet had never expected this. After everything she went through, nothing prepared her for the huge wash of pure love that she felt when that warm, wriggling, squealing little bundle was placed gently into her arms. The baby was beautiful, with the longest eyelashes Violet had ever seen, and looking so like her father that she wanted to laugh.

She was allowed to hold him and bond with him and feed him for the next few days, as even Sister Helga decreed that she was too weak to work.

I have to tell my father, Violet thought. *He has to know that he's a grandfather now to the most beautiful, strong, robust little boy you ever saw.*

Of course he was still bound to be angry, because she'd had the baby out of wedlock, but all that would change as soon as he saw the baby, she knew. Her father had always wanted a son; someone to play football with and take to matches and who might, in time, become a property developer too. Well, now he had a beautiful little grandson, and wasn't that almost as good?

Violet just needed to get word to him, that was all, and maybe, *maybe*, he would fall in love with the baby just as she had and take all three of them home to Primrose Square. She even named him Frederick Junior, knowing how much her father would like that.

Then, on another bright sunny morning about three days later, a priest barged into Violet's sickroom, with Sister Helga obsequiously bowing and scraping beside him. She was all, 'Yes, Father' and 'No, Father', and it almost made Violet sick to see this about-turn in her manner.

'So, this is our Magdalene then,' said the priest, sitting on the edge of Violet's bed, uncomfortably close to her. 'Well, it seems that you're a very lucky girl. God has taken great pity on a sinner like you, and you should be down on your knees thanking him for this miracle.'

'What miracle?' Violet asked numbly. The only miracle she was interested in was getting her and her baby as far from this hellish place as possible.

'You've a grand healthy little boy now,' the priest went on, speaking to her as if she were an idiot. 'And I'm sure you want the best for him, like all good mothers, don't you?'

'Say "Yes, Father",' Sister Helga prompted.

'Yes, Father,' Violet said automatically.

'In that case, I have news for you,' the priest went on. 'Sister Helga here has managed to find a lovely married couple all the way from New York who'd like to give your baby a good home. Isn't that wonderful, now? You might thank Sister Helga for all the trouble she went to on your behalf?'

Violet sat up in bed, terrified. 'You mean you want to take the baby away from me? Frederick Junior? But you can't do that, I won't allow it!'

'Didn't I tell you, Father?' Sister Helga said sorrowfully. 'The sin of arrogance and pride is strong in this one. We have a long way to go with her before she learns manners and humility.'

'This is a good Catholic couple we're talking about,' the priest explained. 'And they'll give your baby the best of everything with them in America. Once the adoption has gone through, we can even have him baptised properly. Isn't that what you'd want for your little fella?'

'Of course it is,' Sister Helga finished the sentence for her. 'Sure, what has this worthless sinner got to offer the baby anyway? Even her own father wanted nothing more to do with her.'

'That's not true,' Violet said spiritedly. 'If you'd just let me write to Father, or better yet telephone him, I know he'll come here to take me and the baby back home . . .'

'But you don't seem to understand, you wilful, ignorant girl,' Sister Helga said smoothly. 'Your father wrote to me himself and said this baby was to be given up for adoption the minute the poor, unfortunate creature was born. And you needn't think that you're going anywhere for the foreseeable future either. Mr Hardcastle's clear instructions are to keep you here, with us, well out of his sight for good. At least here you can work hard and learn to purge your sins.'

'Isn't it great all the same, Sister?' said the priest, looking so utterly delighted with himself that Violet wanted to throw up. 'To think that an illegitimate little boy like this now has the chance of a decent life, with a good, Christian mother and father to look after him. Isn't the will of God a wonderful thing?'

Emily

Somehow, Emily managed to haul a still-sobbing Violet up the stairs to her bed. Somehow, Emily undressed her, got her shoes off and managed to get her under the heavy counterpane that covered her bedsheets. Somehow.

'It's OK,' she kept whispering to Violet over and over again. 'You're here now and you're home and you're safe and it's over. I faithfully promise you, it's over.' She felt Violet's thin, bony hand tightly grip onto hers.

'It's never over,' Violet said. 'Never. Not for me.'

'I promise you, it is,' Emily insisted, trying to sound confident, even though she didn't feel it. Violet's story had terrified her. Of course she knew that Magdalene laundries existed all over the country – for God's sake, it had been the mid-1990s before the last one in Dublin finally shut its doors. They were no better than gulags and a shameful part of the country's history – and of the Catholic Church's appalling treatment of women. But the thought that Violet had been sent to one was what truly shocked Emily. Someone like her, from a good home with money behind her and a family too?

There were photos of Freddie Hardcastle all over the house, and the minute Emily got the place to herself, she vowed to fire one of them out the nearest window just as soon as she possibly could.

Violet wasn't improving. She was still lying, agitated and twitchy, in the bed, unable to sleep, even though Emily was lying fully clothed beside her, cradling her in her arms and trying to shush her fears away. So when Emily heard Francesca coming home, tiptoeing quietly up the stairs, she felt a huge sense of relief.

Help is here, she thought as she very gently slid away from Violet and went out to tell her everything. Reinforcements. Francesca would know exactly what to do; she always did.

With poor Violet in no state to argue, Francesca made a quick phone call to Jayne across the square and asked her to get here as fast as she could. It was well past midnight at this stage, but still Jayne came running. Emily felt an overwhelming surge of gratitude when she saw Jayne's warm, concerned face appear at the front door, still wearing her dressing gown with tracksuit bottoms on underneath it. Emily had met Jayne a few times through Susan, as the two were next-door neighbours. Jayne was the heart of Primrose Square; everyone thought the world of her, and apparently she and Violet went back decades. If she wasn't able to help, who could?

Jayne, Francesca and Emily held a quick, huddled confab in the kitchen.

'I just came home and Violet was in bits,' Emily said. 'I'm worried sick about her; it's like the woman is having some kind of breakdown. She's been reliving the most nightmarish time you could imagine. I had no idea she's suffered the way that she has.'

'I did notice that she didn't seem quite like herself over the last few days,' Francesca said to Jayne. 'You'd warned me about it, of course, but I'd no idea it was quite this bad.'

'It's the date,' Jayne nodded wisely. 'She's always a bit wobbly in the middle of August. And this year was bound to be worse than ever.'

'Why this particular year?' Emily asked.

'Because it's been fifty years, you see,' Jayne said. 'Her son, her little baby that was taken from her, would have been fifty years old today. It's not something she ever talks about – even with me she pretends it never happened – but it's still with her, every single day of her life.'

It must have been close to one a.m., but the house was still up and awake as Francesca made tea and toast served on the good china and brought it upstairs on a tray to try to coax Violet to eat something. Violet had always adored Francesca – or Frank, as Violet still knew her – and if anyone could soothe her, Emily thought, it was her. Meanwhile she and Jayne sat together at the kitchen table, talking, talking, talking.

'It's trauma, pure and simple,' Jayne said. 'Can you imagine what it must have been like for Violet in one of those awful places? Think of those young, vulnerable women who were abused so badly, then just expected to get on with their lives as if nothing happened?'

But Emily couldn't answer. All she could do was beat herself up for being so catty about Violet when they first met. She felt mortified when she thought how cutting she'd been about Violet's snobbery and her waspishness and all her odd ways.

But no one is born like that, she reminded herself. *Life is what made Violet the way she is.*

'I wrote to her at the time, you know,' Jayne said quietly. 'Because as far as I was concerned, Violet had just disappeared into thin air. One day she was here and the next day she was gone, it was as simple as that. Of course, I called to this house time and again, trying to find out what had happened to her. She was my friend and I was worried sick. Her father was a complete tyrant, though, and wouldn't even let me through the front door. But there was a very nice housemaid who worked here at the time, Betty, and she told me as much as she knew.'

'Did you know then where Violet had been taken to?' Emily asked.

'No,' Jayne said. 'No one did. It was as if she'd just been brushed under the carpet and forgotten about. Betty thought she might have been sent down to the country to live with a relative, but couldn't tell me any more. She did say that if I wanted to leave letters here for Violet, she'd do her best to see if she could forward them on to wherever the poor girl had been spirited off to. It was years later before I found out that not a single one of my letters ever reached Violet. Her father burned them all and never said a single word.'

'What a bastard!' Emily muttered hotly, glaring at a photo of Freddie Hardcastle on the dresser.

Jayne sighed deeply. 'Normally, I try to look for the good in other people,' she said, 'but I'm afraid in Freddie Hardcastle's case, it wasn't easy. He adored Violet, you see – he'd pinned all his hopes on her bringing great glory to this house, then when she got pregnant . . .'

'He just shunted her off where he wouldn't even have to look at her,' Emily finished the sentence for her. *Jesus*, she thought. *And I thought my own family was dysfunctional. Compared with this lot, I came from the shagging Waltons.*

'So how did Violet eventually get out of that place?' she asked, dying to know. 'Did they let her go once the baby was born?'

Jayne couldn't answer for a moment.

'I wish I could say yes,' she said after a long pause. 'I wish I could tell you that Freddie forgave her and welcomed her home with open arms and that all was well again.'

'But . . . what?' Emily prompted.

'But that's not what happened at all. He still refused to have anything to do with Violet, so he just left her where she was, airbrushing her from history. His business had run into difficulty by then though, and towards the end of his life, I know he was under huge financial pressure.'

'You said towards the end of his life,' Emily said. 'Did he live long after all this?'

'Another decade,' Jayne said. 'Ten more years, can you imagine? And what's worst of all is that at any point throughout those awful years, he could have sent for Violet and brought her back home at any time, but he was a proud, stubborn man and never did. Not once. According to Betty, he even burned every photograph of her that was in this house. Every single last one.'

'Please tell me Freddie Hardcastle died a horrible, screaming death?'

Jayne just looked at her wryly.

'I know, I know,' Emily said. 'Kindness and tolerance and all of that shite. But honestly, someone like him doesn't deserve any sympathy, does he?'

'Freddie Hardcastle died a good ten years later,' Jayne said simply. 'When he did, this house went to Violet, although there was precious little money left over for her, just a string of debts he'd left behind.'

'So she got out of that laundry and got to come home?'

Jayne nodded. 'And from that day on, I don't think she ever set foot outside her own door again. Home became her safe space, her sanctuary, her refuge. Once she got away from that terrible place, and back here, she never stepped outside again.'

'And what happened to her baby's father?' Emily asked.

'Andy,' Jayne said thoughtfully. 'That was his name. He was a cousin of my late husband Tom's and I'm afraid to say he didn't behave very well at all. He was trying to make it in the music business, you see. He wanted to be the next Paul McCartney, but he had no success at all. So he went back to England, moved to Manchester and settled there. He married and went on to have a large family, and even though Tom and I told him what had happened to Violet, he didn't want anything to do with her.'

'He didn't even want to know his own son?'

'No,' Jayne said sadly. 'Although by then, Frederick Junior had long since been taken to the States for adoption. But still, though. All that unhappiness. All that pain and suffering for poor Violet. Those were very different times, you see. The past, as they say, is another country. Thank God it's all changed now.'

They were interrupted by Francesca, who came into the kitchen, looking white-faced and worried.

'Violet's asking for you now,' she said. 'She says there's something very important she needs to tell you.'

'I'm on my way,' Jayne automatically said, rising to her feet.

'No, not you,' Francesca said apologetically. 'It's actually Emily she's asking for.'

❧

Emily knocked gently on Violet's heavy oak bedroom door, let herself in and perched gently on the bed beside a deathly pale Violet.

OK, she thought. *Here goes. Either I can treat her like a complete basket case on the verge of a breakdown, or I can do the woman the courtesy of acting exactly the way I always do around her.*

Emily decided on the latter. 'Jesus, old woman,' she said lightly, 'that was some heart attack you gave me earlier. Thought we'd have to check you into St Michael's there for a minute, and as an ex-inmate, I can tell you, you'd bloody hate every second of it there. There's no telly, for one thing. You'd lose your reason.'

'So now you know,' Violet said, propped up against a mound of silky, lacy-looking pillows.

'Now I know.'

'I'm sorry about all those grow baby bags, or however you refer to those dreadful things,' Violet said. 'I will of course replace them, in due course.'

'Just give me a month off rent and let's call it quits,' Emily said cheekily and was rewarded with a wan half smile.

There was a comfortable silence before Violet spoke again.

'You and I have something in common, Emily,' she said.

'What's that? Because I ain't no lover of the royal family, if that's what you're getting at.'

'I was about to say,' Violet went on, 'that people don't like you and me, really, do they? They get the wrong idea about you, just like they do about me.'

Emily looked at her, unsure where this was going.

'But they're quite mistaken, aren't they?' Violet said. 'Because I know that there's a real diamond inside you. I know from the little kindnesses you showed me, when I was nothing but foul to you. You're a good person deep down, Emily Dunne. And now it's time to let the world see that too.'

It surprised Emily, how genuinely touched she was.

'And what about you, Violet?' she asked. 'What are we going to do with you? Are you just going to stay here in this house, never going out, filling your days by firing off letters to strangers and crucifying yourself for something that no one even cares about anymore?'

'And what, pray, is the alternative?' Violet said, with a hint of her old haughtiness returning.

A very good sign, Emily thought.

'Or, you could do exactly as I suggest.'

Gracie

Meet in a public place, Beth had wisely advised, and Gracie was bloody glad that she'd paid attention. Everyone was always on their best behaviour in public. Rows would be overheard and, God forbid, if Ben didn't handle this well, it would be significantly harder to storm out in a strop from a packed restaurant, with onlookers taking everything in.

She'd chosen the Trocadero restaurant in town quite purposefully, as she knew Ben was a big fan of the head chef there and would be on his best behaviour. Amber was excited too, as she'd been pestering to be brought there for ages and was bird-happy when they did manage to get a reservation.

'Oh my God, Mum!' she chattered, as she, Gracie and Ben were shown to their table. 'There's, like . . . loads of celebs here . . . Loads!' Then Amber took out her phone and she and Ben were so engrossed in snapping a TV presenter at the table right beside them, craning their necks to get the perfect selfie without the unsuspecting celeb being any the wiser, that neither of them even noticed a tall, slim, elegant lady gliding into the restaurant and slipping quietly into the booth beside them.

Showtime, Gracie thought. Nor could she have stage-managed it any more smoothly.

Gracie didn't remember much about the meal. She couldn't even say for certain what she ate – or didn't eat, more likely.

She remembered next to nothing about the conversation, which was perfectly normal, almost mundane. Exactly the kind of run-of-the-mill, ordinary things that they used to talk about as a family all the time, prior to Frank moving out. Everything, she thought, was as it always was and always had been, except that Francesca looked a helluva lot glossier and more groomed than Frank ever did.

From the moment she arrived, Amber burst into a wide, broad grin, and even Ben seemed at peace with it all. Not only that, but Francesca was far more light-hearted and secure in herself today, surrounded by all her family. She was fun and funny and an all-round joy to be with. She was in her prime, she was glorious, she was her true self.

All Gracie could remember, with any degree of certainty, was strolling back to the car with Ben, as Francesca and Amber were a pace or two ahead of them.

'Well, love?' Gracie prompted her eldest. 'That wasn't too awful for you, I hope?'

Ben walked on in silence for a bit before answering.

'The weird thing is –' he shrugged, shoving his hands deep into his pockets – 'is that it wasn't weird at all. Not in the least. I mean, I thought Dad was going to show up in a dress like some kind of bad drag act, but it wasn't like that, was it?'

'No, love.' Gracie nodded in agreement. 'Not at all.'

'Dad did show up,' Ben said, 'but it's like today I got to see the real him, and up until now, he's only been play-acting, going around the place in suits and shirts the whole time. It's like he's been acting a part for the last eighteen years and now he doesn't have to do that anymore. He can just be who he is.'

'The real him,' Gracie repeated softly. 'That's exactly what I thought when I first saw Francesca. I thought, this is who your dad was meant to be all along. And now it's his time to shine.'

They both looked in front of them to where Francesca and Amber were striding on ahead, the two of them laughing and giggling at some shared joke. Happy and relaxed in each other's company. Just like always.

'I've been a bit shit to Dad lately, haven't I?' said Ben.

Gracie gave a half smile. 'I think that's something we're both guilty of.'

'And you know something else?' Ben added. 'I thought I'd hate this. I only came because of you and Amber, and I was all set to leave after half an hour. But it was . . . well, it was all . . . OK. Fine. Normal. Isn't that, like, seriously . . . *whacking*?'

'You know what I think, love?' Gracie said, turning to face Ben in the warm summer sunshine. 'I think that families aren't perfect. They never are, no matter how much they try to be. But as long as we can all live our truth in our little family, then that's OK, isn't it?'

'Suppose.'

'If we can do this as a family, together, then we've got to doing something right, haven't we?'

Emily

'Come on, old woman. Move your arse, would you?'

'If you would kindly refrain from corner-boy language,' Violet said primly, 'then I would find this process a whole lot less degrading.'

'We're here with you, Vi, love,' Jayne said soothingly. 'Nothing bad is going to happen to you, I promise. We won't allow it.'

'I would feel greatly more encouraged,' Violet said, 'if your hand wasn't trembling as you spoke.'

Jayne and Emily were linking Violet through one arm each and trying to coax her to come outside. To cross the threshold of her own front door, something the woman hadn't done in decades. Between the two of them, they'd been cheerleading her on for days, and as it was such a fabulously sunny afternoon, they'd decided this was as good a time as any. The hall door was wide open, with Primrose Square looking at its sunshiney best in the late summer sun.

'Come on, you're so close!' Emily said enthusiastically. 'I'll get you a dirty big cream puff if you manage it!'

'One more step, Vi, and you're almost there,' Jayne tried her best to encourage her.

But Violet's nerves had got the better of her. She'd started to shake by then, uncontrollably.

'No,' she said quietly. 'No, I don't think so.'

'Oh come on, please try, Violet,' said Jayne. 'This is the closest you've come in years. Think of how good it'll feel to be out in all that lovely fresh air!'

By then, though, Violet was having a full-blown panic attack and there was no budging her.

'No,' she said breathlessly. 'I can't. Not now. Not today. Maybe not ever.'

'But look, you're almost there . . .' Emily tried to say. 'Just one more step and you're home and dry!'

It was pointless, though; they all knew it.

'She's upset, so we should leave her,' Jayne said quietly to Emily. 'You've come this far, Violet, and I'm so proud of you. But I think that's probably enough for one day, don't you?'

'Enough for one day,' Violet said, pale-faced and trembling as she was led back into the hallway, back to safety, back to where she belonged.

Not long afterwards, Emily had a meeting with her boss, Julie Flynn at Flynn's Stores' headquarters on George's Street. Punctual to the dot, she was shown into Julie's office and rewarded with a big, warm smile and the very welcome offer of a coffee.

'Your first few weeks here have gone fantastically,' Julie said, handing Emily an Americano and perching on the edge of her desk. 'Line management tell me you're first here every morning, last to leave in the evening and always so helpful and cooperative with customers on the shop floor. You're working your ass off, and I don't want you to think it hasn't been noticed.'

'Wow, thank you,' Emily said, totally unused to being complimented. Up until then, her sole experience of meeting with any boss had always been a prelude to her being fired. She'd never in her whole life known what it felt like to work at a job you actually enjoyed, for a boss you respected and admired. It was a good feeling. In fact, more than that, it was a bloody amazing feeling.

'I've got my beady eye on you, you know,' Julie joked. 'And if you ever wanted to chat to me about design, my door is always open. Although I know that's not the reason why you and me need to talk today.'

'No, no it's not,' Emily said, bracing herself for her big pitch.

'It's about sponsorship, isn't it?' Julie asked. 'That's what my assistant told me.'

'Yes, it is, actually. If it's not too cheeky of me. It is for a very good cause, though. That much I can promise you.'

'Then let's hear what you have to say. I'm all ears.'

Francesca

'You're sure it's not too much blusher?'

'Stupid question,' Emily replied. 'You can never have too much blusher.'

'And I look . . . you know . . . passable? Not too scary? Professional?'

'Oh, come on!' Emily said, as Francesca pulled the car into the underground car park at one of the spaces reserved for her office. Arriving punctual to the dot, thanks to a convenient app that told them there was a nine-minute tailback on the M50. 'You're utterly glorious,' Emily said. 'If I could look a fraction as good as you on my way to work in the morning, I'd be one very happy lady.'

'I'm nervous,' Francesca said, with every right to be. It was her first day at the office as Francesca and she knew, without even trying, that she'd be the sole focus of the day and the main topic of discussion among her co-workers.

Emily had offered to come as far as the door to Creative Solutions with her, and Francesca was bloody glad that she had. Somehow Emily's reassurance and cheerleading had got them both this far. Just another few steps and Francesca would have made it to the office lift, and just another few steps after that and it would all be over, bar the shouting.

'Not a single thing to be nervous about,' Emily said confidently, taking Francesca by the hand as they both stepped out of the car. 'Are you ready, then?'

'Ready as I'll ever be.'

'You're sure you don't want me to come in there with you?'

'Certain, thanks,' said Francesca, exhaling nervously. 'You're an angel to come this far, but from here on, I'm better going in alone.'

'Then give them merry hell, babes. Call me if you need me and remember I'm only a phone call away from you at all times.'

Emily walked Francesca right to the door of the lift, giving her a quick, tight hug before she slipped off to start her own day's work at Flynn's Stores' HQ.

Left alone, Francesca focused on taking nice, deep, soothing breaths before stepping out of the lift at the third floor. Then, the very minute she appeared at the glass office door, Hannah from HR bounded over, twitchy and edgy and seemingly desperate to say and do exactly the right thing.

'Good morning, *Francesca*,' she said, stressing the name and shaking hands, as every head in the office swivelled around to have a good, proper ogle.

Good, Francesca thought. *Let them. Let's get it over and done with. Let them talk all they like and then let it all blow over for the nine-day wonder that it is.*

'I just want to say welcome to the office today . . .' Hannah went on.

'But I was only here yesterday,' Francesca said. 'I worked till almost ten p.m. You were here – you saw me. I even gave you a lift to your bus stop last night.'

'Yes,' Hannah fumbled nervously, 'but that's when you were still *Frank*. Today you've come to work as Francesca and I just wanted to say that here at Creative Solutions, we pride ourselves on being completely inclusive and gender blind.'

'I'm the same person, you know,' Francesca said. 'I just look a little different, that's all. But I'm still me.'

'And that's wonderful,' Hannah said, by far the most nervous person of the two and tripping over herself with political correctness. 'I want you to know how happy we are that you've chosen to express yourself this way. And by the way? If you wanted to tweet about how supportive we've been at Creative Solutions, that would be terrific.'

'Hashtag: freakshow,' Jake muttered loudly enough for a few people in the office to hear.

But Francesca heard him too.

Ah, Jake, the office bully boy. *How do you solve a problem like Jake?* she wondered. In her old life, Frank would have blushed and cowered and crawled quietly away to his desk, where he'd keep his head down and bury himself in work for the rest of day.

But not Francesca.

She strode over to Jake's desk, towering over him with her hands on her hips, looking fierce and glorious and magnificent all at the same time.

'What did you just say, Jake?' Francesca demanded. 'Because if you've something to say to me, you might at least have the good grace to say it to my face.'

Met with the combined presence of Francesca and Hannah from HR, Jake backed down. 'Nothing,' he hissed under his breath.

'Glad to hear it,' Francesca said. 'One more word out of you, mate, and you'll end up as the hashtag. Hashtag: dole office.'

'I'd like to apologise profusely for any upset that comment may have caused you,' Hannah stumbled over herself to say, with a furious glare in Jake's direction. 'Jake, please come to my office at ten a.m. sharp.'

'Hey, I'm a big girl,' Francesca said, feeling a surge of pride like she hadn't done in years. 'And I can tell you, the Jakes of this world are a piece of cake to me.'

There was a ripple of applause as she glided to her desk, which grew steadily louder and louder. A few of her co-workers waved and mouthed words of encouragement.

'You look fabulous!'

'You're amazing!'

And that's when she knew.

In that single moment, that's when Francesca knew absolutely everything would be OK.

Emily

It took another few weeks of grafting and incredible hard work on Emily's part, throughout all of which Francesca, Jayne and even Violet herself offered nothing but encouragement. Every single step and every single setback of the way.

'You're doing a fine thing, you know,' Violet graciously said to Emily, as the two stood together in the hallway, before Emily left Primrose Square for the evening ahead. Leon had very kindly offered her a lift before he started his night shift, and the last thing she wanted to do was be late for him.

'I'm a big bag of nerves,' Emily said to her. 'Wish me luck, will you?'

'She'll be proud of you,' Violet said. 'How could she fail to be?'

'Who do you mean?'

'Your mother, of course. Isn't all this for her benefit?'

We'll see, Emily thought.

'You're sure I can't persuade you to join us, Violet?' She chanced her arm, already halfway out the hall door.

But Violet just shook her head.

'Not tonight, dear. But that doesn't mean I won't be thinking of you. Now go. Shine. Enjoy. And I'll be waiting up for you to hear all the news.'

Emily gave her a spontaneous little hug, marvelling at the distance she and Violet had come back from the days when they were at each other's throats. Now there was a genuine fondness between the two women. And more importantly, there was trust.

Leon drove her, but when Emily tried to twist his arm and get him to come inside with her, he batted it away.

'Gotta start my shift, you know yourself,' he said. 'But have a great night, won't you?'

'I'll do more than that,' Emily said as she clambered out of the car. 'I'll even buy you breakfast tomorrow morning, so I can tell you all about it. At the greasy spoon café of your choice. How about that?'

Leon wasn't a great one for outward shows of emotion, she knew well by now, but still. She could have sworn he smiled as she said it.

You've been a real pal, she thought fondly as she waved him off in his taxi. At a time when friends were thin on the ground for her, Leon had been there, and she'd never forget him for it.

So now, here she was, ready to go. Showtime, as Francesca would say.

Emily had done her prep work thoroughly and had taken care to issue handwritten invitations to each and every one of the residents at Ambrosia Independent Living. She'd given them loads of notice and had written out the start time in giant block capitals, so no one could blame their cataracts for missing out on all the fun.

The staff at Ambrosia had been wonderful too.

'We never have treats like this,' said one young, smiling nurse from Manila. 'Never!'

'And it kicks off at half seven on a Saturday night,' said Norma, utterly delighted. 'Unlike boring crappy old flower-arranging classes and prayer meetings, which all seem to start at three in the afternoon. I always say, nothing good in this life ever began in the afternoon, trust me. You did good, kid,' she added with a little side wink in Emily's direction.

Emily grinned back. 'I had a lot of help. The good folks at Flynn's Stores sponsored all this, right down to the barbeque food, so I can't take any credit for it.'

'You worked in event management once, didn't you?' Norma asked.

'How did you know?'

'Just a lucky guess,' Norma twinkled, before drifting off to grab a hot dog and a seat with a view.

It was early autumn by then, and Emily had billed this as an end-of-summer outdoor party, with a firework display to round the evening off. Her previous life working in party planning had indeed helped her, as she'd called in every favour imaginable to pull together an evening like this for all the residents.

They'd been blessed with the weather too; it was dusky and just getting dark, yet it was still mild enough that guests could drift about without freezing their arses off. The grounds were filling up fast, and everywhere you looked, people were setting out garden chairs or else laying thick blankets on the ground to plonk down on. The staff had decked the park with trestle tables for the food, and already residents were nabbing seats or gently being guided in wheelchairs to wherever they'd get the best view. Grandkids were running excitedly all over the place, loving the candyfloss that Jayne's son Jason was serving from his ice cream van, which was parked right at the side of the main reception area.

The invitations had stressed that families were of course welcome too, and they turned out in force. Although there was really only one family that Emily had her eyes peeled out for.

No sooner had she thought the thought, when she felt a warm, supportive arm slip around her shoulders. It was Francesca, looking as breathtaking as ever, even wearing a neatly tied apron and laden down with trays, where she'd been serving freshly barbequed food for all and sundry.

'Any sign?' she said, correctly reading Emily's concerned expression.

'Not so far, I'm afraid.'

But then they just had to come. They couldn't not turn up, could they? After all her weeks of preparation, after all this hard work?

'Stay strong,' Francesca said. 'Here, have a cheeseburger. That's bound to cheer you up.'

Emily couldn't face food, though; she was still too nervous.

'Hey, we're not all like you, you know!' she said jokingly. 'You eat what you want and you never gain a single gram – unlike the rest of us.'

'I'll have you know,' Francesca said so primly that Emily had to smile, 'that my figure is all down to a particularly tortuous pair of Spanx knickers that are killing me right about now.'

Emily was about to come back with a smart remark – except that's when she spotted him.

Jamie, her little nephew. Patiently queuing up at the ice cream van for a 99. When he saw Emily, he instantly abandoned his place in the queue and ran squealing over to her.

'Auntie Emily!' he said, throwing his pudgy arms tightly around her legs and almost making her fall over. 'This is so cool! I normally hate coming to see Granny here because it's boring and it smells of wee, but tonight is amazing!'

'Hey, big guy!' she laughed, bending down to brush the hair out of his eyes and have a good look at him. How tall he'd got. Had it really been so long since she'd seen him? 'It's so good to see you!'

'It's good to see you too, Aunt Emily. I miss you lots. Like Jelly Tots.'

Emily smiled. 'This is a family night, pet,' she said, 'so you just make sure you have a great time. OK?'

'I'm already having, like, the best time *ever*!' He giggled happily, with an adorable smile that showed about five teeth missing. 'I *love* firework displays – especially if they're really loud and noisy!'

'Oh, and I almost forgot,' Emily said, reaching into her back pocket and fumbling about for her wallet. 'This is for you, pet,' she added, handing over two crisp fifty-euro notes.

'What's this for?' Jamie asked, looking back up at her in bewilderment.

'It's the money I owe you,' she told him. 'Remember back to when I was very naughty and I stole from your piggy bank? Well, it's all there for you now. Every single cent of it.'

Jamie looked back at her in shock.

'But this is *way* more than you borrowed!' he said, stunned. '*Waaay* more!'

'Consider it an interest payment,' she smiled. 'And just don't spend it all on candy floss. Or if you do, don't tell your mother.'

'Don't tell your mother what?' Emily heard a voice say from behind her. She whipped around to see Sadie standing there, wearing jeans and a big Puffa jacket, and smiling. Wow. Sadie never smiled at Emily, ever. The last time her sister smiled at her was on her wedding day.

'You came then,' Emily said, unsure whether to hug her or not, and deciding not to, in case it just ended up being embarrassing.

'Try keeping us away,' Sadie said, and this time, there was no mistaking it – there was most definitely a smile.

'Would you like me to get you a good seat for the fireworks?' Emily stammered, nervous in spite of herself. After all, she'd done all of this for her family, and for one person in particular, and now here they were, in front of her.

CLAUDIA CARROLL | 408

Actually here, being civil to her for the first time that she could remember.

'Me and Jamie have the best seats in the house right here,' Sadie said, pointing to some garden chairs with blankets draped over them to keep out the chill. 'But you know what?' she added.

'What?'

'There's someone over there, who I think would very much like to be shown to a good seat.'

Emily followed Sadie's eyeline all the way over towards the row of apartments where her mother lived. And there she was, neat as a pin in her 'good' M&S suit, with her comfy flat brogues, just standing there with a curious look on her face. Still on her walking stick, but looking robust and healthy in spite of it.

Her mother. The one person who Emily had gone all out to please, more than anyone else. The one person who she'd done all this for.

'Go on,' Sadie said encouragingly. 'Go over to her. I'm pretty certain she wants to talk to you.'

Emily did as she was told, glad it was dark so you couldn't really tell how flushed and red in the face she was with nerves.

'Hello, Mum,' she said tentatively, now that they were standing beside each other, for the first time in God knows how long.

'Well, well, well,' her mother nodded, drinking in Emily from head to foot, as if she were really seeing her properly for the first time in years. 'Isn't this just marvellous?'

'It's about to begin,' Emily said. 'The fireworks, I mean. So if you'd like, I could help you to a good seat? Maybe beside Norma and some of the ladies she's with?'

Her mum thought for a moment before answering. 'That's very kind of you,' she said, 'but if it's all the same, I'd prefer to sit with my family.'

'Of course,' Emily said. 'I'll get a seat beside Sadie and Jamie for you, so the three of you can be together.'

'I meant you too, Emily. We're not a proper family without you.'

Emily looked back at her, stunned into silence.

'You've done terribly well, you know,' her mum said, taking a step forward and linking Emily's arm as they both walked towards the main park area, where the fireworks were about to begin. 'The residents have all been so excited about tonight. Everyone is greatly looking forward to it.'

Emily blushed. 'That's . . . that's really great to hear. Thank you.'

'Sadie tells me you've got a good job now,' her mum went on, 'and that you've found somewhere nice to live too.'

'Well, yeah,' Emily smiled. 'I mean, I'm doing OK. I'm in a good place, Mum. Finally. I'm gaining on happiness and I actually think I might just be getting there.'

'That's all I ever wanted for you, you know,' her mother said. 'You have so many gifts and talents, Emily. It broke my heart to see you wasting them for so many years, and now it's wonderful to see you put them all to good use.'

'Thanks, Mum,' Emily said, deeply touched. 'All this is . . . tonight, I mean, is just . . . well . . . to say sorry to you, really. I don't think I'll ever forgive myself for what I put you through, and I can't undo the past, but I can at least show you that I'm trying to be a better person.'

'I know you are,' her mum said softly.

'I've got a long journey ahead of me, Mum,' Emily said. 'But it'll be so much easier knowing that you and me are at peace.'

The sound of fireworks swelled in the background as her mother smiled, her cornflower blue eyes catching the light.

'Do you know something, Emily?' she said lightly, as if mother and daughter chatted like this every day of the week.

'What's that?'

'I was thinking I might have a little family dinner next weekend. Would you care to join us? Say yes, love. It really wouldn't be the same without you.'

The first fireworks of the night sparkled off into the sky as Emily smiled and said yes. And, for the first time in over a decade, she sat down with her mother and nephew and sister.

A family again.

Six months later

'Come on, old woman!' Emily yelled up the stairs of number eighty-one Primrose Square. The newly redecorated stairs, as it happened – given that, between them, she and Violet had finally begun to declutter and redecorate the house.

Francesca and her family, particularly that big, strapping son of hers, Ben, had been fabulous too and had done a lot of the heavy lifting. But the whole project had really been Emily's redesign and she was bloody delighted with the way it was turning out.

Turning out so far, she corrected herself, as there was still so much more to do. But so far, they had redone the entire hall, stairs and landing in a clean, crisp artic white, which showed off to perfection the newly varnished staircase. Which was now looking grander than ever, with the tatty old carpet consigned to a skip and with a gentle, elegant cream stair carpet in its place.

A lot done, a lot to do, but still. Every time Emily turned her key in the hall door, she felt a surge of deep pride. Even Violet herself was delighted with the results.

'It's getting back to the way it used to be!' she'd often say. 'Back when I was a girl – back to when this house was the envy of the whole square.'

Not that restoring the house was high on Violet's list of priorities on a day like today, though.

'Now?' she called back down to Emily, appearing on her walking stick at the top of the stairs and slowly making her way down. 'Really now?'

'Now.' Emily nodded, trying hard to keep calm and sound confident. It had taken so much investigative work to make a day like today come about, and she knew that Violet was sick with nerves.

If she sees me anxious too, she thought, *then we're done for.*

'And he's there? Actually there?'

'Sitting on a bench in Primrose Square, talking to Jayne. Waiting for you, Violet. Just waiting for you. His taxi arrived from the airport about half an hour ago, and he's come all this way to see you. So come on, you don't want to be late.'

'How do I look?' Violet asked, coming down the last few stairs and walking as far as the hall door.

Emily smiled at her. The truth was that Violet had never looked better. She'd finally filled out a bit and had lost that bony, gaunt, pinched look on her face, so now there was a softness about her features, which took years off her. It was a mild spring day and she was wearing a light lavender raincoat that Emily had bought her with her staff discount from work for Christmas.

'You look great,' Emily said truthfully. 'You look like the Queen on her way to open a sausage factory. All you need is a miniature bottle of gin in your handbag and you're good to go.'

Violet was about to retort, as she always did with Emily – the two sparred off each other constantly and a sizeable part of Violet actually seemed to enjoy it. But then they were distracted by Jayne, who'd just left the square and was crossing the road over to the house, waving and smiling happily.

'Well, Violet, don't you look wonderful!' she said, seeing her old friend framed in the doorway. 'He's here and absolutely dying to see you.'

'He's there?' Violet repeated nervously. 'Really there?'

'Really there, sitting on a park bench. And wait till you see him, Vi. He's the living image of . . .' But Jayne broke off there, not wanting to shatter the mood.

'The image of his father, I imagine you were about to say,' Violet finished the sentence for her.

'Yes,' Jayne said quietly. 'Yes, that's exactly it. Andy McKim, God have mercy on him.'

In their investigations over the past few months, Emily and Violet had discovered that Andy McKim had passed away only about two years previously. In a nursing home in Kent, they'd discovered, having only had minimal contact with his extended family for years.

'Yes, well, never mind about him now,' Violet said crisply, double-checking her lipstick in the mirror just inside the hall door. 'What's past is past.'

'Well said, old woman,' Emily smiled, giving her an affectionate pat on the back and handing over her good gloves. 'It's the future that we all need to focus on.'

'I can't believe Freddie Junior is fifty years of age,' Jayne chatted away excitedly. 'He looks so much younger. All that sunshine and Vitamin D in California, I suppose. And you won't believe this Vi, but guess what he told me? He plays the piano in his spare time. Isn't that astonishing? He's musical, just like you!'

'He's come halfway around the world to get here,' Emily said quietly, gripping Violet's arm as Jayne took the other and gently guided her to the front step. 'I think he's finally ready to meet his mum.'

'All right then,' Violet eventually said, taking a very deep breath and composing herself. 'In that case, it would be unconscionably rude to keep him waiting much longer. Just help me out of here and let's do this.'

With one last grateful look to both women supporting her, Violet steeled herself, stood tall with her shoulders back, and for the first time in decades, stepped past the threshold of her own front door.

Outside.

Free.

Two years later

'And now my next guest on Morning FM is a woman with a truly astonishing tale to tell. Francesca Woods, welcome to the show and thank you for coming in to talk to us today.'

'Delighted to be here,' Francesca smiled, feeling a little nervous, but determined not to let jitters get the better of her.

'Let me just say this to our listeners out there,' said the over-caffeinated morning radio presenter, a chirpy, perky twenty-something called Kirk. 'Obviously none of you can see Francesca but let me give you a visual: she's radiant – and wow, what a smile!'

'Oh, now, stop it,' Francesca beamed, swatting away the compliment.

'But let me begin by asking you this,' Kirk went on. 'You weren't always Francesca, were you? In fact, you've been on quite a journey, it's fair to say.'

'I certainly have,' Francesca said, with a confident toss of her hair. 'And now I'm here to help others who may find themselves in a similar situation.'

'Will you share your experiences with us today?' Kirk prompted.

'I'd be delighted to,' said Francesca, gearing herself up for what she knew would be a lengthy interview. 'But first of all, can I just say a few very quick hellos?'

'Of course, be my guest.'

'I wouldn't be here without three very special people,' Francesca said simply. 'They were always there for me, just as I am for them.'

'I'm guessing you mean your wife and kids?' Kirk replied, referring down to the notes in front of him. 'That's . . . let's see . . . Gracie, Ben and Amber?'

Francesca shook her head. 'They're not just my family,' she said firmly. 'They're my sanity, my reason for getting out of bed in the morning. They're the joy in my life.'

At that, she turned to the production booth behind her, which was separated from the studio by a thick glass partition. There stood Gracie, waving proudly and giving two very big thumbs up.

She knows what a big deal this is for me, Francesca thought, *so she came with me for support. My best friend. The best friend I ever had.*

'My family are my whole world,' she said, turning back to the interview. 'Always were, always will be.'

Acknowledgements

Thank you, Marianne Gunn O'Connor. Always and for everything.

Thank you, Pat Lynch.

Thank you, Vicki Satlow.

Very special thanks to Sarah Bauer, for her tireless hard work and for being such an all-around joy. Thank you also to Katie Lumsden, who has the most incredible eye for detail – it's a privilege to work with you both.

Thank you, Kate Parkin and Perminder Mann.

Thank you, Eli Dryden.

Thank you to Francesca Russell, for the amazing work she does in Publicity.

Thank you, Alexandra Allden, for the most glorious book covers.

Thank you so much to James Horobin, Stephen Dumughn, Nico Poilblanc, Vincent Kelleher, Imogen Sebba, Ellen Turner, Carla Hutchinson, Sahina Bibi, Angie Willocks, Victoria Hart, Carrie-Ann Pitt, Jamie Taylor, Alex May, Natalie Braine, Laetitia Grant and Dean Cornish – for everything.

Special hello to Margaret Stead. I'm so looking forward to meeting you, so I can thank you in person for all your kindness.

Thanks to Simon Hess, who works so hard and does so much for all of us.

Thanks to all the team in Dublin: Declan Heeney, Helen McKean, Eamonn Phelan and, of course, the man himself, Gill Hess.

Hi there,

Huge thanks for picking up *The Women of Primrose Square*, and I only hope you enjoyed reading it? I had an absolutely ball writing the book – it was magic to be able to revisit the location where *The Secrets of Primrose Square* is set, and to introduce a whole new set of characters.

So where did the idea for this book come from? Well, now, there's a tale!

At my (scarily advanced) hour of life, I find I'm going to a lot of birthday parties, 'with a naught at the end of them', and that's where the idea for this little book baby came from.

I had an idea: supposing your family were throwing a surprise fiftieth birthday party for you and pretty much everyone you'd ever met in your entire life had been invited? But because the surprise was so well hidden, you genuinely thought everyone had forgotten about you. Meaning that you strolled home to an empty house completely unsuspecting and looking forward to a peaceful evening alone – only to open the door, click the lights on – and realise you were suddenly front stage and centre, starring in your very own mini-drama.

And that's when the character of Frank came in – a shy, unassuming man who's effectively been living a lie for most of his life. Except of course that he's outed in the most public way imaginable on the night of his special birthday. Poor Frank! I adored writing this character and then Violet Hardcastle, who lives just down the road, seemed like the perfect foil. Violet just flew off the page – but then, I always think, no one is born nasty and horrible, are they? It's life that makes people like that, isn't it? So I was dying to work out why Violet was as – well, just as vile as she was to all around her. What had happened to the poor lady that moulded her that way? Then there's the character of Emily Dunne, who made a cameo appearance in *The Secrets of Primrose Square* and who, quite literally, nagged at this author until her story could be told in full. Emily is a recovering alcoholic and her journey on the twelve-step programme was one I was absolutely dying to explore.

And if you'd like to know a little bit more about the background to *The Women of Primrose Square*, here's a little suggestion.

We all love to read, don't we? And what's even better than a great book? The inside scoop on one – the DVD extras, if you like, the bits that only a select few dedicated readers get to read. Which is why the good folk at Bonnier Towers came up with an absolute diamond of an idea: my very own Readers' Club.

I'm ridiculously excited to be a part of My Readers' Club. It's full of exclusive content you'll love, and my job is to make sure that if you sign up, you won't regret it. Anyway, head over to **www.bit.ly/ClaudiaCarroll** if you'd like to join and it goes without saying all your information is entirely confidential.

I really do hope you'll enjoy the little extra treats I've included in My Readers' Club and till then, feel free to review the book on Amazon or Goodreads, or on social media – because it's always good to talk books, isn't it?

Big thanks and warmest wishes,

Claudia xxxxx

Want to read
NEW BOOKS
before anyone else?

Like getting
FREE BOOKS?

Enjoy sharing your
OPINIONS?

Discover

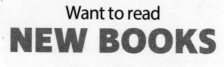

READERS FIRST

Read. Love. Share.

Sign up today to win your first free book:
readersfirst.co.uk

For Terms and Conditions see readersfirst.co.uk/pages/terms-of-service